NEIL WHITE

Last Rites

AVON

A division of HarperCollins*Publishers*
77–85 Fulham Palace Road,
London W6 8JB

www.harpercollins.co.uk

This production 2012

A Paperback Original 2009

Copyright © Neil White 2009

Neil White asserts the moral right to
be identified as the author of this work

A catalogue record for this book is
available from the British Library

ISBN: 978-0-00792-630-5

Set in Minion by Palimpsest Book Production Limited,
Grangemouth, Stirlingshire

Printed and bound in Great Britain by
Clays Ltd, St Ives plc

MIX
Paper from
responsible sources
FSC® C007454

Acknowledgements

As a lawyer and a writer, I feel blessed to have two jobs that I enjoy, but like in everything, it isn't always the job itself that is the most rewarding, but the people you meet on the way.

I work with the police regularly, a body of people whose dedication to their jobs helps us all to sleep a little safer. Throughout all of my books is admiration for them, and if that doesn't come across enough, then that is my fault. Then there are the others, from the people who have emailed me, sometimes from the other side of the world, to the other authors I've met, some new, others with names that adorn my own bookshelves. You have all made my job a lot less lonely, helped me to get through those late night moments when the story isn't going so well and the next deadline looms ever closer. For that, I say thank you.

Of course, becoming a writer isn't an overnight thing, and I've got the rejection slips to prove it, but there are some people who have always said the right things. I know who you are, how you helped, and I will always remember that.

What has made it a joy is that the people at Avon have been great to work with from day one, especially Maxine Hitchcock and Keshini Naidoo, both pillars of support and sound advice, but most of all, good company. For that relationship, I have to thank my agent, Sonia Land, always a font of great wisdom on all things book-related.

Underlying all of these things are the people who knew me before, who know me now, and will be friends and more long after. Like Duncan, who has kept the beer flowing through the years, and most of all, Alison, my wife, who bears the burden of my lost evenings too charitably, keeping my three boys in good health.

To Thomas, Sam and Joe, as always

Chapter One

Abigail Hobbs looked up and shivered as she opened the door to her stone cottage. The wind was blowing hard from the west, October ending with a snarl, the first bad mood of winter. It roared along the sides of Pendle Hill, a huge mound of millstone grit covered in grass and heather. The hill dominated the surroundings, dark and gloomy, and kept the sunlight from her windows. She pulled her coat to her chest and flipped the collar to her ears. She was too old for mornings like this.

'Tibbs? Tibbs?'

She couldn't find her cat, a grey British Shorthair, all smile and floppy paws. He was always there when she woke, waiting on her windowsill, blinking at her. But not that morning.

'Tibbs?'

She looked around. Still nothing. Her voice wasn't as strong as it had once been, and it died on the breeze, but she knew something wasn't right.

Abigail stepped onto the path, the stones sunken and uneven, and listened out. She could hear something, but

1

at first she thought it was the wind. A knocking sound; a fast rattle. She edged along the path, her slippers making slapping noises on the stones. There was the noise again, like metal banging against wood. And there was something else. A crying sound, distressed.

'Tibbs?'

Abigail got nearer to the end of the house, long grass trailing against her ankles. The noise seemed louder. She called out again. The sound was still there.

She reached an old outhouse, a brick add-on to the cottage that was used to store garden tools. The door was banging, the metal latch clattering, and as her footsteps got closer, the crying got louder.

'Tibbs, wait there. What have you done?'

She pulled on the outhouse door but it didn't give at first. It felt stiff, like someone was holding the other side. She could feel the vibrations in the door, the cries from inside louder now. She yanked at the door, and then as it opened she saw Tibbs, her cat, suspended in mid-air, struggling, thrashing, something wrapped around him.

Abigail was confused. She reached out, went towards him, but then there was a flash, a loud bang. Something wet hit her in the face, sharp and small, making her stumble backwards, losing her balance. As she fell, she saw that Tibbs was no longer there.

Chapter Two

I didn't hear my phone at first.

I was walking up the steep hill to my house, legs working hard, chin tucked into my scarf to keep out the cold. The morning walk was my break from the mundane, where I could forget about the bickering at home or the long stretch of the day ahead. The air in the Lancashire hills woke me up, crisp and fresh, so different from when cotton ruled the valleys, when the giant chimneys filled the towns with smoke and every life centred on the huge redbrick mills clustered around the canal.

My walk wasn't just about the cold in my face though. The last year had seen too many chocolate runs or long nights in with takeaway and wine, and we'd both put on weight. We'd settled into each other. Maybe too much.

I turned as I walked and looked back on what had made me: Turners Fold – a tired old collection of steep terraced streets, cobbled scars in the lush green view, like a museum of lost industry. But for me it was more than just that. As I looked, I saw all the haunts of my childhood. The park where I'd braved my first kiss, the sweeping crescents of the estate where I'd grown up, the school that had educated me so I could leave the town, which I did for a while, but the lure of home brought me back.

I smiled at the view. The mills were all empty now, the chimneys cleaned up, the buildings redeveloped as offices and apartments, or just left to crumble as grass grew through the floor and the windows fell in. But the town glowed from October dew and stood in silhouette against the sun spreading from the east, making me forget the bitterness of the wind.

I turned back and saw my house ahead, halfway up the hill, dry-stone walls lining the road, the old slate tiles and stubby chimney set against the fields behind. I thought I saw Laura through the window, just a shadow as she moved about inside. I waved but she didn't wave back.

Then I heard my phone, the ringtone set to the horns of 'Ring of Fire', an old Johnny Cash tune. I flipped it open and recognised the number. Sam Nixon, a local defence lawyer. He didn't call me that often and so he must have something good for me.

'Hi Sam,' I said, as I went into the house.

Laura looked up as I answered, but I turned away. She was making Bobby his breakfast but I could tell that she was listening.

I listened to Sam, and then said, 'Okay, I'll see you then,' and closed my phone. I turned to Laura and tried to look innocent.

'What did Sam Nixon want?' she asked.

I sneaked my arm around her to pinch one of Bobby's soldiers. 'He said he would tell me when I got there.'

'Don't get mixed up in anything stupid,' said Laura, and when I glanced back I saw her eyes flash me a warning.

'What do you mean?'

'You know what I mean,' she said wearily. 'Defence lawyers can mean trouble. Most don't see the line that separates their client from themselves.'

'Sam's not like that,' I replied. 'And you know how it works.'

And Laura did know. As a detective in the local police force, she saw too much of her hard work undone by crafty defence work, silence or lies peddled in the name of human rights. My side of crime was different. I sat at the side of the courtroom, writing up cases for the local paper, usually just sidebar stuff. I'd done some feature work, even used to do freelance in London, but it was too uncertain, sometimes dangerous, and it wasn't a good time for me to take risks.

Laura sighed heavily and gave Bobby a kiss on the top of his head. 'Not now, Jack,' she said. 'We can't afford to mess this up, not so near the end.'

I turned away and walked into the kitchen, a small windowless room partitioned off from the living room. I didn't want an argument, not so early.

Laura came into the kitchen behind me. 'Jack, talk to me.'

I turned around, the kettle in my hand. 'It's all we talk about these days,' I replied sullenly.

'I just don't want you getting wrapped up in anything stupid, that's all,' said Laura.

'I know, I heard you,' I replied. 'Our lives are on hold, just so we don't upset your ex-fucking-husband.' The words came out harsher than I intended.

'Do you think I'm enjoying it?' she snapped back at me. 'Waiting for someone else to decide who my son can live with? Is that what I had in mind when I moved up here?'

I paused and took a deep breath. 'I'm sorry,' I said, putting the kettle down and holding my arms out to her, trying to pull her towards me. 'I wasn't having a go. I know it's harder for you.'

Laura shrugged me off. 'No, you don't know how it is for me,' she said angrily. 'I'm the one who has made the sacrifices. I moved north with you, with my son, made a new life for us. No, hang on, that's wrong. I moved north *for* you, and sometimes I just wonder whether I did the right thing or whether we should have stayed in London, where I wouldn't get the fucking martyr treatment every time the situation gets a bit inconvenient.'

I looked to the ceiling. We'd had the same row too many times now, but I knew it wasn't us. We were good together, in those quiet moments we shared, when the custody battle for Bobby was forgotten for a few hours and we got the chance to relax – but those moments were getting further apart.

'Look, it's okay,' I said. 'Sam just said he had a story for me.' When Laura didn't look convinced, I added, 'It will be nothing. Some tip, an overnight case or something.'

'So why didn't you just say that?' she said, before she turned and walked away.

I sighed heavily, all the pleasure from the walk now evaporated. How had we got to this? And so quickly.

I went back into the living room and saw that Laura was getting Bobby's school bag ready. Bobby was silent, eating his breakfast slowly. He had been here before with his father – Laura's ex-husband – and he deserved more than that. He was the sweetest boy, just six years old, with Laura's brightness and Geoff's height, but how did you stop a child getting hurt?

It wasn't us, though, I knew that. It was the situation, Laura's ex-husband fighting to take him back south, to her native London. He claimed that it was for Bobby's benefit, that Laura's police work made his home life chaotic, but it had never been about Bobby. It was all about me, Laura's new man, stranger in the nest, the one who made her happy, who had made her give up her London career and settle instead in a small northern town, a detective job in nearby Blackley replacing the London Met. So now we had the fortnightly trip to some motorway services near Birmingham for Bobby's handover, Laura quiet all the way home, only really happy again when he was collected two days later.

Laura looked up at me, Bobby's bag in her hand. I tried a smile.

'C'mon Bobby,' she said, turning away from me. 'Finish your breakfast. We need to go.'

Chapter Three

Inspector Rod Lucas dusted down his tatty brown corduroys, slammed the door on his battered old Land Rover, and looked at the scene.

The cottage was just as he expected it. Like most houses in the shadow of Pendle Hill, it was set back from the road, dark grey stone against the sweep of green fields stretching away behind it, the slate roof low and overhanging.

He looked up at the hill, the exposed, barren summit making him feel cold. He pulled on an old waxed jacket and turned away, thought about Abigail Hobbs instead, still in hospital, burns on her face and stitches in her head from when she'd hit the stone floor. He knew that it wasn't the physical injuries that would hurt her the most. It would be the emotional scars that would last.

The two constables by the door straightened as he approached, both young women, their hands thrust into the pockets of their luminous green coats, their hips made to look big by the large belts around their waists. He glanced down at his own clothes. He lived in a barn conversion, access gained by a mud track overhung by branches, and he had been pruning a tree when he'd got the call. His hands were still covered in dirt and he hadn't changed into his uniform. He would oversee the scene, and then go back to his garden.

'How bad is it?' he asked, his voice quiet, a slow Pennine drawl.

The two officers exchanged glances. 'It's not nice, sir,' said the older of the two.

'Are Scenes of Crime on their way?' he asked.

'As soon as they can,' came the reply.

Lucas knew what that meant: that this was a rural area, a few miles from the nearest town. Scenes of Crime would be busy with more urban crimes: burglaries, glassings. They'd come out here when the day warmed up and they fancied a drive in the country.

He looked around. Brambles overhung the path and the paint on the windows looked flaky and old. The windows didn't give away many secrets though.

'Third time in two weeks,' he said to himself.

'Is that why you're here, sir?' asked the other constable. 'An inspector, I mean. Is it more serious now?'

'Someone has been hurt,' Rod replied. 'It's gone beyond routine vandalism.'

'So what do you think?' she asked. 'Kids?'

He looked around, noticed the small track that meandered down to the cottage from the main road, grass grown over the stones so that it was sinking back into the land as the years passed. 'No,' said Rod. 'It's too far from everywhere else, so getting away would take too long. It would increase the chance of getting caught. This is something else, some kind of a message.'

'But why her?'

Lucas's lips twitched. 'I don't know. Why any of them?' He straightened himself, and when he asked where it had happened he was pointed towards an old outhouse along the path. As he set off walking, he felt his trousers become damp from the trailing grasses. He swept back his thinning hair, his head golden with freckles, grey sideburns reaching down to his jaw-line.

He slowed down as he got near to the outhouse. The remains of the cat were still scattered over the path, the tiny severed head by the door, its mouth open, the sharp little teeth set in a final grimace.

He pushed at the door with a pen, careful not to leave any forensic traces, and saw the wire hanging from the latch. Just like the others, the wire led to a small metal pipe, filled with gunpowder. Once the door opened, it pulled at the wire, which set off a small blasting cap and exploded the pipe. In the other attacks, the pipe had been left on the floor. This time it had been strapped to Abigail's cat and suspended from the top of the door by a clothes line. This was more than just kids, he knew that.

He let the door close slowly as he turned away, the rusted hinges creaking, and walked back to the house, deep in thought. The constables by the door stepped aside as he went to go into the house, curious to find out more about Abigail, but he caught their exchange of glances, the raised eyebrows.

'What is it?' he asked.

They both looked at each other again, unsure what to say, and so Rod Lucas brushed past them and pushed at the door. It opened slowly, the interior dark, and as he peered in, his eyes adjusting to the gloom, he whistled.

'What the hell?' he muttered to himself, and then stepped inside.

Chapter Four

I was heading for Sam Nixon's office, walking quickly through Blackley along the paved precinct, chain stores on one side and the entrance to an indoor mall on the other. Victorian shop-fronts used to line the street, back when the town was the glamorous big brother to Turners Fold, but the area had tried to shake off its past a few decades earlier. The modern town plan that had come along in its place looked tired already. Not many people walked the streets, just earnest young college students and shop assistants clicking their way to work in high heels.

I could see Sam watching my approach. His office was above a print shop, accessed through a glass door at the bottom of some stairs, his name spelled out in gold leaf. His clients congregated there sometimes, somewhere quiet and warm to swap dealer names, but Sam's wife, Helena, acted as the bouncer. She used to be a lawyer herself, straw-blonde with stick-thin arms and a pinched nose, but years out bringing up children and being on the wrong end of a breath test turned her against it. Instead, she managed the paperwork, the money, and allowed Sam to do the law.

I exchanged quick greetings with Helena, just a peck on the cheek. Her face was cold, her complexion pale.

'How's business?' I asked.

Helena grimaced. 'Crime's no game for a sole practitioner.'

'Not busy?'

She laughed, but it sounded bitter. 'People through the door are not the problem. Getting a decent rate of pay for it, that's the problem.'

I didn't respond. I reckoned our views on decent pay might be different. Instead, I let Helena show me through the reception area and into Sam's office, a large room with just a chipboard desk and worn-out chairs bought in a clearance sale. The desk was busy with files, the dark blue of *Blackstone's*, Sam's preferred legal reference, acting as a paperweight, but the room felt bare and cold. Sam Nixon & Co. hadn't brought in enough money to think about comfort.

Sam stood up as I entered, smiling, his hand out to shake. 'Hello Jack, good to see you.'

I shook his hand and noticed the tiredness behind his smile. Sam looked like business was tough. He wasn't much older than me, both of us moving through our mid-thirties, but his face looked filled with worry, his hair was working its way backwards quickly, and whatever was left was sprinkled with grey. He had lost weight and lines had started to appear around his eyes.

Sam Nixon fed me stories, often just a nod as he came into court, a tip that a case was worth hanging around for. My write-ups shamed his clients, but it kept his name in the paper and a steady footfall through his door. For me, it was my job. For Sam, it was free publicity.

'How's Laura?' he asked.

'She's on CRT.'

'Good hours for the family,' said Sam, nodding his approval.

I smiled, played the happy boyfriend for a moment, aware that there were other people in the room.

Laura was a detective on the Custody Reception Team at Blackley Police, who dealt with the overnighters, the burglars and the domestic bullies. The nightshift officers would be long gone to their beds, leaving behind a disgruntled prisoner and a bundle of paperwork, and Laura's team had to sort it out. It gave her regular hours, but it meant she spent most days interviewing hostile prisoners in the belly of the old police station, where the smell of the cells, sweat and vomit, seeped into her clothes.

I was suspicious of Sam. If a criminal lawyer asked me first about the welfare of my detective girlfriend, I assumed that he didn't want her around.

'You know what Blackley is like,' I said. 'It's full of criminals. They keep her busy.'

'Blame it on the lawyers for setting them free,' Sam replied.

As he was talking, I turned towards the other people in the room, a middle-aged couple perched uncomfortably on chairs. I recognised them immediately. Their faces had filled the local news for the last week. I looked back at Sam, who seemed nervous now.

'Jack, this is Ray and Lucy Goode,' he said.

I smiled a polite greeting, but I knew who they were. Their daughter had made the headlines, a pretty young teacher, the photograph from the school prospectus showing her with straight auburn hair and freckles like splashes. Sarah had a boyfriend, Luke, a fitness instructor at her gym. It was normal girl–boy stuff, until Luke had been stabbed to death in her bed a week earlier and Sarah had disappeared.

It had played out in the local paper for a few days, had even brushed the nationals, but the television got the best angle – the news conferences, Mr and Mrs Goode tearful and scared, begging for Sarah to come home – but then it went quiet when there was nothing new to report. I'd guessed the subtext: it was officially a missing persons investigation, but, for the police, Sarah Goode was a murderer on the run.

'This is Jack Garrett,' Sam said. 'Our local hotshot reporter.' When I didn't respond, he added, 'They want to speak to you. Is that okay?'

I nodded at them politely, but then I asked Sam, 'Why me?'

Sam looked embarrassed. 'It's probably for the best if they tell you about it.' He went towards the door. 'I'll be in the next room if you need me.'

I watched him go, surprised, and wondered why he didn't want to be a part of it. When the door clicked shut, Sam left behind an uncomfortable silence, broken only by the ticking clock on the wall and the creaks of the chairs as Mr and Mrs Goode shuffled nervously.

I tried to weigh them up. They were in their fifties. She was in a blue suit, knee-length skirt and blazer, navy blue with gold buttons, her hair in tight grey curls. He looked uncomfortable in a dated brown suit, as if he hadn't worn one for a long time, and I could see the shirt collar digging into his neck. His sandy hair had receded to just wisps of a comb-over.

'This is about Sarah, I presume?' I said.

They glanced at each other, and I saw a nod, a look of comfort. It was Mrs Goode who took the lead.

'Yes, it's about our daughter,' she said. Her voice was firm, but the way their knees touched told me that they needed each other for support. She licked her lips and repositioned her bag on her lap. Then she said, 'We want you to help us find her.'

It was said simply, as if she assumed I would be interested.

I wasn't. I didn't write features any more. I'd sacrificed that for family harmony, for our bright future.

I tried to sound sympathetic. 'I'm sorry, but that's not the sort of journalism I do, the campaign stuff. I write up court hearings, that's all.'

'But you used to do more than that,' said Mrs Goode. 'Mr Nixon told me about some of the stories you wrote.'

'That was then. And I'm a reporter, not a private detective.'

'But we thought it would be a good story if you found her,' she pressed.

I shook my head slowly. 'I don't see a story, not the type I write.'

They looked down, disappointed. Mrs Goode clenched her jaw and a tear dripped onto her eyelashes.

It was Mr Goode who spoke next. 'Not even if you found her first?' His voice was quiet, hesitant.

I gave him a smile filled with fake regret. 'The police will have to speak to her before me, and if Sarah is charged I won't be able to write anything that might affect the case. It's called *sub judice*. It would just sit on an editor's desk for six months, maybe longer.'

'There might not be a court case,' Mrs Goode said, her eyes imploring. 'If you could find her and bring her in, once we know what she is going to say, she might have a defence.'

My eyes narrowed at that. 'What about Sam Nixon?' I asked. 'Will he speak to Sarah before she goes to the police?'

Mrs Goode looked down and didn't answer. That told me all I needed to know. It wasn't about a story, it was about Sarah's parents getting her story straight first, before she handed herself in.

'I'm sorry, I really am,' I said as I headed for the door, 'but I don't see a story, not yet anyway.'

They both turned to each other and exchanged desperate looks. Mrs Goode put her hand over Mr Goode's hand and squeezed it. He looked like he was about to break down. It stalled me.

Mrs Goode turned back to me. 'Thank you for coming down, Mr Garrett,' she said softly. 'At least you listened.'

'How much have you told the police?' I asked.

'Whatever they wanted to know.'

I sighed. 'If they can't find Sarah, I don't see how I can,' I said, and this time the regret was genuine.

As I left the room I saw that Sam was waiting in one of the reception chairs. 'How was it?' he asked.

'You know damn well how it was,' I said.

'What do you mean?' Sam replied, as he picked at his fingers and tried to look innocent.

'They came to you because they know the police want to arrest her for murder,' I said. 'Is that right?'

Sam started to say something, but then he stopped himself. He nodded and tried to shrug an apology instead, but then he realised that it was pointless.

'They're decent people,' he said. 'They're worried about their daughter.'

'And someone is dead,' I replied harshly. 'His family will be decent people too.' Sam looked down, so I continued, 'They need someone to help them find her, but they can't afford a private investigator and they thought I would come cheap. About right?'

'But it would be a good story if you could find her.'

'I wish it was like that, Sam, because I need the money – Laura's lawyers are taking most of what we have – but you don't understand journalism. I deal in court titbits, pub talk.' Sam looked confused, so I said, 'My point made. Papers want the pub tales: *Man Bites Dog*, that type of thing. This is feature stuff, an in-depth analysis, and I can't afford to take the gamble of someone being interested. And anyway, if I find her, *I'm* the story, and that's not how I want it right now.'

Sam nodded in apology. 'I'm sorry, Jack. They came to me for help. They're desperate people, and they're good people. You were the only avenue I could think of.'

I sighed. 'So what's your interest?'

Sam looked sheepish at that. 'We're struggling, Jack,' he said. 'We've got the work coming in, but it's all small stuff. Shoplifts, car breaks, Saturday night bust-ups. It's turnover work, but the bills come in faster than the clients.'

'You need a murder to put you in the big league,' I said, acknowledging his admission, and then nodded back towards the room I had just been in. 'And so you need their daughter in a cell.'

Sam looked ashamed, but he added, 'This is my living. I didn't kill that man, and someone has to represent her. Why not me?'

I thought about Mr and Mrs Goode and the look they both had – confused, helpless, wanting help. 'I think they want a bit more,' I said, and headed for the exit. 'Thanks for the tip, Sam, but I can't see a story in it.'

Sam didn't answer, and so I was back on the street, heading towards the Magistrates Court, ready for another day of routine crime stories.

Chapter Five

As Rod Lucas pushed open the door to Abigail's cottage, the smell hit him first. It was strong, sort of smoky. Incense-burners, he guessed. His eldest daughter had gone through a phase of burning them in her room. It helped her sleep, or so she claimed at the time. It was to cover up the smell of cigarettes, he learned later. She was away at university now, and her twenty-a-day habit was one of a list of concerns.

But he remembered the cloying smell, the way it made him cough and wrinkle his nose. He could understand an experimental teenager burning them, but why a pensioner living in a remote cottage?

He looked around. Rod had expected chintz: patterned sofas, high-backed chairs, china ornaments everywhere and pictures of grandchildren, but the cottage wasn't like that. The walls were painted black, with thick red cloth covering the windows and tall mirrors on the walls, ornate and Gothic. There were candles everywhere – on the mantelpiece, the sideboards, the windowsills – everything from deeply scented ones in small jars to large black altar candles.

He saw a rug pushed up against the wall, revealing the stone floor, large slabs worn smooth over the years. His eyes widened when he saw why it had been moved, and what was in its place, the thing that dominated the space.

White lines criss-crossed the room, jagged and uneven, made up of something sprinkled onto the floor, like small white grains. There was a table and chair set in the middle of it all, as if the old lady sat in it when she was alone. Lucas stooped down to dab his finger into the lines. He tasted it. Salt.

The lines made a shape. It wasn't perfect, as if it had been done in a rush, but he could make it out: a five-pointed star, with things placed at each point. A small posy of flowers; a large red candle; a sea-shell.

Rod thought back to the explosive device. Why would anyone target this woman? Was her lifestyle the reason? This was the third explosion like this, but no one had reported anything strange in the other houses. Or maybe they just hadn't looked hard enough.

He would go to the hospital next. Maybe Abigail could provide the answers.

I shuffled on the bench at the side of the Magistrates Court in Blackley as I tried to get comfortable. It was still before ten and the court hadn't started yet, although I could hear the corridor getting busier. I looked up to the ceiling, at the flaking paint, and wondered how I had got to this point. I used to write crime features for the nationals when I was a freelancer in London, had always had the dream of writing a book, maybe ghostwriting a gangster memoir. Now, I churned out the small stories: incidents of local shame, drunken fights, domestic violence, sexual misbehaviour. The local paper paid me for each story rather than a salary, so if the crime scene went quiet, or if the police started another new initiative to keep people away from courts, then I didn't get paid. I worked my own hours, though, and it still left me to peddle the better stories to the nationals, but I used to do so much more.

But I knew that Laura was right. The stories were steady work and provided a stable home. Laura was doing the same, working regular hours, no shifts, so that we were home each evening, and there was nothing for the judge to criticise when the trial for Bobby's custody started.

I looked around the courtroom, empty apart from the prosecutor at the front, sorting out his pile of files, ready for the morning slog. The defence would arrive soon, wanting their papers for the overnight clients.

'Anything decent for me?' I asked.

The prosecutor looked up. 'Uh-huh?'

He was one of the old guard; when the mood was right he was effective, but most days his job was just a plough through Blackley's grime.

'Anything to report?' I asked. 'I'm not here because I like your suit.'

He smiled at that, just a glimmer. 'Just the usual,' he said. 'We've got a drink-driving teacher, crashed his car leaving school, if that's any good.'

I raised my eyebrows. Another reputation ruined, but his shame was his problem. My mortgage was mine.

'Don't get too excited, though,' said the prosecutor.

'Mick Boreman's defending. There'll be no guilty plea today.'

'Too middle class to be guilty?' I queried.

'Something like that.'

I exhaled and sat back. I couldn't write the story properly until he was convicted. It was good for a paragraph reporting his name and profession, but not much else.

I thought about Mr and Mrs Goode as I waited for court to start. Was I right to turn down their request? Looking for Sarah would be a break from the mundane, and it might be a good feature to have written up and ready just in case she was caught and convicted. But then I thought about the bills that dropped onto the mat most mornings, how we needed the steady production line of small tales from the courtroom just to keep ahead of those, and if Geoff went all the way with his custody case then Laura's lawyers would soak up the rest, and quite a bit more.

The tapping of my pen got faster.

The family future was nearly resolved though. Anything I wrote now would be published later, long after the custody case had finished, and if the court was going to be quiet then it might be worth looking into Sarah's case, just to see if there was something to grab the headline. I could write the feature at night, after Laura had gone to bed.

I felt some guilt creep up on me as I thought of Laura, but I dismissed it, perhaps too quickly. I was a reporter; selling stories was what I did.

I put my notepad back in my pocket and rushed out of the courtroom.

Chapter Six

Sarah Goode panted as she looked around the room. Stone walls all the way round, with a door at one end, cell-like, just twenty-foot square with no windows, no view out, a dirt floor scratching her feet.

She looked up to the ceiling and then winced, shielding her eyes. The lights there were like car head-lights, bright halogen on full beam, searing into her retinas.

She tried to stretch her legs, but they hurt, all cramped up. She knew she had to keep moving, had to get her muscles working again. She limped to the walls and thumped them, but the sound came back as a dead thud. They were solid, sound-proof, old Pennine stone.

Sarah felt her way round the length of the room, using the wall as support, looking for a weak spot, maybe a loose stone, until she got to the door, wooden and old, the edges uneven and dry. It was bolted on the other side; she had heard it slide back whenever he came into the room. She knew it was a man from his hacking coughs and his deep throaty laugh when he taunted her, when he had kept her in the box.

She looked over to the corner of the room. The box was still there, one end open, from where she had crawled not long before. She turned away from it swiftly and looked up at the lights again, shielding her eyes. Would they stay on all the time? She leapt at them, tried to break one just to reduce the glare, but they were too high. She hurt herself instead when she landed, the dirt cutting into the soles of her feet.

Sarah sat down and put her face in her hands, gripped her hair with her fingers. Why was she there? What had she done? Why her?

She started to pull at her hair, wanting to scream, but then she looked up, startled. She could hear the buzz of speakers. Sarah shielded her eyes to see past the lights, and then she saw them, dark shapes behind the brightness. She sat still, waiting for whatever was going to come out of them. Then the sound came out at high volume, so loud that she had to cover her ears. It was the sound of a heartbeat, fast and anxious, a relentless thump-thump, the noise pulsing around the walls.

Sarah clamped her hands tighter over her ears and screamed, tried to drown it out, but the sound still made it through, making her own heart race to keep up.

She looked back to the box. Maybe it would be quieter in there.

She turned away. She couldn't go back in there, she knew that. Her life had once been normal, but those days in the box meant that it would never be the same again.

Chapter Seven

Laura McGanity swung her bag onto her desk and sat down with a slump. She leaned back and closed her eyes for a few seconds.

'I'm not sure I can cope with another day of this,' she said, almost to herself.

Pete Dawson grinned at her. 'Turning on tape machines and filling out forms not exciting enough for you?' he said.

Laura looked at him, took in his crew cut, and the scar over his eye that was a remnant of his last jaunt with the Support Unit in the Saturday night van.

'Don't be offended, Pete, but you don't look the agony aunt type,' she said.

Pete laughed. He had been Laura's sidekick for most of her time in Blackley. He was an old-style detective, a head-cracker who had not yet accepted the committee style of police politics, and Laura liked him for that. Pete had learned one thing in his police career: criminals are ruthless and devious, and don't feel much remorse for those they hurt on the way. So Pete liked to let them know what he thought. Sometimes it was just a quiet word on a dark street, although it came with a snarl. Mostly it was just about being relentless, so that the criminals knew that if he became an enemy it was time to change their turf.

'This was your choice,' he said. 'Regular hours.'

She rubbed her eyes. 'It's not just that, though.'

'If you want to have a moan,' he said, 'you've got around ten minutes, because the cells are full, and if we're ever going to see daylight today we need to get the first one out of the way.'

Laura shook her head. 'I'm not talking about it,' she said, and then she turned her head quickly when she heard laughter further along the corridor. It was the murder squad, assembled for the Luke Howarth murder, all chasing down Sarah Goode.

'It's not just Bobby's custody case, though, is it?' he asked. 'Or Jack?'

'What do you mean?'

Pete pointed towards the door. 'I thought maybe you'd grown tired of me, but it seems like you just want in on the big case.'

Laura didn't answer straight away. It was more than being out of the loop, she was about to say. It *was* about Jack, and Bobby, and home, and Geoff and the custody case, and missing London. But she didn't say that. Instead, she exhaled and forced out a smile. 'You've got me, Pete. Maybe we should get into interview quickly if you're in this kind of detecting form.'

'You don't want to be with them,' he replied. 'The creases are too sharp in their trousers.'

'Is that how you judge people?'

'It's just one way.'

Laura sighed. 'C'mon then, what have we got first?'

Pete tossed over the papers. 'A fight in The Trafalgar. Someone almost lost an eye.'

'Is this a joke?'

'It's barely a case,' Pete replied. 'We've got the right man, but no one is making statements, not even the victim.'

'Let me guess,' said Laura, smiling now. 'An argument over a woman, and the victim is married?'

'And you said I was the great detective,' Pete replied, standing. 'C'mon, let's turn the tapes and see what we get.'

I sat in my car and pondered the view.

I had made a few calls around some contacts to get the address, and so I was outside Sarah Goode's house in Blackley, the scene of the crime, in the middle of a long terrace halfway up a steep hill. Or down it, depending on your outlook on life. It seemed like nothing out of the ordinary. The street was long and straight, its lines broken only by the roads that criss-crossed it, so that driving down became a game of dare, a dicey rat-run for those trying to avoid the town-centre jams. The houses were in traditional glazed red brick, with the doorframes picked out in painted white stone, no gardens, the front doors straight onto the street, and the slope so pronounced that it took only a tilt of my head to make the street look like fallen dominoes.

I looked along the street, trying to gauge the neighbourhood. I felt my car windows vibrate from R&B

played too loudly on bad speakers, and a car filled with young Pakistani men drove past slowly, all of them staring at me. Their community had grown in the sixties, when the cotton mills needed night-shift workers and the newly prosperous white working class didn't want to do them. The Asians worked at night, the whites during the day. When the mills closed down, both communities had found themselves jobless.

A group of women watched me from further up the street, as the wind pushed their silk pants against their legs and made their headscarves flap around their faces. I took some pictures. Maybe there was something here. How Sarah came to be a killer, an analysis of small-town murder. Truman Capote for the industrial north. I could follow the investigation, something in the bank for after Bobby's custody case, a story better than the ones I churned out most days.

Sarah's house looked still. There were wicker blinds in each window, all down, so nothing about the house gave away its secret. I decided to leave the neighbours for a while. There'd been a flurry of interest just after the body was discovered, and not all journalists were courteous. There's no story in a slammed door.

I checked my watch as I pondered where I should go next, and then I saw something, some movement in my peripheral vision. I stepped out of my car and moved closer. Sarah's house looked the same as before, deserted and cold, the blinds still closed.

Then I saw it again, in the front-room window, just a finger on the blinds. Somebody was watching me.

Chapter Eight

Inspector Lucas looked at the floor as he was led through the ward. There were the usual smells, antiseptic and illness, but it was the hopelessness that made him look away. The ward was a series of rooms, each containing four beds, the occupants old and disinterested, just staring into space. He was on the dark side of fifty. How long was there until this?

He noticed that the nurse had stopped walking and was gesturing towards one of the rooms. The occupants were all women, with no empty beds, but he guessed which one was Abigail from the freshness of the bandages. He followed the nurse into the room. No one looked at him as he went in. He saw that Abigail was sleeping.

'How is she?' he asked.

'The cuts on her legs have been stitched, and the burns are not too bad,' the nurse replied, her voice low. 'Superficial mainly. But she's in shock, and we're worried about her sight.'

'What do you mean?'

'Some of whatever it was that exploded hit her in the

eyes. Her right eye is just sore, but she might lose her sight in her left.'

Rod didn't want to tell the nurse that it had been pieces of Abigail's cat that struck her in the eye.

'I'll just wait,' he said.

'It might be a while,' she said. 'I don't want you asking her questions before she's ready.'

'I won't,' he said, and nodded that he understood. The nurse looked unsure at first, but when he gave her a reassuring smile, she relented and left him in the room.

Rod pulled up a chair next to her and sat down. Abigail wasn't like he expected. He knew her age, sixty-eight, and so he had expected grey hair and pale skin, but Abigail was different to that. Her frizzy hair was long and dyed black, her silver roots showing through, and it was back-combed, spread in a tangled mess over the pillow. Her fingers were covered in rings, and her nails were long and painted purple. Despite the plaster over her eye, Rod could tell that both eyes were ringed by bruises. Abigail's legs were out of the bedcovers, bandages over her wounds.

He looked closer at her hands. There were grazes on them, but something else drew his attention. It was one of her rings, the one on her right hand, third finger. A screaming face, silver on black, set into a silver band. He had seen it before, he was sure of it, but he couldn't remember where.

'Abigail,' he whispered, just to check whether she was awake. There was no response. 'Abigail,' he said once more. Still nothing.

He settled back in the chair. Sometimes the art of being a good copper was patience.

I knocked on the door of Sarah's house. The women at the top of the road looked at me again and then chattered to each other. I waited, but there was no response from inside.

I knocked again, more insistent this time. Then I heard a noise, and when the door opened I flashed a smile. It had no effect.

I was facing a dark-haired woman in her early twenties, in jeans and a loose T-shirt. Her hair was short, elfin-style, tucked just behind her ears so that it showed off her face, pretty and porcelain pale, with high cheekbones and bright hazel eyes.

'Yes?' she said curtly.

My mind raced through what I knew about Sarah's story. Luke's body had been discovered by her lodger, a young student. There was a pause as I grasped for her name, but it came to me just as she was about to slam the door.

'Katie Gray?' I asked.

She didn't answer at first, but then asked, 'Who wants to know?' Her voice was cautious.

I smiled again, tried to disarm her. 'My name is Jack Garrett and I'm a reporter.'

'I guessed that.'

'I'm interested in Sarah Goode,' I continued.

'I guessed that too,' she snapped, but I put my hand in the way as she went to close the door.

'Sarah's parents contacted me. They want me to write about her.'

She paused at that.

'I understand she used to live here,' I continued, trying to engage her.

'She still does,' she replied, but her tone was less hostile than before.

'Her parents just want to find her,' I said. 'They want to help her, make sure she's all right.' My voice was soft and low, my hand still on the door.

'Have you got any ID?' she asked.

I reached into my pocket and found a business card. I passed it over and waited, but how could she refuse once I had produced identification?

She looked at the card, then at me, and then at the card again.

'Okay, Mr Garrett, you'd better come in,' she said, and then turned and went into the house.

I followed her into the hallway, narrow and dark, the light coming from a small window above the front door. Katie led me into the room at the back of the house, a chill-out room, with saggy old sofas and family photographs on the wall, but I glanced into the room at the front as I went past the doorway. It was more formal, with better furniture and an old black fireplace, the light dim behind the wicker blinds.

Katie turned around. 'Do you want a drink? Coffee? Tea?'

I chose coffee, it would keep me in the house for at least fifteen minutes, and Katie disappeared into the kitchen, a long and thin extension with views into a concrete yard.

'How long have you been living here?' I asked her, as

one of the pictures on the wall caught my eye. It looked like a family tree, framed, the branches spreading out, but it was the symbol at the top that drew my attention. It was unusual, like a screaming face, with hollow eyes and open mouth.

'I thought you were here to talk about Sarah,' Katie shouted from the kitchen.

'I am, but you're part of the story.'

Katie returned with two coffees. 'No, I'm not,' she said, and handed me one of the cups.

I sat down, and I felt my knees rise up as I sank into a broken old couch.

'You found Luke. That makes you part of it,' I countered.

She sat down on a chair opposite and thought for a moment. She pulled her legs onto the cushion and took a drink, watching me over the top of the cup. 'So what do you want to know?'

'The story,' I replied.

Katie drank her coffee for a while, and then said, 'If you've read the papers you'll know most of it. Sarah's a teacher. She couldn't pay for the house without a lodger. She put a notice on the college notice-board. I saw it and got in touch.'

I nodded and smiled, played at being the interested journalist: sympathetic glances; faked empathy. I noticed that her body language was less defensive, and that her voice was quieter now. 'I presume I'm talking to Katie Gray,' I said, more as a comment than a question.

Katie paused, and then smiled properly for the first time, her eyes twinkling.

'You have read the papers,' she said.

'It's my job,' I replied, and then asked, 'What do you study?'

'History,' she said, and blew into her coffee as she watched me, the cup cradled in both hands. She looked younger now, more vulnerable. 'So if you've seen the papers, you already know the story,' she said. 'You must want something more.'

'Sarah's parents just want me to find her,' I said, shrugging. 'They are convinced she had nothing to do with her boyfriend's death, but the only way to prove it is to get Sarah to come home.'

Katie nodded as she listened.

'I know how Luke died,' I continued, 'and I can guess what the police think, but I need to know more.'

She put her cup down on the floor and leaned forward. I thought I saw something in her eyes. Sadness? Loneliness?

'Where have you been so far?' she asked.

'I've started here.'

'Where else are you going to look?'

I looked at her carefully when she said that. Katie seemed interested in my movements and I wondered why.

'Wherever the facts take me,' I replied cautiously.

'How are Sarah's parents?' Katie asked.

'How well do you know them?'

'Not much at all really. I'm just the lodger.'

I thought back to the meeting in Sam's office. 'Somewhere between frantic and sad,' I said.

Katie looked back and ran her fingers through her

hair. She smiled at me and then asked, 'What do you need to know?'

'Just tell me about Sarah,' I said simply.

Katie watched me for a few seconds and I felt myself shuffle in my seat. I looked away, tried to take in the room. The walls looked sparkling clean. No cobwebs around the light-fittings, and the tabletop gleamed so that the scuffs and scratches seemed to catch the light and shine it back. Katie still lived in the house. Maybe the house had been cleaned to wipe out the memories of what had happened there.

'She was fun,' Katie started, making me look back, her voice low, so I had to lean in to catch what she was saying. 'She wasn't like a teacher. She was more fun than that. Her parents live close by, but she wanted her own place. She moved in, but she bought the house at the top of the boom and so needed me to help with the mortgage, and that's it.' Katie smiled wistfully. 'We got on. We went out together, met some men together, just normal stuff. She started seeing Luke, and the rest, well, you know how it ended.'

'Who was Luke?'

'He was a personal trainer at the Pendle Gym. I reckon Sarah was different to most of the women he met. He could have had anyone at the gym. You know, he had the body, the smile, but Sarah was cooler than that. She was a bit prim and proper on the outside, and I think he liked that.'

'And on the inside?'

Katie laughed, blushing slightly. 'I used to hear them in the night. She wasn't always so reserved.'

'So Sarah liked him,' I said.

'Oh, it was more than that,' she replied, grinning now. 'He was handsome, six foot and muscular.' She traced the top of her cup with her finger. 'She was falling in love.'

'Was he?'

Katie sat back and thought for a few moments, more solemn now. 'I really don't know,' she said. 'You know what men like him are like.'

'You mean he was seeing other women?'

'Don't men like Luke always see other women?'

Would it make her grab a knife and stab him, I thought to myself, as Katie twirled her fringe with her finger, watching me as I jotted down her quote?

'So what do you think happened?' I asked.

Katie watched me, almost studied me. 'Why do you think my opinion matters?'

'Because you knew both of them. The police didn't, and they've got an opinion.'

'Have they?'

She was teasing me, trying to make me uncomfortable.

'My guess is that the police think she killed him,' I said.

She shrugged, her eyes never leaving mine. 'They're the experts,' she said.

That surprised me. It seemed like Katie agreed with the police hints, that Sarah was Luke's killer.

Katie glanced at her watch and put her cup down. 'Have you got many more questions?' she queried. 'I've got to go somewhere.'

'Lectures?'

She nodded.

'Can we talk again?' I asked.

Katie waved my business card at me. 'I've got your number. I'll call you.'

I went to stand, but she leaned forward and grabbed my hand. Her fingers were warm and soft, her grip gentle, almost a caress.

'Thank you,' she said.

'For what?' I asked, surprised.

'Just for being nice. It seems like people avoid me now.'

I nodded and smiled, felt my cheeks flush. 'That's okay,' I said, and dropped her hand. I turned to go. I thought she was going to show me out, but she stayed in her seat, tapping my business card against her cheek.

'Another time then,' I said. I felt awkward but I didn't know why.

When Katie didn't answer, I let myself out. I looked back at the house and wondered at how much I had learned in there. And then I felt my cheeks. They were hot, and my fingers trembled slightly.

Chapter Nine

Sarah Goode scrambled backwards as the sound of the heartbeats stopped and the door at the end of the room slid open. It was heavy, and it scraped noisily against the soil in its runner as it was pushed open.

She saw the hood first, and she screamed out loud. It was black cloth, pulled over his head, ragged around the neck and tied by thin rope, scarecrow-like. It was a man, she knew that from his height and broad shoulders, but he seemed different. She had seen the hood before, when she had been taken out of the box to stretch her muscles, to ease out the cramp, to have the chance to breathe properly, and it had terrified her. It was faceless, emotionless, but that person had seemed different. Younger, slimmer.

He stepped into the room slowly, deliberately, his heavy boots shuffling on the floor. His arms didn't move as he walked towards her, his back ramrod straight so that he almost seemed to glide. The hood billowed out slowly as he breathed.

'Hello Sarah,' he said, his voice muffled.

Sarah felt the stone wall against her back as she reached

the end of the room. 'Who are you?' she asked, her breaths coming fast.

He stopped and stood still for a moment, watching her. 'Why do you need to know?'

'Because you kept me in a box for a week,' said Sarah, her voice cracking. She could feel him watching her and so she looked at the floor, tried to suck in some deep breaths to regain her composure. 'I just feel like I've got a right to know,' she said, her voice stronger this time, but she flinched when he moved closer to her.

Sarah gasped as she heard him laugh, just a deep chuckle under the hood.

'You don't have any rights,' he said quietly.

Sarah moaned and put her head in her hands. 'What are you going to do to me?' she pleaded.

'I haven't decided.'

Sarah could feel the panic rising through her chest. Tears welled up in her eyes, but she fought them, didn't want to look weak in front of him. But it was hard. She knew what he was capable of, ever since her nightmare had begun a week earlier.

It had started with a knock on the door, close to midnight. She had almost ignored it – it was cold and dark outside and Luke felt good next to her, sleeping naked – but the second knock had been more insistent, louder, and so she had slipped on Luke's shirt and some old jeans and gone to answer the door.

All she had seen was the mask, like a shadow, and then his hands shot forward and grabbed her, an arm around her neck and a hand over her mouth, rough and callused, smelling of cigarettes and oil. She had tried to bite him and lashed out with her feet, but his arm went tighter around her neck as he dragged her out of the house.

She had heard Luke shout out, asking who was there, but a rag had been pushed into her mouth, petrol and grease, and the pavement tore the skin of her heels as she was dragged to a car, the street quiet, no one around.

The boot had been open, ready for her, but it had been cramped and filled with dirty tools and a spare wheel. She was pushed in there anyway, head first, her arms pulled behind her back, her wrists tied together quickly, before he slammed the lid down.

The memories flooded back as Sarah looked at him, in the same impenetrable black hood.

'Why me?' she wailed.

He tilted his head as he looked at her. 'I'm here to look after you, Sarah. Is there anything you need?'

Sarah looked at him, incredulous. She glanced behind him, at the way out of the room, to the stairs that seemed to lead upwards.

'I want to go home,' she replied, meekly now.

'Anything else?'

Sarah swallowed as she felt the tears come again. She shook her head, knowing that if she spoke she would show her weakness.

He didn't answer. He watched her for a few moments, until he suddenly turned to go.

Sarah almost ran at him, to beg him not to lock her in, that she would do anything to get out, whatever he wanted, but something stopped her. Perhaps it was the fear of what he really wanted from her. Instead, she

41

watched him walk out and then listened as the bolt slid back into place.

She was alone once more, and she let the tears flow as the heartbeat noise started again, her hands clamped tightly over her ears.

Chapter Ten

I went to Luke's gym next.

It was part of a new development, all glass and steel girders, built on the site of a demolished mill on the outskirts of Blackley. Shops were on one side, entertainment on the other, as long as you liked bowling and pizza. Luke's gym was in-between, a guilt trip as you walked back to your car.

I could see the metal frames of the equipment and exercise bikes as I got near to the entrance, the poseurs gallery lined up in rows near the huge windows. I could hear music thumping out of speakers as I walked inside, accompanied by the occasional clang of weights. There was a bored young woman in a polo shirt at the reception desk. She glanced at my midriff and reached for an application form. I put my business card on the counter.

'I'm writing a story on Luke Howarth,' I said. 'Is there anyone I could speak to?'

I detected a change in her mood. 'The press came here last week,' she said, her voice timid. 'I thought you'd all got bored.'

I shook my head. 'Luke deserved more than that,'

I replied, guessing that she might be a friend. 'I want to find out what happened to him. Were you one of his friends?'

'Not really,' she said, but then looked apologetic. 'I don't mean that I didn't like him. I haven't been here long, but he seemed pretty nice. Callum was Luke's best friend.' She looked at her watch. 'He'll be on a break soon. I'll page him to come down.' Then she pointed me towards the coffee bar in one corner of the gym.

I was halfway through my latte when I saw a tall man walking towards me, his skin dark, his hair shaved afro. He wore the same uniform polo shirt as the girl on reception, but he filled it, the sleeves tight against his arms, his broad chest visible through the cloth. I stood up to greet him, my hand outstretched. 'Callum, I presume.'

He didn't take it.

'Thanks for seeing me at short notice,' I added.

He sat down and folded his arms.

'Had your fill of journalists in the last week?' I ventured.

He paused for a moment, and then relaxed, and his eyes lost some of their hostility. 'I just can't see what good they have done. Luke was just a passing story to them, but he was my friend.'

'Well, I'm not writing for the dailies. I'm writing a feature.'

'On what?'

'On Luke. A tribute.' I tried to hold his gaze as I said it, so that he wouldn't spot the lie.

'What do you want to know?' he asked.

I tapped my pen on my lap and asked, 'How about Luke and Sarah? What kind of couple were they?'

'You'll need to write two stories to get that,' he said.

I was confused. 'What do you mean?'

'They weren't a couple,' Callum replied.

I was still confused.

'C'mon, get real,' said Callum, shaking his head at me. 'They were fucking each other, that's all. Have you been out of the game that long?' Before I could ask him what he meant, he added, 'No offence, but you don't look like a man on the hunt.'

'But I get the impression that they were "Luke and Sarah" – you know, a couple,' I said, looking down at myself, seeing the old boot-fit jeans and tatty jumper, bought the year before and worn too often.

Callum snorted. 'That's because she killed him. Go back a couple of months, maybe even less than that, and Luke was my friend, and Sarah was just one of the girls he was seeing.'

'So it was casual?' I asked, still surprised. Katie had talked like it was a whirlwind, that special one.

'Casual? Oh yes, very casual,' Callum answered, laughing slightly, his eyebrows raised. 'Yeah, sure, Luke liked her. She was good-looking, and had a great body. He met her in one of the clubs in town, and it seemed like most of the eyes were on her.'

'A good notch on his belt?'

Callum shrugged, unapologetic. 'Think of the women you wish you'd been with, and I bet one is a teacher. Something about it, isn't there? The discipline, the respect.'

'Maybe for schoolboys,' I replied.

Callum blinked, spotted the jibe. 'Maybe in ten years' time I'll think like you,' he responded.

A smile flickered on my lips. He'd won that point. Then I remembered about the rage, the knife in the chest. And I thought about what Katie had told me, and so I said, 'What if I told you that Sarah was getting in deeper, perhaps much deeper than Luke?'

'She knew the score, they all did,' he replied, and then it was his turn to smile. He had spotted me for what I was: settled. But he presumed that I wanted his life. Sometimes I liked the idea of being single, but it was like waiting for summer: you expected the sunshine but only ever got showers.

'What do you mean "all"?' I asked.

Callum laughed at me. 'He was a fitness instructor. Do you have any idea what it's like?'

I shook my head.

'Middle-aged women try to hang on to their youth by booking one of us,' he continued. 'They try and get back to a shape that they haven't had since they were teenagers, and in between breaths they try and seduce us.'

'And do they?'

'That depends. Some of the women look good, and sometimes there are some young clients, maybe young women trying to burn off the pregnancy weight. Our only rule is that they have to be single; we don't want angry husbands coming down here.'

'Cramp your style?'

'Don't look at me like that,' he snapped at me. 'We

all know the rules. Do you think the women care about us? Course not. We're just muscles to them, something different from their ex-husband. Sarah was the same. All coy and reserved on the outside, but once you take them home, well, you can guess the rest. Luke said it was like peeling off a mask, you know, like the angel was really the devil in wings and a white dress.'

'So there were other women?'

'Luke was a good-looking bloke – there were always other women.'

'Anyone special? Or any who didn't like being unsuccessful with him?'

'He didn't tell me that much,' Callum said, softening slightly. 'Just man-talk, you know, all about the conquests, not the losses.'

I made some notes, scribbles that I knew I would have to make sense of later. He had some good quotes, but I was starting to feel uneasy. Katie had described the relationship as close, but now Luke's friend had described it as relaxed, and whatever it had been, Luke had ended up with a knife buried into his chest. The two things didn't add up.

'Did Luke have a temper?' I asked.

Callum looked surprised by the question. 'What do you mean?'

'I'm just wondering why Sarah would stab him, if it was so casual. Self-defence?'

'No,' Callum replied warily. 'Luke was a pretty chilled-out kind of person.'

'But maybe there was something affecting his mood.'

'What like?'

I sensed some defensiveness in his question. I pointed at Callum's arms, the veins being throttled by the knitted sleeve of his polo shirt. 'You work in a gym,' I said. 'You'll know what goes on in the pursuit of physique.'

'Are you saying Luke was on drugs?'

I cocked my head. 'I don't know, but you don't end up looking like you do on chicken and pasta.'

Anger flashed across Callum's face, his jaw clenching as he glared at me.

'Roid rage,' I pressed, trying to guess the answer from his response. 'Perhaps Sarah was just defending herself?'

Callum stood up quickly, his chair rocking back on its legs. 'Is that what you're going to write?' he demanded.

'I'll write the truth,' I replied.

'It doesn't sound like much of a tribute,' he said.

'You haven't given me much to admire about him.'

'Please leave,' he said, his voice low and angry, his brow furrowed as he stared at me.

'Nothing else to add?' I asked, pushing for one more quote.

Callum didn't answer, and we both knew the interview was over.

I thanked him for his time and walked towards the door. I stopped for a moment and thought about apologising. His closest friend had died and I was making allegations without proof. I had lost both my parents and so I knew how raw grief could be. Had I sold out my humanity for the value of a good quote? I glanced back at Callum, but from the hostile stare he was giving me, I could tell that any apology would be pointless.

When I got back to my car, I threw my pad onto the

passenger seat and wondered whether I was wasting my time. Sarah Goode was missing, and her occasional lover was dead. It sounded straightforward. If I wanted to use it there had to be an angle, something different from the average murder report.

But there was something different. I sensed it. If Katie was right, Sarah had killed Luke in a lover's rage, passion gone wrong. But if Callum was telling the truth, it was a murder without reason.

I checked my watch and wondered what Laura would say if she knew what I was doing. No, I knew what she would think; the memory of the argument that morning was still sour. So if I was going to write the story, I wanted Laura to find out from me.

Laura McGanity tried not to look at the prisoner in front of her, as she sat on a plastic chair that was bolted to the floor to stop prisoners throwing them, in one of the interview rooms at the end of the cell complex. No windows, no natural light. The floor was dotted with old chewing gum and scarred by cigarette burns, souvenirs of life before the smoking ban. Pete was next to her, leaning forward to make the cramped space seem even smaller.

The prisoner in front of her had been arrested from the middle of the brawl, dishing out black eyes to anyone who came close, until a blast of parva spray sent him to the gutter, crying at the pain in his eyes. His bravado had melted now, and he had slept off most of the drink, but he was trying hard to keep his breakfast down. He'd been sick down his jumper, and he held it in his hands, putting it to his mouth whenever another wave of nausea hit him. Laura kicked the bin towards him and shook her head, trying to breathe through her mouth. This wasn't on the recruitment poster.

Pete Dawson was frustrated. 'Doesn't look like he wants to explain himself,' he said to Laura. 'Looks like the court will form its own conclusion.'

'Do you really think it will get that far?' asked the prisoner's legal representative, a young police-station runner in shiny pinstripes and gelled hair who looked like he wanted to be much further away from his client than the bolted-down chair would allow.

'I wasn't talking to you,' barked Pete.

'Okay,' the legal rep replied, his smirk forcing Pete to take a deep breath to keep his anger at bay. He turned to his client and said theatrically, 'For the benefit of the tape, let's hear it one more time.'

The prisoner held his jumper to his mouth. 'No comment,' came the muffled reply.

Laura turned away as the smell of the jumper wafted towards her. She was frustrated by the no comment mantra, but she knew the advice was right. The other fighters didn't want to help, so if he didn't confess, he would win the day.

'Let's suspend the interview,' she said. 'I think we all need some fresh air.'

As Pete clicked off the tape machine, a twin-deck black cube, Laura said, 'We're going to check out the CCTV. Your client can think about that as he sits in his cell.'

As she headed for the door, Pete just behind her, she

heard a groan, and then the splash of the prisoner's vomit as he lost his battle with his stomach. From the curse that came from his rep, it seemed that he hadn't quite made it to the waste bin.

Laura stepped into the corridor and smiled at Pete. 'That's one interview room out of action for a while.'

'Do you think we should have waited?' he asked. 'Let him recover? He can't think straight.'

Laura shook her head. 'The advice would have been the same, except the rep would have kept his shoes clean. I think I prefer it this way.'

'So what now?'

Laura checked her watch. The cells were full, the others on the CRT working their way through the list, and so when they had finished with this prisoner, it would be time to move on to another.

'Like I said, I'm heading out to the town hall, see if the cameras picked anything up. Maybe we'll get something more than midnight lovers.'

Pete scowled. The camera operators used to liven up their evenings by looking out for drunken couples snatching romance in alleys, just behind the bottle crates and dustbins, but two people had lost their jobs when the cameras missed an assault that put someone in a coma. Pete had been the one who had explained that to the victim's parents, and the memory wasn't a pleasant one.

'And if we've nothing?' he asked.

She joined him in a scowl. 'Then he walks, like always.'

Laura felt her phone buzz. As she looked down, she saw that it was a text from Jack. *'Coffee somewhere? Got some info for you.'*

'Got to go,' she said to Pete. 'Get him in a cell and write up the interview summary. I won't be long.'

As she turned to walk away, the legal rep opened the door, his face white, his mouth set in a grimace. He glanced down towards his trousers. 'Have you got a towel?'

Laura was smiling as she left.

Chapter Eleven

Rod Lucas had been to the hospital shop, and he looked up from his newspaper when he heard Abigail stir.

He checked his watch. He had been there for a couple of hours.

Abigail groaned and tried to roll over.

'Miss Hobbs?'

She turned towards him and reached out. There was a bandage over one eye, and the other one looked swollen and red. 'Who is it?' she asked, sounding quiet and weak.

'It's all right,' he said, and took her hand. Her skin was cold and her hand felt brittle. 'There's no need to move, Miss Hobbs. I'm a police officer.'

Abigail raised her head, and then she winced and lay back down again. 'Am I still in the hospital?' she asked, her Lancashire accent slowed down by the drawl of the countryside.

'Yes, you are,' he replied, his voice gentle and soothing. 'You'll be home soon.'

She took a few short breaths, and then asked, 'What happened?'

'Someone set you a trap,' he said.

She swallowed, and Rod could tell that she was thinking back to the events of the morning.

'Tibbs? I could hear Tibbs. Is he all right?' she asked.

He took hold of her hand and gave it a squeeze, as if the action would make her stronger. 'Tibbs is dead, Miss Hobbs.'

Abigail gave out a small cry as the events of the morning came back to her. She gripped his hand tightly as she realised what had exploded in front of her eyes.

He let her cry it out for a while, but when her quiet sobs died away, he asked gently, 'Who would do that to you?'

He passed her a tissue, and as she wiped her nose, she replied, 'I don't know. I've done nothing to harm anyone.'

'No enemies?'

Abigail waved her hand dismissively. Rod took that as a no, but he wasn't too sure.

'It's happened to other people, not just you,' said Rod, watching her face for some recognition, but Abigail didn't respond. 'Have you heard that?' he pressed. 'Do you know these other people?'

She turned away.

'Miss Hobbs?'

'Go to your family,' she said.

'How do you know I've got a family?'

'You have a kind voice,' she said softly. 'That comes from contentment. And your family are waiting for you.'

That stalled him for a moment, but he asked again, 'What's going on, Miss Hobbs?'

Abigail didn't answer. She rolled over in the bed so that he couldn't see her face any more.

He stood. 'Sorry to have disturbed you,' he said. 'If you want to tell me anything, get in touch.' And he wrote his name and number on a scrap of paper and placed it on the small cupboard next to Abigail's bed.

His footsteps were just light taps as he left the room. No one else stirred. He took one last look at Abigail, but she hadn't moved.

I waited for Laura in a coffee bar a few minutes' walk from the police station, in a cobbled backstreet with views over the cathedral gardens. It had a mocha-coloured shop-front and rickety metal tables, none of the bright lights of the chain coffee-houses, but it sold good coffee and that was enough.

I had been thinking about Katie Gray, how she had been with me, that touch of her hand before I left. But then I saw Laura at the end of the street, and I felt a jump. Was it guilt? Or was it something better than that? Perhaps it was the excitement I used to have when I saw Laura, that feeling that I had got luckier than I deserved.

She flashed a quick look down the backstreet but then she waved when she saw me looking out of the window. I asked the café owner for another cappuccino and reached out my hand as she sat down. My fingers brushed over her knuckles, like we were stealing moments together.

'I'm sorry about this morning,' I said softly.

Laura moved her hand away. 'Are you softening me up for something I don't want to hear?'

'What do you mean?'

Laura sighed and then it turned into a smile. 'I love you to death, Jack Garrett,' she said, 'but if you need to see me, and it's to do with work, I need to worry.'

I reached out for her hand again. She didn't move it this time, and I felt her fingers grip mine. They felt different to Katie's. Older somehow, her skin dry, the veins showing on the back of her hand.

'I went to see Sam Nixon this morning,' I said.

'I know. Keep going.'

'He wanted me to meet someone. Two people in fact.' I paused for effect, to make sure I could properly gauge Laura's response. 'They were Sarah Goode's parents.'

Laura didn't react at first. Then I saw her eyes widen. 'The teacher wanted for murder?'

I nodded slowly.

'Jack, what are you playing at?'

'Nothing. That's why I'm telling you.'

'What did they want?'

'In an ideal world, to turn the clock back,' I answered. 'But as they can't, they want me to find their daughter.'

'Why? Do they think she is innocent?'

'I don't know. Perhaps they just want to stop her from doing something stupid.'

'But why you?'

I gave a small smile. 'I'm cheaper than a private detective. If there is a story in it, I'll do the research. They just want to find their daughter.'

'But why go through Sam Nixon?'

I didn't answer that. I knew that Laura would work it out as quickly as I had.

'They want you to find her so that they can bring her in on their terms,' she said. 'They want to get her story straight.'

'Maybe. I just don't know,' I said. 'But they know that Sarah is in trouble and so went to a defence lawyer first.'

'So why are you telling me?' said Laura, and she pulled her fingers away again.

'What's wrong?' I asked.

Laura looked into her coffee for a few seconds, and then she said, 'I've put my career on hold for Bobby, to make sure he stays with us. I'd even give it up completely for him, if I had to, but you won't even give up a story.'

'It's not like that,' I protested. 'It won't affect the custody case, because it won't go to print for a long time, at least until after she is convicted.'

'So why are you telling me, if it won't affect anything with Bobby?' she asked.

'Because if I'm being used, someone else is in control of what happens, and I don't like that. So I want you to tell the murder team what I'm doing. They won't like it, but if I find out where she is before they do, I'll tell them.'

Laura folded her arms. 'Have you met the murder team?' When I shook my head, she continued, 'They've been strutting around the station ever since Luke's body was found. We're just the small-town hicks who can't cope, waiting to be saved by headquarters, and you're worse than that, because you're not in the job. All you'll do is antagonise them if you get in the way.'

I raised my eyebrows. 'You don't sound pleased with them.'

Laura sighed. 'I'm just bored, Jack. I didn't join the police to process prisoners. I joined it to solve crimes, as corny as it sounds.'

'So maybe you know how I feel?'

I saw her soften, felt her fingers grip mine again.

'The judge isn't going to give Geoff custody of Bobby just because you're good at your job,' I said.

Tears flashed into Laura's eyes. She took a deep breath. 'We've been through this too many times now,' she said, 'and I know that nothing is dead certain in a courtroom. I'm not taking that chance.'

When I didn't respond, she added, 'You're going to get involved, though, aren't you?'

'I think it's worth a look.'

Laura thought about that for a few seconds, and then she stood up to go. 'I've got to get back to work,' she said.

'Laura?'

'You'll do what you want to do, Jack,' she said wearily. 'You always do.'

And then she went.

I saw the waiter looking at me when I turned around. He shrugged. I didn't have a response to that. Instead, I watched Laura disappear out of view, her head down, and I thought that she looked a long way from home.

Chapter Twelve

Sarah was kneeling on the floor, her hands over her ears, the deep bass of the heartbeats booming out of the speakers making her dizzy, her own heartbeat keeping time. Then the speakers went quiet.

She paused for a moment, relished the silence, but when she heard the bolt slide on the door, she scuttled back against the wall.

He walked slowly into the room, the black hood silhouetted against the lights from the ceiling. For a moment, Sarah saw the gap behind him, the way out, but as he got closer all she could see was his dark shadow, the room filled with the rasping breaths emanating from under the hood.

He didn't move as he stood and looked down at her.

Sarah thought of her parents, and she felt tears choke her up. She took a deep breath, tried to swallow them away, and asked, 'What do you want me to do?' When he didn't respond immediately, she added, 'I'll do what you want, if you'll just let me go.' Her voice broke as she pleaded with him and a tear ran down her cheek.

'Take off your clothes,' he said, his voice deep and muffled, almost gravelly.

Sarah closed her eyes and grabbed the open neck of her shirt, pulling it tight. This was it now, the reason, what it was all about. Just close your eyes, she told herself. Don't think about it. Give him what he wants, and then get out. She started to shake, felt her chin tremble, more tears on her cheek. She took a deep breath and shook her head, tried to find some reserves of courage.

He took one step forward. Sarah took one step back. 'Why are you doing this?' she shouted at him.

He kept on walking towards her. Sarah stepped back again, but the wall stopped her. She could smell cigarettes on him, rolling tobacco, strong, pungent.

Sarah looked down and reached for the top button of her shirt.

'Don't hurt me,' she screamed, and then she began to sob, unable to stop herself. She flicked at the button, her hands trembling, and the top of her shirt fell open. It was one of Luke's shirts and it was too big for her. She flicked at the next button and felt the coldness of the room against her breasts. She was exposed to him, goose-pimples across her chest, and she could smell oil on him, and sweat.

Sarah yelped as he grabbed her chin and made her look at him. She could see only the black cloth of the hood, moving in and out faster now, his breaths deeper.

He grabbed at the next button down, his fingers rough and dry. Her cleavage was flecked with sweat despite the cold. He ran his finger between her breasts and rubbed the moisture between his fingers. It seemed almost tender, caring, and then he said softly, 'If you don't do as I say, I'll hurt you.'

Sarah choked on a sob, and as she closed her eyes, she steeled herself, tried not to think about what she was doing.

She undid the rest of her buttons and let the shirt fall to the floor. She looked down, saw the dirt on her jeans. She undid them and let them fall to her ankles, stepping out of them so that she was naked in front of him. She felt exposed, vulnerable, so she put her arms across her chest and pressed her thighs together. Make it quick, she thought, and looked at the ceiling. Don't make it hurt. Just do it and let me go. Please.

Sarah opened her eyes when she heard movement. He was no longer there. She stepped away from the wall just as he came back into the room, except that this time he was carrying something. A hosepipe.

She was confused at first, but then she looked down and saw how dirty she was. Her skin looked mottled and cold, and her legs were soiled from when she had been trapped in the box.

She cried out as the blast of water hit her. It was icy, the stream coming at her like a punch. Sarah twisted, tried to get out of its way, but it followed her. The dirt around her feet turned into mud. She thought she heard someone else in the room, but maybe it was the water bouncing off the walls. It smacked into her chest, against her legs, her stomach. She cried out but the sound was lost in the noisy rush of water.

Then the water stopped. Sarah gasped with cold as the water dried on her body, her hair still dripping wet.

He moved towards her, his boots squelching in the mud. She didn't look up, just cried and flinched when she felt his hands on her shoulders. They felt warm and clammy against her frozen skin.

'Why are you doing this?' she asked, her teeth chattering with cold.

'I do it because I like it,' he replied. 'Isn't that a good enough reason?'

Sarah looked at the hood, tried to guess at the face behind it. All she saw was black cloth. No features. No eye-holes.

'That's evil,' she said quietly, shivering.

He stepped back in fake shock. 'Evil?' he asked, and Sarah heard the pleasure in his voice. 'What does that mean?'

'You know what it means,' she shouted, angry now, tears running down her face.

He shook his head, enjoying himself. 'I give power to my imagination, that's all,' he said. 'You live your life in fear, scared of consequences. I don't. That's what makes us so different.'

'You don't know me,' she said.

'Oh, I do, Sarah Goode. Better than you think. Everything has consequences, even the things that you do. Your little games, Sarah, they all mean something.'

Sarah swallowed, started to shiver again, but this time it was through fear.

'And what if I don't want to play your games?' she asked.

'Then you will die,' he said simply. He gripped her hair in his hands and whispered into her ear, 'but I could show you a different way. No more fear, no more being held back.'

Sarah closed her eyes.

'Will you live your life my way?' he asked, letting go of her.

Sarah looked at the floor and nodded her head slowly. 'I'll do whatever you want me to do.'

She screamed as the water hit her again, smacking hard against her chest and then her face. She tried to curl up, her arms wrapped around her head, but the water carried on until she could feel herself slipping in the mud.

When the water stopped, she looked up at her captor. He was standing over her, the hosepipe dripping in his hands. He stepped forward and pressed his hands onto her shoulders, turning her around. Sarah could feel his eyes on her even through the hood, examining her, as if he was searching for something. She stared at the floor, tried not to think what he might do. Once he had turned her full circle, he grabbed her face in his hands and pulled her towards him. Sarah tried to look away, but he held on to her cheeks, made her look at him.

'What do you see?' he asked slowly, his breath smelling stale and unclean, even through the hood.

'I see you,' Sarah replied.

'Not me. What do you see ahead, for you? Your future?'

Sarah swallowed, and then closed her eyes.

'I don't see one,' she said quietly.

'Have you ever wondered about the end?' he whispered. 'What it will be like to draw that last breath, to look into the abyss, to know that you'll know the answer soon enough, life after death, or is it just nothing?'

Sarah swallowed back tears and small moans of fear escaped.

'I want to see the end flicker across your eyes so clearly that I can feel it too,' he continued. Sarah could hear him licking his lips, and then he let go of her and turned to leave the room.

When he'd gone, Sarah saw that he'd left no food. And her clothes were gone. She was naked. No blankets, no bed, the incessant beam of the headlights illuminating the room and her feet cold in the wet dirt.

Then she heard the speakers pulse back into life, and the heartbeat sound filled the room once more as she sank back against the wall, sliding downwards, the stone cutting into her back, her cries mixing with the repetitive thumps.

Chapter Thirteen

Rod Lucas looked down at the addresses on his lap, the two other victims of recent explosions, and they were all on his patch, a rural area around Pendle Hill. Although he had worked in the towns nearby earlier in his career – Blackley, Turners Fold – he had spent most of his career patrolling the tight lanes around the hill. He understood the crime in his area, mostly diesel thefts or large brawls in remote pubs, country boys settling their disputes in the old-fashioned way. The explosions were different. They seemed planned, targeted.

He was outside one of the addresses. He checked his list against the number on the house, peering through the mud smeared on the windscreen of his Land Rover, and stepped out onto the pristine new tarmac of a modern housing estate. He looked along and saw a succession of green lawns, square and flat. As he walked towards the door, faux Georgian, with wooden panels and a frosted glass arch, he heard only the hard smack of his boots on the paved driveway, the curved streets quiet. It took just one knock to get the door to open.

'Hello?' said a female face from behind a security chain, young and cautious.

'I'm Inspector Rod Lucas,' he said. 'I want to talk to you about the explosion in your garden last week.'

'You don't look like the police.'

Rod looked at his outfit. He couldn't argue with that. He was still wearing his pruning clothes, a checked shirt and grubby corduroys. He pulled out his wallet and showed the Lancashire Police crest.

The door closed for a moment, and Rod heard the rattle of the security chain. When the door opened fully, the face at the door turned into a teenage girl running down the hall. College girl was Rod's guess.

'Mum?' she shouted. 'There's a policeman to see you.'

The girl turned round and pointed to a room at the front of the house. 'Go in,' she said. 'Mum won't be long.' When Rod smiled, she blushed and then skipped into a room at the back of the house.

Rod opened the door to the living room, and he was surprised. He had expected a modern look; laminated flooring, coal-effect fire, maybe a large television. Instead, it was similar in style to Abigail's cottage, like a Gothic lair, with a heavy black chandelier and dark red walls. The fireplace was high and open and made of dull grey stone, more suited to a castle than a modern box in a faceless estate.

He turned around when he heard the door open, and in walked a woman in her early forties, her hair dark and long, crimped into waves, wearing a long linen dress, her feet bare.

'Isla Marsden?' Rod queried. When she smiled

whimsically, he said, 'I'm here to ask some questions about the recent explosion in your garden.'

'It was in the shed,' said Isla, her voice soft, an almost dreamy quality.

'It's happened to someone else,' said Rod. 'Except that someone was hurt today.' When Isla didn't respond, he said, 'It was an old lady called Abigail Hobbs.'

Rod saw the flinch, just a widening of her eyes, before Isla quickly brushed her hair from her face, a reflex action, and resumed her faraway smile.

'Do you know her?' he asked.

Isla made a bad show of thinking about her answer, and then she shook her head. 'I don't think so.'

'Her cat died, and Abigail is in hospital, hurt quite badly. Are you sure you don't know her?'

Isla shook her head again.

'Do you have any more ideas about who might have caused the explosion?' he asked.

Again, Isla responded with just a shake of the head, and then she said, 'I thought I had to ask you that question,' her voice defensive.

'We're trying our best,' he said solemnly. When she didn't answer, he nodded and said, 'Thank you, Mrs Marsden. I'll keep in touch.'

As he walked out of the room, heading for the front door, he paused. 'It's funny, though, Mrs Marsden, about the coincidence,' he said.

'What do you mean?'

He turned round and saw that her composure had slipped. He looked down at her hand. 'You share the same taste in jewellery.' As her cheeks flushed, he pointed at her right hand. 'You even wear it on the same finger. Third finger, right hand. The screaming face, silver on black. Abigail has one too.'

As she looked at him, her eyes worried now, Rod nodded at her.

'Thank you for your time,' he said. 'Call me if you want to talk,' and then he clicked the door closed as he went back to his vehicle.

I was heading for the college, trying to shake off my unease about my private life. I wanted to speak to Katie again, to find a reason why Luke's friend had described Sarah's relationship with Luke so differently. I remembered that Katie said she had lectures, so college seemed like a good place to start.

I didn't normally feel old. I was thirty-four but had kept my hairline, just speckles of grey spoiling the dark waves, but suddenly I felt a generation gap as I hung around the college building. It was an offshoot of one of the Manchester universities, a seven-storey concrete slab in the middle of Blackley, next to a one-way system, so that lectures were disturbed by posing young men driving the loop, watching the girls and playing music at distorted levels, making the shop windows rattle as they went past. Young students with rucksacks and attitudes stared at me as I looked around, their faces obscured by hoods, their legs stick-thin in baggy denims. The security guard was chatting up the young female students, his chest puffed out, feet apart.

Katie had said she was studying history, so I made my way inside and searched for the history department.

It didn't have much of one, not what you could call a faculty, just lectures taking place on different floors, marked out by timetables printed on notice-boards. I walked the corridors but I couldn't see her.

I headed out and decided to take a drive past the house. I struck lucky. Katie was just locking up the house as I drove up the street, and she looked startled as I scraped my wheels against the kerb, squeezing behind a scruffy green Fiesta. When I jumped out of the Stag, she relaxed and smiled. 'Back so soon?'

'I've got a few more questions,' I replied.

'Well, I was just going out.'

'Let me take you,' and I went to open the passenger door.

Katie looked up and down the street before throwing her bag into the passenger footwell and climbing in.

'Where do you need to be?' I asked.

Katie thought for a moment, and then said, 'College will do.'

'Again? How many lectures do you have a day?'

'I need to go to the library, that's all,' she replied. When I didn't respond, she turned towards me and asked, 'What do you want to know?'

'Just more about Luke and Sarah,' I replied. 'There are a few things I can't get straight.'

'What like?'

I set off driving, the Stag struggling up the steep hill. 'You told me before that Luke and Sarah were close, that Sarah loved him,' I said. 'It would explain a jealous rage, I suppose, the knife in the chest, but Luke's friend tells it differently. He talked like it was a casual thing

69

on both sides. That makes a rage less likely. So which one is real?'

Katie looked out of the window as old houses were replaced by traffic lights and a quick route out of town, the grey strip of the inner ring road, trees and flowers along the edge to break up the concrete. 'The real Sarah is different to what people think,' she said.

We were near the college again, and so I found somewhere to park and turned off the engine. Katie turned towards me, one knee onto the seat, and ran her fingers through her hair. 'What do you think about Luke's murder?'

I could smell Katie's perfume, sweet and cloying. 'I don't think anything,' I replied. 'Not yet. So tell me, why do you think Luke saw it differently to Sarah?'

'Does it matter?' she asked.

'Maybe. It can't be a lover's rage if it was just a fling.'

'Are you in love, Jack?'

I found myself about to say no, I didn't know why, like I'd been caught off-guard, but then I stopped myself and asked her why she wanted to know.

'You're a man, Jack,' Katie continued. 'When have you ever told your friends that you loved a woman? I don't mean find attractive, or wanted to fuck, or whatever. I mean told a friend that you truly loved a woman?'

I didn't answer when I realised that she was right. And Callum too. That living up to being a man is all about the conquests, not the losses.

'Sarah was in love,' she said, her voice low and soft. 'She talked about Luke all the time, like she was making plans. If Luke thought differently, well, that was his choice. He wouldn't be the first man to say I love you and not mean it.'

'So that's it then?' I said incredulously. 'This all happened because Sarah loved Luke, but he didn't respond? Was she that unpredictable?'

Katie pulled at some strands of hair, twisting it between her fingers before letting it fall to her head. 'Some people are like that,' she said. 'Great fun when things are going well, but she could be nasty and hurtful, very hot-tempered.'

'A lot of people snap,' I said, 'but they don't all plunge knives into their boyfriend's chest. They'd just been in bed together. It seems quite a leap.'

'I wasn't there when it happened, so I wouldn't know,' Katie said, and she sounded hurt, like I was pushing it too much. Then she sighed. 'I've never seen a dead body before,' she said quietly, and she dabbed her nose with her sleeve, like a nervous reaction, her cuff over her hand. 'He was just sort of splayed out,' she continued, although I was surprised at the evenness of her voice. 'There was this knife, just there, sticking out, with blood all over the bed. I've never seen so much blood before.'

'What did you do?'

Katie gave a small laugh, embarrassed. 'It sounds stupid now, but I called an ambulance. I don't know why, I could tell he was dead, but it was like an automatic reaction. When they came, they called the police.' She rested her elbow on the car door and looked at me, her eyes filled with worry. 'I'm scared, Jack.'

'You've no need to be,' I replied.

'Because you're here?' She shuffled closer towards me

and put her hand on my leg. 'You seem like a kind man.'
Her eyes stared into mine. Before I could answer, she
said quietly, 'Hold me.'

I was surprised, her touch unexpected. I closed my
eyes, knowing that I had to end it as her hand stroked
my leg. An image of Laura flashed into my head, and I
took hold of Katie's hand.

'It's okay,' she said softly, 'it doesn't mean anything.'

'It would mean something to me,' I said firmly, and
lifted her hand from my leg.

'I just needed someone to be there for me,' she said,
sounding hurt. 'I'm sorry. Just forget it.'

'No, no, it's not like that,' I protested, feeling guilty
now. 'It's just, well . . .'

'You might get caught?' She shook her head. 'Like I
said, it doesn't matter,' and then she reached for the door
handle.

'Don't,' I said, too quickly.

Katie turned around, a half-smile on her lips. 'What
is it?'

'I just want to finish the story,' I said. 'There are more
things I want to know.'

'Call me then, so we can spend more time together,'
Katie replied, flirting, and then she opened the door and
stepped onto the pavement.

I leaned across the passenger seat and asked, 'Do you
think Sarah killed him?'

Katie leaned into the car. 'Who else could it be?'

'If Sarah had killed Luke and run away,' I replied, 'she
would go somewhere she felt safe, maybe a favourite
holiday place, or with friends who didn't know about

Luke. Did Sarah ever talk about anywhere away from Blackley?'

'Everyone in Blackley dreams of being somewhere else,' she said.

'Except that not everyone leaves,' I responded. 'So did she talk of anywhere else?'

Katie shook her head. 'She's nearby.'

'How do you know?'

Katie looked round, seemed worried that someone might be listening, and then whispered, 'She has written to me.'

I was shocked. 'What do you mean?'

She gave me a knowing smile. 'Just that,' she said. 'I've been getting letters from Sarah.'

'There's been nothing in the papers about that,' I said.

'The police are keeping them quiet, and they told me not to say anything about them,' she replied.

I knew that sounded right. It was the sort of thing that the police would keep back, they had done ever since the Yorkshire Ripper tapes misled everyone and allowed Peter Sutcliffe to kill more women.

'What do they say?' I asked.

Katie shook her head at me. 'Give me a call, Jack Garrett, and you might just find out,' she said, and then she walked away, her bag swinging in her hand.

I jumped out of the car and shouted, 'Wait!', but Katie just kept on walking.

I watched her go, intrigued. I wanted to know more, I knew that, but I wondered what risks came with that, from the story and from Katie.

Chapter Fourteen

Blackley police station was on the edge of the town centre, in an old Victorian building next to the court, with steps to the front door and Roman arches over the windows. The interior showed its age, as paint flaked from the walls and cold draughts blew along the corridors. That would all be changing soon. The police were moving to a new-build station on the edge of Blackley, so the station was filled with boxes and crates as officers packed up exhibits and personal effects.

Laura was at the custody desk in its basement, a high wooden counter with dingy lighting and posters advertising prisoners' rights. The sergeant was hovering over a clipboard, watching Laura's prisoner count his change, making sure that he couldn't accuse anyone of stealing from him, before he got him to sign the custody record. An end to another fruitless day, thought Laura.

'There'll always be another time,' growled Pete.

'You said that last time,' came the reply, the prisoner smirking as he threaded his belt around his waist.

Laura placed her hand on Pete's arm as she saw him

tense, but then she saw someone through the glass in the custody door. DCI Karl Carson.

He was hard to miss, a large man in a lilac shirt and navy trousers, his tie bright purple, knotted large, like he had lost count when doing the final loop. His bald dome glowed bright pink, more scrubbed than shaved, his face just the same, with not even the trace of eyebrows to break up the shine. Laura knew his name, and his reputation had been whispered around the station when the murder squad moved in. Ruthless and rule-bending, sometimes arrogant, but he had a squad of eager young men devoted to him, knowing that Carson got results, either through sheer persistence, or often by persuading witnesses to talk to him when they had resisted the polite way, his squad happy to swap their social lives for long hours of overtime and the occasional glimpse of the spotlight.

Laura thought about her meeting with Jack, and she felt her anger bubble to the surface again, that he was interfering in a live case, and that it could affect her; she hadn't been in Blackley long enough to fall back on too much goodwill. But she realised that he was right about one thing: that it would look worse for both of them if it appeared that he was secretly helping Sarah Goode.

She mumbled to Pete that she would be back in a moment and buzzed herself out of the custody office with the swipe card that hung around her neck whenever she was in the station. Carson was moving quickly along the corridor, heading for the Incident Room. Laura caught up with him just as he was about to step inside.

'Can I have a word, sir?'

He stopped and looked at her, and then gave a quick smile.

'How can I help?'

Laura paused for a moment as she saw those in the Incident Room stop what they were doing and look at her. The scene was as it had been since their move from headquarters, a temporary stop-over from their normal base on the outskirts of Preston, just in Blackley for the Sarah Goode case: paperwork and coffee, fingers tapping on keyboards, eyes concentrated on computer monitors, pastel shirts and bright ties. But now the activity had stopped, and all eyes were on Laura.

'Can I have a word about the Sarah Goode case?' Laura asked.

She noticed Carson tuck in his stomach and puff out his chest. The trips to the gym didn't keep off the weight, but it turned his bulk into something solid. He looked to his colleagues before he answered, a smirk on his face. 'Fire away, sweetheart.'

Laura looked into the Incident Room again and wished she had waited. Most of the faces were smiling, but they weren't friendly. They were waiting for the show – and Laura knew that it was too late to back out.

'My boyfriend is a reporter,' she said, 'and he's been approached by Sarah Goode's parents.'

Carson blinked, the information registered, but then he started to grin. 'Boyfriend?' he said, turning to his team. 'How old is he? Sixteen?'

Laura went red, but from anger, not embarrassment. She didn't respond, knowing that she would say something she would later regret.

'Tell me more,' he said, smiling. 'What's your name?'

'DC McGanity,' replied Laura. 'On the CRT.'

'First name?' he said.

'Laura.'

'Okay, Laura, what did Sarah's parents want with your boyfriend?'

'They want him to find Sarah,' she replied. 'They went to their solicitor first, and he set up the meeting.'

'So it's coming through a lawyer?' Carson queried, sounding sceptical. 'And if he finds her?'

'He's got to tell her to hand herself in.'

'Why are you telling me?'

'Because he asked me to,' she replied.

'And what if he tells you more but doesn't ask you to repeat the favour? Will you still come and speak to me?' Before Laura had the time to respond, he said aggressively, 'Because pillow talk is not confidential. You hear anything, little lady, come down here and tell me. Understand?'

'I just thought you ought to know,' Laura replied, feeling humiliated, her heart pounding with anger. When she turned to leave the room, someone spluttered a laugh behind Carson, and he started to grin.

As she walked quickly back down the corridor, she was aware of a pause, and then she heard the noise of Carson's team laughing. She guessed that Carson was leading the chorus.

When Laura burst back into the custody office, she saw her prisoner's arrogant grin.

'If you hit him because he was messing around with your girlfriend,' she said to him, her stare hard and direct, 'you might have chosen the wrong tactic.'

The grin wavered. 'Why?'

'Us girls don't like to get lonely,' she said, stepping closer. 'I can bet who she spent last night with.' Laura looked at her watch theatrically. 'Do you want me to call her, to give him time to leave?'

The prisoner's face turned into an angry flush before the custody sergeant buzzed open the exit door. Laura stomped away quickly, slowing down only when Pete caught up with her.

'I could learn from you,' he said, as he got alongside her. 'Menace with a smile.'

Laura sighed. 'I let myself down,' she replied.

Pete laughed and waved it away. 'No, it was fun.'

As they walked along the corridor from the custody area, Laura heard laughter ahead. She guessed what was coming even before Carson appeared in the doorway, a few members of his team just behind him, sharing the joke.

They went quiet as Pete approached them, although the smiles remained. As Carson went past, Pete nodded and said, 'Afternoon, sir', more out of obligation than respect. Carson didn't respond. Instead, he looked down at Laura, before raising what should have been eyebrows at his team.

Laura looked down and took a deep breath, not yet ready for formalities. As their footsteps receded, she glanced back. One of Carson's men looked back towards her at the same time. He was dressed differently to the rest, in a dark polo shirt and casual trousers, bulky pockets on his thighs. As Laura looked, he smiled and nodded.

'If ever you need a reason not to get promoted, there's a few to choose from there,' said Pete.

Laura didn't respond at first. Instead, she walked on ahead, stopping only when she was back at her desk, holding another handover package.

'C'mon,' she said quietly. 'There's another cell to empty.'

Chapter Fifteen

It was cold, and getting colder. Sarah Goode walked quickly around the room, her arms wrapped around her chest as she tried to keep warm, but it was no protection for her naked body. Her skin was pale and goose-pimpled, and she dreaded the thought of the night ahead. When she looked down, she saw how dirty her feet were, made grubby as she walked around, the soles of her feet numb, the soil floor turned to mud by the hose-blast from earlier.

She knew she had to stay strong, but she was cold and she was hungry. Her primal instincts took over, her need for food and warmth and sleep.

The pulsing heartbeat still reverberated around the room. She tried to walk in time to it, to use it as a distraction, to get some strength from it, but every time she got close to the speakers she had to clamp her hands over her ears.

Then the noise stopped.

Sarah went still, listened out for a noise, some hint at what was to come. And then the lights went off.

It was dark and silent for a few blissful seconds, but

then she saw a sliver of light under the door. Someone was there. She heard the click of the lock, and, as the door slid open, someone holding a bright torch stepped into the room. All she could see was the light. She looked away and her vision swam with bright speckles.

Sarah shielded her eyes with her arm. 'Who's there?' she shouted. Maybe it was someone come to rescue her. 'Please, who is it?'

The same voice she had heard before answered.

'Have you thought any more?' he asked, his loud whisper filled with menace. He walked into the room and started to circle her, the torch beam constantly shining into her face, blinding her.

Sarah tried to move her face away, but the light was too direct. She tracked him, not letting him get behind her. 'I don't know what you mean?' she said, her voice filled with desperation.

'We talked about it before,' he said. 'Your future. What awaits you?'

Sarah shook her head. She tried to see behind the torch but it was too bright. 'I don't know, you tell me,' she said, and then she started to cry. 'I don't know what you want.'

'Don't be scared,' came the reply, followed by a low chuckle. He was enjoying this. 'Consequences, Sarah,' he said. 'That's all you are interested in. Fear of them. They hold you back.'

Sarah sank to her knees. 'I don't know what you mean,' she wailed, but then she scuttled backwards as she heard his steps in the dirt floor, coming towards her, slow and deliberate.

'Your time is running out,' he said as he got closer. 'I am not your enemy. Fear is your enemy.' And then he laughed again, this time low and mean.

Her head hung down and she dug her hands into the mud, cold between her fingers. 'Please, please, please,' she sobbed. 'Let me go. I won't say anything. Just let me go home. Please.'

He paused, and then said, 'That's a lie, and it's wrong to tell lies.'

Sarah looked up, sucked in air, tried to calm herself down. 'I can't do this,' she said. 'I don't know what game you are playing, but I don't want to play any more.'

'It's no game,' he said. 'I want to see what you see, that's all, just that moment.'

'What moment?'

'The final moment,' he answered, his voice turned into a growl. 'It's unique, that glimpse, when you know what lies ahead, the answer to everything. The final look back on yourself, and that last look into the future. Is there life beyond what we know?'

'So I'm going to die?'

He laughed. 'We're all going to die, Sarah.'

Sarah put her face in her hands. 'What about Luke?' she said quietly. 'He'll tell the police.'

He laughed again, but louder.

'What's so funny?' asked Sarah, but she felt her stomach turn as she guessed what he'd done. She put her arms over her head and leaned forward, so that her forehead touched the soil. It was cold on her face, and images of Luke flashed through her mind. Smiles, laughs, good times, all rushing into her head. She started to tap her head lightly against the soil. Then she got faster, and her moans turned into screeches, the pain as she banged her head a distraction, until she was rocking up and down, her arms clasped around her body.

She looked up at him. 'You've killed him,' she screamed. 'You fucking monster!'

He knelt down so that the hood was next to her face. 'He didn't come to help you, did he?' he mocked. 'He stayed in bed as we took you to the car. What was it? Drunk? Or just not bothered?'

Tears streamed down her face. She clutched her stomach, his words making her want to retch.

'Maybe he thought it was you running up the stairs,' he continued. 'He was still under the sheets when I ran in there.'

When Sarah didn't respond, he leaned into her ear and whispered, 'Would you like to kill me? Right now, if you had the weapon, would you do it?'

Sarah didn't answer.

'You could do it, right now. Your hands around my neck. I would fall over, you would overpower me.'

Sarah stayed silent, but as she felt his eyes on her, even through the cloth, she spat at him.

He wiped off her spittle. 'You see,' he said, 'there's not much that separates us. Just my courage, and your cowardice.'

He stood up and left the room. And as the door slammed shut, the lights came back on, and the sound of the heartbeat returned, louder this time.

Chapter Sixteen

Bobby was playing on the floor as I browsed the internet, looking for information on Sarah Goode. He was talking to himself, soft chirrups, all part of his game. I liked the distraction. I worked better with a background sound, much different to the hush of Blackley Library.

The library had been my first stop after leaving Katie, to get copies of the stories written about Sarah. It was a long Victorian building, an old workhouse, with stained glass and arched doorways, incongruous among the glass shop-fronts further along the street, where bored sales assistants stared out of the windows and fiddled with their necklaces, the lunchtime rush long gone.

I was able to spend an hour making copies of the articles that had been written about Sarah, and now they were spread across the table. They all had the same theme: a pretty young teacher had killed a boy and run away. It wasn't explicit, but all week long there had been tributes to Luke, about what a nice young man he had been, sporty, outgoing, good looking. The comments about Sarah were different, tinged with surprise, at how a popular young teacher, vibrant and pretty, could kill someone.

I started to trawl through the Google hits once I'd read the newspaper articles, to find out more about Sarah, and it only took a few pages to start to build up a picture of her life. Sarah was listed on Friends Reunited, a jokey entry, saying how she had left school but then gone back, alongside her graduation picture, showing Sarah with a proud smile, her face dotted by freckles, her parents alongside. On other websites, I found news from her workplace, a state school on the edge of Blackley, not often a first choice when the applications went in. A school play. Ofsted reports. A charity event.

I browsed Facebook for her, it was always good for a quote, and wasn't surprised when I found her. I couldn't access her page, though; Sarah would have to accept my 'friend request' for me to be able to do that. I sent a request anyway, it only took one click, and then I turned to look at Bobby. He had found the play dough made by Laura a couple of days before, just salt dough laced with food colouring. He was cutting into it with a plastic knife, his tongue darting onto his lip with concentration.

'What have you got there?' I asked.

He looked up, distracted from his game, and then he beamed at me, the dimples he'd inherited from Laura flickering in his cheeks. 'I've made you a pizza,' he said, and held up a lump of green dough criss-crossed with lines.

I found myself smiling back at him, but I felt a kick of guilt as well. He shouldn't be making things for me. He should be making it for his father. What was I doing, making him live up here, so far from everyone close to him?

'That looks great,' I said. 'Do you want me to eat it now?'

Bobby smiled proudly and brought over the lump of dough and placed it on the table in front of me. I sat him on my knee and tickled him, enjoyed his squirming and his giggling.

'When's Mummy back?' he asked between laughs.

'I don't know. Soon.'

'Do you like your pizza?'

I mimicked some lip-smacking sounds. 'The best one I've ever had.'

When he looked pleased with himself, I asked him if he could make me a cake. Bobby hopped off my knee and went back to his place on the floor.

I was about to pick up my papers when I heard a car crunch onto the gravel outside the front door. Bobby looked up and then ran to it. As he looked outside, he shouted, 'Mummy's here.'

I felt some of his excitement; I always did when Laura came home. While we hadn't been getting on recently, as soon as I heard the car I wanted to see her smile, wanted to feel that sense of excitement of us all being together. Her dimples, the hint of red to her brunette, the colour of the London Irish. And those private moments always came to me, of the Laura that only I knew: the feel of her skin under my hand, the way she kissed, soft and slow, those breathless whispers.

But when Laura strode into the house I sensed the darkness of her mood. She threw her bag onto the table and smiled a hello, but it was perfunctory and brief. Bobby ran to her and wrapped his arms around her waist. Laura kissed him on the top of his head, then gently peeled his arms from her and marched towards the kitchen.

'Everything okay?' I asked.

'Why shouldn't it be?' came the shout back, but I could hear the frustration in her voice.

I joined her in the kitchen and found her browsing the wine we stored in a rack by the fridge.

'It must have been a bad day,' I said.

Laura picked out an Australian white, selected on price, not reputation, and put it in the freezer to cool.

'Sometimes alcohol *is* the answer,' she said.

'What's wrong?' I asked.

Laura folded her arms and looked down. I didn't think she was going to say anything, but then she blurted out, 'I went to the murder team and told them what you were doing.'

'And how did it go?'

She looked up at me and scoffed. 'Oh, just fine, once they'd stopped laughing at me.'

'Why would they laugh?'

'Because they're pricks,' Laura snarled. 'I'm just the skirt who spends her life processing other people's arrests. They put them in a cell and go home, and then leave me to sort out the mess. I'm the one who works late when we need more evidence, not the person who brought them in.'

'It's not for much longer,' I said, cajoling. 'The Court Welfare Officer is coming round the day after tomorrow, you know that, and then the hearing is after that. Once we have it formalised that Bobby stays with us, you can go back to a normal police job.'

'I want my career to amount to something, Jack, but it seems like I'm the only one making sacrifices,' she said, her voice getting angrier. 'Geoff's job hasn't changed, and he doesn't have the day-to-day stuff like I do.'

'Like *we* do,' I corrected her. 'It's both of us, not just you.'

Laura stopped for a moment, and then she sighed. She stepped forward and put her arms around me. She put her head into my chest, and as I kissed her hair I could smell the cells, the scent of stale bodies and stress. I put my hands on her cheeks and lifted her head up. There were tears brimming onto her lashes.

'Just be patient,' I said softly. 'We're nearly there.'

She wiped her eyes. 'Sometimes I just wonder at how much I want it, how there must be an easier way to live my life.'

'What, go back to London?' I queried, and then regretted voicing it, putting it out there for discussion. I felt my throat go dry as soon as the words came out.

'Would you want me to?' she asked.

I pulled her closer, put her head tight into my chest. 'You'll need to improve your interview technique if you're going to get on,' I whispered, 'because you can't ask stupid questions like that.'

We stayed like that for a few minutes. When Laura pulled away from me, wiping her eyes, she asked, 'How was your day? Is the story getting any better?'

'It's getting interesting,' I replied. 'I spoke to Katie again, Sarah's lodger.'

Laura raised her eyebrows. 'You're getting keen. She'll think you're a stalker. Good looking, I presume.'

I shrugged noncommittally. There was no answer that would be the right one.

Laura turned away, about to go back to Bobby, when I said, 'Can I ask you something about the Sarah Goode case?'

Laura stopped, and then turned back slowly. 'Probably pointless. If I know the answer, I won't tell you anyway.'

'Nothing about letters sent by Sarah Goode, after she went missing?' I queried.

Laura paused at that. 'What kind of letters?'

'Are there different types?' I said. 'Just normal letters. I've been looking at the newspapers and there is no mention of them, but Katie mentioned them.'

'What if they are so significant that the rest of the press have agreed not to say anything about them?'

'That's what Katie said to me,' I said, 'and that's why I'm interested.'

Before Laura could respond I heard a ping from my laptop. It was an email arriving. I walked through, expecting an offer of fake Viagra, but what I saw made me gasp.

Laura must have heard my reaction. 'What is it?'

'It's Sarah Goode,' I said. 'I guessed she would be on

Facebook, and I found her. I sent a friend request, just so I could write up that there was no response.'

'And?' asked Laura, coming close.

I clicked on the link in the email, just to make sure, and then I stood up and grinned.

'She's accepted the request,' I replied, pointing at the screen. 'Now that makes an interesting angle.'

Laura leaned forward, curious.

'She looks happy,' said Laura, looking at the profile picture.

I clicked on Sarah's pictures, and there was a succession of family photos and ones of Sarah at play: at a party, a bottle of beer raised for the camera; on a fun run, her arm around some friends, their faces flushed. It was fun-loving young woman stuff, the story of a life she used to have that would never be the same again. She didn't update her page very often; perhaps she had joined on a whim – there were few friends in her profile. I noticed that she listed her status as single.

'This means one thing,' said Laura, 'that she must be near a computer. I wonder if we can get the Facebook people to tell us where she is posting from.'

I printed off the page and clicked the events section, where people listed their diary.

'Shit!' I exclaimed.

Laura tapped me on the arm, pointing at Bobby. I held up my hand in apology and then tapped at the screen. From Laura's gasp, I realised that she had read it too.

In the events section of Sarah's Facebook profile, for 31st October, were the words, '*I die.*'

I gave a slow whistle. 'That's four days away,' I said.

Laura looked grim-faced. 'It looks like I'm going to have to go to the murder squad again.'

Chapter Seventeen

Morning already. Sarah guessed it from the way it seemed a little warmer, although not much. She reckoned it had been eight days now, but it was hard to mark time when days and nights seemed almost the same: the constant spotlights, the relentless, steady noise of thumping heartbeats.

Sarah had shivered through the night so that every minute crawled by, her arms wrapped around her chest, no bed, no bedding, no clothes. She had paced around the room to generate heat, twelve paces in an oval pattern before she was back where she started, so she did twelve more, and then twelve more after that, the dirt getting stuck between her toes. She rolled in the mud on the floor, cold at first, but it was like an extra layer of skin once it set hard onto her body.

Maybe the mud had saved her. The early hours were torture, but she knew time was the only cure, that soon the air would become warmer, just. She waited for the sounds of movement.

But as she got warmer, Luke came back into her thoughts. Had they really killed him, or was that all part of the game? Maybe he was still alive and in a room just a few feet away? If she could get to him, maybe they could work together.

She paced faster, but the view never changed. Just a stone wall, and then another after that, broken only by her shadow cast by the spotlights, shifting as she walked faster, more heat, more sound, her feet moving in time with the pulsing coming from the speakers.

She had taken to chanting. As she paced, and then as she jumped on the spot, Sarah would say, 'Keep strong, keep strong', like saying it would make it come true.

But it was easier to be strong when she was on her own. There was no one to hurt her, just her own thoughts and dark despair.

Just then, the speakers went silent. Sarah heard someone outside the room. She froze, felt her stomach lurch. What was coming now?

Her strength disappeared when she heard the lock turn in the door.

Laura looked down at the arrest handover package in front of her. It was an A3 piece of paper, folded over, holding a print-out of the incident log and custody record, the former telling her how the job had been called in, the latter telling her what had happened to the prisoner since his arrival.

Pete buzzed around her desk, trying to see what she had.

'A scrapper,' she said, her voice struggling to hide her contempt.

'Todd Whitcroft?' he asked.

She checked the name on the front sheet. 'Yeah, that's him. Do you know him?'

Pete raised his eyebrows. 'Blackley's premier-league scrapper. Feeds his kids by stripping the town's roofs of their lead and cashing it in at the scrap yard. He's moved on to cables now, because he thinks they're less traceable.'

'Maybe he's got scared of heights,' Laura said as she skim-read the front-sheet. 'It looks like they caught him with a van full of them.'

Pete sighed. 'Oh great.'

'What's wrong?' she asked.

'Todd Whitcroft never admits anything. He will say he had permission, or else he will say nothing at all.'

Laura sensed the day stretching ahead, and she was overtaken by a sense of gloom.

'So we have to catalogue it all,' she said, her voice weary, 'just so that we can prove where it came from.'

'That's about it,' he said, as he hopped off the desk and headed for the door. 'No time like the present.'

Laura got to her feet wearily, and then followed Pete out of the room. As they walked along the corridor, Pete bouncing small talk off the walls, Laura heard conversation coming out of the Incident Room further along. Her cheeks turned red as she remembered the humiliation from the day before, but she couldn't help glancing in as she went past. It looked like most were working the phones, chasing down old leads just to check if they had missed something. Only one person looked up, the cop in the polo shirt with the crew cut from the day before. He was still casually dressed, much different to the suits around Carson, and he smiled a greeting to Laura as he noticed her, a nod of reassurance.

Pete pressed the security button and they both went into the cobbled yard at the back of the station. Laura groaned as she saw the dirty cables spilling out of the back of a battered Transit van.

Pete passed her the clipboard. 'You make notes, and I'll get in the van and shout out what we have.'

Laura was about to object that she wasn't his secretary, but then she looked at her hands, clean and scrubbed, and then at her suit. Maybe there was a time for chivalry.

'Have you thought some more?' the masked man asked Sarah as he walked into the room. He was still again, his arms by his sides.

'About what?' She covered herself as best she could, arms over her breasts, her thighs clamped together.

'About killing me,' he answered.

Sarah shook her head in exasperation. 'I don't know who you think I am, and I don't know what you want from me.'

He nodded at her. Sarah thought she saw the shape of a ponytail sticking out of the cloth, bobbing up and down in time with his head. 'I know what you are,' he said. 'But you have to work it out too.'

Sarah turned away and faced the wall.

'Do you think you are the only one here with compassion?' he asked.

Sarah took a few deep breaths before she answered. 'It feels that way,' she said quietly.

'You'd be wrong at that,' he replied. 'Morals suit everyone differently. But what of the things you really want? Not the fantasies people tell you you should have, but your real fantasies, the ones you don't tell anyone about, the ones that come to you in the night? They're your real morals. You should embrace them.'

'And what do you want them to be?' Sarah asked, her voice rising. 'Murder, like you, or worse? Torture? Rape? Is that what you want me to tell you I think about? Or maybe me being raped, how I like to be hurt?'

He said nothing.

'Or perhaps I just want normal things,' Sarah continued. 'Like hoping I meet someone I love and settle down, have a happy home. What's wrong with that?'

'Cowardly,' he said. 'Everyone has a darker side. Feed it, grow it.'

'And what are your morals?' Sarah asked as she turned back around. 'What sick things do you dream of?'

He gestured around the room. 'I dream of this. Of you, in here, my butterfly fastened by the wings. And of this,' and then he turned and dragged something into the room. Sarah saw that it was a camp bed. 'I feel like showing you a kindness. There is no trick. This is just how I feel today.'

Sarah looked at the bed. She craved the bed. She saw a blanket on top. Maybe if she could get in, she could drown out the noise and get some warmth. She closed her eyes as they became filled with tears. She had wanted to be strong, but she had more basic needs.

'You have seen what I can do,' he continued. 'I will

follow my emotions. You have to make me want to be kind, if that is how you want me to be.'

'And if I make you feel different? If you don't feel kind?'

'I'll just follow my feelings,' he said, his voice sinister, and when Sarah swallowed, he added, 'and my imagination.'

'I'll do as I'm told,' Sarah whispered.

He dragged the bed further into the middle of the room and unfolded the blanket.

'Can I have my clothes?' she asked.

'Do as you are told and be rewarded,' he whispered. And then, as Sarah climbed under the blanket, grateful for the warmth, he slipped out of the room.

The noise of the heartbeat returned, but it seemed more bearable now.

Chapter Eighteen

I had been sitting in my car for nearly an hour before I saw Katie walking up the hill to her house. It was steep, and so she didn't see me until she reached her front door, her head down as she climbed.

She had looked deep in thought, but brightened when I stepped out of the car.

'Mr Garrett,' she said coyly. 'Do you have some more questions?'

'You're too perceptive,' I replied, playing along. 'Is that okay?'

'Depends on the questions,' she said, and she smiled.

I glanced towards the door. 'Shouldn't we go inside?'

She considered that for a moment, and then reached for her keys. 'Follow me,' she said.

As I went in, I noticed different things to our first meeting. The house seemed quieter, like it had become used to silence. The wind chimes in the hall tinkled like broken glass as we entered, but they sounded too loud. I noticed the smell this time. It was bleach, cleaning fluids, a touch of fresh paint. I glanced into the living room, tried to get an impression of Sarah, but Katie went straight into the back room again, dumped her bag onto the sofa and sat down with a sigh. 'What do you want to know?'

'You mentioned letters,' I said bluntly.

She pulled off her shoes. 'Did I?'

'You know you did. Yesterday. It was the last thing you mentioned before you walked away.'

'I can't say anything,' she said eventually. 'I told you that too.'

'So why did you mention them?'

Katie smiled at me. 'You look sweet when you get all serious.'

'I might get really sweet soon then,' I replied. 'Why can't you say anything?'

'DCI Carson,' she said, the words coming out with a grimace. I guessed that she hadn't been impressed. Laura had told me all about him the night before.

'I'm not asking for a copy of the letters, but just tell me what was in them,' I said.

Katie played with her hair, just teasing it around her ear. 'I can't. I'll get into trouble. And I'll get you into trouble.'

'Don't worry about me,' I said. 'Knowing a secret isn't a crime. And I would protect my source. All journalists would.'

I let the silence hang there, hoping Katie would say something, but she stayed quiet.

The silence became too long, so I said, 'Okay, I get the message. Pass on my congratulations to DCI Carson. He's got an obedient student.'

'Come and see me later,' said Katie quickly.

'Why?'

'About the letters.'

'Why not now?'

'Because if you want something from me, it will be on my terms. And I don't want to talk yet.'

'So it has to be later?'

Katie nodded. 'Come here for six. We'll talk then.'

I looked at her, hoping that she might change her mind, wondered how I would explain it to Laura, but Katie just smiled at me.

'Later it is, then,' I said, and started to walk towards the door.

'Jack!' she shouted out.

I turned around.

'I'll look forward to it,' she said, and then she giggled.

I turned and left the house, and as the door closed I looked down at my hands. They were shaking.

But it wasn't just the story, I knew that. Katie intrigued me. Maybe it was just the looks, but I knew that it was something else too: that she thought she was in charge, that she had something I wanted.

I knew I would have to be careful.

Chapter Nineteen

Rod Lucas took a quick look at Pendle Hill as he walked towards Abigail's door. The skies looked darker than the day before, the bracken top covered in gloom, and it made him raise the collar on his waxed jacket to shield his ears. His wife pestered him to wear a hat and gloves, but Rod wanted to feel the countryside, not just see it through his windscreen. It was what made his patch special.

He knocked on the door and then stepped back. Abigail was out of hospital, but he knew he would have to wait. She lived on her own, not even a cat for company any more, and Rod recalled her injuries. She wouldn't be moving quickly.

He put his hands into his pockets and stayed still. A couple of minutes went past and so he gave another rap on the door, just so that Abigail would definitely know someone was there. Eventually, he heard the rattle of a key, and when the door opened he was surprised at what he saw.

'You look well, Miss Hobbs,' he said, and he meant it. There was some bruising around her chin, and one of her eyes was covered by a patch, the other one red and sore, but some of the swelling had gone down and she was walking proudly upright, even with the bandages on her leg.

'I heal well,' she said, suspiciously at first, but then she recognised Rod. 'I'm sorry, but you were dressed differently yesterday.'

He glanced down and remembered his gardening clothes from the day before. It was shirt and tie today, but there was still dirt ingrained into his fingers.

He nodded and smiled. 'I wonder if we could have a talk,' he said, just a hint of reproach in his voice.

'There's nothing much else to say,' said Abigail. 'Young vandals or trouble-causers. I can't add anything to that.'

'What about Isla Marsden? Can she help?'

Rod watched her carefully, looked for a reaction, but she was more prepared for the question than Isla had been. Her eyes narrowed slightly, but the sweet smile never wavered.

'Thank you for calling round, Inspector,' she said. 'If I hear of anything, I'll get in touch.'

Abigail started to close the door, but Rod stuck out his hand.

'Do you want me to come in and make sure everything is secure?' he asked.

Abigail guessed his motives. 'I can still turn a window key,' she said.

'If you are being targeted for a reason, then someone else might get hurt, or even worse,' he said, appealing for her help.

Abigail looked at him for a moment, her smile shifting

for a second, before she thanked him again and closed the door slowly.

Rod Lucas was left facing the closed door. He stood there for a short while, thinking about what he should do next, before turning around and walking slowly back up the path.

I was in the same coffee shop as the day before, halfway through a cappuccino, when I decided to call Laura.

When she answered, I asked, 'What are you doing?'

'Wading through a pile of stolen cables,' she said.

'Sounds like you've had better times.'

Laura laughed. 'No, just routine. Just another morning of preparation before we get the no-comment interview.'

'Doesn't anyone answer questions any more?'

'We can't make them, Jack,' Laura replied, 'but I still have some faith in the system. It succeeds more times than it fails.'

'That's not the impression I get.'

'Yeah, but that all depends on how you report it.'

I exhaled loudly. 'You need a break,' I said softly. 'When it's all sorted out with Bobby, we'll go away somewhere warm, just me and you, where we can lie down for a couple of days and watch the sea and feel the sun on our faces.'

The line went quiet for a few seconds, and then Laura said, 'That would be nice', her voice soft. 'I miss you, Jack.'

'I haven't been away.'

'It feels like you have,' she said.

I shook my head. 'I've always been here,' I told her. 'I'm just not sure you saw me.'

'Why have you called?'

'I just wanted to hear your voice, that's all,' I replied.

Laura stayed silent, and I tried to picture the Laura that had first captivated me. The brightness to her smile, the way she bit her lip when she was feeling mischievous, how she giggled at my jokes.

'I'm glad you called,' she said quietly, and then she took a deep breath. 'How was your morning?'

'Interesting.'

'More than yesterday?'

'I didn't know about the letters yesterday.'

'Are you still going with that? I told you: you need to be careful.'

'But you still haven't heard anything?'

'I told you last night – even if I did know, I wouldn't tell you. But I don't.' Then she asked, 'Where are you going next?'

'The head teacher at Sarah's school,' I replied, 'and then I'm chasing down the letters.'

Laura paused, and then she said, 'Be careful, Jack. She's killed someone, so everyone believes, and murderers can be desperate people.'

'So you need to keep the murder squad informed of my whereabouts.'

'Huh!'

'So they can find my body,' I said jokily.

Laura laughed. 'If you keep on, I don't think Carson would bother looking too hard.'

Chapter Twenty

Sarah was under the blanket, some warmth tingling back into her feet, the mud cracking off her skin, when she heard the screech of the door moving on its runner, just audible over the sound of the heartbeat blasting through the speakers. There was the crunch of feet in the dirt again, but faster than normal. Sarah peered over the top of the blanket. She saw the familiar hood, but the shape of the head looked different. Leaner, smaller. It was the other one, the one who had come to her when she had been in the box.

She shrank back, shaking suddenly. She remembered the time in the box.

It had been waiting for her when she first arrived in the room, after the cramp of the car ride, squashed into the boot, gripped by panic, hyperventilating, her breath coming out as short rasps that echoed under the lid. There had been voices in the car, just murmurs, too quiet to make out, not rising above the hum of the tyres on the road. Sarah had tried to work out where they were going from the turns and the stops, but she got lost pretty quickly. The car was old, so the suspension had bottomed out of every pothole, sending a kick to her back.

When the car came to a stop, Sarah had been pulled out by the rope around her wrists, her arms twisted back, and then dragged along a path, sharp gravel under her feet, hands over her eyes. She was taken down some stairs and thrown into the room, her chest breaking her fall in the dirt.

He had untied the rope, his mask still on, but then she had been dragged to the corner of the room, towards the box.

The box was lying on the floor, long like a rifle chest. Entry was at one end, and she was put in head-first, like a corpse in a mortuary drawer, on her back, her arms by her side. It was only just wide enough, so that her arms were wedged against the sides, impossible to move. Her head pushed against one end, and when the open end of the box was slammed shut, it banged against her feet so that she had to curl her legs up to fit.

The sides or front had no give to them, no cracks in the lid to allow a view out, and the top was only inches from her face, so that her breath made the air condense around her cheeks, warm and stale, just a vent by her feet to let it out. She wanted to stretch out but couldn't. She had screamed, she had cried, but none of it made a difference. She thought hard on how to stay calm, how to think and how to rationalise, to work out time. But then another night had come, obvious from the cold, and another one after that. Hunger gnawed at her, Sarah's survival instinct superseding her fear, her mouth dry.

But then he had returned and turned the box over.

Sarah had spent the next day face down, unable to move her arms, not knowing when she'd ever be able to move again. She felt her captivity against her head, her feet, her back, her front. No water, no food, trapped in her own piss and shit.

She was tipped out of the box on the third day and allowed some water and a crust of bread. He had stood over her, the light from the room blinding her after those days in darkness, and she spent a few precious moments of movement trying to get used to the glare. He had said nothing. He just watched her, nothing to see but the hood, stood still, his arms by his sides. But then she was slotted back into the box. She struggled and screamed, begged not to go back in, but he was too strong for her.

This went on for another three days. No talk, no reasons given. Just captivity and silence.

But there had been the other person, the one in the room with her now.

Sarah could tell he was younger, from the excitement in his voice when he came into the room, calling her name, taunting, tormenting her. One day he turned the box on its end so that Sarah was upside-down, his groans of effort loud against the lid. She couldn't stop her body slumping down so that her neck bore her weight, unable to get her arms free to provide support. All that kept her in place was the tight dimensions of the box. Sarah wasn't like that for long, just a few minutes, but she thought she was going to suffocate on the weight of her own body pressing down on her, but he returned and threw the box back onto the floor.

Another game was banging the box with hammers. Just noise, the only break in the silence, but the hammers banged around her, thudding, too loud in the box.

Although the room scared her, she did not want to go back in the box.

'What do you want?' asked Sarah, looking up, a tremor to her voice.

He threw a bag onto the floor. Sarah looked. It contained clothes. Her jeans were clean, and the shirt too, and there was a jumper in there, home-knitted, warm-looking. Sarah climbed out of the bed and began to pull them on, almost smiling at the warmth. He left the room and then returned almost immediately with a plate of food, soup and bread, with coffee, along with something else.

Sarah looked at the food. 'More kindness?' she asked.

'Nothing for free,' he said. 'But you must do something for me,' and he held up a clear plastic bag.

Sarah saw the pen and paper inside, and then she noticed his latex surgical gloves and the way he was holding the bag away from himself.

'Another letter?' Sarah asked. She remembered the other times, the only respite from the box. She had gone along with it, hoping for some reward, maybe some comfort, but the words were disturbing, frightening.

'I want people to know that you're still alive,' he said. He sounded excited. Sarah noticed that he seemed twitchy, shifting his weight from one foot to the other.

'But why like this?' she asked. 'They don't make sense.'

'Because I say you should,' he replied.

He put the food on the floor, out of her reach. He walked over to her and passed her the pen and paper.

He then reached into his pocket and put some pre-prepared scrawl of his own in front of her.

'You know what to do. Copy that and you can have the food.'

Sarah looked at him and she felt angry. It was time for a little victory of her own.

'Let me eat first and then I'll do it.'

'Do it now,' he said, some irritation creeping into his voice. 'If you don't, I walk out and you won't eat.'

Sarah looked down at the tray of food, the aroma of the soup making her salivate. She looked down at the scrawl she had to copy. 'Okay, okay,' she said. 'I'll do it.' Tears began again. 'Don't go. Please.'

The shuffling of his feet seemed to get faster, almost gleeful. He was enjoying it too much. She wiped away the tears, ashamed, and looked more closely at what she had to write. It made her shiver.

'What does it mean?' she asked.

He shook his head, and Sarah knew she had no choice, so she wrote, her cold fingers struggling with the pen.

She put the pen and paper back into the bag, which he held open for her. Once satisfied, he walked out of the door, holding the bag in front of him.

Sarah looked over at the food and felt her hunger rush back at her. She ate the soup quickly, the spoon clattering against her teeth, and then gulped down her coffee. It was hot and strong.

She lay on her back, feeling stronger, and looked at the grain in the wood of the beams that crossed the ceiling. She looked at nothing else for around twenty minutes, but then she realised that she could see the grain clearer than she could before. The grooves were sharper, showing shade. The light bounced around them, made them move like a slow pulse, rainbows flashing around each swirl, the knots moving in time with the noises that came from the speakers. She was transfixed, wanted to see where the lines went. They moved towards each other as she looked, seemed to get tangled, and then she shrank back as the beams came hurtling towards her, as if the ceiling was collapsing, her arms over her eyes. But there was no pain. She looked up again, and saw that the beams were still there. But they were vibrating in time with the heartbeats that blasted out of the speakers. She scuttled backwards, scared, feet kicking against her blanket as she sought refuge. But there was no safe place to hide. She ended up on the floor, on all fours, her eyes darting around, looking at her cell. She saw that all the walls were moving, beating in time with the noise, and then in time with her own heartbeat, which went faster as her fear grew. The stones of the wall started to blur together and grow darker, making shadows that seemed to blot out the glare from the spotlights.

Sarah screamed and wrapped her head in her arms. It came to her quickly, a dead certainty. Something had been in that food. She didn't feel right. Her thoughts felt like they were being pulled backwards through a small hole, reality imploding, the unreal taking its place.

She felt herself panic. She knew what was happening, but she knew that she couldn't stop it. Her legs turned heavy and she slumped to the floor, unable to move.

Sarah closed her eyes quickly, but the lights were still

there. First red, lighting her eyes, then purple, then blue. They went to green, then to yellow, then back to red. Then it started again, only this time faster, the rhythmic change becoming a streak, becoming a blur, the noise of the colours screaming in her head like pressurised air.

She opened her eyes in fright. The ceiling rushed at her. She covered her face, but when she moved her arms away the ceiling was back at the top of the room.

Sarah screamed, but she couldn't hear herself over the metronomic pound of the heartbeat.

Reality was hell. This was worse.

Chapter Twenty-one

Sarah's school was a sixties comprehensive on one of the hills overlooking Blackley, in the more derelict end of town, where the kids would go for gang fights with the Asian kids at the next school along. Time hadn't been kind to it. Paint flaked from the metal window frames in all three storeys, and the bricks looked damp where the flat roof drained the rain down the front of the building.

I made my way to reception just as the classes were emptying. Most of the kids were in uniform, although the ties were slack, the shirt buttons undone, their rucksacks slung lazily over their shoulders. Some wore their coats over their faces and tried to intimidate me as I went past. I ignored them. They were teenagers. Being pleasant wasn't in the script.

The school secretary looked up at me as I approached the counter. I smiled.

'Hello, my name is Jack Garrett, and I'm . . .'

'A reporter?' she asked, her eyebrows raised, completing the question.

I nodded, could do little else.

She stood and put her arms onto the counter. 'No,

we haven't seen Sarah. Yes, she was a good teacher. Yes, it took us by surprise. Did she do it? We don't know.' She pointed towards the door. 'That's all your questions answered. Please leave.'

I noticed weariness in her eyes. She knew Sarah, maybe even liked her, and people just like me had interrupted her life for the sake of a throwaway quote.

But that was the game. I didn't take part to be popular.

'Thank you,' I said. 'If I can't speak to any members of staff, I'll wait outside and ask the kids.'

'We've had that threat before.'

'So you'll be used to it then.'

And then I turned to walk out.

I knew she would shout me back. She was pissed off with reporters because she had no choice but to speak to them.

'Okay, Mr Garrett, I'll see what I can do,' she said, and when I turned around she pointed at a low seat by the main entrance and barked, 'sit there, and don't you dare move.'

I smiled, tried to get her back on my side, but the glare she gave me told me that she wasn't interested in making friends.

I watched the school kids slouch by, and then the secretary appeared at the counter again. She pointed along the corridor. 'That door,' she said curtly.

As I looked along, I saw a man by a door, hands on hips, his grey jacket pulled to his sides.

I nodded thanks, but she had looked away before I'd finished it. As I walked, I heard her bellow, 'Don't run!', and the sound of adolescent footsteps slowed down.

The head teacher looked more tired than angry. He was wearing a cheap grey jacket over a thin white shirt, with black trousers and scuffed suede shoes. His moustache was bushy, obscuring his top lip, and so it was hard to see whether he was smiling.

'Hello, I'm Jack Garrett,' I said, and I held out my hand.

He shook, too polite to refuse an outstretched hand, and then beckoned me into his office. His room was neat and functional. A filing cabinet filled one wall, and there was a bookcase on the other. His desk was beech-effect with a plastic in-tray, but there were few personal effects, no family pictures or potted plants.

As he sat down, he said, 'So, what do you need to know about Sarah that hasn't already been told to the press?'

'How are the kids about it?' I asked. 'It's not just about Sarah.'

'I haven't seen the kids as excited in a long time,' he replied. 'Their work improved for the first couple of days. If she's caught near exam time, we could get record results.'

I laughed politely. 'Did the kids like her?' I asked.

He nodded. 'She was a good teacher. Enthusiastic, engaging, confident.' He gave a wry smile. 'There wasn't a hope in hell of her staying around. For teachers, this school is either a launch pad or a retirement home.'

'Do you know anything about any letters she might have sent since she went missing?' I asked, watching his response carefully. If the headmaster knew, the police were taking them seriously.

He paused. His fingers went to his moustache and pulled at some of the whiskers.

'No,' he said eventually.

I didn't believe him.

'You don't sound sure,' I said.

He took a deep breath and glared at me. He gave a theatrical look at his watch.

'Tell me about the letters, and let's see how far we get,' he said.

I couldn't respond to that.

He smiled, knowing that I was just fishing for information. 'I've got to get on, Mr Garrett.'

'What about 31st October?' I countered, remembering the Facebook entry. 'Three days away. Do you know if it means anything special to her, or to anyone?'

'It's Halloween, and so other than trick or treat, nothing.'

'What about any special friends at school?' I asked, as a final gambit.

'What do you mean? Anyone who would allow a murderer on the run to sleep in their back room?' he replied, his voice filled with sarcasm. 'No,' he said, answering his own question. 'Sarah turned one or two heads in the staff room, but nothing special, and I suspect there were one or two schoolboy crushes.'

'Sounds interesting. Any names?'

'This school is full of teenage boys,' he said wearily, his boredom showing. 'They would spend all day with their hands down their trousers if it was allowed. It would be nothing unusual if there were crushes, but I suppose their mothers would spot the leggy beauty hogging the bathroom every morning.'

When I looked amused, he rose to his feet and said, 'Goodbye, Mr Garrett.'

I held up my hands, smiling. 'Okay, thanks for your time,' I said.

As I left his room, I heard the head teacher pick up the phone. I gave the receptionist a wave as I went. She glared at me.

I was unsure what to do when I got outside and idly looked around at the pupils as they left to go home. Then I became aware of someone next to me. I looked down and saw a boy of around fourteen, with his head shaved around the sides and a fringe gelled to his forehead. He was wearing the school uniform, but only just. The tie was hanging down to his breast pocket and the trousers were black denims.

'You a reporter?' he asked.

'How can you tell?' I replied.

'Because you all look the same,' he said. I shrugged my apology, and then he said, 'I hope they find Miss Goode. She was nice. A good teacher.'

I smiled at him. 'But what if they find her and lock her up?'

He thought about that for a moment, and then said, 'Nah. I was talking to my dad about it, and he said his solicitor was the best, and if she goes to him she'll get away with it. She's too nice to go to jail.' And then he walked off, placing some headphones into his ears.

I smiled to myself as I watched him walk away.

I realised that I had a better quote by chance than I'd had from the head, straight from a pupil. Sometimes it is best just to let things fall into place rather than push them through.

Chapter Twenty-two

Sarah was curled up in a corner of the room, her knees to her chest, her eyes staring forward. She was screaming. Long, hollow, frightened screams, while she tore at her hair, feet scrabbling at the floor.

She thought she had seen people watching her, laughing, their faces close, too close. She had squeezed her eyes shut, but then she heard something. Moans, shouts. When she looked, two people were fucking, the bright colours of flesh moving on the floor, thrashing excitedly. And then the images were in her head. Laughing, grinning, moving fast into one another, like machines, the noises echoing, the heartbeats getting faster, the colours turning blood-red.

But then the colours stopped. Now it was the door that moved. It opened and closed, sliding noisily, like glimpses of hope, but when she reached out for it she saw the runners had teeth. Whenever the door slid open, they snapped at her with giant jaws, just clipped her feet, and pushed her back into the wall.

When the door closed, the teeth receded, and for a second she could see out. She saw light, like sunlight.

Bright, clean, warm. It glowed yellow and soft and drew her in, like the shape of her dreams, moulded from clouds, pulling her forwards. She moved again to the door, left the safety of the wall and tried for the light, but the door banged shut, the noise echoing, making her scramble backwards. And when the door was shut, it became thick and heavy, no more hope.

She looked around. She thought she could hear something. Chanting, singing. People were swaying, rhythmic, enchanting.

Sarah reached out, wanted to feel some contact, but then the door opened again, teeth bared, and the people were gone. She was back in the corner, crying with fear, the noise of her cries being sucked from her and out of the room.

And the spiders. They scuttled in front of her, a mass of them, like a moving carpet, crawling over her feet, their legs like soft kisses on her skin, moving out towards the walls and then creeping upwards, heading for the lights.

Sarah clamped her eyes shut.

Hell.

Chapter Twenty-three

Laura was writing a summary of the interview she'd just conducted with the cable thief. As she'd expected, there had been no answers to her questions. Now it was the paper trail: the case summary, the form for the prosecutor, a final read through to see whether any more evidence was needed.

A shadow fell over her desk. When she raised her head, she saw it was Karl Carson. He stood right over her, so that when she looked round quickly the first thing she saw was his crotch.

'Why didn't you tell me about your boyfriend and the letters?'

Laura looked up. She thought he looked flushed.

'How do you know that I know?'

'Because he knows,' he said angrily, 'and so I guess that you two smooched over it last night.'

'If he knows, it didn't come from me,' said Laura, 'and if you think otherwise, prove it.'

His flush deepened. 'Don't make it difficult for yourself,' he said, his voice low. 'The headmaster's been on the phone. He told me what lover-boy was asking about.'

Laura smiled as sweetly as she could. 'So he mentioned Facebook too?' When Carson looked confused, she continued, 'Maybe you should listen to Jack, because please excuse me if I don't come rushing to you. You didn't seem too receptive yesterday.'

'What do you mean, Facebook?'

'Events diary for 31st October. "*I die*" is the entry, and she's near a computer, because now she and *lover-boy* are friends.'

Carson looked down at her, his cheeks nearly purple now, the colour spreading over his head. Then he turned and stalked out of the room. When Laura was alone, she put down her pen and checked her hands. They were trembling. She didn't know how far she could push him before she found herself in front of the disciplinary department, but she knew that she didn't feel much like helping him. Why was the arsehole ratio so much greater the higher up the pole she looked?

The station was quiet when Rod got back. It wasn't large, looked like a church hall from the outside, and was used as a training centre for the new recruits. If anything happened in his division, everyone dashed out, hoping for something interesting, making it quiet for those left behind. When he went into his office he saw that someone had placed some fax messages onto his desk. They were updates on the explosions. He leafed through them as he sat down.

The sleuth report on the fingerprint analysis was first. It had come back as negative.

The other document was the explosives report. That

121

interested him more. He skimmed through. Like all expert reports, it was filled with technical jargon, explaining the background to the conclusion – so Rod did what he always did: he went to the conclusion. And there it was: ammonium nitrate, a fertiliser-based explosive, the anarchist's favourite. Easy to get hold of, and when mixed properly it could make quite a bang.

He heard a knock on his office door. One of the young constables peeped through and said, 'There's a young girl to see you, sir. Emily Marsden. She said you would know what it's about.'

Rod sat back. 'Show her in.'

The constable stepped aside, and Emily walked in, shy, smiling. He recognised her from the visit to Isla's house – the daughter. 'What can I do for you, Emily?' he asked, and pointed her towards one of the seats.

Emily sat down, her knees tightly together, a canvas bag in her lap.

'Do you think my mum is in danger?' she asked.

'I don't know,' Rod replied, 'because your mother won't tell me anything about herself.'

'Maybe she doesn't want you to know.'

'That's her right,' said Rod, nodding, 'but I don't want anything to happen to her.'

Emily wrapped the handles of her bag around her fingers and took some deep breaths. Then she said, 'My mum will kill me for saying this, but it's about Abigail.'

Rod nodded. 'Go on.'

'It's the craft group that Mum goes to, where Abigail goes too. I think it's more than just craft, making rings and stuff.'

'Why do you say that?'

'Because they meet up a lot, and whenever she goes, she spends ages getting ready.' Then Emily smiled. 'And I've seen the rings and bracelets they sell.'

'Not very good?'

'Rubbish,' she replied, and laughed, embarrassed.

Rod smiled back at her. She was a nice girl. A bit flaky, maybe, the sort of girl who would prefer to sit in a field making daisy-chains rather than hang around in bus shelters, like most of the kids in his area seemed to prefer.

'How often do Abigail and your mother meet?' he asked.

Emily thought about her answer, and then said, 'Once a week, but then once every month they have a really big meeting, and Mum comes back really late. I think they meet somewhere near Newchurch. I know that because I heard her arguing with my dad about it.'

'Why does your dad get all worked up about it?'

Emily shrugged, and then she toyed with the handles of her bag again. 'He gets jealous, but I know Mum wouldn't do anything like that.'

'So what do you think they get up to in the craft-group meetings?' he asked.

'I just don't know,' she replied, 'but I don't want anything to happen to her. Someone set off an explosion in our shed, and now Abigail has been hurt. I'm worried that they'll come back.'

'Can you find out when the next craft-group meeting is, and where, and call me?' he asked, and he passed her a business card with his details on. As she looked at it, he leaned forward. 'Thanks for coming in, Emily. I'll make sure your mum stays safe.'

Emily looked pleased by that, and headed back out of Rod's office.

When he was left alone again, Rod wondered for a moment about Emily. Teenagers do strange things in their quest for attention, and the craft group was causing problems in the family. How did she feel about that, and was there less innocence to her than it seemed?

Chapter Twenty-four

I checked my reflection in the car mirror before I stepped out. I was nervous about seeing Katie. I was secure with Laura, and I knew I shouldn't be feeling like that, but her flirting made me wonder what lay ahead.

I'd parked a few streets away, as the parking spaces were all taken outside Sarah's house; Victorian terraces weren't made for two-car families. The steep hill reminded me that I hadn't been for a walk that day, and I was panting when I knocked on the door.

I looked around as I waited. The street was quiet, dark now, the end of British Summer Time bringing the winter forward with a slam, but I thought I could see someone in a van further up the hill. It looked green, but that could be the orange sodium lights playing a trick.

I looked back when I heard the door open. It was Katie. I saw that her hair looked wet and she was wearing only a towel.

'I'm sorry,' I said, embarrassed. 'I must be early.'

Katie smiled at me, her stare direct, challenging. 'No, you're not,' she said. 'Come in.'

I went inside and heard Katie lock the door. When I looked round, she said, 'Force of habit,' and then brushed past me. I watched her go up the stairs, saw how pale and slender her legs looked, her muscles well-defined. Before she got to the top she slipped off her towel, as if to get ready, and I felt my cheeks flush. She saw me looking at her, nude, unashamed, and then she turned onto the landing. I thought I saw the trace of a smile. When I heard the blast of the hairdryer, I went into the room I had been in the day before.

I felt fidgety, my cheeks red. The look in her eyes and her naked body had aroused me, but I didn't want to think like that, and so I filled my mind with thoughts of Laura to stay focused. I needed to hear Katie's story about the letters, about what the police had said to her.

I closed my eyes, but I saw an image of Katie again, naked, flirtatious. This wasn't fair on Laura, or Bobby. And it was unfair to myself; I had spent my life looking for someone to love in the way that my father had loved my mother. They had been happy, a strong couple, until cancer took away my mother.

I knew what my father would have done: he would have put my mother first, before his job, and walked out. That was the thing to do. I moved towards the door, but Katie was there, wearing tight leggings that hugged her figure and a cropped shirt that showed her flat stomach, her skin creamy and pale, a steel ring in her belly button.

She must have sensed what I had been thinking. 'I thought you wanted to know about the letters.'

'I do,' I replied.

'So sit down.'

I faltered, and then did as she said. I checked my watch.

Katie went into the kitchen. When she reappeared, she was holding two glasses of wine. 'I don't like drinking alone,' she said.

As I took a drink, Katie sat just along from me on the sofa. She had her feet up on the cushions and was staring at me over her glass.

'So tell me about the letters,' I said.

'All in good time,' she responded.

'Okay,' I replied. 'Answer me this question instead: what kind of person can live in a house where someone was murdered?'

'What kind of person do you think I am?' she asked, raising an eyebrow.

'I'm still trying to work that one out.'

Katie thought for a moment, and then she said, 'What do you think about history?'

'You're the history student,' I replied. 'You go first.'

Katie shuffled closer to me. I could smell the soap from her shower, flowery and clean. 'I think of this street and wonder how many people have walked up and down it, have looked at the same view. Go back a hundred years and the view would be the same. Same houses, same doorways. There would be cobbles instead of tarmac, and no cars, and maybe the houses are a bit ragged now, you know, the roofs sag and you can wake up to find kebab smeared over your front window, but the street hasn't really changed.'

'Isn't that just like everywhere?'

'I suppose so, but these things used to feel important. History felt important. It's what drew me, to go back to the start. That's what I was told, that to understand anything, you have to go back to the start, to know what went before. But now, I'm not so sure. So many lives have been lived in this street. Births, deaths, fights, marriages. All of those things behind these bricks, all of them important at the time, but now,' and she clicked her fingers, 'all gone. It means nothing in the end, and one day someone will look back and say the same thing about Luke's death, but we'll all be gone, and this conversation will mean nothing.'

'So you can live here because ultimately what happened will fade?' I asked.

'Something like that,' she replied. 'Whatever happened doesn't really matter, not in the long run. Doesn't matter at all.'

'That seems disrespectful to Luke,' I said. 'As if he never mattered.'

Katie shook her head. 'I just want to go back to how it was, when this was just a tatty little street in a worn-out mill town and I don't have to think of the things Sarah made me see.' She sounded distracted, her voice sadder than before.

'Why do you say that Sarah made you see them?' I asked.

She looked at me, and as she took a deep breath, some of her sparkle returned. 'The letters,' said Katie, 'the ones you're so interested in. They're confessions to Luke's murder, and they're addressed to me.'

I was silent, stunned. Confessions? That changed things. Did Sarah's parents know?

128

'Where are they?' I asked. 'The letters?'

'The police have them,' she replied.

'What do they make of them?'

'The police don't tell me anything.'

I chewed on my lip. If there were confessions, it would add something to the story, I knew that. 'What did the letters say?' I persisted.

Katie smiled. 'I'll show you, if you'll come upstairs.' I must have looked confused, because she said, 'I've scanned them into my computer, for reference purposes.' She stood up and walked to the kitchen. When she re-emerged, she was carrying the bottle of wine. 'C'mon, bring your glass, I'll show you,' and then I heard her feet pad softly up the stairs.

I looked at my empty glass and wondered at the wisdom of following her. But when I thought of the story, I knew I would do only one thing.

Chapter Twenty-five

Sarah lay in the middle of the floor, laughing out loud.

The images had passed, the nightmare was fading. The room was beginning to look normal again, becoming the shape it had been before her meal. The lights were still on, but they were no longer the kaleidoscopes they had been for the previous few hours. She was back in her cell, so it seemed, with only her fears to keep her company.

But she didn't feel fear any more. Just an overwhelming sense of relief. He had attacked her mind, where it was harder to fight back, but now it was over and she had survived. She rolled around and laughed, pointed at the walls, at the door. She held her stomach as it ached. Too much laughing.

The walls had stopped moving, the door stayed closed.

Sarah carried on laughing as the day turned cold once more.

Chapter Twenty-six

Katie's bedroom surprised me. She seemed smart and pretty, but her room was untidy, with nothing really settled or put away. Clothes were scattered over the floor, as if she had just discarded them en route to the bed, and there was a stack of history textbooks at one end, some open, some closed. There was a feminine smell, a mix of cosmetics and mild perfume, but the hum of the computer fans disturbed the karma. The machine was blinking away on an old desk in front of the window, and Katie jiggled the mouse to get rid of the screen-saver. She sat on a battered old stool, and I leaned against the wall nearby.

'When I said they were confessions,' she began, 'they are not like confessions in the strictest sense. In fact, I'm not really sure I understand them.'

'What do you mean?'

'It's the language used. It's English, but not spoken English. It just doesn't sound right, like there's something off-key.'

'Did you say this to the police?' I asked.

Katie laughed. 'When did that become my job?' She

put her wine glass down on the desk and beckoned me over, patting her hand on the end of the bed. 'C'mon, you want to see it, don't you?' Her top fell forward as she leaned towards me, and I could see that she wasn't wearing a bra. Or maybe I was supposed to see that. She smiled, her pupils large, and she held my gaze.

My stomach fluttered, but it wasn't through lust; it was fear. I knew I should go, I was worried about what would happen if I stayed. I hadn't been out of the game so long that I couldn't recognise the signs. Katie was flirtatious, staring into my eyes, toying with her hair. But it didn't feel right. I was being played, I sensed that, but I didn't know why.

I sat down on the end of the bed as Katie started to navigate through folders.

'I encrypted it so the police wouldn't know I still had it,' she said, 'but it made it invisible, so I'm trying to remember where I put it.'

I watched the screen change and flicker like a quickly turned book, until eventually she stopped clicking and leaned back. 'There you are,' she said. 'That's the first one. See what you think.'

An image of hand-written text appeared on the screen. It looked neat and tidy – necessary writing for a school-teacher, I supposed – set down on lined paper. I shuffled towards the screen and scratched my chin absent-mindedly as I read.

Such was the nature of my offences, and the multi-tude of my crying sins, that it took away all sense of

humanity. The murder I had committed, laid open
to the world, did certainly produce contempt amongst
people.
    Sarah

I stared at the screen, puzzled, and looked at Katie, who just shrugged, so I read it again, but it still made no sense.

I turned to Katie. 'What do you make of it?'

'Just about the same as you,' she said. 'I don't get it.'

I sat back and exhaled loudly. I had the scent of a story, but it was too insane.

'Are you sure it's from Sarah?' I asked. 'Murders attract crackpots.'

'The handwriting,' she said. 'I recognised it straight away. It's controlled, a bit like her, all repression and formality.'

I fell silent and wondered about the message. It was as if she was quoting something, had taken something old and inserted her name. *'Crying sins.'* That certainly wasn't everyday language.

'Where's the second letter?' I asked.

Katie went to the same folder on the computer and brought up another image. It was the same handwriting as before.

    Such is the horror of murder, and the crying sin
of blood, that it will never be satisfied but with blood.
    Sarah

I ruffled my hair, confused. I didn't know what to say. I read it again, tried to decipher it, and then asked, 'When did these arrive?'

Katie thought about that and then answered, 'The first one was around three days after I found Luke. The second came a couple of days ago.'

'Was Sarah religious?' I asked. 'The phrase "crying sins" appears in both. Did she ever go to a church? Will there be a priest she might be confiding in?'

Katie shook her head. 'We didn't agree on that. I go to church, always have done. Sarah never went, and she used to say that she never would. She said that her family were Church of England but didn't really practise, and the Bible was just something that washed over her at school.'

'So her talk of sin is something that she wouldn't normally say,' and I glanced back at the screen. 'And there: *such is the horror of murder, and the crying sin of blood, that it will never be satisfied but with blood.* It sounds like a threat, that she has sinned, and that she will sin again by killing again?'

Katie took another sip of her wine. 'I hadn't thought of it that way,' she said, 'but you could be right.' Then she looked at me quickly, a frightened look in her eyes. 'Do you think it's a threat aimed at me?'

'Why do you think that?'

'Because the envelopes were addressed to me,' she said, and then let out a deep breath, brushing away her fringe once more. The flickering light from the monitor was reflected in her eyes, and I saw a film of tears in them too. She put her glass down and moved closer to me.

'I'm scared,' she said, her voice soft and vulnerable. 'Luke is dead, and I will see his corpse in my mind for the rest of my life. The only person who can really tell me what happened has run away, and the only contact we have with her are these letters, and I can't make sense of them.' She turned her face to the screen again and dabbed at her eyes with her finger.

I couldn't respond to that. I wasn't there to protect Katie. I was there to write a story, and it was getting more mysterious every time I looked at it.

'Could I have copies?' I asked, and nodded towards the monitor.

Katie nodded, and after a few clicks a printer by her feet whirred into action. Within five minutes of entering Katie's room I had copies of the so-called confessions.

I took another sip of wine and looked again at the letters. What could Sarah see when she wrote them? Where was she? What was she thinking? Would she make contact again?

Something outside distracted me. The yard was a short concrete one with a high back wall that led to an alley, but I could see over it from Katie's bedroom upstairs. I thought I saw movement in the alley.

'Did you see that?' I asked.

'See what?'

I looked at Katie, and caught her wiping her eyes. I wondered for a moment about her. Maybe it was harder on her than I realised.

'Nothing,' I said. 'I must have been mistaken.'

I thought she was going to start crying, but she steeled herself and reached for the wine instead. 'I liked Luke, he was a nice man,' she said, smiling thinly, and then sniffing as a small tear appeared in the corner of her left eye. 'Oh, I'm just being selfish,' she said tearfully. 'You know, why did it have to happen to me? Why did it have to mess up my college year? Why must I have to get over seeing Luke's body?'

'Why don't I ask the questions?' I said. 'Perhaps talking about it will help.'

Katie smiled back. She wiped her face and took a deep breath, as if to start over. 'Okay.'

'Tell me what you found, in detail,' I began.

Katie exhaled and thought for a moment, and then began.

'I'd been away for a few days,' she said, 'back to my parents in Leeds. I moved here for college, and Luke was planning to stay over while I was away. I got back early afternoon, about one thirty on the Sunday, and when I came in it was quiet. I thought nothing of it, and I'd been in the house for a couple of hours before I thought about going into Sarah's room.'

'What made you go in?' I asked.

Katie curled her mouth as she thought about it.

'With hindsight, I probably suspected something was wrong. I don't normally go into her room. I remember seeing her toothbrush in the bathroom, so I knew she hadn't gone away. But for all I knew, she could have just gone for a drink.' She shrugged. 'Maybe I just wanted to chat to someone. I'd left my family again, and had a shitty journey, been on the train for a few hours. I knocked on her door but there was no answer. I waited a few moments, and then I went into her room, and . . .' She paused there, her voice breaking. She steeled herself and took a sip of wine before she continued, trying to be matter-of-fact. 'Luke was on the bed, there was blood on the floor and on the walls, and there was a knife sticking out of his chest.'

At that her voice broke again, but this time the tears came.

'Hey, come on,' I said, trying to cajole her. 'None of this is your fault.'

She wiped her face and I saw her steady herself again.

'I didn't know what to do,' she said quietly. 'I could tell he was dead. He was still, his face had kind of sunk, you know, and the blood on the floor was dry. The room was a mess. There was blood on the walls, like small teardrops, as if the knife had been pulled out and plunged back in again. It was on the door, on the floor, it was everywhere. But he was just in bed, a sheet still covering his legs, his arms spread out as if he'd been laid on a cross.'

'Was he naked?'

Katie just nodded.

'Was there blood anywhere else in the house?' I asked.

'I didn't notice, but the police said they found traces in the bathroom, around the sink and on the taps. Only traces though.'

'Was anything taken?'

'Not as far as I could tell. Her toothbrush was still there, her books, clothes, letters, all still there.'

'Purse? Handbag?'

'I couldn't see it, but the police said they found it on the other side of the bed.' She paused. 'I didn't go that far into the room.'

I thought for a moment. Things were looking bad for

Sarah. It couldn't have been someone else breaking in for money, because her purse was still there. But if Sarah was running, she didn't have any cash. So what about the blood around the taps and plug? Washing away the evidence is calculated. But if it was Sarah, why not be calculating enough to take some money if her life was about to be on the run? Empty her account and hit the road? Cash is more invisible than plastic.

Something was bothering me. I knew it sounded like Sarah was the killer, but the facts didn't fit. No known motive. No known history of mental health problems. No means of support. Calculated cover-up after the event.

But Luke must have known the killer. His feet were still wrapped in the sheet, so he hadn't got out of bed to struggle with an intruder. He felt safe enough to stay in bed until the moment the knife had gone into his chest. The fact that only his feet were covered might be the result of trying to move out of the way when he realised that he was in the last split-second of his life, but until then he was happy to lie in bed, naked, vulnerable.

'Can I look at the room?' I asked.

Katie wiped her eyes and pointed to the front of the house. 'Help yourself,' she replied.

I folded the letters and put them in my back pocket before I went to the next room along, and when I swung the door open I was surprised at how normal it seemed. I'm not sure what I expected, some kind of butcher's apron, but the walls looked bright and clean, and in the corner of the room there was a dresser covered in photo frames. There was no carpet, though, and the bed had gone.

I opened the curtains and looked out over the street. Just an ordinary view. I turned back to the photographs. There was a picture of Sarah's parents, relaxed in a town garden. There were pictures of friends, a black Labrador, and one of a group of young women, maybe an old college photo. I spotted Sarah, and as with the Facebook photograph, it seemed that the newspaper photographs hadn't done her justice, with her bright smile, carefree, her white teeth showing as she laughed, her hair falling over her face.

I wanted to get a sense of the real Sarah, and so I opened a drawer. T-shirts were stacked in two piles, one or two pulled about as if she'd gone for one at the bottom. Or maybe that was the police, just checking them for information. The next drawer was more disorderly, knickers and socks thrown in as if she had done it in a rush. There was a box of condoms in the corner, and a quick count showed that three of the twelve were missing.

I quickly checked the other drawers. Oddments of clothes, some sanitary products, but nothing else.

I sighed to myself. I knew that the police would have removed anything useful. I turned back around to survey the room. I took a couple of photographs and then went to stand where the bed used to be, judging from the knocks and nicks where it had banged against the wall. I saw Katie watching me. I looked around the room again, tried to see it from Luke's viewpoint, his last look at the world. There was the window looking out over the street, but he would have been too low down to see anything outside. I looked towards the doorway. I could see the landing rail, where the stairs came up.

I tried to imagine the scene, Sarah walking into the bedroom, her hands behind her back. Luke was naked, so maybe they were fresh from making love. What had he seen when she walked back in? There must have been something in her eyes, anger or revenge. Had he done something to her? Perhaps he had started to climb out of bed but she got to him first, he would have been low down, and used all of her downward pressure to fend off any attempt at defence, made sure that the knife plunged in deep. It would have to be deep, as Luke was young and fit; she wouldn't get many chances. Katie had said there were blood splashes on the wall, and the knife was still in his chest, so there must have been more than one thrust with the knife.

I wondered about the scene of crime report. Were there footprints in the blood, or fingerprints on the knife handle? Was that why the police believed that Sarah had killed him?

I looked to the doorway and saw Katie there. She had regained some of her poise, and was watching me as I took some more pictures of the room.

'Did you find anything that helps?' she asked.

I shook my head and answered no. It was a lie. Anything can be useful in a story, if it's used right.

'None of this makes sense,' I said instead, running my fingers through my hair. 'Everywhere I look, I see an ordinary girl seeing an ordinary boy, and then she did an extraordinary thing.'

'I know,' said Katie softly. The tears welled up once again and she looked at me, her expression all doe-eyed.

I felt a burst of pity for her, wanted to comfort her, but then I stopped myself, thought about Laura. I had to go.

'Thanks for the wine,' I said, 'and for the letters,' and I patted my back pocket.

She looked surprised. 'Are you going?'

'I've got a story to write.'

'But I'm worried,' she said. 'The letters were hand-delivered, and so Sarah is still nearby.'

'I can't help you with that,' I said. 'You need to call the police.'

I went towards the door, wanting to get away, to feel the cold wind in my face. Katie didn't move, and so I had to squeeze past her.

As I got to the bottom of the stairs, Katie behind me, I glanced back towards the kitchen. I saw a knife block, six black handles sticking out. But it was made for seven, and one of the slots was empty.

I went to the front door, and as I opened it, I turned back just to say goodbye. Katie was leaning against the wall, her head tilted, smiling softly at me. Before I could say anything, she reached out and caressed my cheek. Images of Laura flashed into my head again. I stepped away.

'I can't,' I said.

'That isn't the same as you don't want to,' she murmured.

I shook my head. 'The reason is the same,' I said, and I turned to walk away.

141

As I walked down the street, I could feel her gaze on me. I took a look back and she was still there, watching me. When I rounded the corner I let out a deep breath. I saw my car ahead, the Stag, but then I heard an engine behind me, and the soft rumble of tyres. It made me nervous, as if it was being driven at my walking pace. I looked round. All I could see were two headlights.

As I looked, it sped up and then pulled alongside me. I felt my stomach take a plunge when the window was lowered and a voice said, 'Get in, we're going for a ride.'

Chapter Twenty-seven

Sarah barely looked up when the door opened.

The laughter had gone, replaced only by a deep despair, so that all she could do was trace small circles in the mud with her finger. She was beyond fear now. It was worse than that. Her limbs felt heavy, her movements sluggish.

She could feel him standing over her, gazing down, but she couldn't bring herself to look up. The speakers were silent, so she could hear his steady breaths through the hood, rasping, hoarse. It was the older one, she could tell that from the more deliberate way he came into the room, the slow shuffles on the soil floor.

She heard a clink as he put some more food on the floor, and then he grunted as he straightened. He walked slowly out of the room and then slammed the door shut.

Sarah could smell the food; it was hot and she was hungry. But she didn't want to eat it, scared of what might happen if she did.

She turned over and put her head under the blanket, tried to make a dark space for herself, just so that it would seem like she was somewhere else, if only for a few minutes.

Then she heard the buzz of the speakers, and she knew that even that brief sanctuary was lost.

Chapter Twenty-eight

My mind raced.

I was in the back of a silver Mondeo, wedged in between two large men, both silent and moody, as we rumbled along narrow terraced streets and under the high stone viaduct that bridged the town centre. Then we began to climb. The houses began to space out, and through the windscreen I saw the streetlights come to an end. We were heading into the countryside.

They were detectives. When they'd showed me their cards, I'd thought about leaving, but I didn't want to provoke an arrest. However, I could tell it wasn't good news. They had been silent all the way, and I knew that they were saving good-guy bad-guy for later.

We drove along a country road, winding upwards, until we levelled out. I looked to one side and saw my companion watching me.

'Strong silent type?' I asked him.

He grinned back at me, his teeth bright in the darkness.

I looked to the front as the car swung onto a track. It was rutted, and the car pitched and rolled before we skidded to a stop on a patch of gravel. There was another car waiting for me, a black Audi, barely visible except for the silvery reflection of the moonlight. There was someone standing next to it, tall and bald, his head gleaming despite the darkness.

As I stepped out of the car, I saw that we were in a clearing, a break in the trees, the track cutting a path through dense woods. I could see the lights of Blackley below me, orange dots in the valley.

'Why have you brought me up here?' I asked. I tried to sound calm, but my heart was pumping fast and my cheeks felt hot from adrenalin.

The driver of the car walked up to me. 'We thought it was time for a talk,' he said menacingly.

He was dressed the same as the rest: pressed white shirt and sharp creases in his trousers. They had all been quiet during the journey. If it was meant to intimidate, it worked. I thought of running. I wasn't in cuffs, and a good push would put a few yards between us, but I didn't know the area, and they all looked like they could run if they had to.

'Why didn't you make an appointment?' I replied.

He smiled, but even in the darkness I could sense the menace. 'We thought you might take more notice this way.'

The bald man stepped forward. 'Mr Garrett. Good of you to agree to help us like this.' His voice was hoarse, like he was a long-time smoker, and the politeness was fake.

'I don't remember agreeing to anything.'

The bald man smiled. 'You weren't forced into the car.'

146

I tried hard to look casual. I was meant to be scared, and I was, but if I showed fear, the battle was over.

'Go on then, talk away,' I said. 'Let me guess. DCI Carson?' When he looked surprised, I added, 'People don't speak that highly of you, so it wasn't hard to work out that you're the prick they're talking about.'

I heard someone gasp behind me. I was banking on the fact that I wasn't the normal criminal he dealt with, whose complaints aren't taken seriously. I could go public without having to complain. The power of the press.

He stepped closer and stared at me with deep blue eyes.

'I want you to tell me what you've been doing,' he said. 'There's no rush. We've got time.' His voice was quiet but firm, his manner businesslike.

'Am I under arrest?'

He shook his head.

'So you've kidnapped me,' I said.

He laughed at that, and everyone else followed his lead.

'You came voluntarily,' he replied. 'You can go any time you want.'

I looked around, saw them all smiling. Two leaned against the car, another one lit a cigarette, the tip just a flash of bright orange.

'Let's go then,' I said. 'I don't want this conversation.'

He gestured along the path. 'Town's that way.' He looked up at the sky. 'You should have brought your brolly. It looks like rain.'

Then I understood why they had brought me up here. It was answer questions or walk. I'd heard the tales before

147

of long drives in a police car, intelligence-gathering. Now I realised that I was the newest target.

'Don't fancy it?' he asked mockingly. 'No. I'll tell you what you will do, and that is talk. You will tell us what you are doing. You will tell us where you have been, where you are going when you leave here, and what you have found out so far.'

That answered my main question: Why have I been brought here? I knew now that it was to do with Luke, or Sarah. I thought hard about what I should do. My eyes wandered around the group. The smoker had thrown his cigarette onto the floor and was grinding it out with his shoe. The others were starting to look bored.

Then I thought about Laura. I couldn't afford to make enemies because they might turn on her. Our jobs clashed sometimes, she knew that, but sometimes the trouble could get too big. I decided that truth was probably the safest of the options. Or at least an edited version of it.

'I've been asked by Sarah Goode's parents to try and find out what happened to their daughter,' I said. I held out my hands plaintively, as if there was nothing more to say.

'Who is Sarah Goode?' Carson asked.

'C'mon, you know who she is,' I replied. 'You're trying to catch her because you think she killed her boyfriend, because you think she's a murderer.'

'I know what she is. I want to know who she is, who she knows, where she goes.'

I thought about what he was asking. It was clear

that she was still the suspect, the target. I reflected on how little I knew. 'I haven't found out much yet,' I said.

'But what do you know?'

I shrugged. 'Same as you. Pretty young teacher who hasn't been seen for more than a week, not long after her boyfriend was killed.'

'Tell me about Katie,' Carson said.

I gave a look of surprise. 'Is she a suspect?' I asked.

He grew impatient. 'Just tell me!'

I sighed and continued. 'She seems like a nice young woman caught up in a bad situation. Sarah was land-lady. Katie was tenant. As simple as it sounds.'

'What did Katie think of Luke?'

'She didn't say too much,' I replied. 'He was her land-lady's boyfriend, just a routine thing, you know: he passes through the house, they talk, she goes away, he dies. Nothing more to it.'

'Where had she gone?'

'When?' I queried.

'The night of the murder. Where was she?' Carson sounded insistent.

'I would have thought she'd already told you,' I said warily. 'Is she a suspect?'

Carson laughed. 'The conversation is one way, Garrett. I know what she told us. I want to know what she told you.'

I could see the way the questions were going. They were checking out alibis, weren't sure of Katie. But I could judge character, journalists need to, and I had no sense that she had lied to me. So I decided on caution.

I wasn't going to raise inconsistencies that would put her under suspicion.

'She hasn't told me,' I lied.

'Mr Garrett,' Carson said, his voice rich with mock disappointment, 'I thought we'd agreed on co-operation. Are you trying to tell me that you've spoken to Katie Gray about Sarah Goode, and about what might or might not have happened, and you didn't ask where she'd been before she found the body?'

'Why? Did Katie find him?' I said sarcastically, but realised instantly that I'd gone too far.

I gasped as someone behind me gripped my collar. Before I knew what was happening I was on the floor, my ears filling with the sound of gravel as I was pushed into the ground.

'Now why don't we just stop fucking around!' came the shout. It wasn't a question. 'We ask questions, you will fucking answer them. If you don't, you'll find yourself in a cell for the night.'

'But why the fuck would I go into a cell?' I shouted, the pain of the landing raising my anger a notch.

'Police assault would be a good start,' the voice hissed.

'But I haven't assaulted anyone.'

'That's not what the report will say, and how do you think that will help your girlfriend's career?' And with that he grabbed me by my shirt collar and hauled me to my feet. 'So do as we say.'

I took some deep breaths, tried to calm myself down. I looked at Carson. He was leaning against his Audi, and I could sense the enjoyment.

'I'm sorry, Mr Garrett,' said Carson, his voice filled

with sarcasm, 'but he can get a bit impatient. I tell him that it isn't the way, that co-operation is always better, but he sometimes gets ahead of himself. Now, where were we?'

My eyes flashed between the two detectives, and I thought of Laura.

'We were talking about Katie,' I said quietly, my chest burning with anger.

'That's right, we were talking about Katie. Tell me, Mr Garrett, where did she tell you she was before she found the body? She did tell you she found the body, didn't she?'

I nodded a yes.

'Good. So where was she before she found the body?'

'Her parents,' I said. 'She'd gone to see them, and when she came back she spent the night watching television, and then she went into Sarah's room.' I paused. 'That's when she found Luke.'

'Why did she go into Sarah's room?'

I was starting to feel weary. 'Can't you ask her that?'

I saw the first detective step closer to me again, but a touch on his arm kept him at bay.

'Okay,' I said in resignation, 'she said she went in because she felt something just wasn't right. All the signs were that Sarah and Luke were staying there, but she'd heard nothing from them. She says she walked in and just saw Luke on the bed with the knife in his chest.'

I watched Carson exchange glances with someone and give a slight nod.

'Who else have you spoken with?' Carson asked.

I shrugged my shoulders. 'Why should I tell you?'

I asked, and then gasped as someone grabbed me again. I tried to keep my focus. 'Get the fuck off my neck.'

Carson was smiling. 'Tell me about Callum West,' he ordered.

I raised my hands as if to say I'd co-operate, and a nod from Carson made the other detective release his grip.

'Okay, okay,' I said, my anger spitting the words out, 'I spoke to him. He didn't have much to say, just told me a bit about Luke, just general stuff. You know, that Sarah was just a girl he was seeing, nothing serious, and he thought she had probably killed him.'

'Why did he think that?'

'For the same reason as you, that she's the obvious solution. He didn't provide me with anything that would help me find her. We had a brief chat and then I left.'

'Tell me about the letters. What do you know about them?'

I stared at him, tried not to blink. 'Just something I heard,' I said.

'Have you seen them?'

I held his gaze, wondered if he was right up to date, but then I remembered that they were in my pocket and they hadn't thought about searching me. I shook my head and said, 'No.'

'You mentioned them to the head teacher.'

'I was fishing.'

The detectives all looked at each other, exchanged shrugs and shakes of the head and the odd mumbled word. 'Who else are you going to check out?' asked Carson.

'No one, no one at all,' I answered. 'You've just named them all.' I felt my lip. It was bleeding. 'I could sue for this.'

Carson smiled. 'Proof might be a problem. No one knows you're here. You weren't booked in, you're not under arrest, and you're outnumbered four to one. Or we could just tell that little sweetheart of yours how cosy you're getting with Miss Gray.'

'I'm not getting cosy with anyone.'

Carson looked around to his men and asked, 'Did you all see it?'

They all nodded back, laughing among themselves. 'Very lovey-dovey,' someone shouted. 'Lots of kissing and hugging.'

'Laura would never believe you,' I said.

'Not on the surface,' Carson replied, 'but the doubt would always be there, chipping away at her.'

I wiped my mouth again. I could feel it swelling. 'Do you do this a lot? Take people for evening rides?' I asked.

'There's a body and so we need a result,' replied Carson.

I shook my head. They were clichés. 'There are rules,' I said.

'There are killers,' he responded, 'and a lot of nasty people out there. I want to lock them up. Go speak to Luke's parents and make the complaint, and then see how much sympathy you get.'

I didn't answer that.

'My father was a policeman,' I said.

The detectives looked at each other in a silent conference. I could make out the slightest shakes of the head, the odd raised eyebrow, and then Carson spoke again.

'What's your point?'

'He was a good man, an honest man, and he would not have done this.'

Carson grinned. 'So he stayed in uniform,' he said mockingly, and when he realised my silence meant that he was right, he said, 'You can go now, Mr Garrett. We're done with you here.'

I nodded towards the car. 'Who's driving?'

The driver of the car who had brought me up there waved the keys in my face. 'I am,' he said. 'You, however, can walk,' and he pointed along the dark woodland track. 'The country air will be good for you.'

And then I watched them as they climbed back into their cars. The engines started with a roar, and then spat gravel at me as they drove off. When they had gone out of view, it was silent. I looked back down towards Blackley. It looked a long way, but I patted my back pocket and felt the pieces of paper in there. The letters. At last, the story was starting to write itself. What Carson didn't realise was that he had just earned himself a starring role.

Chapter Twenty-nine

I was trying to write the story in my head as I walked, my pace fast to keep out the cold, when for the second time that evening I heard a car slow down alongside me. But as I looked, I saw a familiar charcoal-grey Golf. It was Laura.

I leaned into the car. 'What are you doing here?' I asked.

She glared back at me. 'Get in or keep walking.' She almost spat the words at me.

I climbed in, and she had slammed the car into gear even before I had the door closed. She turned it around in the road and tore up the verge on the opposite side.

I looked in the back and saw Bobby. He was in his pyjamas, wrapped up in a dressing gown and holding a hot-water bottle.

When I looked back towards Laura, I realised why she was angry.

'Look, I'm grateful, but you didn't have to come out for me,' I said. 'I would have called a taxi as soon as I could get a signal on my phone.'

Laura shook her head. 'Not now, Jack.'

'Why not now? I didn't ask for this to happen.'

'But it did,' she hissed. She checked in her rear-view mirror, and I knew that she was looking at Bobby.

'I've got the Court Welfare Officer coming tomorrow, to see if I'm a suitable mother,' she said quietly, although I could still hear the anger in her voice. 'They'll speak to Bobby. What if he says that he was taken for a ride in his pyjamas because you were left on the moors? It makes me look bad.'

'I thought it was "we" and "us"?' I said.

Laura looked towards me quickly. 'What do you mean?'

'You said the Court Welfare Officer was coming to see you, to see if you're a suitable mother. They're coming to see all of us, to see if we're a suitable family. It's not just about you.'

Laura didn't answer that.

We drove in silence for a while, the lights of Blackley getting nearer. As we started down the hill that led down to the viaduct, Bobby asked, 'Did you get lost in the woods, Jack?'

I didn't know how to answer that. *No,* I thought of saying, *a car full of policemen kidnapped me and dumped me in the middle of nowhere,* but I realised that maybe Bobby was too young to get cynical.

'I was with a friend,' I said, 'but my car broke down.'

'Where's your friend?'

'He lives in the other direction.'

Bobby seemed satisfied with that, and turned to look out of the window.

I glanced at Laura. 'How did you know where I was?' I asked.

'I got a call from someone at the station. They were laughing about it, how they left you up there. I was told where you would be, so I came looking for you.'

I thought of Bobby. And the Court Welfare visit.

'You could have stayed at home,' I said.

'I know,' she replied, calmer now, 'but as you said, the Court Welfare Officer is coming for a family visit. It's not much good if you're dead from hypothermia, or knocked down at the side of one of these unlit roads.'

Laura's hand was on the gearstick. I placed my hand over hers, just for a second, and gave a squeeze.

Laura looked down at it, and then back out of the windscreen. She softened. 'I'm sorry you were treated like that,' she said, and then a smile broke through. 'Don't read too much into it. I checked your life insurance before I came out, and I wasn't sure I'd get paid out.'

I laughed at that.

We went under the viaduct and started to drive through Blackley's centre, past a line of takeaways, the Saturday night flashpoints.

'C'mon,' she said. 'You can tell me all about your adventure when we get home.'

Chapter Thirty

Sarah had a few moments' rest, the bed soft beneath her, some comfort after the hardness of the floor. Mercifully, the speakers had fallen silent, and she used the blanket to blot out the lights.

The fear passed as the drugs subsided. She suspected LSD, but it was only a guess. She had never tried it, but she'd heard The Beatles, all those 'marmalade skies'. The soup had been mushroom soup. Had it been that?

She tensed when she heard a noise above her, and then soft steps, steadily descending. She'd been without the heartbeats from the speakers for a few minutes now, and instead her ears strained for the slightest sound from outside. There was never anything. Just silence. So when she heard something, it had to mean a visit. She flinched when the door slid open with a bang.

She could smell the food before she saw it, and it scared her. She remembered the last time she'd eaten. She had tipped the previous lot of food away, fearful of the same thing happening, but now hunger gnawed at her. She had got through what happened last time.

Maybe she would again. The food smelled good and she needed to be strong.

Her hands gripped the edge of the blanket. She could rush him, wrap the blanket around his neck, pull hard, use all of her weight. And use her anger. She could do just enough to get out of that door. She didn't care if she killed him. She wanted to kill him. She wanted to hear him beg for mercy, wanted to rip off his hood and look into his eyes as surprise crossed to fear and then to a realisation that he had lost.

Sarah knew that she would have to get used to the routines so she could work out when to strike. Then she thought about the food, because if there was food then it couldn't be her time yet.

Sarah lay perfectly still, listening to the sounds, and finally heard the footsteps come into the room. One step, two steps, three steps, and then a pause. The tray went onto the floor, and then he let out a breath as he straightened himself.

Then there was nothing. Sarah knew he was watching her. She lay still, all quiet, just the sounds of his breaths filling the room. What was he doing?

'Who do you trust?' he asked, the voice deep and muffled.

Sarah turned around. 'What do you mean?'

'The food or your body? You want it, but you are scared. Overcome your fears. I have.'

'And what fears have you had to overcome?' Sarah replied angrily.

'It doesn't matter what the fears are. It is the inability to overcome them that holds you back. You live your life scared, most people do. Worried about money, about death, about doing something wrong, being found out.'

'And don't those things worry you?'

'Do I seem worried?' When Sarah didn't respond, he shook his head. 'Of course I'm not scared. That's why I'm different to you.'

'Aren't you scared of being found out?'

He laughed. 'We're back to consequences, Sarah. That is all that stops you from being like me. That's why men fight in wars. They can kill without consequence. If you can shake off your fear, then you become free.'

'And that makes you a better person than me?' she asked scornfully.

'I am a better person than you. I see things, Sarah, see them the way they ought to be. I could show you the way. No more restrictions. No more fear. Think of all your fantasies, and reach for them.'

'I just want out of here.'

'That's good, Sarah. Reach for that. No fear.'

And then he turned around and left the room. Sarah was alone once more, the slam of the steel bolt the only sound.

She looked over at the food. It was on a tray, against the wall, the same place as last time. He was showing a habit, a weakness. He had turned his back on her to place it there.

Sarah got out of bed and went to the door. From there, she walked to the tray. She did it in three paces. So that's the routine. Three paces, and then a pause as he puts the tray on the floor, his back to her.

She was getting an idea. But first, she needed strength.

She looked at the food. Fresh bread, bacon, eggs, water. The bread looked edible, drug-free, and the eggs and bacon looked divine. It must be hard to lace that. Perhaps if she ate that and avoided the water?

But she needed water.

The thought of the food took over. She wanted it now, more than anything.

Sarah felt her stomach. It ached. He was right, in one way. To defeat him, she had to get over her fear. If the food was drugged, she would suffer again, but she would suffer more if she didn't eat.

She broke off a piece of bread and examined it. It looked just like bread should. She nibbled it. It tasted fine. She took a bite, chewing slowly, carefully. She groaned. It tasted good. And Sarah knew that if she was going to make it out of there, she had to be strong.

She sat down and devoured the food. When she had finished, she looked at the water. It seemed fresh. It looked just like water. She sniffed it and couldn't smell anything.

She took a deep breath, put the cup to her lips, and drank the water quickly. She sighed when she finished and let out a small laugh. It felt good not to be thirsty.

She stood up and began to pace around the room, which was echoing now with the noise of her feet in the dirt, beating a time, walking off the days.

She felt stronger. She was going to make it out. She knew it now, and as she got near the door, she kicked it and then laughed at the noise, the dull thud. She hit it again, this time with her fist. It made her feel better, so she pounded at the door, grimacing with the effort. When she stopped, panting, Sarah smiled.

Chapter Thirty-one

We drove along the lane to our house, the lights of Turners Fold blocked out at times by trees as we climbed up the hill. Bobby was dozing in the backseat.

As we got nearer, I saw someone there. It was a petite woman in a large coat and a woolly hat, blowing into her hands. I couldn't see a car.

'Who is that?' asked Laura.

I looked closer, unsure, but then her face was caught in the sweep of the headlights and I recognised her.

'That's Katie Gray,' I said, surprised. 'Sarah Goode's lodger.'

I saw Laura's eyes narrow. 'How did she find out where you lived?'

I shook my head. 'Not from me. Only my number is on my business card.'

I stepped out of the car and walked towards her. 'Hello,' I said. 'What are you doing here?'

She was about to come towards me, but as Laura got out of the car, Bobby in her arms, she stopped herself.

'I'm sorry,' she said hesitantly. 'I rang around for your address. You're quite well-known in Turners Fold.'

I paused at that. I couldn't remember telling her I lived near Turners Fold.

'I'm frightened, Jack,' she said, her voice quiet. She stopped talking when Laura went past her, heading upstairs. I saw that Bobby hadn't stirred.

'Why, what's wrong?'

Katie looked around, watched where Laura had gone, and then reached into her pocket. I watched her hand as she pulled out something white.

'I'd just got back,' she said, sounding strained.

I was curious now, less concerned with how Katie had found out where I lived. Something had happened – the light from the house showed the red rims under her eyes. She'd obviously been crying, and she looked like she was about to start again.

'It's okay,' I said, touching her lightly on the arm to reassure her. 'What's wrong? What's happened?'

She wiped her eyes and took a huge breath, appeared to steady herself.

'I'd just got back,' she continued. 'After you'd gone, I needed some things, and so I went to the shop. When I got back, I found this posted through my door,' and with that she held up the folded piece of paper she had pulled from her pocket.

'What is it?'

Katie took a deep breath and wiped her eyes again.

'It's another letter from Sarah,' she said.

I looked at the piece of paper, and then back to her. My hand went to my pocket, just to check that I still had my copies of the first two. 'Hand-posted?' I asked.

Katie nodded slowly and then held it out to me.

I took it from her carefully. I didn't want to open it, but I wanted it in my possession. I turned the piece of paper in my hand. It was cheap ruled-line paper, the sort that would be found in any high-street stationer's. Difficult to trace.

'How long were you out for?' I asked.

She thought about the answer, and replied, 'Not long. Half an hour.'

'Have you asked around the neighbours? You know, did they see who delivered it? Did they hear anything?'

Katie shook her head. 'I just came here when I saw it.'

I paused for a moment, worried about Laura's re-action, but when I thought of the letter I knew I wanted to know more. I pushed open the door. 'You'd better come in.'

Rod lifted the cup to his mouth, the coffee from his flask making the windscreen mist over.

He had found a spot on an old farm track that gave him a view of Abigail's cottage, the grey block of stone now just a shadow, broken only by the soft red glow of her windows. He had been watching for over an hour and nothing had happened.

He reached down for a sandwich, roast chicken, made by his wife, who worried that he might starve if he went more than a couple of hours without food. As he took a bite, his radio fizzed at him with news of someone staring into windows in one of the villages further along. And there was a new alert for diesel thieves. Another normal night.

Rod didn't respond to any of the messages. He had

settled in for a long evening. He would wait until midnight, and if there was no movement, he would go home.

It had been quiet so far. He folded the tin foil over his sandwiches and put his cup back on his flask. His vigil still had a couple of hours to run.

As he looked back through the window, he saw some movement. Wasn't that always the way? As soon as he stopped looking, something happened.

He lifted his binoculars again. Abigail's front door was open. Then he saw something at the front of the house, a shadow moving along the path. He put the binoculars down and tried to get a better view, so he could track where the shadow was going. Then he realised that the shadow was heading straight for him.

He flicked on the headlights and then sighed. It was Abigail, and as she reached him, he saw she was holding a blanket.

'If you're going to watch me,' she said, pushing it towards him, 'stay warm,' and then she turned round to hobble back to her cottage.

Rod looked at the blanket, and then at Abigail disappearing back into the shadows. He laughed to himself and then started his engine. He knew he wouldn't see anything else that night.

Chapter Thirty-two

Laura came downstairs just as Katie followed me into the house. Laura looked angry at first, and I knew she was wondering what Katie was doing there, annoyed with me as Katie was a witness, but she softened when she saw that Katie had been crying.

'I'll make a drink,' said Laura.

I pointed towards the settee. 'Make yourself comfortable,' I said, and then went to join Laura in the kitchen.

As I got there, Laura whispered, 'What the hell is going on?'

'It looks like Sarah Goode has sent another letter,' I said, and I held up the piece of paper.

Laura looked at the paper, and then at me. Her eyes widened. 'You've got something there from a murder suspect. You can't keep it.'

I nodded. 'I know. It looks like I'm going to have to meet up with my friends from the murder squad again.'

Laura's jaw clenched. Then she looked at the piece of paper. 'What about forensics?' she asked.

'That's why I haven't opened it,' and I showed Laura

that I was holding it by one corner. 'Have you got something to open it with?'

Laura paused for a moment.

'I need to see what it says,' I pleaded.

'Wait there,' she said, and left the kitchen, returning with some small steel eyebrow tweezers.

I went back into the living room, Laura behind me. I put the piece of paper on the small table. Laura put a hot chocolate next to it for Katie.

Katie smiled her thanks, and then wrapped her hands around the cup. She must have been outside for some time because she looked cold.

I opened the piece of paper on some tin foil, to catch anything that might fall out, and spread it out, my fingers using the tweezers delicately. I felt a flutter of excitement, or was it nerves, knowing that I could be on the verge of a good story after months of jotting down court tales. Katie didn't seem to share my excitement. She looked vulnerable, hurt, lonely.

I started to read.

> There is no one alive more unwilling to pronounce this woeful and heavy judgement than myself: but the blood of that innocent child, whom cruelly and barbarously I have murdered, has brought this heavy judgement upon me at this time.
> Sarah

My skin crackled into goose-pimples. It seemed to confirm the obvious, that Sarah had gone mad and killed Luke – but the obvious seemed incredible.

I looked at Katie. She began to cry. 'What does it all mean?' she wailed through the tears.

Laura sat next to her and placed a comforting arm around her shoulder, although I saw the wariness in Laura's eyes.

'It's okay,' said Laura, her voice soft. 'We'll take it to the police in the morning.'

I read the letter again, tried to work out a hidden meaning. But nothing jumped out at me.

'I don't know what it means,' I said, answering Katie's question. 'Why so mysterious?'

I looked at the letter. I read again the reference to *'the blood of that innocent child'*. Was Sarah referring to Luke? Is that how she saw him? He was her child, and she was in control? Or, at least, so she thought. Or was Sarah that child, describing her own inner turmoil, battles between her good side and her bad side?

But she talked about *'whom cruelly and barbarously I have murdered'.* There couldn't be too many ways that it could be misinterpreted.

The language puzzled me. Was she trying to set up an insanity defence? If Sarah wrote the letter, had she recognised that she had done a bad thing and deserved to die? *'There is no one alive more unwilling to pronounce this woeful and heavy judgement than myself.'*

I pulled at my lip. Maybe I was reading too much into the syntax? But the words must be important, as why else would they be so strangely constructed, with the language old English in style?

I sighed and ran my hand through my hair. I was

puzzled, but I realised that the story was getting even better.

'Well?' Katie asked. 'What do you think?'

I wasn't really sure what I thought. 'It reads like a confession,' I said, still looking at it. 'But it's an odd one, which makes me wonder if it's something else.'

'What, some kind of hint as to where she might be?' asked Katie, her eyes wide now. 'Can we find her, do you think?'

'Leave that to the police,' warned Laura.

I smiled. 'But it would be a hell of a story if we could.'

'No, Jack,' repeated Laura, her voice sterner.

'Even if I don't look for her,' I said, 'I'm going to write the story. There isn't much else I can do.'

Laura looked angry at that, but what else could I say? I knew that I wouldn't leave the story alone, not now. I thought of the murder squad. I imagined how angry it would make them. That made it all seem worthwhile, but it wasn't just that. I felt like I'd recovered some of my excitement in the job, that buzz of chasing a story that no one else had, my name as the byline.

'It is her handwriting,' added Katie, watching us both. The smile disappeared again. 'Poor Sarah,' she said sadly.

'Why poor Sarah?' asked Laura. 'If she killed someone, she needs to be punished.'

'But what drove her to it?' replied Katie. 'Whatever has been going on in her life to make her do this, it makes me feel sorry for her, that's all.' She shook her head in disbelief. 'I know Sarah did it, that's what the police say, but it just isn't like her.'

'From all the crime I've covered,' I said, 'it always

seems that the obvious answer is the right one.' But when Katie looked down and nodded her agreement, some sadness in her eyes, I added, 'One thing bothers me though.'

Katie looked up. 'What is it?'

'Why did she tell you?' I asked. 'If she wants to confess, why not just do it? Go into a police station and tell them everything.'

'It sounds like a cry for help,' Laura said. 'Maybe she wants to be found, and she is scared, not sure what to do.'

I shook my head. 'If she's making a cry for help, she doesn't give away many clues. There is nothing here that would hint at her location.' Then I thought of something. 'What period of history do you study?' I asked Katie.

'The modern histories,' Katie replied. 'You know, the sixties, the Kennedys, that kind of thing. Why?'

'Just because of the language used,' I said. 'It sounds antiquated. If you're a historian, maybe you are supposed to spot something, like a coded message.'

'But I don't,' replied Katie.

'Let the police think about that,' said Laura. 'I want you to promise me that you'll take it to the police first thing tomorrow.'

'Of course I will,' said Katie, sounding offended.

'At least let me photograph it,' I said, 'so I can use it in the feature.'

Laura looked sternly at me when I came back with my camera. As I took pictures, Katie said quietly, 'I don't want to go home.'

'Why not?' I asked.

'Because Sarah has now hand-delivered three letters to me,' she replied, 'and the last person she spoke to in my house ended up with a knife in his chest.'

'You can stay here, if you want,' I blurted out, although when I caught Laura's angry look, I added, 'just for tonight, though.'

Katie gave me a watery smile. 'Thank you, Jack. I appreciate it.'

From the look Laura gave me, I realised that she wasn't as grateful.

Chapter Thirty-three

Sarah woke with a start. The speakers were back on, the heartbeat sound pumping out again. She wrapped the blanket around her head, tried to muffle the noise.

It was getting late, she could feel that from the way the end of her nose had gone cold. The glow from the food was still there, but she was getting hungry again. And she was tired. It came at her in waves, an overwhelming desire just to lie down and drift away, but the lights made it hard, and now the noise was back.

Sarah looked at the floor. She had worn a smooth path in the dirt from the tight circles she'd walked earlier in the day. She leaned over the edge of the bed and let her hair fall forward, until it trailed in the dirt. She stared at her hands, saw how her nails were dirty and broken. She dug them into the soil and then put them to her face, so that she streaked dirt down her cheeks. She did it some more, and her skin tightened as it dried, until the only part of her face that was visible were her eyes, white and wide.

She realised now that she wasn't going to be released any time soon, and so the only way she would get home would be if she fought her way out.

But first she had to overcome her captor, and she shuddered at the thought of what might happen if she failed.

I collected some blankets and a spare duvet. Laura was on the other side of the bedroom.

'What the hell are you playing at, Jack?' she said, her voice low and angry.

'It's one night. What if I'd said no and you heard that she'd been found dead in that house?'

'That's not the point,' Laura snapped back.

'What is the point?' I said. 'That's she's young and attractive?'

Laura's eyes widened. 'Is she, Jack?'

I cursed myself as I realised how it had come out. 'I didn't mean that,' I said testily. 'She's not you.'

'What about the Court Welfare visit?'

'What about it?' I asked.

'How will it look, with someone sleeping on the sofa?'

'She'll be gone before then, I'll make sure of that.'

'And how will you do that?' Laura hissed angrily. 'Breakfast in bed?'

I walked downstairs, not wanting an argument, and put the duvet on the sofa. Katie's eyes were red, her cheeks streaked where grubby hands had wiped away tears.

'You don't mind me staying, do you, Jack?' She looked up at me, wide-eyed, innocent.

'No, it's fine,' I said. 'Make yourself comfortable.'

She smiled and stood up. I saw her put together a makeshift bed, and then she turned back to me.

'Do you think I'm in danger?' she asked, her voice softer now.

I shrugged. 'I just don't know.'

'But if I am, you'll help me, won't you?'

'I'm a reporter,' I replied. 'The police will look after you better than I can.'

She seemed happy with that, and I detected a glint of something in her eyes that I couldn't work out. She started to get changed for bed. Without taking her eyes off me, she undid the buttons on her jeans and let them fall to the floor. She stepped out of them without dropping her gaze.

I turned to go.

'It's okay, Jack,' she whispered.

I didn't know what to say, how to respond. One minute she was scared, vulnerable, and the next she was like this, provocative, sexy.

She took off her jumper and threw it to the floor. She was in her underwear, her stomach tight, her hips slim, her breasts pushed forward. She reached behind her back to unclasp her bra, looking directly at me all the while.

As her bra fell to the floor, her breasts pert, her body pale and lean, she hooked her thumbs into her panties, ready to slide them down. I turned to leave, embarrassed and confused. I didn't know Katie's game any more.

As I turned around, I saw Laura. She was standing at the doorway, glaring at Katie. As I went past Laura, her stare never moved. I went upstairs, but not before I glanced back and saw that Katie was smiling at Laura, but it was superior, threatening. Laura threw one of my

T-shirts onto the settee and turned away, taking deep angry breaths.

Laura went past me, her cheeks red, her eyes blazing. Before I followed her, I saw Katie look at me. She smiled, made no attempt to cover herself up.

I went upstairs.

When I went to the bedroom, I heard Laura in the bathroom. I waited for her, not quite sure what she would say. When she came into the bedroom, she got into bed without saying a word, and turned over.

I realised that it was a discussion best left until morning.

Chapter Thirty-four

Laura stood over Katie, watching her sleep, the morning sun streaming in through the window.

Then Katie opened her eyes, and when she stretched, the duvet fell off her and her T-shirt rode up her stomach.

'I want you out of here now,' said Laura icily.

Katie yawned into a smile. 'What's the matter?' she whispered. 'Worried about Jack?'

Laura knelt down so that her face was close to Katie's. 'Look, you little tramp, I don't know what your game is, but Jack is not part of it.'

'Isn't that Jack's choice?' Katie gave a small laugh. 'I reckon he wasn't far from making it last night.'

Laura took a deep breath. Don't hit her, she said to herself. Think of your career. More than that, think how it would look to the Court Welfare people.

'You don't look bad, though, for a woman your age, I mean,' Katie continued. 'What are you, thirty-seven? A bit older? Time has given you a couple of kicks, you know, a few sags and bumps that I don't have, but you make the best of what you've got. I can see why Jack finds you interesting.'

Laura's hand snapped forward, her eyes angry, her jaw set, ready to grab Katie's neck, but Katie grabbed her wrist and held it.

'Be careful, officer,' Katie said, her eyes hard now. 'That wouldn't look good on your CV.' She pushed Laura's hand away.

'Why do you want him?' asked Laura. 'You're not really interested in him, are you? This is just a silly little game for you, like that strip-show you gave him last night.'

'Did he enjoy it?'

'I want you out of here in five minutes,' said Laura, getting angrier, 'or I'll throw you out.'

Katie laughed. 'You could have joined in, you know,' she mocked. 'It might have been fun.'

Laura felt her hand clench into a fist, her mouth set firm in anger. She ought to punch the little bitch, wreck those looks of hers, but she took some deep breaths instead. Don't give her the satisfaction.

Then she heard movement upstairs. Jack was coming down.

'Get dressed and get out,' said Laura, and then she walked to the kitchen.

I was surprised to see Katie awake when I got downstairs, although she was stretched out in her underwear, smiling at me. I went to the kitchen and Laura was in there, and when she looked round I thought she looked tired, as if she'd struggled to sleep. Her hair was sticking up and her eyes looked heavy.

'How are you feeling?' I asked her.

Laura snapped a smile at me, but her eyes didn't

178

match it. 'Oh, just great,' she said, and then she pointed towards the living room. 'What kind of game is she playing?'

I exhaled and then stepped forward, tried to put my arms around her, but she shrugged me off.

'I don't know,' I said, 'but if it's about me, you've no need to worry. I wouldn't do it to you. I love you too much to throw it away on Katie.'

Laura turned away at that and poured herself a drink. 'I've been here before, remember, with Geoff,' she said quietly. 'I know all the lies, and I'm not going there again, not when I've come this far.'

'I'm not Geoff. You can trust me.'

Laura looked at me, and then her eyes softened. She smiled at me and kissed me on the cheek. I could smell the sleep on her, musty and familiar. 'I hope I can,' she said.

'I need to stick with Katie, though,' I said. 'The story centres around her somehow, and I sense a good story when it all comes out.'

'Well, just be careful. For me.'

We both looked round when we heard movement, and we saw Katie get to her feet from the sofa. Her hair was tousled, and she smiled as she stretched, looking at me all the time, my old T-shirt riding up to her panties, her legs long, her eyes challenging.

'Can I use your bathroom?' she asked sleepily.

Laura nodded her assent and pointed up the stairs, but there was little welcome in it.

Katie walked off, and I made sure that I didn't watch her go. Once Katie had gone upstairs, Laura turned round to me, and I thought she was going to be angry, but then she smiled at me.

'I would trust you more if you weren't doing that,' she said, her voice deep in pity.

'Doing what?'

She reached over and put her hands on my stomach. 'Sucking it in.'

I looked down and saw my T-shirt billowing over her fingers. I blushed.

'Automatic reflex, I bet,' she said, and began to chuckle.

I didn't have an answer for that.

Chapter Thirty-five

I ran up the court steps, hoping to catch Sam Nixon. The two security guards slowed me down, as I was made to empty my pockets and was then hand-scanned as an old packet of mints set off a beep, but I still entered the court corridor at a rush.

Blackley Magistrates Court was next to the police station, as they all once were, where an overnight remand meant a short walk along the cell corridor and into the holding cells underneath the court, nothing more than cages where the prisoners swapped stories and talked about their lawyers. When the new police station was completed, prisoners would arrive in shiny white vans and be taken into the building in chains.

Not many people looked up as I searched for Sam Nixon. It was busy, as always, the plastic chairs filled by young men in tracksuits and old men with glazed looks in their eyes. No one was talking. The nervous ones stared into space and awaited their fate. The cocky ones smoked outside and laughed and joked, court just an interruption to their chaotic schedule.

The courtrooms were large and imposing, with high

ceilings and glass docks, the Magistrates high on wooden benches in front of the court crest, the lion and the unicorn. A porthole in the door allowed me to see inside. I could see a prosecutor on her feet, and I recognised her. It was Alison Hill. She used to work with Sam Nixon, but not many people stayed in defence work now. The hours were bad, the clients were bad, and the money wasn't what it was. Like most, she had crossed the line and prosecuted.

I could see Sam further along the desk, waiting for Alison to finish, making her perform in front of her old mentor. Alison eventually sat down, and when Sam rose to his feet he blackmailed the Magistrates, held up a pre-sentence report and asked them to agree with the conclusion, which would contain a recommendation for something other than prison. It was the hidden hint that would win him the day. I had heard it so many times: read the report, and if you agree with it I'll say nothing more. But if you don't, I'll go on for hours. I saw the Magistrates glance down at Alison's files before they left the court, the prosecution work piled high on the desk. If they didn't go along with the report, they would be there all day.

I went to the press bench at the side of the court and caught Sam's attention. When he came over, I asked, 'Could you give me a legal opinion?'

He looked surprised. 'For free?'

I nodded. 'The price of publicity.'

He held out his hands in submission. 'Fire away.'

'What happens to someone who is acquitted of murder because of insanity?' I asked.

Sam opened his mouth to answer, and then he stopped himself. 'Is this connected to Sarah?' he asked.

I smiled. 'Potentially.'

'I thought you weren't interested.'

'You shouldn't always believe journalists. So what's the answer?'

Sam sighed. 'Well, it's not really getting off with it. You just get locked up in a secure hospital until you are fit to be released, which usually means never. Why do you ask?'

'Just curious, that's all.' When Sam raised his eyebrows, I added, 'If you were going to run an insanity defence, and were planning it, how would you start?'

Sam's look darkened. 'What are you suggesting?'

'Nothing,' I replied, my voice filled with innocence. 'I just wondered how hard it would be.'

'Very hard, is the answer,' said Sam. 'You win very little with an insanity defence, if it isn't true. Maybe it was useful when the hangman was still around, but not any more.'

'So you wouldn't set out to fake it, to set it up before you hand yourself in?'

'Not if it wasn't true and you had taken legal advice first. Which, of course, Sarah hasn't.'

'Okay, thanks, Sam.'

As I turned away, I felt my phone vibrate against my leg. When I picked it up, I saw a message from Katie. '*Meet me outside college in 10 mins. If no can do, ring. Kt.x.*'

It looked like my next appointment had just made itself.

Chapter Thirty-six

Laura was once again in the queue to see the custody sergeant, the tapes of interview in her hand, the prisoner next to his solicitor, who held his file across his chest and looked at the floor. Not wanting to look at the exhibit bag, Laura guessed, filled with rocks of crack cocaine that had once been hidden inside the prisoner, a drop of his trousers and a touch of the toes revealing the secret, a knotted end of a plastic bag sticking out of somewhere that wasn't designed for storage.

Laura had handled the interview badly though, had bickered rather than questioned. It was an interview tape she would not want played in court.

She was angry with herself, although she knew what was on her mind: the Court Welfare visit. It had been all she had thought about during the morning, worried that the wrong word, a bad attitude, or just a clash of personalities, would see Bobby taken away from her, transported to London to live with Geoff, just so that he could get bored and pass Bobby over to babysitters.

Laura looked round when she heard a voice. It was

her prisoner's solicitor, a young Indian man in pinstripes and gelled hair.

'What did you say?' she asked.

The lawyer looked at her, his eyes filled with arrogance. 'I said, are we going to spend the day in the corridor?'

Laura clenched her jaw. She knew she had been distracted, thinking about Bobby, but there was no reason to be rude.

She stepped forward. 'I've just got a few enquiries to make, so unless you want to share your client's cell, be quiet.' Laura looked at Pete. 'There's something I've got to do. Can you sort him out?'

She turned and walked away, not giving Pete any time to respond. She needed some fresh air, and so she headed for the exit, for a few minutes with the smokers. Her head was down, she was still berating herself for letting the stress of the impending court visit spill over into her job, when she heard a loud guffaw. As she looked up, she saw Carson stepping out of the Incident Room, heading for the toilets.

All her rage from the night before came rushing back at her. Her anger at Jack, at Katie, the memory of her drive to the moors with Bobby in the back.

She stalled for a moment, knew that she should walk away, but her anger was too strong. She marched after him.

As she pushed open the door, she saw white tiles and mirrors, and then, further along, three stalls. Then she saw his back in one of the mirrors. He was at one of the urinals, his concentration fixed downwards.

Laura marched over and stood right next to him. He jumped, startled, saw Laura looking down at him.

'What the bloody hell are you doing in here?' he shouted angrily as he tried to cover himself up.

'I received a complaint, sir,' she said. 'A member of the public told me that he had been abducted, taken onto the moors and left there.'

Carson's eyes narrowed, and then he smirked. 'Pretty boy upset?' he said arrogantly. 'I'll tell you what: you tell him to keep out of my case, and I'll keep away from him.'

Laura shook her head. 'I don't think he's going to do that. You see, he's a journalist, so he thinks he's got a right to free speech. And free speech means that he can make a complaint about his treatment.'

Carson sneered at her. 'I hope he earns good money, because his might be the only wage when you try and answer for being in here.'

Laura stepped even closer. 'I'm sorry, sir, but I knew how serious the complaint was, so as soon as I saw you I rushed straight in. I should have realised that you would be . . . what's the word . . .' and she looked down. 'Embarrassed?' Now it was Laura's turn to smirk. 'I've spoken to the member of the public,' she continued, 'and advised him that it's not going to happen again, I'm sure of that. If it does, he'll take it further.'

At that, Laura turned to go.

Carson turned around and zipped himself up. His cheeks were flaming red, his mouth set in a scowl.

Just before she got to the door, Laura turned back. 'You might want to get the dryer on that,' and she pointed down to Carson's trousers.

Carson cursed when he saw the piss patch on his groin, and Laura was smiling when she slipped back into the corridor.

I saw Katie waiting for me outside college. She was on her phone as I approached, pacing up and down. When she saw me, she ended her call and smiled.

'Glad you could make it,' she said chirpily.

'Your text sounded urgent,' I replied.

Her hand brushed away her fringe. 'It's not really urgent. The police didn't seem that impressed by the letter when I took it in, and so I thought some more about it. Then I had an idea.' When I raised my eyebrows to suggest that she should continue, Katie said, 'It was the language that made me think. Old-fashioned, almost Tudor.'

'Go on.'

'Have you heard of the Pendle witches?' she asked.

I was surprised by that. I had heard of them, everyone had around Blackley. It was embedded in local folklore, tales of covens from four hundred years earlier, when two local families were in dispute and witch fever was at its height. King James had just come to the throne, and he'd brought with him a hatred of witchcraft. When one of the local families was accused of bewitching someone to death, members of both families fell over themselves to accuse each other of witchcraft. A number of local people went to the gallows at Lancaster Castle, and the Pendle witches passed into infamy.

'Yeah, I've heard of them,' I replied, 'but what has that story got to do with Sarah?'

Katie looked around, at the students heading into the college building. When there was no one around her, she said, 'Sarah is a descendant of a Pendle witch.'

I laughed. When I noticed that Katie didn't laugh with me, I asked, 'How do you mean?'

'Just that. One of her ancestors is Anne Whittle, the head of one of the main families involved.'

The wording of the letters started to rush through my head again. Old in style, with talk of murder and sin. And what about the angle for the story? *Descendant of Pendle witch is a murderer?* It would sell, I knew that.

'How do you know this?' I asked.

'She told me. She's got the family tree on the wall, framed. It shows the line, from Anne Whittle right down to her.'

'Why are you telling me?' I asked.

Katie blushed. 'Because you were kind to me last night, letting me stay. And you know what they say, that an act of kindness comes back at you threefold.'

'And a bad deed?'

'Threefold too.'

'So that's the favour returned once over,' I said. 'What about the other two times?'

Katie looked back at the college. 'I'll get you into the college library.'

'Why?'

'Because,' she replied, smiling coyly, 'if the letters have any connection with the Pendle witches, then maybe a search through the textbooks will find it.'

I followed her gaze, and then I thought about my next planned move. Or, rather, the lack of it.

'I like the idea,' I said. 'Are you going to help?'

'If you want me to.'

'Good,' I said. 'That's a threefold return. We're quits.'

Chapter Thirty-seven

Sarah's eyes opened, instantly awake, when she heard footsteps on the other side of the door. They were slow and steady, as if he might be carrying something. Maybe more food. Her stomach grumbled at her, but she had to push her hunger aside.

She gripped the bedclothes tightly and closed her eyes, tried to keep her breaths low and steady. The bolt slid slowly across, creaking, and then the door started to open.

Sarah stirred, just to keep it natural, but her body was tensed, her fingers gripping the edge of the blanket. Wrap the edge around his neck, she thought, pull on it hard, and keep pulling until his struggles stopped. The blanket would be cumbersome, but she would get just one chance.

Her breaths were heavy, her stomach turning with nerves.

The footsteps came into the room slowly, deliberately, just soft crunches on the dirt. Sarah counted the steps, three paces, just like before. She was poised to run, but then he paused. Sarah listened keenly, and then she heard him exhale as he bent down with the food.

She jumped off the bed and ran towards him, the blanket between her hands. He turned, the tray falling to the floor, the clatter of cutlery lost in her screams as the blanket went over his head.

She pulled hard on the blanket, felt it tighten around his head, his hands scrabbling at her. His fingers clawed at her face, and then her hair. She pulled tighter and tried to pull him to the floor.

'You bastard!' she shouted. 'I'm going to kill you.'

He tried to struggle out of the way. He was stronger, and Sarah could feel herself being thrown around. He caught a fistful of hair and yanked at it. Sarah lurched to one side but tried to ignore the pain. She pulled again at the blanket, tried to snap his head back, and so he dug his heels into the dirt and pushed at her. She was slammed against the wall, her grip loosening for a second as she felt her breath knocked out of her, her vision blurred as her head banged against a stone.

He elbowed her hard in the stomach. Her grip slackened some more, and so he used his weight to push Sarah against the wall again. As she grunted, he reached back and grabbed her hair, except this time when he pulled at it, she went with it, one hand letting go of the blanket.

He threw the blanket from his head and stood over her, the black hood billowing out in quick bursts as he gulped down air.

Sarah scrambled backwards, her feet kicking at the dirt, but he went towards her, faster than normal, his fists clenched hard, his control lost.

He reached down to her shirt and pulled at it, sending

the buttons to the floor. Sarah could hear his anger in his growl as he pawed at her.

'Why are you doing this?' she screamed. 'Leave me alone. Do you hear? Just leave me alone. Not this.'

He pulled at the shirt again until it ripped, his hard, callused hands clawing at her breasts, reaching down to his trousers, pushing them down to his thighs.

Sarah kicked out, but it just made him angrier, his hands grabbing at her, pulling at her waistband, the button on her jeans popping open. 'No, no, no, no,' she cried, and tears streamed down her face, but he yanked at her jeans, brought them down to her ankles, and then she felt the coldness of his thighs between hers. His hand was over her mouth, pressing hard, the hood near to her face as he panted in her ear like a dog. His hand tasted of oil and cigarettes.

She let out a cry when he put himself inside her. She went rigid, couldn't move. There was no fight left, no anger. She became limp, passive, her eyes stared at the ceiling as he moved on top of her, his hand pressing into her face, fingers clawing at her cheeks. But she stopped feeling the pain. It was as if it was happening to someone else, like she was a spectator. She didn't scream or thrash. She just stared at a spot on the ceiling, at the bright lights, but she was beyond tears.

It was over quickly. She became aware of his breaths as he lay on top of her, as he crushed the air out of her and pushed her head into the dirt.

He stayed like that for a while before he clambered off her, fastened his trousers, and stood over her.

Sarah didn't move. She could hear him panting,

hoarse and angry. She wanted to turn round and scream, wanted to hurt him like he had hurt her.

She didn't do any of that. Instead, she wiped the dirt from her mouth and lay there on the floor, semi-naked, her clothes tattered, and stared at the ceiling. She knew his eyes were on her, but she felt lifeless, uncaring, unable to move.

He walked out of the room. When the door shut, she began to feel the pain. And when the sobs came, they sounded like a long scream.

Chapter Thirty-eight

As we headed towards the college building, Katie said, 'Do you know what's funny? No one talks to me now. But I'm not the one that was killed, and I'm not the one who has disappeared. I pray nothing bad has happened to Sarah, but I want things to be normal again. I've assignments to complete. I found this tragedy, but I'm not part of it, and I want my life to go back to normal; there's a lot of it left.'

'I can understand that,' I responded. 'Maybe once Sarah is found, you'll move on properly.'

'What about you?' she asked.

I was confused. 'What do you mean?'

'What does the story mean to you?'

I smiled and sighed. 'I'm a reporter. I write the story, I get paid, and then I move on to another one.'

'So this means everything to me, but as far as you're concerned, I'm just a small part of a story you'll soon forget.'

'That's life,' I said, 'and I don't see how I can apologise for that.'

'It's no wonder that reporters don't have a good reputation.'

'I'm doing what I've always wanted to do. I've got plenty of free time, and I don't worry about what people think of me.'

'Do you really not care what other people think of you?' Katie asked.

I shook my head. 'I'm a freelance reporter who lives in a little hillside cottage, and I'm happy with that.'

'And Laura?'

I flinched at that. 'What about Laura?' I asked.

She stopped and looked at me. 'Do you think you'll get married?'

I laughed too loudly. 'That's too far ahead for us to think about,' I said, and then wondered about her interest. 'Did something happen this morning, between Laura and you?'

Katie smiled. 'Just girl talk,' she said, and then headed into college, holding the door open for me.

When we got into the college library it was smaller than I expected, just a room on the top floor with views over Blackley. Desks ran along the window, separated by partitions, and the college books were stacked in dark aisles. It seemed much different from my own university, where the library had occupied a whole building, with views through latticed windows. This was bright and modern, but it seemed like an afterthought, a space they had to find when the college grew.

Katie handed me a piece of paper. 'I scanned in the letter that arrived last night, before I took it to the police. You take that, and I'll take the first two. Let's see what we can find.'

As Katie set off down one of the aisles, I wondered

about her theory. If there was a link, Sarah might be sending messages, but it was too damn cryptic.

I set my coat down at a desk and walked to the same area of the library as Katie. There was a section devoted to local history, with books on the industrial revolution and religious strife. But there was a shelf devoted to witchcraft, and most books focused on the Pendle witch trials: perspectives on the trials, transcripts of evidence, studies of the reasons and the theories behind the reasons.

I returned to the desk with a few useful-looking tomes, including a verbatim account of the trials, or at least as verbatim as you could get before the days of stenography, and two books on the characters and personalities of the trials. I couldn't see Katie when I returned to our table, so I ploughed through the books on my own.

I reached into my pocket and put Sarah's letter on the table. I read it again:

> *There is no one alive more unwilling to pronounce this woeful and heavy judgement than myself: but the blood of that innocent child, whom cruelly and barbarously I have murdered, has brought this heavy judgement upon me at this time.*
> *Sarah*

I sighed. I wondered whether Katie had tried too hard to find a reason behind what Sarah did. But I remembered the name of Sarah's ancestor: Anne Whittle. At least I had a starting point.

The books were tough going and I found myself drifting as I read. I thought about Sarah's parents, no doubt wondering what Sarah was doing at that moment, as I sat huddled over dusty pages reflecting on events of four hundred years earlier. And I wondered what DCI Carson would say if he knew what I was doing.

I'd heard of the Pendle witch story, and I knew some of the names – Bulcock, Alice Nutter – but as I read, I realised that the story was more complex than just the trial of a few local women. The Pendle witches were just like any others accused of witchcraft: they were poor, uneducated, and regarded as outsiders. There were two families involved, the Southerns and the Whittles, each headed by two bitter rivals, Old Demdike and Old Chattox, who for years had sought to outdo the other in their outlandish claims of witchcraft and spell-casting. But when Demdike's granddaughter, Alison Device, was accused of causing the death of a passing peddler by witchcraft, the local Magistrate became involved, and that started it, the chain of blame. Alison herself blamed witchcraft, foolishly hoping it would excuse her, and then she accused others of witchcraft too, and so the accusations spread.

I began to flick, racing through transcript after transcript, page after page, my eyes glazing, and I was on the verge of giving up when I was stopped dead by words that seemed to leap out at me.

It was just a phrase I recognised. I had been making my way through the documents when I spotted words that rang familiar. I turned again to Sarah's letter and read the last part of it, my hands fumbling with the paper:

> . . . *the blood of that innocent child, whom cruelly and barbarously I have murdered, has brought this heavy judgement upon me at this time.*

I looked now at the text in front of me and felt a rush of adrenalin. It was virtually the same. I had been scanning page after page of accusations when I came across it: the judgement in Anne Whittle's case, Sarah's ancestor. I spotted a familiar phrase:

> *But the bloud of those innocent children, and others his Maiesties Subjects, whom cruelly and barbarously you haue murdered, sollicited for satisfaction and reuenge, and that hath brought this heauie iudgement vpon you at this time.*

I looked up and saw that nothing had changed, that students were still sitting around, making notes or just reading. But it seemed noisy to me, the excitement of a good story unfolding in front of me, making me want to thump the desk or shout out. And it confirmed that Katie had guessed right: the Pendle witch connection was not a coincidence. The letter from Sarah had paraphrased part of the judgement, the finding of guilt.

I returned to the books in front of me. I could feel my breath begin to shorten as my fingers turned pages quickly, looking for more words and phrases that might leap out at me, my eyes racing over the text.

I raised my head and saw Katie pass an aisle, engrossed in a book. I returned to my own study, wondering whether she had found something, and just as my mind began to speculate and wander again, I saw another familiar phrase. It was from the same passage. I'd gone past it first time around.

I almost shouted out this time. I was getting somewhere, I knew it, although I wasn't sure where. Page after page rushed past my eyes as I looked for more signs, and the more I looked, the more I saw. Some from the letter I had, some from the first two, the ones Katie had. I scribbled fast, made notes, flicked page after page over until I thought they would rip and tear in front of me.

I grabbed my papers and went to Katie, rushing through the library. I found her with a look of shock on her face. I wondered if she had found the same.

'We need to go,' I whispered urgently into her ear, and I was pleased to see her grab her papers and follow me out.

Chapter Thirty-nine

Laura looked up when the door opened, knowing that Carson would have complained; after all, she had stood over the boss of the murder squad as he took a piss. She expected her sergeant, maybe higher, but when the door opened she saw that it was someone else from the murder squad, the guy who had smiled at her, the one in the polo shirt and the crew cut.

Pete looked up, and then said, 'How you doing, Joe?'

'You know him?' she asked.

'Everyone knows Joe Kinsella.'

'I don't.'

Pete smiled, and then he gestured with his hand towards the other man. 'Laura, this is Joe. He cut his teeth in Blackley before he hit the big time and moved to headquarters. Too groovy for us.' Pete gestured towards Laura. 'Joe, this is Laura McGanity. She's from London, but I've forgiven her for that.'

Joe smiled, and then said, 'It's Laura I've come to see.'

'Are you the forward party?' she asked. 'Come here to soften me up before Carson comes down.'

He shook his head. 'It's not like that,' he said, and

then he sat down on a chair next to Laura's desk, which was cluttered with papers: the statements from the case and her handwritten account of the police interview.

Laura looked at him. He was around thirty, slim and toned, his body hidden by black clothing, with just the occasional grey hair, his eyes deep brown and dreamy. 'What is it like then?' she asked.

'I've come to say sorry,' he said, and when he spoke, he sounded measured, comforting.

Laura paused at that, her face suspicious. 'Why?'

'For what my team did, the adventure with Jack, the trip to the moors.'

'Isn't it Jack you should be apologising to?'

Joe nodded. 'You're right, and I will, if I get the chance. It might not mean anything, because I wasn't there, and Carson won't say sorry, but someone should say it.'

'So why are you bothering?' she asked suspiciously.

'Because it was wrong, and I'm on that team,' he said. 'And because I wanted to speak to you.'

Laura was confused. 'Why me?'

He smiled. 'I heard what you did to Carson, giving him a dressing-down in the toilet. But his problem is that he doesn't complain, he just gets even. He's got enough yes-men to help him out, so you won't win, and from what I've heard, you deserve better than that.'

'What have you heard?' she asked.

'Just your reputation for being a good detective, that people respect you. Don't get dragged into a battle with Carson. We'll be back at headquarters soon, and none of this will matter.'

'You don't sound like you fit in,' said Laura.

He laughed. 'I don't, and that's why Carson likes me. He likes the yes-men around him, but he is a good enough copper to realise that he needs a different opinion sometimes. Carson is a prick, I know that, but he is good at what he does.'

Laura smiled ruefully. 'Thanks for the tip.'

'There'll be no complaint from Carson,' said Joe, 'but watch your back,' and then he turned to leave.

When he'd gone, Pete chuckled to himself. 'He has that effect,' he said.

'What effect?'

'Blushing,' said Pete, pointing at her. 'He makes women blush.'

Laura shuffled her papers together, flustered. 'It's not that,' she said. She checked her watch. She knew she had to speak to the CPS before she could charge the prisoner, but the Court Welfare meeting was fast approaching. 'Will you go to the CPS with this for me? I've got to be somewhere else pretty soon.'

Pete held out his hand, grinning, and as she left the room, Laura felt in a better mood. The sun had come out and the day seemed unseasonably warm for the end of October. She checked her watch. Time to get home to make sure that it was all tidy, so that it looked like a good home for Bobby.

When Laura jumped into her car, she saw something on the passenger seat. An envelope. She looked around. Who had been in her car? It had been locked, she was sure of that.

Laura reached for the envelope and opened it slowly. There were photographs inside, A4, colour. The top one was of two people in a doorway, close to each other. It was dark, and so they were indistinct, but Laura could see that it was a man and a woman, and the woman was reaching out to the man, her hand on his cheek. She went to the next one, and her stomach turned over, a sob welling up in her throat.

It was Jack, and she recognised Katie, reaching out to him, stroking his cheek.

Laura looked around, trying to see who had put it there. As she looked towards the back door of the station, she saw Karl Carson. He waved, just to make sure she had seen him, and then he turned to go inside.

She threw the envelope onto the seat next to her, angry. With Jack, with her situation, but also with herself, because she realised that she'd made a powerful enemy.

She took a deep breath and tried to compose herself, remembering the Court Welfare visit. She had the most important battle of all to come: to keep Bobby with her.

Chapter Forty

We ended up in a fast walk through Blackley. My mind was still racing, and I didn't want to speak until I had assembled all I'd found into something real.

'Why the rush?' asked Katie, trotting to keep up.

I stopped and looked at her. 'You were right,' I said. 'The Pendle witch connection is no coincidence.' I was breathless, almost shouting, the words coming out in a rush.

'What do you mean?' Katie asked, although I could tell it wasn't a simple question. She said it quietly, watching me intently.

I looked around and saw a fast-food restaurant. Not my preference, but the lights were bright and the tables large. I pulled her towards it, and once we'd seated ourselves in a large alcove, Katie asked, 'What is it, Jack?'

I wondered how to approach it, but then I realised that directly was the only route. I spread my papers over the table, photocopies of Sarah's letters.

'I found this first,' I said, and I jabbed my finger at the line about the blood of children. 'Now look at this,' and I pulled out a photocopy of the textbook page, my highlighter pen making the passage bright orange. 'See how close they are. The spellings are modernised in Sarah's letter to you, but the words used are too alike to be just coincidence. Same phrase.'

Katie looked dolefully at me, not showing the excitement I was feeling.

'Do you know where this is from?' I asked. When Katie shook her head, I said, 'Anne Whittle's trial. Sarah's ancestor. The same words.'

Katie didn't say anything, so I picked up another photocopy of a textbook, adding more highlighter pen. 'So next,' I continued, speaking quickly, 'I carried on going through the volumes, and I found something else from Anne Whittle's case.' I paused for breath. 'The phrases from Sarah's letter are taken from the trial of Anne Whittle, just twisted and given a different meaning. Look at this sentence from Sarah's letter,' and I pointed at the page. *'There is no one alive more unwilling to pronounce this woeful and heavy judgement than myself.'* I pushed the photocopied sheet across the table at her. 'And now look at this quote from the trial,' I said excitedly, jabbing at the page with my finger. *'There is no man aliue more vnwilling to pronounce this wofull and heauy Iudgement against you, then my selfe.'* I smiled at Katie in triumph as she read. 'Can you see?' I asked her. 'They are almost the same.'

I paused to look at Katie. She looked serious.

'That quote is from Anne Whittle's trial,' I repeated, 'the witch Anne Whittle, back in 1612. It was the judgement in the case, finding her guilty of witchcraft. There is a slight difference though. In 1612 it was the judge who was racked with unwillingness. In the letter, it is Sarah Goode who pronounces the judgement against herself. She has turned it around, but it's near enough to be more than just coincidence.'

Katie looked unsure. 'Maybe the police have already worked it out,' she said.

'Perhaps,' I replied, 'but that wouldn't change anything.' I pointed down at the paper. 'This is the sign of a troubled mind. Sarah has turned the original finding of guilt into a confession. "*Cruelly and barbarously you haue murdered*" into "*cruelly and barbarously I have murdered*".'

Katie didn't look pleased.

'What's wrong?' I asked. 'I thought you would have been pleased. You know, we're starting to make progress.'

'I know I said that, but it was just a daft idea,' she answered softly. 'Now that we have discovered a link, it seems scarier somehow, that if there is a connection with the Pendle witch trials, for Christ knows what reason, then something is seriously wrong.' She let out a deep breath and looked upwards. I thought I saw her blink back some tears. 'I just want all of this to be over,' she continued. 'Before today it all looked like a moment of madness. I could deal with that. We all feel passion. We do things we regret, bad things. I can deal with that, can empathise, but what I can't deal with is talk of witches and ancient trials and executions. This is not a witch hunt. This is Lancashire in the twenty-first century.'

'I'm sorry,' I said. 'Perhaps I've got a little carried away with myself. But tell me this: why aren't you dismissing it out of hand? If it bothers you, it must be because you believe there might be something in it.'

Katie didn't say anything. Something was wrong.

'What did you find, Katie?' I asked, although I knew that it was the same as me.

She looked at me. 'I found the same as you,' she said quietly. 'Just the same.'

I struggled to contain my excitement. 'Show me.'

She delved into her bag and passed her notes over. 'I found it all straight away. I just didn't know what it meant.'

I looked at them, the photocopies used by Katie covered in arrows and underlines, her handwriting turning into scribbles as she found things, as if she was trying to get it all down as quickly as possible before the chance slipped away. I felt my eyes widen as I read.

'This is no coincidence,' I said in astonishment.

Katie looked at me with sadness. 'I knew it meant trouble. When you came over I hoped you'd found something different. I was wrong.'

'But Katie, this gives a direction.'

'No,' Katie said in protest. 'For you, it makes a story, that's all.'

I couldn't respond to that. Instead, I said, 'Let's look at what you found.'

I looked at Sarah's first letter:

Such was the nature of my offences, and the multitude of my crying sins, that it took away all sense of humanity. The murder I had committed, laid open to the world, did certainly produce contempt amongst people.

Then she passed me a photocopy of a page from a textbook, yellow highlighter over one passage:

. . . But such was the nature of her offences, and the multitude of her crying sinnes, as it tooke away all sense of humanity. And the repetition of her hellish practises, and Reuenge; being the chiefest things wherein she always tooke great delight, togeather with a particular declaration of the Murders shee had committed, layde open to the world.

I felt that same cold shiver, that same rush. Something was going on here, something revealing, important.

I looked at Katie. 'Where is this from?' I asked.

She looked up solemnly. 'The arraignment against Anne Whittle.'

'What, the accusation itself?' I asked.

Katie nodded. 'The arraignment outlined the actual allegation and what each witness would say.'

'So,' I said, trying to follow the path, 'in sending these letters, Sarah, for the wording of the first letter, uses the beginnings of the legal proceedings against Anne Whittle. She twists the words, but it's unmistakably the same. Am I right?'

Katie nodded. 'That's how it appears.'

I pulled on my lip. 'What about the second letter?' I asked.

Katie leaned over and pulled out a piece of paper from the middle of the pile. 'Here it is.'

I looked first at Sarah's letter.

> *Such is the horror of murder, and the crying sin of blood, that it will never be satisfied but with blood.*

Then I looked at a quote Katie had found.

> *Svch is the horror of Murther, and the crying sinne of Bloud, that it will neuer bee satisfied but with Bloud.*

I whistled. 'Where's that from?'

'It's from the arraignment of Ann Redfern,' Katie said.

'Not Anne Whittle?'

Katie shook her head. 'Ann Redfern was Anne Whittle's daughter.'

'And a witch too?'

'It was a family dispute in reality,' Katie answered. 'It was bound to drag the children in.'

'And if Anne Whittle was Sarah's ancestor,' I said, 'then so was Ann Redfern. The connection with Sarah is still there.'

I was deep in thought, my mind turning over solutions and possibilities, when Katie spoke. 'I wonder what it all means?' she said, almost to herself.

'Does it have to mean anything?'

'Of course it does,' she said. 'There are so many questions, but perhaps the first should be why were those particular sentences chosen?'

I looked at the notes and scratched my head. 'There is a path,' I said, 'some logic.'

Katie looked puzzled. 'What do you mean?'

I leafed through the papers again. 'Think about it,' I said, reading them again. 'The letters have gone full circle, through the whole legal process.' I pulled out the copy of the first letter written by Sarah. 'This letter starts with the description of what the case will be against Anne Whittle. The next letter is the same, but against her daughter. Both are ancestors of Sarah. Then go on to the last letter, the one I looked up,' and I pulled out the copy of the letter, the one I'd been working on. 'We move straight on to a twisting of the judgement in the case, the conclusion of the judge. We are in the next stage of proceedings.'

'Except,' Katie said, understanding my thread, 'Sarah confesses rather than there being a judgement against her.'

I nodded grimly. 'Maybe that's why the letters were sent in the first place, to confess. She sends a letter to point to the allegation and evidence against her, perhaps in the early stages of her decline, the early signs of paranoia, of self-blame. Not yet ready to confess, she just wants to blame herself. Then the decline hits a lower level, and so she seeks absolution in confession.'

Katie looked upset. I could see her becoming distant, looking scared.

'Are you all right?' I asked.

'I'm worried,' she said, her voice trembling. 'Because look at what she has written, and look where she sent them. Why is she writing to me?'

I looked her in the eye, saw the fear, the worry.

'I don't know,' was all I could say.

Katie just looked at the table.

I dipped my head so that I was able to catch her eyes, and I smiled. I was pleased to see her smile back.

'She won't hurt you,' I said, trying to reassure her. 'She's asking for your help. Do you believe me?'

Katie nodded silently and smiled again.

'C'mon,' I said, 'we've both got things to do. You've got college, and I've got a story to write.'

As I collected my things, Katie asked, 'If the letters follow the witch trials, the accusations and then the judgement, how did they end?'

'What do you mean?'

'Judgements of guilt are not the end of the trial,' she said. 'There is the sentence as well. That's the end of the case. If the letters follow the witch trials, then what came next?'

'You know what happened to them,' I said.

'They went to the gallows,' she said quietly. 'Anne and her daughter.'

I nodded. 'And quite a few others.'

Katie collected her papers together, her expression grim. 'Sarah's going to die, isn't she?' she said.

I remembered the Facebook entry for 31st October. *I die.*

'If we don't find her and stop her,' I replied grimly, 'then my guess is that she will.'

Chapter Forty-one

Sarah didn't move when the door opened. She was staring into space, ignoring the noise, the light.

She could feel him on her still. It was the smell on her shirt, his staleness, sweat and old cigarettes, the scratches his rough hands had made between her thighs. And she could still feel his body, the way he felt between her legs, the sound of him in her ear. Invasive, abusive.

He stepped into the room and stood there for a few moments, just watching.

'You're just like me,' he said quietly.

Sarah turned to look at him, her eyes filled with contempt. 'I'm nothing like you,' she spat at him.

'You tried to kill me,' he said.

'I had no choice,' Sarah replied.

He chuckled at that. 'The door was open. I left it open, wanted to know what you would do. You could have raced through it and slid the bolt. I would have been locked in.'

'There would have been someone waiting for me.'

'Maybe, but would it have been any different if you

had killed me?' he replied. 'You were consumed by hate. That was your weakness.'

'No, you are motivated by hate, not me,' she said. 'You have kept me captive, you have hurt me. I am not like you.'

He shook his head. 'You're wrong. You are more like me than you think. We are all evil, all killers. You weren't scared of the consequences, and that's why you could kill me. And who would criticise you, killing a monster like me? Make a murder free of consequences, and you make a murderer. One like you, Sarah Goode.'

'So was rape in your master plan?' she asked, her voice getting angrier, tears flashing across her eyes. 'Go on, tell me, you're the fucking genius here, the criminal mastermind. Did you always intend to rape me?'

He flinched. It was barely visible, but Sarah spotted it, the first chink in his armour. Just a hunch of the shoulders, a shrug of uncertainty.

'No, that was just weakness, wasn't it,' she continued, her venom growing. 'You claim some kind of special insight, but when it comes to it, you're just another man, someone who wants to fuck women because it makes you feel good. You just couldn't control yourself.'

He didn't answer.

'And look at you, behind that ridiculous mask,' she continued, her voice getting more strident, snarling, angry. 'You say you aren't scared of consequences, but you hide from me so I can't describe you. Or is it because if I saw how you looked, I wouldn't have any fear? Do you seem so ordinary on the outside?' Sarah stood up, threw the blanket to the ground. 'So go on then,' she screeched at him. 'Fuck me again, if that's all you want.' She started to unbutton her shirt. 'One more time. Now.'

He turned away and went towards the door. Sarah went towards him, but before she could get to the door, he slammed it shut and locked it, the bolt slamming home loudly.

Sarah banged on the door with her fists, screamed at him to come back, but when it stayed silent on the other side, she sank slowly to her knees and wrapped her arms tightly around her chest. She waited for the heartbeat sound to return, and she knew that he wasn't coming back for a while. He was going to leave her to rot.

Sarah thought of her parents. Of her mother, proud of her teacher daughter; and her father, strong and protective. And then more tears came. Tears of despair, of knowing that this was the end.

Chapter Forty-two

I pulled up outside the home of Sarah's parents, a semi-detached bungalow on one of the roads out of Blackley, with views towards the countryside and a neat front garden. The gate opened onto a small driveway with a carport at the side and a garage further along. Sarah's father was in there, and the clang of the gate must have alerted him because he looked up as I walked towards him.

His garage looked like it hadn't housed a car in years, filled from front to back with tools and half-finished projects. Old bolts sat in jars of oil, and a gnarled wooden bench ran along its length, the line broken by a metal vice and a half-finished go-kart. I don't think he recognised me at first, but as I got closer he wiped his hands and came out to greet me.

'Hello Mr Garrett,' he said, surprised, recovering to hold out his hand to shake. Before I could take it, he noticed the oil on his palm and withdrew. He looked down, embarrassed. 'I'm glad I've seen you. About the other morning. I hope you don't think we were using you or anything. It's just that, well . . .'

'You're desperate,' I said. 'I understand. And it should be me who apologises. You are having a difficult time. I didn't mean to be rude.'

Mr Goode nodded at me, accepting the apology.

I pointed towards the garage. 'What are you making?'

He looked back. 'A go-kart,' and then he smiled, the first time I'd seen it. 'It's for the little lad who visits next door. His grandma lives there.' He sighed. 'He'll have a much better one at home, with an electric motor so that he won't need a hill to make it go, but it keeps me busy.'

I smiled with him, but I could tell that the project was just a distraction to keep his mind busy until Sarah came home.

Then he looked at me. 'What can I do for you, Mr Garrett?'

'It's about Sarah,' I replied. 'I've got a confession to make.' When he looked quizzically at me, I continued, 'I've been looking into Sarah's case. I thought there might be something to write about.'

'But you didn't seem interested,' he said, taken aback.

'I know, but that was to protect myself, just so that I could drop the story if it came to nothing. If I had promised to look into it, stopping would have been hard.'

Mr Goode didn't respond straight away. He picked at some loose skin in the palm of his hand, and then said eventually, 'So have you found something?' He looked up, and I saw that his eyes had turned moist. 'If you're telling me now, you must have found something.'

I nodded. 'I want to talk to you. There might be some things that you don't know about, but you might clear some things up for me.'

He walked slowly past me and went to his back door. He turned to invite me inside. When I walked in, I saw Mrs Goode sitting in a chair, reading a newspaper. She looked up, surprised.

'He's writing the story,' blurted out Mr Goode.

I held up my hands in protest. 'I'm looking into it, that's all.'

'So why are you here?' she asked. When I didn't respond, she said, 'Because you want to know more, so you're interested.'

I smiled an apology. It didn't seem like a good time to start an argument.

'I just want to find out more about Sarah,' I said.

Mrs Goode put down her newspaper. 'Sit down, Mr Garrett,' and as I settled into a high-backed chair by the fire, Mr Goode going back outside, she asked, 'What do you want to know?'

'Just about Sarah,' I replied. 'Her interests. Her likes and dislikes. Hobbies.'

Mrs Goode looked out of the window as she spoke. I could tell it was hard for her, going back to a time when everything was normal. 'She had a lot of interests,' she said quietly. 'Music, films, just the usual stuff. She was just an ordinary girl, our only child. She cannot have done what they say she has done.'

'What sort of music?'

'Oh, stuff I didn't understand,' she replied. 'She went through a phase when she was younger. It's always the bright girls who go through it, so they say. She dyed her hair black, eye-liner to match. Long black dresses. Even had a stud in her eyebrow.'

'Goth?'

'I think that's what they call it. I used to tell her not to hide herself, but she just wanted to shock. I tried to tell her that young people can't shock any more, and I could never understand why someone would hide away a lovely figure like hers, but she did. And some of the boys she brought home,' she said, shaking her head, and then she laughed. 'They frightened me at first. Long dark hair, like Sarah's, but big boots and long black coats. But you know what?'

I raised my eyebrows.

'They were the nicest boys,' she continued. 'They cared for Sarah, and were sensitive and polite. And then I thought that if I was still proud of Sarah, however she looked, then their parents must be proud of them.'

'When did Sarah stop dressing like that?'

Mrs Goode gave a small laugh. 'I don't think she ever really stopped. She stopped dyeing her hair, and the black clothes went, but she still had the same interests.'

'What kind of thing?'

'Spooky stuff. She used to fill the house with candles when she lived here, and incense burners, crystals, symbols, things like that. I don't think she opened her curtains for a year. Her house was just the same.' She sighed. 'It was just the way she was. Innocent fun.'

'Did she ever mention the Pendle witches?' I asked.

Mrs Goode looked surprised. 'Why do you ask?'

'I heard someone say that Sarah had a connection with them.'

Mrs Goode looked at me for a few seconds, and then stood up. 'Follow me,' she said, and shuffled towards the hallway. When I got there, she had stopped at a large picture frame.

'Sarah bought me this a few years ago. She thought it was interesting.'

I stepped forward and looked at the frame. There was a symbol at the top that looked familiar, a screaming face in outline. Underneath it, there was some kind of a family tree. I realised that I'd seen it before, on the wall in Sarah's house. I went to the bottom line, the words written small and difficult to see, but I saw Sarah's name there. Above it, I saw Mrs Goode's.

'Your family tree,' I said, stating the obvious. I guessed what it would reveal, but I knew that I had to let her tell the story.

'It's not just that, though,' she said, and pointed to the top of the frame. 'Start with the beginning, not the end.'

My gaze shifted, and I squinted as I read the name at the top.

'Anne Whittle?' I asked, feigning ignorance.

'That's right,' she said, nodding. 'Don't you recognise the name?'

I shook my head.

'Anne Whittle was one of the Pendle witches,' she said dramatically, and I did my best to look surprised.

'Tell me about Anne Whittle,' I said, trying hard not to smile. The small-town murder stuff had been interesting before, but this was in a different league. Descendants of witches. Cryptic letters. Family trees. I relished the thought of pitching the story, knowing that one of the nationals would be interested.

Mrs Goode looked at the framed family tree. 'It's something Sarah is quite proud of.'

'Proud?'

'Why shouldn't she be? It's a part of history, and I'm connected to it, according to this. So is Sarah.'

'Did Sarah talk much about the Pendle witch connection?' I asked.

'A lot of people around Pendle talk about the witches. Sarah said that we were just a bit more special because we were descendants, but there are a lot of people around Pendle who can claim that.'

'So it didn't make her feel cursed in any way?'

Mrs Goode looked at me, confused. 'Why would it? It's just a piece of history from four hundred years ago.'

I thought about telling her about the letters, but the police were trying to keep the letters secret, and I wasn't sure how they would view it if I told the Goodes all about them.

'Have you got any photographs of Sarah that I could use in my story?' I asked, trying to steer the conversation away from the witches, and hoping I would be left alone for a few minutes.

Mrs Goode nodded and shuffled off towards the stairs. When she was gone, I pulled out my phone and took some shots of the family tree, hoping that the words would still be visible when I put it on my computer. I zoomed in and tried to get all of the branches.

When Mrs Goode came back downstairs with some pictures, the phone was back in my pocket.

She seemed proud as she leafed through the pictures, looking at them herself before passing them over. There were some of Sarah's school photographs, an awkward girl, lanky, ungainly, her face pale and freckled. In the later pictures she had blossomed, but she had gone darker. Her face was still pale, but her hair was long and dyed jet black, and I could make out the glint of metal around her eyebrow.

Mrs Goode must have caught me glancing back towards the family tree, because she said, 'It's funny that you should mention a curse.'

'Why?'

'Because I started to research some of the names. We would be related, and I thought it would be nice to meet them, these distant cousins, but it seemed like some were people who had died too young.'

'People die all the time,' I said. 'In fact, most people on that tree are dead, if you think about it logically.'

'There is no need to be facetious, Mr Garrett. I thought you seemed interested, that's all. And now, Sarah has gone missing.'

And Luke is dead, I almost said, but instead I sighed and apologised. When Mrs Goode didn't respond, I asked, 'Who are you talking about?'

She walked back to the picture and pointed at a name close to the bottom. It was one level higher than Sarah.

'April Mather?' I said. 'Would that be one of your cousins?'

Mrs Goode nodded. 'A distant one, I suppose. We never met, but I remember seeing it in the paper.'

'Seeing what?'

'About her suicide. She hanged herself. It was quite dramatic, so I recall, jumping from Blacko Tower. It must be, oh, around ten years ago now. And her,' she said, pointing at another name.

'Rebecca Nurse?'

She pulled a face at that. 'That was another tragedy, a couple of years after April,' she said. 'She was young and pretty, with her whole life ahead of her. She went to the pub one night, but she never made it home. She was found next to a stream just near to Pendle Hill. Her clothes had been torn off, and she had been strangled.'

'Did they catch her killer?'

Mrs Goode shook her head. 'I don't think so. Or at least if they did, I didn't hear about it.' Then I saw her brightness dim, the interest she had in the story spoiled by a realisation that people would talk about Sarah as the next in the curse, just a conversation piece.

As I looked at her, I saw her retreat back into herself as she thought about her daughter. I sensed that I wouldn't get much more from her. I took her hand and thanked her for her time. She looked up at me and I saw tears in her eyes. She squeezed my hand and then nodded that she knew the meeting was over.

As I headed for the door, I wondered how strange the story was going to get before I would get the chance to write it. But when I looked at my watch, I realised with a jolt that I had something more important to do first.

I was late for the Court Welfare meeting.

Chapter Forty-three

Rod was unsure what reception he would get as he stood on Abigail's doorstep. He had her blanket over his arm, to give him the excuse that it was a courtesy call.

As the door opened, Abigail looked at him, and then at the blanket.

'You didn't have to bring it back, officer,' she said.

'It gets cold around here in winter, Miss Hobbs. It would stay on my conscience if anything happened to you.'

Abigail smiled and then turned to walk into the house. As Rod followed her, he saw that she had touched up her hair, the grey roots disappeared now, her hair frizzy black right down to her scalp. She was wearing a long purple dress, loose and flowing over her large frame, but as Rod looked, he got the sense that she was naked underneath, everything in her dress moving around too freely.

He looked away, uncomfortable, and then as he entered the living room, he saw a sprig of rosemary pinned to the doorframe. The living room itself was tidier than the first time he'd been there, with the rug back in its place and the intersecting lines of salt swept up. And there was some light coming in from one of the windows, catching the small trails of smoke coming from the incense sticks dotted around the room, making the air hazy. The back of his throat tickled and made him cough.

'That's strong stuff,' Rod said.

Abigail turned around and wrinkled her nose. 'It helps me think,' she replied slowly, and then pointed to a chair. 'Sit down.'

Rod nodded and took his place in the chair while Abigail shuffled off to the kitchen. He waited, looking at his fingernails, no sound in the house except the tinkle of some wind chimes by the window and the regular clunk of an old clock on the mantelpiece.

When Abigail returned, she was carrying a small tray with two cups. Rod got to his feet to help her, but she shook her head that she didn't need it. He noticed another sprig of rosemary over the door to the kitchen. As Abigail set the tray down, she offered Rod a cup and then asked, 'How can I help you?'

Rod took a sip of his tea. 'I want you to tell me what is going on,' he said, pausing to pick some tea leaves from his lips.

'Why do you think anything is going on?' she asked.

'Miss Hobbs, I don't mean to upset you, but someone blew up your cat, there was an explosion in Isla Marsden's shed, and in someone else's before that. Isla pretends not to know you, but you both wear the same rings.'

Abigail looked uncomfortable and shuffled in her

seat. 'I don't want to do anything that would cause harm to anyone,' she said quietly, 'but I cannot say anything.'

'But if you don't say anything, someone else might get hurt.'

Abigail shook her head slowly. 'No, Inspector. I just can't.'

'What about your craft group?' he asked.

Abigail looked surprised, and Rod saw the cup tremble in her hand.

'I know that you are in a craft group with Isla,' he pressed. Still Abigail wouldn't respond. 'Would anyone have any reason to want to harm you?'

Rod looked at her, waiting for her to continue, but she stayed silent.

'What about the salt pentagram on your floor?' he continued. 'The rosemary over the doorframe?'

Abigail just shook her head.

Rod sighed as he realised that he wasn't going to get anywhere. He reached out and took her hand. 'Take care of yourself, Miss Hobbs,' he said, and then stood as if to leave.

Abigail kept hold of his hand. 'Finish your tea,' she said.

Rod looked back at the cup, saw the black leaves swirling around. He paused, unsure, and then he reached down to drain it. When he'd finished, Abigail said, 'Spin the leaves.'

Rod looked at her, confused.

'The cup,' she said. 'Rotate it three times, and then put it on the saucer, upside down.'

He did as he was told, and then watched as Abigail

reached for the cup. She concentrated, turning the cup back over, holding it up to her face, looking closely, starting with the rim and then looking further into the bowl.

'Can you see that?' she said eventually, holding the cup up to him.

Rod leaned forward. All he could see were tea leaves scattered around the inside of a white china cup.

'Near the handle,' she continued. 'Can you see the leaves are in a hammer shape?'

Rod couldn't, but he nodded anyway, just out of politeness.

'It means you will be rewarded for your hard work,' she said, and then she smiled.

Rod nodded slowly. 'Thank you,' he replied, although he was unsure what he was thanking her for.

Chapter Forty-four

I was driving too fast, but I knew I was late, the Triumph Stag skittering around corners. I checked my watch. The Court Welfare meeting was at three, and it was already quarter past. Our cottage was sometimes hard to find, tucked away on a quiet road in the hills around Turners Fold, so I hoped the visitor would be late.

As I rounded the corner close to our house, I saw Laura's car parked outside, pulled onto the small patch of gravel at the front. In front of her car was another, a stranger's car. I cursed to myself and rushed inside.

Laura looked up at me. She smiled, but I could see that it was forced.

'I'm sorry I'm late. I got held up with work.' I tried to show my regret and make it sound official, that there was nothing I could do, but I knew that Laura would know the truth, that I had become distracted.

The woman on the sofa with Laura stood up to shake my hand. 'You must be Jack,' she said. 'I'm Jenny.'

I shook hands and tried to assess her like I knew she was assessing me. She looked like how I expected, cords and blazer and a short haircut. No rings. I guessed that she had no children herself. It was the earnest look in her eyes, that she knew best, which gave it away. People with children tend to be more forgiving.

'I came a bit early. I'm sorry,' Jenny said.

To catch us how we really are, I thought, rather than as the package we would present.

She smiled at me and sat down again.

The rest of the meeting went in a whirl, just lots of talk about plans for us and plans for Bobby, about contact arrangements, schooling. All aspects of our life disclosed to a stranger so that she could recommend what should happen to Laura's child. But Laura had already made that decision, that he was best with us. Geoff was disputing it only because of me, as I was the intruder in the nest, although he hadn't been so protective when he had been unfaithful to Laura, and more than once.

As I looked at Jenny, I wondered whether she would see through Geoff. I told myself that most families she saw would be riddled with more problems than our little unit. Maybe this visit was a break from the routine. Or maybe it was routine to her, the absent father making trouble for the new boyfriend.

I answered her questions honestly, about our plans for Bobby's schooling, how our jobs interfered with looking after him. I stammered a bit when I was asked about marriage plans, but Laura stepped in with an explanation that we had none. Bobby was playing upstairs most of the time, I could hear him rattling his toys and talking to himself. Jenny asked if she could speak to him. Laura said it was okay, and as soon as

Jenny's flat shoes disappeared around the bend in the stairs, I whispered, 'I'm sorry I'm late. I got held up in the library, and then I went to see Sarah's parents. I just lost track.'

'Were you with darling little Katie?' she snapped at me.

'What do you mean?'

'I've seen photographs of a loving goodbye,' she said.

'Carson?' I asked angrily.

'Probably, but that's not the point.'

'Nothing went on,' I said. 'You saw what she was like last night. It doesn't mean I responded.'

Laura stared at me, clenching her jaw, and then she said, 'Well, you were supposed to be here. Do you remember all that crap you keep saying, that this is our fight, not just mine? It didn't last long, did it?'

'It wasn't like that,' I protested.

'Oh no? I might just decide I don't want the fight any more, and that will take me away from here. Will you fight then?'

Before I had the chance to respond, Jenny came back downstairs, Bobby just behind her. When he came into the room, he sat right next to me. Jenny noticed that. I couldn't have scripted it better.

We answered a few wrap-up questions, Laura's smile switched back on, although I still sensed the frost, and then Jenny grabbed her things. I let Laura show her out as Bobby ran back upstairs, his game not complete. When Laura didn't come back inside, I went to look for her, and found her at the end of the garden, on an old bench I'd bought from a reclamation yard, the wood gnarled and bent. I'd put it where we had a good view along the valley, the height of the wall cutting out the slate-grey of the town.

She looked up, and I saw that she had been crying. I sat next to her and linked my fingers into hers.

'So that's it then,' she said quietly.

'What do you mean?'

'That woman will go and decide our future, and we just have to sit here and wait.' She sniffled and wiped her eyes. 'Do you know what was the strangest thing?'

'No, go on, tell me.'

'I found myself explaining for the first time why I had moved up here. No, that's not right, not explaining. Justifying. That's what I was doing. You wanted to come home to the north, you had something to come back for, but I just sort of followed, with dreams of a new start, all that romantic stuff.'

'This conversation doesn't sound good,' I said.

'No, it is good,' she said, 'because I had to tell Jenny why I wanted to stay up here. The fields. The view. The job. Even the people. I loved London, still do, but it is nice to be out of it. I've slowed down a bit, and that has to be good. For the first time since I moved here, I had to convince someone else that it was not only good for me to be up here, but also that it was good for Bobby.'

I kissed her on the cheek, and she put her arm around mine, rested her head on my shoulder. We stayed like that for a while, neither of us speaking, and then Laura broke the silence. 'Tell me again, why were you late?'

'Like I said, it was about work, and I'm sorry, but this Sarah Goode story has taken an interesting turn.'

'Tell me.'

I looked down the valley, away from Turners Fold and towards Pendle Hill, sprawled across the view. Its summit wasn't high, but it always seemed like the clouds were not too far away, as if the hill pulled them towards it.

'Do you see that hill?' I asked.

'What, the long one?' she queried.

'That's the one,' I said, and I knew what Laura meant. It didn't just rise up, it seemed to lie along the landscape, more barren than the green fields around it, the sides darker, bleaker somehow.

'What about it?'

'It's seen some strange things.'

Laura shuddered. 'I don't like it,' she said. 'It's strange, it spooks me.'

'Pendle Hill,' I said. 'It's a landmark in these parts. Tales of witchcraft and dark deeds.'

Laura smiled at that. 'Hubble, bubble, toil and trouble, and all that.'

'You're not far off the mark with that,' I said. 'The *Macbeth* reference, I mean.'

She looked up at me. 'What are you talking about?'

'Have you never heard of the Pendle witches?'

She curled her lip. 'I've sort of heard about them, in that I've heard the name, but I don't know anything about them.'

'Well, let's go inside. It's nearly Halloween, and so it's a good time for some ghoulish local history.'

Chapter Forty-five

Sarah pulled her knees closer to her chest.

She knew she had to escape. She wasn't going to be kept so that she could be used by him whenever his urges were too strong. Escape or die trying. But she needed to be strong, had to keep a clear mind. He was right, she had let hate distract her. The door had been open. She could have rushed for that. Instead, she had become consumed by hatred, wanting to kill him more than she had needed to get out.

She needed to draw on some strength, some inner resource.

Sarah stood up and began to walk backwards in the room, dragging her heel in the dirt, making a straight line, bold and clear, from one corner of the room to the centre of the opposing wall, and then back down to the other corner. Then she went across to another wall, dragging her heel still so that it became raw and started to bleed. But she carried on, knew she had to keep going, and so she went back across the room again, another line, before making her way back to the corner that she had started from.

She looked back at what she had done. It wasn't perfect, but it was good enough.

It was a pentagram, drawn into the dirt.

Sarah knelt down in the middle of the pentagram, so that its five arms stretched out all around her. She closed her eyes, tried to conjure the images in her head that she needed. It was hard. The speakers beat out that steady heartbeat rhythm, so that she fought hard to banish it from her mind. Then she realised that it was easier if she went with the sounds, so she swayed with the rhythm, backwards and forwards, then to the side, her eyes closed, her lips closed in a half-smile.

Then the right thoughts came. She thought she could feel the warm breeze in the room as she thought of it tugging at branches, or brushing the soft hairs on her arms. Her hair seemed to flutter over her shoulders.

'Watch over me, Air,' she said softly. 'Guard me, guide me, protect me during whatever lies ahead. Blessed be.'

Sarah felt stronger. She tried to think of a flame, swaying like the flickers of a roaring fire. She rubbed her arms, felt them become warm under her touch.

'Watch over me, Fire. Guard me, guide me, protect me during whatever lies ahead. Blessed be.'

Then it was a fast-flowing stream. She thought she could hear the ripples over the sound of the heartbeats, softening the sound.

'Watch over me, Water. Guard me, guide me, protect me during whatever lies ahead. Blessed be.'

Her voice was getting stronger as she swayed in time to the heartbeats.

Sarah thrust her hand to the floor and grabbed a handful of dirt. Her nails felt broken, her fingers raw, but she held her hand aloft and let it fall over her.

'Watch over me, Earth. Guard me, guide me, protect me during whatever lies ahead. Blessed be.'

Sarah's voice grew louder, more strident, seemed to echo around the room, over the sound of the heartbeats coming from the speakers. She clenched her fists and felt tears roll down her cheeks. She held out her arms and looked upwards.

'Lord and Lady, I call upon you to watch over me. Guard me, guide me, protect me during whatever lies ahead. Blessed be.'

Sarah reached out with her right hand and began to draw a circle around herself, turning clockwise on her knees.

'I make this circle as a place between the worlds,' she shouted, turning still. 'It will protect me. Blessed be.'

As she overlapped the end of the circle over its beginning, she slumped forward, panting. All she could do now was wait.

Chapter Forty-six

As we checked that Bobby wasn't listening, I sat down at the table, my bag next to me.

'That's why I was late,' I said to Laura. 'I was researching the Pendle witches.'

Laura didn't look pleased by that. 'You were late for the Court Welfare meeting because you were looking at some local history? You said it was about your story.'

'No, I was late for the meeting because I was researching the Sarah Goode story. It's just that it's all about the Pendle witches.'

Laura started to smile. 'What, she's got herself a pointy hat?'

I smiled back, my eyebrows raised. 'It's much more interesting than that,' I said. I checked Bobby again. He had eyes and ears only for the screen, *SpongeBob* keeping him quiet. 'Sarah is descended from one of the Pendle witches.'

Laura waggled her fingers and made her eyes wide, tried to cackle like the Wicked Witch of the West.

'It's true,' I said, laughing. 'Anne Whittle. She was one

of the witches, one of the main ones. Sarah is a direct descendant.'

'So that's the angle of your story: murderer has witch blood?' she said, sighing. 'It's a bit *Sunday Sport*, isn't it? You're better than that.'

'Do you remember the letters?'

Laura nodded.

'The wording is taken from the witch trials,' I continued. 'Made more modern, but undeniably the same.'

Laura tugged at her lip. I went to the bag I had put on the table and pulled out some papers. I held them up. 'Look at the language,' I said. 'Sarah Goode is sending confessions to murder, and using the words spoken four hundred years earlier by her direct ancestor.'

Laura cast her eye over the letters. I pointed out the similarities to her, the ones I'd discovered with Katie earlier in the day.

Laura wasn't smiling any more.

'And Sarah isn't the first descendant of Anne Whittle to suffer tragedy,' I continued. 'There were two more that I know of.'

'Who?' Laura still didn't look convinced, although I wasn't sure if it was at the truth of what I was saying, or at her willingness to be dragged into the story.

'Two more women have died,' I said. 'Both descendants of Anne Whittle.'

'You said the story was four hundred years old. There are bound to be other deaths.'

'These were in the last ten years.'

Laura looked interested now.

'The first one was called Mather,' I continued. 'April Mather. She killed herself ten years ago. A suicide. Hanging. The second one was Rebecca Nurse. She was killed and found dumped near a stream around eight years ago, just at the base of the hill.'

Laura thought about that for a moment, but then she said, 'The list of descendants will be huge. Four hundred years is a lot of generations. Of family-tree branches. They will have spread out like veins across your back. It could just be a coincidence?'

I shook my head. 'The family tree I saw wasn't that big.'

'Where was it?'

'At the home of Sarah's parents. And you know what: at the top it had some strange kind of symbol, maybe a symbol for the family, like a screaming face. Sarah had the same symbol on her wall, framed and prominent.'

Laura looked intrigued. She went to the window and looked along the valley, towards Pendle Hill. I didn't interrupt her. Laura was strong-willed, and so I had to let her decide herself that it was an interesting story.

'Who were these witches?' she said eventually, turning to face me.

'Four hundred years ago, eleven of them went to the gallows for witchcraft, and one died in prison,' I said. 'All local women, and it was all to do with King James and a quarrel between two local families.'

'What, the Gunpowder Plot King James? The Bible King James?'

'Witches sound silly to us, I know that, but not to King James,' I said. 'He didn't like them. No, more than

237

that, he thought they were a source of evil. He published a rant about witches even before he came to the throne, blamed them for some shipwreck. This was a man who had a downer on witches, and what do people do when their king doesn't like something? The answer is that they don't like it either.'

'Emperor's new clothes?'

'Something like that,' I said. 'So those people who wanted to impress the new king turned on witches to do so. Even Shakespeare.'

'The *Macbeth* thing?'

I nodded. 'He wrote *Macbeth* just after King James came to the throne. From what I've read this afternoon, it was written as a tribute to the king. Banquo was an ancestor of King James, and in one of the scenes there is a parade of kings, like a chance to salute James and all of the great kings that went before him.'

Laura sighed. 'I don't know too much about Shakespeare, but I never took him for a royal toady?'

'You pander to your crowd, I suppose,' I replied. 'The witches in *Macbeth* were the villains of the play, and so Shakespeare was just playing to the king's favourite subject. And do you think the people up here were any different to the people in the south? The local bigwigs could make a name for themselves by rooting out witches, gain a bit of local power.'

'And that is what happened around here?'

'Pretty much so,' I said, nodding. 'There were just four at the start, but then the two families got together to sort out a truce, to get their loved ones back, maybe even exact some revenge, the infamous Good Friday

238

gathering at Malkin Tower. Unfortunately for them, the local Magistrate found out about the meeting and had them locked up as well. Four months later, they were all tried at Lancaster Castle. Most of them were found guilty, and most of them were executed.'

'And the local Magistrate was made to look good before the king,' Laura said, guessing the subtext.

'That's about the size of it.'

Laura rubbed her eyes. 'I've had a stressful day, and this is too much.' She sighed, 'Go on, tell me where Sarah Goode fits into all of this?'

'That's what got me thinking.'

'Uh oh,' said Laura. 'This is where I get worried.'

'Maybe,' I said, 'maybe not, but the Pendle witches tie in somewhere because of the letters. Perhaps the witch connection sent her crazy, and so she killed Luke.'

'Or maybe she is pretending it did, getting in her insanity defence early,' replied Laura.

'You are a cynic, Laura McGanity,' I said. I didn't tell her that I had already talked about the same thing with Sam Nixon.

She smiled at that. 'I've seen too many things to make me anything but one.'

'There is, of course, another possibility,' I said.

'Go on.'

'Maybe Sarah Goode is somehow a victim, not a killer.'

Laura looked surprised. 'What makes you say that?'

'Just a hunch, because no one has said she was crazy, and if she isn't crazy, why is she writing letters based on the witch trials? And if you think about it, she is either a killer or she isn't; there is no middle ground. And if she isn't a killer, she must be a victim in some way, and it must tie in with the witches because of the letters.'

'But remember that one of the dead descendants was a suicide,' said Laura.

'I know that, but it's a story that is getting stranger, and I need to look further into it.'

'When?'

'Tomorrow', I said. 'I'm going back to where it all started: Pendle Hill.'

Chapter Forty-seven

The police station was quiet when Rod went in. There had been a report of a disturbance in the street, some kind of road-rage incident, so all the new officers had headed out, hoping to bag the arrest.

Rod checked his diary. He had a meeting with a residents' committee in an hour, everyone concerned about kids hanging around and causing damage. Kids have been hanging around and worrying older generations for decades, thought Rod, but that view never went down well. Nods of understanding and the occasional visit by the police van usually placated neighbourhood nerves.

His phone rang. When he picked it up, he was told that Emily Marsden was on the line.

'Put her through,' he said, and after a pause, 'Hello Emily.'

'Hello Inspector,' said a soft voice, the one Rod recognised from the day before. 'You asked me to call you if I heard anything.'

'That's right, Emily. And have you?'

Rod could hear the nervousness on the other end of the line, as Emily fought her betrayal. 'My mum told me this morning that she wouldn't be around this evening,' she said eventually. 'She said that she's got a craft group meeting.'

'Do you know where?'

'Not really, but she said she was setting off soon to pick up Abigail.'

Rod smiled to himself. 'Thank you very much, Emily,' he said. 'You've been a great help. I'll make sure your mother stays safe.'

As he put down the phone, he reached for his diary, to get the number of the residents' committee. The meeting would have to be rescheduled, and the neighbourhood kids would get a few more days' grace to hang around on street corners.

The sun shone through the gaps in the branches as I drove towards Pendle Hill. Summer had stayed late, so that most of the leaves were still on the trees, but the sun was low and the road was dappled by shadows.

The landscape changed as I got nearer to the hill. The houses around Turners Fold were built for the cotton industry, stone-built terraces for workers near the mills, and grand Victorian town-houses further away, suitable accommodation for their bosses. The houses around Pendle Hill were different, built before the Industrial Revolution, stone cottages with tiny windows, the stones uneven, the gaps filled with lime mortar, so that the houses looked like they had tumbled straight out of the hill.

I headed to Newchurch, a small village at the foot of the hill. I knew from my research the night before that it was at the heart of the witch story. I wound my way along tight country roads and then suddenly a wide valley appeared in front of me. I could see Newchurch ahead, a cluster of grey stone and whitewashed cottages on a steep hill out of the valley, using Pendle Hill as shelter from the north winds.

The hill overshadowed everything though. Even though the sun was shining, I could see clouds gathering at the top, the hill pulling them in like a magnet. As I climbed out of my car, I saw how the houses matched the greyness of the clouds, and a sharp breeze made me button my coat to my chin; it seemed colder in the shadow of the hill.

I looked around for a suitable starting point, and I saw a shop further along, hidden by white-painted lattice windows, just an ice-cream placard outside giving it away.

As I walked, I felt self-conscious, just a feeling that I was being watched. I turned to look and I thought I saw movement out of the corner of my eye, but maybe it was just my imagination getting the better of me.

A bell tinkled as I went into the shop. I had to duck to go inside, and I squinted when I got there. The shop was dark, shelves filled with bread and tins, and the only source of brightness was a refrigerated unit against the wall. There were two women talking, just local gossip, the lady behind the counter joining in.

She turned to me, the talk stopping for a moment.

I tried a smile and then said, 'I hope you don't mind, but I'm a reporter, and I'm researching some deaths that occurred here a few years ago.' I thumbed through my notes. 'April Mather and Rebecca Nurse. Do you remember them?'

I saw an immediate change in her. The trace of a smile disappeared and she glanced at her friends. 'I'm sorry,' she said, too quickly. 'Those names don't sound familiar.'

I wasn't convinced by the answer. 'Do you know anyone who could help?' I asked, probing a bit more.

She shook her head. I looked at the other two women in the shop, but they just stared at me. I held up my hand. 'Okay, thanks, but if anyone remembers anything, give me a call,' and I left my business card on the counter.

No one said anything as I left the shop, with just the sound of the bell disturbing the silence, and when I got back onto the street I felt that anxiety again, the sensation that I was being watched. I turned round to look back towards the shop, and I was sure someone had just ducked away from the window.

I walked down the hill, just to see what else there was in the village, and I saw a church. It was old, with a square bell tower and graves lined up in the yard. Something occurred to me: the women who had died were local people, and so maybe they were buried there. As I crossed the road, my footsteps were loud clicks on the tarmac that turned into soft crunches as I went onto the gravel path in the church yard, the tall metal gate creaking loudly, announcing my arrival.

The church yard was surrounded by trees, allowing just glimpses along the valley. The graves were clustered tightly together, stone headstones mostly, old and worn, but there were some grander ones too, more like small monuments. I saw the sunlight break through and reflect back off the modern ones at the bottom of the yard, the moss-covered slabs giving way to shiny black granite.

I walked slowly among the graves, and I started to notice the same names repeated, generations laid under through the years, but I couldn't see the names I'd written down.

I looked around, tried to spot something familiar, and then I thought I heard something, a quick rustling noise. I turned, but there was no one there.

I started to walk again, tried to make my footfall silent so that I could listen out for movement. I could hear the creak of branches as they were blown gently by the breeze. The autumn leaves blew along the path, just scratching sounds against the gravel. I turned as I walked, and I thought I saw something again. Or maybe it was just the light flickering through the trees, making the shadows move. The headstones were high and were right against the path, so that I was tensed, waiting for someone to appear from behind them. I looked up towards the church at the top of the path, and all I could do was keep walking.

Once I'd done the full circuit, I took a deep breath. I knew I wasn't alone. I took some pictures and then turned to go, anxious to get out, when I noticed a grave against the church wall, a large slab of stone lying flat. I stopped, curious.

The lettering on it was hard to make out, the grooves washed away by the rain through the years, but I saw the name emblazoned across the top. *Nutter*. Names were listed underneath. And the years. Seventeenth century, but I couldn't make out much else. I recognised the name from my research though. Alice Nutter had been one of the Pendle witches. Was this her grave?

Then I saw it. A symbol at the top. A screaming face, just in crude outline, with hollow eyes and open mouth. The same as on Sarah's family tree.

I heard something behind me, a crunch on the gravel. I whirled around. It was a man, standing, watching me. He was dressed in a black suit, a scarf around his neck, with dark hair and a black goatee, grey strips at his temples and in his beard.

'That one always makes people look,' he said, his voice quiet, precise. 'People come here to see it.'

He started to walk towards me, and just as I was about to back away, the scarf slipped and I saw the dog collar underneath.

'So this is all yours,' I said, casting my hand around me.

He tapped at his collar, his eyes watching me all the time, ice blue over the dark clothes. 'A bit of a giveaway,' he said. Then he looked towards the gravestone and said, 'It's not what you think it is.'

'How do you know what I'm thinking?'

He smiled at that, but it didn't thaw the icy look, his thin lips showing through his beard.

'Most people who come here do so because of the witches,' he said. 'If it wasn't for them, this would be just another small Lancashire village. And that gravestone always brings a crowd.'

'It says *Nutter* on it,' I said. 'Alice Nutter was one of the Pendle witches. Is there any connection to her?'

'Alice Nutter was hanged at Lancaster Castle for being

a witch,' he said. 'Witchcraft is heresy. Do you really think she would be buried in consecrated ground?'

'"Was" heresy, you mean? Not "is".'

He watched me for a moment, and his eyes narrowed. His hands were clasped in front of him. 'This is the Nutter family grave,' he said, his voice even. 'They were a wealthy family back then, but Alice isn't one of them down there. She married into the family, and then her husband hit bad times.'

'There's an emblem at the top,' I said, watching his expression. 'It's like a screaming face. Is that normal?'

He didn't look down, didn't need to. 'It's to ward off evil spirits,' he answered.

'That isn't normal on graves.'

He smiled again. 'This isn't a normal valley,' he said. Before I could answer, he continued, 'Perhaps the family felt they needed more than being next to the church wall. That was a family with a past. Look at the dates. 1651 is the earliest. The people in there lived through the witch trials. And look at the church tower.'

As I looked, I shrugged. 'I see a clock.'

'Go round to the other side.'

I didn't move at first, curious as to why he was taking such an interest, but then I remembered that if I was going to write the story, I had to follow it first.

As I moved round to the next face of the tower, the vicar pointed upwards.

'Do you see that?' he asked.

'Another clock,' I said, nonplussed.

He turned to look at me, his eyes boring into me.

'The Eye of God. Are you telling me that you can't see it?'

'Can't see what?'

The vicar pointed again at the church tower. 'That oval set into the stone, below the clock. The Eye of God, keeping a watch over the village.'

Halfway up the church tower, there was an oval with a painted black centre. It did look like an eye, I had to agree, but I wasn't convinced.

'That tower was built not long after the second witch trials,' he said, still looking upwards.

'Second witch trials?'

'Oh yes,' he said. 'There was a meeting of witches at Hoarstones, just twenty years after the first trial, over that hill,' and he pointed away from the village. 'The Nutters were involved again. More trials, more infamy, more guilty verdicts.' As I looked around and wondered what it must have been like back then, he added, 'Think how small these villages are, how tiny the population must have been back then, and then think how many people were lost to witchcraft. The village needed someone to look after them.'

I looked around again, tried to get a feel for the church yard. I felt the hairs on my arms prickle.

'The witch stories are nothing new around here,' he said. He stepped closer. 'How are you going to write them up?'

I was puzzled by that, and uncomfortable with his presence. 'I don't remember telling you that I was a reporter,' I said, my voice wary.

His cheeks glowed a little redder, but then he pointed

towards my camera. 'You have a voice recorder in your hand and a camera dangling from your wrist. I made an educated guess.'

I didn't respond, but I wasn't convinced by his answer.

'So, to the local people back then, the witchcraft thing was more than just a family fall-out that ended up in the courts?' I asked.

A half-smile played on his lips. 'In those days, witchcraft was a crime against God.'

'And now?'

He thought about that for a few seconds. 'It depends on who you ask. To some, witchcraft is the black arts, Satanism in its earthly form.'

'And to others?'

'Some people see it as harmless, just a haven for hippies to follow a religion that isn't proscribed.'

'And what do you think?'

His eyes narrowed. 'If a faith doesn't worship God, it must be ungodly. There is but one God, not two or more.'

'You talk like there is still witchcraft around,' I said, watching for how he answered.

'Even valleys like this have dark corners,' he replied, his glare piercing. Then he changed the subject. 'What are you looking for?'

I told him that I was looking into two deaths. He blinked when I said the names. He paused as he thought, although I got the impression that his decision was whether or not he *should* help me, not whether or not he could.

'Follow me,' he said eventually, and then he turned

and walked through the church yard. He was small, but he walked quickly, his steps fast along the path, kicking the leaves as he went. I tried to work out where he was heading. I'd gone through the recent graves and I hadn't seen any of the ones I was looking for.

He came to a halt by a hawthorn tree overlooking the valley. I could see the fields rolling away from me, broken by stone walls, twisting jaggedly towards the horizon.

'Here she is,' he said. 'April Mather.'

I saw that he wasn't pointing at a headstone, but at a small granite plaque, the lettering in gold and topped with white lilies. *Treasured memories of April, our dear daughter, and mother to our precious grandson, Tom.* It was separate from the graves, at the other side of the path, on a verge at the edge of the church grounds.

'No grave?' I asked.

He shook his head. 'Her husband didn't want that. He had April cremated, but her parents were church-goers and so they put the plaque there, so that it was looking out over the countryside she loved.'

'I asked about Rebecca Nurse as well,' I said. 'The girl found dead by a stream. Is she buried here?'

The vicar thought for a moment. 'The girl by Sabden Brook,' he said. 'I do remember her, and her family too, but I think they fell out with God when Rebecca was killed. She was cremated too.'

'That seems like a lot of tragedy in one small place,' I said.

'Even small places have tragedies. They just stand out more.'

I backed away from the plaque, and I started to get the impression that he wasn't going to leave me on my own in the church yard. This village was marshalling me, keeping a close eye on the outsider in its midst.

I bade my farewells and headed back to the gate. As I glanced back as I got onto the road, I saw him watching me still.

I shuddered slightly, and then I checked my voice recorder. He might have spotted the voice recorder, but he hadn't noticed that I'd clicked it on as soon as he began speaking to me and put my thumb over the red light.

The story was growing.

Chapter Forty-eight

Laura looked along the corridor, waiting to see Joe Kinsella. She knew she ought to pass on what Jack had discovered about the letters the day before, and she sensed that he would be the only one to listen. However much she disliked Carson, Laura was still a policewoman, and she wanted to see bad people behind bars.

She sighed. There was plenty of movement coming from the room, but no sign of Joe.

'He's got you, hasn't he?' said Pete, grinning.

Laura whirled around and felt herself go red. 'Who?'

'Don't give me "who",' Pete replied, laughing. 'Joe Kinsella. You're looking out for him.'

'No, I'm not,' she lied, and then, 'Maybe I've got something to tell him.'

'Like, you would like to take him out for a drink?'

'Pete, I'm attached.'

'So why have you doubled your perfume and put on your best suit?'

Laura looked down. 'This isn't my best suit,' she said, and then she smiled. 'Maybe I just look damn good in it.'

Pete shook his head. 'Better people than you have failed with him.'

'Thanks a lot!' Laura spluttered, laughing.

'I tell it like it is. Joe doesn't have relationships at work, that's all. He keeps his private life and his work life separate.'

'So what is his private life about?'

'He keeps it private,' said Pete.

Laura sighed in exasperation. 'You're making me sound interested and I'm not. I've just got something to tell him, that's all.'

'Fine, if you say so,' said Pete, looking back at his paperwork.

Laura tried to concentrate on her own work again, but she struggled. Pete had distracted her. But then she saw some movement in the corridor. It was Joe Kinsella. She was about to get up when Pete followed her gaze and said, 'Go on then, stalk him.'

Laura glared at Pete. 'It's not like that.'

Pete said nothing. He just smiled to himself.

Laura watched Joe walk away.

'Not going after him?' Pete asked. 'Maybe for the best.'

He ducked just in time as Laura's pen flew past him and hit the wall, before she rushed out of the room and went after Joe Kinsella.

Chapter Forty-nine

As I pulled away in my car, heading for Sabden Brook, I noticed a white van behind me, an Astra, old and shabby, and as I turned out of Newchurch it turned with me. I watched it in my mirror for a while, but it seemed to hang back as I got nearer to the turn-off, just an old farm track that led to a ribbon of water that ran between two fields.

I turned onto the track quickly and had to brake hard when I came up against a farm gate. The white van seemed to falter, as if the driver didn't know where to go, and as it pulled away I caught a glimpse of the number plate, just the last three letters: DDA.

I watched it go and then pulled out the report about Rebecca Nurse. She had been found by Sabden Brook, but the newspaper write-up wasn't specific about the location. There was a photograph showing a wreath laid against a small rock by a small bend in the stream.

I hopped over the gate and started to walk down the track. The floor of the valley spread out before me, a stretch of green broken by walls and the occasional grey farmhouse. No one interrupted me except for a three-legged dog that hopped towards me, barking.

The brook was exactly as I had expected it, a small country stream that trickled through a gap in a wall, and so I walked along, the old news report in my hand, looking for a match, just so that I could update the story. There was a house in the picture with a low roof, and as I walked along the bank I could see it further along, as if it had stepped out of the past, the scene unchanged. I walked a little quicker, knowing that I was in the right place. I bent down to take some pictures. The grass along the brook was unkempt, and the only sound was the water flowing over rocks in the stream.

Then I saw something that made me stop. I wasn't sure I had seen it right at first, that maybe it was just a trick of the light as the breeze made the Pennine grasses flutter and sway. I stepped forward and brushed the grass to one side. 'Shit!' I exclaimed out loud, and then I fumbled for my camera.

There was a large stone by the brook, smooth and flat, like a large pebble. It had no moss on it, unlike the others scattered around, but it wasn't just that. On its surface, a symbol had been scratched into it, one I was starting to see regularly. The screaming face, in outline, the same as the one on Sarah's family tree and the Nutter family gravestone. It was crude, hand-drawn, but it seemed like it was there as a marker, a tribute.

I took some pictures, but I felt a strong urge to leave, to get away from there. My religious views weren't strong, more a case of hedging my bets than a belief, but even my limited experience told me that there were things going on that went beyond a normal story.

I took one last look around and began to walk quickly

back to my car. I felt nervous, tense, my hands suddenly sweaty. I scanned the landscape as I walked, looking for someone watching me, remembering the van from before, and then I thought I saw someone behind a wall, near to my car.

I started to run. The track was long and curved and uphill and I was soon out of breath, my feet pounding into the mud. I saw someone move away quickly and then I heard a car door slam. I jumped onto the gate and threw myself over to the other side and then scrambled to the road. I heard an engine. It turned over quickly and began to drive away, the clutch dragging as the driver set off in a panic. As I looked around the corner, I saw a white van, an Astra, the same as before, disappear from view.

I put my hands on my knees and took in some deep breaths. I looked around me, at the hill, at the dark cottages, the wide empty spaces. My mouth was dry and I could feel nerves churning in my stomach.

As I leaned back on my car, all I wanted to do was to get as far away from there as possible. But then I smiled to myself. I was a reporter, and so I wrote up whatever happened. And I knew that if things were happening, it just made the story even better.

Chapter Fifty

'Joe, Joe!'

When Joe Kinsella looked round, Laura trotted along the corridor to catch up with him.

He turned around. 'Detective McGanity,' he said, smiling. 'What makes you shout?'

Laura grinned sheepishly. 'I'm sorry,' she replied. 'I just wanted to give you an update.'

'On what?'

'On Jack,' she said. 'He seems keen on keeping you in the loop.'

'He's a forgiving man,' Joe replied, laughing. 'C'mon, I'm going for a walk.'

'Where are you going?'

'Outside, just for some thinking time.' He pushed on the exit door, and Laura blinked as they both walked into the October sunshine. As they strolled up the steep cobbled path that took them out of the station yard and into the shadows of the street, he said, 'Tell me what you know.'

Laura fastened her suit jacket and shivered. 'Pendle witches,' she said. 'You heard of them?'

Joe looked at her, intrigued. 'This seems a strange way to start an update.'

'It's a strange story,' Laura replied, and then she said, 'That's where the letters come from.'

Joe stopped, his brow furrowed. 'Go on,' he said quietly.

'They're extracts from the trial documents,' Laura replied. 'Made modern, but essentially the same.'

'But why?'

'Sarah is a descendant of one of the witches.'

Joe started to smile. 'That certainly makes it interesting,' he said.

'Do you think there's anything in it?'

He shook his head. 'I don't know. We knew the language was odd, but we never thought of that. Is Jack going to print yet?'

'I don't know,' Laura replied. 'I suppose the story doesn't have an ending at the moment, but I know that he's not going to reveal the letters yet. Did you make any progress with the Facebook entry?'

He grimaced. 'Not much. All they told us was that someone would need her log-in details to post it, but we knew that anyway. We can only hope it's not true, that's all.'

Laura didn't respond to that, and they walked in silence for a bit longer, dodging the pushchairs and shopping trolleys of morning shoppers. Laura realised that they were walking a circuit, making their slow way back to the station.

'Do you do this a lot?' she asked.

'What?' was Joe's reply. He looked distracted, chewing on his lip.

'Walking around town?'

'It helps me to get among people,' he replied. 'We move around the towns and never really get a feel for the places, but we should. How can we investigate the town's deaths if we don't understand the people?'

'You used to work in Blackley,' said Laura. 'You should know it already.'

Joe shook his head. 'That was a few years ago,' he said. 'The town has changed – not for the better though; it seems more hopeless now – but getting out helps me connect with the place, and that helps me feel that I know it, that I understand it. How about you? What brought you up north?'

'Love,' she said, blushing when she said it. 'I followed my heart.'

'You were right to do that.'

Now it was Laura's turn to look confused. 'What do you mean?'

'Your heart tells you what you really want,' Joe replied. 'Your head just tells you why you can't have it. But if you can, then you should always follow your heart.' He glanced at Laura. 'What does your heart tell you now?'

'It's all a bit mixed up at the moment,' she replied, surprised at herself for confiding in him.

'You've no need to worry about Jack,' he said softly.

'What do you mean?'

'The photographs,' he said, and he sighed. 'I heard about the photographs Carson left for you. But I heard the talk behind the banter too, about what really went on. They got lucky with the camera, that's all, because it didn't catch the recoil as she reached out to him. I heard that he couldn't get away fast enough. Nothing went on, you can believe that.'

Laura smiled, and had to take a deep breath. 'Thank you,' she said. 'I knew that, deep down, but it is good to hear it.' As she looked up, she realised that they had done the full circuit and were now approaching the cobbled ramp back into the station yard. 'We're back,' she said. 'Was the walk worth it?'

'It was,' he said, nodding, smiling. 'Very useful. Your reputation is deserved.'

'Reputation?'

'You need to expand your horizons,' he said. 'People speak highly of you, despite the London thing.'

'What do you mean, the London thing?' Laura asked, laughing.

'I know what they say about us at headquarters,' he said. 'Stuck up, arrogant, condescending. Some of that's true, maybe, but for a London cop to come up here and avoid those things, then you've shown how good you are.'

'Get me on your team then,' she blurted out, and then blushed when she realised what she had said. 'I'm sorry. I didn't mean it like that. I know there are proper channels . . .'

Joe held up his hand. 'No, stop apologising,' he began, and then he said, 'maybe we could do with some extra help, particularly from someone getting information from the outside. I'll speak to Carson.'

And then he walked ahead, leaving Laura fanning her red cheeks, wondering whether she had done the right thing.

Chapter Fifty-one

I thought about the white van and drove in the same direction, looking for it, driving quickly along the lanes around Newchurch, wanting to know why it was following me. The lanes were tight, all bends and dips with no pathways, usually just space for one car, so that every fifty yards I expected to see the van coming towards me, both of us surprised, but it didn't happen.

It seemed like all the houses were set back, away from the road, accessed only by rutted tracks. The stone cottages were hidden by trees and natural hollows in the landscape, so I had to drive the Stag down roads that classic cars weren't meant to go. And every time I did, I was met by a locked gate or dead-end.

But then on one of the lanes I heard something, an excited chatter.

I got out and peered over the wall, and saw a group of women talking animatedly. There were four of them, and it seemed nothing special, just a meeting of friends, but just as I was about to walk back to my car, something about the group struck me. I looked back over the wall and I realised that I had seen two of the people before: they were the two customers from the shop in Newchurch, along with two others with long black hair streaming over their shoulders, one old and heavily bandaged around her leg, the other middle-aged. I ducked behind the wall and strained to listen to what they were saying. They were talking fast, but I thought I heard one of them mention Rebecca Nurse. I smiled to myself; I must have caused a stir in the village.

I looked over the wall and watched as the women converged on a car and started to unload things from the boot, cloth bags, heavy-looking, before carrying them over to an old stone barn, checking around as if they were scared of being watched. One of the women pulled hard on the barn door, and once it had screeched open they all went inside.

I pointed my camera over the top of the wall to get some pictures, and then ducked down again when the women reappeared, minus the bags. Everyone climbed into the car, and once the engine started and the car pulled away, I stuck my head over the wall and watched them crawl away up the track. When they reached the road at the other side of the field, they slipped away into the distance.

I reckoned I had to be quick. I hopped over the wall and tried to walk nonchalantly down to the barn, hoping not to be seen.

The door to the barn was large and black, the building made out of old grey stone, missing mortar in many places, no windows along the sides to provide any other way in.

I pulled on the door, and the grit in its runner made

it creak and groan as it opened. If anyone could see the barn, they would hear the noise and look over. But I had gone too far to stop.

It was gloomy inside, the only source of daylight being the open door. It didn't let much in, but I could see enough to notice that it wasn't used for farm equipment any more.

I felt a shiver, a worry that I was getting into something that was way over my head. I stepped forward slowly, knowing that with each step I took, the less likely it was that I would be able to make a quick exit.

I had expected dirt and cobwebs, old tools, pieces of machinery, but there wasn't any of that. It had been cleaned out, ready for something.

The walls were painted black, as was the floor, which was around thirty feet square, hard concrete, so that my footsteps echoed as loud shuffles in the empty space. The roof was high, and I thought I could hear animal sounds in the dark corners, a flutter of wings or the scurrying of a rodent. I walked slowly, on edge, waiting for someone to appear from behind a post or out of the shadows.

But it was what was on the floor that drew my interest.

Across the entire barn was painted a white pentagram, a five-pointed star bounded by a large white circle. The lines were ragged, painted free-style, but bold and permanent. I knew what the symbol stood for straight away: the occult, and another link to what I had found the day before, that somehow witchcraft fitted into the story. And I remembered what the vicar had hinted at earlier, that maybe witchcraft wasn't just part of history for some of the local people. As I looked around, I realised that he was right.

There were objects dotted around the circle, pewter candle-holders designed for three candles each. I counted them. Nine in total – the contents of the bags was my guess.

I started to walk across the barn, wanting to explore further, but then I stopped myself as I got to the edge of the circle. I wasn't superstitious, but something told me that walking through the pentagram wasn't a wise thing to do, that it was ceremonial and I should respect it.

I walked around it until I got to one end of the barn, at the top point of the pentagram. There was an old oak table there, scarred and knotted, but it seemed ceremonial, like some kind of altar. Behind it, the wall was covered in a black cloth, and as I got closer I could just make out a symbol, painted in silver. I felt the hairs on my arms stand up and I shuddered. It was that symbol again, the same as the one on Sarah Goode's family tree, the screaming face.

I thought I heard something again, like soft footsteps. I stopped, waiting for the next sound, but there was nothing. Just silence. I pulled out my camera and took some pictures. The flash lit up the scene, and I saw a bag on one side of the circle, in the shadows by the wall. It looked like the one I had seen in the hands of the old lady not long before.

I walked around the circle, never crossing the line, and peered inside the bag. It was filled with candles. I looked around again, and I realised from the placement of the candle-holders and the bag filled with candles that there was to be a ceremony soon. I checked my watch. It was still late morning. From the candles and the darkness of the barn, it seemed like this would be a nocturnal ceremony.

I knew I would be coming back later, so I went behind the black cloth to look for a way to get in, and for somewhere to hide and watch whatever was going to happen.

The space was small, just a gap between the cloth and the wall, and I felt my way along, cursing as I banged my shin on something left there in the darkness, and then I stopped when the cold stone changed to coarse wood. There was a window I'd missed before, boarded up loosely, really just a collection of short planks fastened to a rotting window frame. I pushed a couple out at the bottom, so that the space was big enough for me to slide out and onto the floor outside. I turned around and took some pictures; not for the story, but so that the flash would illuminate the scene and then I could work out if there was anywhere else to hide.

My stomach jolted as I heard a car approach, the hum of tyres turning into a rumble as it made its way down the muddy track. I pushed the boards a bit harder and slid out of the window, slumping to a heap on the outside. The sudden return of daylight made me squint, and I lay still, breathing hard, listening out as the car crunched to a halt. I looked towards the path that I had come down, and I could see the roof of my car over the top of the wall.

I set off walking, stepping away from the barn

wall, my feet swishing through the grass, when I heard something behind me. I tried to turn, but strong arms grabbed me and pulled me back against the barn wall.

Chapter Fifty-two

Laura went back into her office and flopped into her chair, putting her head on the desk.

'Didn't it go so well?' asked Pete.

She groaned, the noise muffled against the desk; she could hear the pleasure in his voice. Then she looked up. 'I told him what I knew, about what Jack had found out, but then I blew it, said something stupid.'

'Go on, tell me,' said Pete, grinning, enjoying himself too much. 'You asked him for dinner?'

'Do you want me to throw another pen at you?' she said, smiling herself now. She sat back. 'No, it was worse than that.'

'I can't wait for this.'

Laura sighed. 'I asked to go onto his team, that's all.' When Pete gasped, she said quickly, 'Only as a temporary thing. A local officer might help.'

'They've got plenty of local officers working for them,' Pete replied. 'Knocking on doors, you know, the routine stuff, like we do.'

'I know that, but I sort of meant in the Incident Room.'

'Are you mad? That's their preserve, the pressed-shirt brigade.'

She put her hands over her face. 'It just sort of came out. I didn't mean to say it.'

'But aren't minor, everyday offences enough for you?' he said, laughing now. 'You can build a career on rubbish like this,' and he waved some paperwork in the air.

'I know, I know,' she said, 'but I miss it, Pete: the high-life, murders. Good crime, not the shit we wade through in here each day.' When Pete looked offended, Laura said, 'I don't mean that I don't like working with you – you're the bright spot – but I'm a girl who needs some excitement.'

Pete smiled at her. 'I used to think that, but I've upset too many people. If you can get on, you do that, but I would like to be there when Carson hears about your request.' When Laura grimaced, Pete said, 'Just tell him that it looked very impressive, you know, when you were looking at his dick.'

'Is that all it boils down to with men, the size of your manhood?' Laura asked.

Pete nodded. 'Either its size, or its use. I'm sure Carson will take one out of two.'

I was pinned against the wall.

'Who are you?' he whispered. He was tall, with thinning blond hair and the healthy, ruddy look you get from living in the country.

'I'm a reporter,' I hissed back at him angrily. 'Jack Garrett. Now it's your turn. Who the fuck are you, and when are you going to let go of my arm?'

I tried to push him away, but he was too strong. He pushed me harder against the wall, so that the stones dug into the back of my head. 'What were you doing in there?' he asked, still whispering. Insistent, not angry.

'I'll answer questions when you answer mine. Who are you?'

He took a deep breath, and then said, 'I'm a police officer. Inspector Lucas. And I want to ask you a few questions.' His grip was still strong.

'Who sent you? Carson?'

He looked surprised at that, and I felt his grip relax. 'Carson? Karl Carson? Why do you say that?'

'Because the last person to grab my arm was one of his monkeys. It seems like freedom of the press doesn't have much of a chance around here. Do you know Carson?'

'Murder squad?'

I nodded.

'I've come across him a few times,' he said, calmer now. 'He comes into town whenever there's a murder, and if it's too tricky for the local boys, he takes over.' Then he looked at me. 'That's not a quote, by the way.' When I shrugged my agreement, he asked, 'How did you get here?'

I nodded up the hill. 'A red Triumph. Just over that wall.'

He didn't look. I realised that he knew the answer already. He just wanted to see if I was the truthful sort. I watched him as he thought about his next move, grinding his teeth as he glared at me. 'Get in my car,' he said eventually, and pointed me towards a dirty cream Land Rover parked next to the barn.

'What about mine?' I asked, as I clambered into the passenger seat. I remembered the last lift I'd had from the police, and I had ended up a long way from anywhere.

'It will still be there,' he said, and then set off quickly, before I had a chance to fasten my seat-belt. 'What are you researching?' he demanded, his eyes never leaving the road.

'I'm looking into Sarah Goode's disappearance,' I answered.

He thought for a moment, and then asked, 'The missing teacher from Blackley?'

I nodded. 'Her parents thought it would be a good story if I found her.'

'Did you think you would find her in a barn on Pendle Hill?'

'I was curious.'

I had to put my arms onto the dashboard as I was thrown forward by the quick stop into a lay-by. He looked at me.

'Why are you here, Mr Garrett?'

I thought about how much to say, and then I realised that I had little to lose by being honest. The story would need quotes, and so I had to talk to get answers. I reached into my coat pocket and laid out the family tree on my knee. I had printed off the pictures earlier, and I pointed at the spider tracks of lines and names.

'The Pendle witches bring me here,' I said.

He laughed, a quiet chuckle. 'Like most people. Why for you?'

And so I told him, all about Sarah Goode and the connection with the Pendle witches, and about the other deaths mentioned by Sarah's mother.

As I was speaking, I saw him looking at the family tree. He took it from me and scoured the names, until he threw it back at me and muttered, 'Shit.' He was silent for a few minutes, just looking out of the window, until he turned to me and asked, 'How long have you been looking into this?'

'I've known about the connection for a day. Why?'

He shook his head. 'It doesn't matter.'

I looked down at the family tree. He had seen something there.

'What is it?' I asked.

I could tell that he was debating what to say, so I made my usual threat. 'If you don't tell me, I'll go to print with what I've got. If there is something else, tell me, and I can hold it back.'

He looked down at the family tree again, and then asked, 'Would that go in the piece?'

'Right in the middle,' I replied.

'I've seen that symbol before,' he said, and tapped the top of the paper. 'People are being attacked around here with explosives, three so far. No one has been killed, but an old lady's pet cat was exploded the other morning. She had that symbol on a ring on her finger, and in the house. So did one of the others.'

I whistled. 'There is something strange going on around here.'

272

'And there's something else,' he said.

'Keep going,' I urged.

His finger jabbed at a name on the family tree. 'Susan Lloyd.' When I raised my eyebrows, he said, 'She was the first victim of the explosions.'

My mouth opened, shocked, unsure what to say.

He sighed. 'Maybe it's nothing. Most local people claim to be descendants of the witches, either Anne Whittle, Alice Nutter, or even Old Demdike. I'm not sure many can prove it, but I suppose there must be Pendle witch blood in most of the people in the villages around here.'

He was trying to sound dismissive, that the witch connection hadn't really surprised him. Was I safe with him?

'And what about her?' I asked, and I pointed to the name of the young girl found dead by Sabden Brook, Rebecca Nurse.

He thought for a moment, and then his eyes opened wide as he remembered it. 'And that's why you were down there,' he said.

'You were watching me all that time?'

He smiled at that – the first time I had seen it.

'And her?' I asked, pointing at the other name that had brought me to Pendle. 'April Mather?'

He nodded. 'A suicide,' he said. 'Hanged herself from Blacko Tower.' He held up the piece of paper. 'Can I borrow this?'

I nodded my agreement, but when he asked me what I was going to do, I told him that I was going back to that barn once it got dark.

'I wouldn't do that,' he said.

'Why not?'

Then he smiled again, although this time more mischievously. 'Because there aren't many hiding places in there, and I'll be there first.'

Chapter Fifty-three

I made it back to the barn just after six, as the sun slipped behind the horizon and the fields all around became shrouded in darkness. I was dressed all in black. Laura had laughed at me when I'd told her where I was going, told me that I was too old to play secret agent, but I knew I was almost invisible as I made my way to the window I had clambered out of earlier in the day.

I listened out for any noise, but it seemed quiet of human activity. I could hear branches creaking, and I thought the trickle of Sabden Brook carried on the breeze. I pulled at the boards, and then slithered through onto the barn floor, careful not to make any sound. I knelt on the floor, listening out, my eyes trying to adjust, and at first it seemed like I was alone. But then I jumped as I heard a noise just behind me and a hand gripped my shoulder.

'I told you I would get here before you,' a voice whispered in my ear.

'Good evening, Inspector,' I whispered back, almost laughing with relief, and then I asked, 'Any movement out front?'

'No, none,' he answered, and then he said, 'There's an old door against the wall over there. I've been waiting behind that. If you kneel down next to me, you should be able to see too. But no photographs.'

I shuffled along the wall, conscious that a discarded tool could make a noise. Once behind the door, I felt our breath warm the small space, and we spent the next hour trying not to talk, worried in case someone came along without us hearing them. So we hid in the darkness, silent, waiting.

We both tensed when we heard steps outside, crunches on the gravel. I felt Rod touch my arm, just to make sure that we both knew to be quiet.

The door screeched loudly as it was pulled open, and then I thought I heard a steady drumbeat, marking time. Goose-pimples sprang up on my arms. I peered through the darkness, waiting for someone to appear.

I saw a flame at first, a large candle making the shadow of the doorway pulse as it flickered, but I couldn't make out any detail on the person carrying it. I could tell it was a man, from his height and the width of his shoulders, but he was wearing a hood, and the brim seemed to move in the candlelight. As I watched, I realised that it was a cloak with a long hood, sack-brown, running the full length of his body. His feet were bare.

'Who is that?' I whispered.

Rod didn't answer.

The steady rhythm continued, and as the first person entered, walking slowly, I saw that there was someone behind him wearing the same cloak. It looked like a woman; she was smaller, moved slower, perhaps older.

And then I saw the bandages on her leg and remembered the woman from earlier. She was carrying the drum I could hear. It was small, held in one hand, and she was sounding a steady beat in time with their steps, like the stop–start rhythm of the death march. As they got further into the barn, they started to walk around the edge of the circle, and I saw that there were others behind, all wearing the same cloak.

They filed in and each took up a position by the large candle-holders I had seen earlier. Their heads were bowed, their hands clasped to the front. The first two to enter had now gone to the head of the circle, nearest to the cloth backdrop, the drum still sounding its steady beat. Then, as the male leader started to raise his hands in the air, the drumbeat stopped. He had a knife in one hand. The blade was double-edged, nearly a foot long, going to a single point.

There was silence in the barn. I thought they would hear the hard pound of my heartbeat. My hands were slick with sweat.

The leader threw back his hood. He had grey hair, long and pulled back into a ponytail, with some kind of a metal headband. It looked like copper. I could see his paunch against the rope tied around his cloak.

'That's Olwen,' whispered Rod in my ear.

'Who is he?'

'Local oddball,' he replied. 'I thought he might have a hand in some of this, but I didn't realise he was the leader.'

'Blessed be,' bellowed Olwen, and then he thrust the knife upwards, holding it high in the air.

'Blessed be,' came the response from everyone around the circle, the words echoing around the barn, the voices a mix of ages and sexes.

Olwen paused and looked at those standing around the white circle. He jabbed the air with the knife again. 'Be it known,' he shouted, 'the temple is to be erected, the circle is to be cast.'

The woman who had followed Olwen started to walk around the circle, her candle still in her hand, using it to light all the other candles. When all were burning brightly, everyone lowered their hoods. There were a couple of older women, a young man with glasses, and the rest were young women, their hair falling in soft curls to their shoulders.

'That's the woman who had her cat blown up, Abigail Hobbs,' Rod whispered in my ear, and I followed the line of his finger to the woman who had been playing the drum.

'She was here this afternoon, with the woman at the back,' I whispered in return, pointing.

'Isla Marsden,' he replied.

We stopped talking when Olwen thrust his knife upwards again.

'I bring light and fire,' he bellowed, his voice echoing around the rafters. 'It brings the breath of life.'

Abigail picked up two small bowls and walked over to him, holding them out at arm's length. Olwen dipped the knife into one and covered the tip with white powder.

'Let us purify ourselves,' he said, his voice deep and serious. 'Cleanse our bodies and spirits with this salt as we dedicate ourselves to the glory of the God and

Goddess.' His shouts turned into a chant, and he dropped the salt into the other bowl and stirred it with the knife. 'Let the sacred salt drive out any impurities in this water, that we may use it in our rites.'

Olwen began to walk around the circle, Abigail behind him, holding out the bowls, limping as she went. He dipped his knife into the water and flicked it along the straight lines of the pentagram on the floor.

'I consecrate thee in the names of the God and Goddess,' he shouted, 'bidding you welcome to this temple.'

When Olwen had walked around the full circle, Abigail put down the bowls and picked up her drum once more. She began to beat out the same steady rhythm. Everyone else joined hands and moved slowly around the edge of the circle.

'This is a coven, isn't it?' I whispered.

'That would be my guess,' Rod replied.

'I consecrate those of you here present in the names of the God and Goddess,' Olwen chanted, 'and welcome you to this, their temple.'

'All hail the air, the fire, the water, the earth,' everyone chanted back.

'We bid the Lord and Lady welcome,' Olwen chanted again, his voice getting louder. 'All hail.'

'All hail,' everyone shouted back.

'Let no one leave the temple until it be cleared. So mote it be.'

'So mote it be,' came the communal response, the words spoken quietly but reverberating around the roof space.

Everyone stopped and held out their candles, the flames flickering shadows around their faces. I was struck by how ordinary they seemed, as if they were just northern men and women playing dressing-up games in a barn. Their eyes were on Olwen. He looked around the circle, enjoying the drama, a smile on his lips.

'Pray for Harmonie, our missing one,' he said, softer this time. 'Keep her safe, and for all who have suffered before, let them find love. Let no one be lonely who is from the family line.'

'Let people come,' everyone chanted, knowing their lines.

Olwen looked around again, from face to face, his knife still high in the air.

'Does anyone know of someone of the family line who seeks entry?' he asked, his voice filled with drama.

Again, there was a pause, but I got the impression that it was theatrical, like the whole evening.

'I know,' said a voice at the far edge of the circle, the younger man, maybe only twenty, but his voice was deep and bold.

'Who do you bring?' asked Olwen.

'She waits outside.'

'Can you vouch for her?'

'I can,' the young man replied, 'because I am her teacher, and I have shown her the Craft. Now she requests entrance.'

'Can she be brought before us?'

'She can.'

Olwen held out his arms. 'Then let it be.'

The young man went to open the door, his movements slow and deliberate. No one looked round as it screeched open. The drumbeat started again, loud and slow.

A woman came into the barn. She was young, in her early twenties, tall and elegant, with short blonde hair and wearing a long dress, her feet bare like everyone else's. She was led into the barn by the young man, her arms held out in front of her. As she got to the edge of the circle, she stopped. Olwen walked slowly around the edge of the circle until he reached her, and then he turned so that he was facing into the centre. He made symbolic slashing movements in the air with his knife, as if cutting an opening, and stepped forward into the circle. Olwen turned to her and took hold of her hands.

'Come with me,' he said, his voice low.

She stepped over the circle threshold and made her way to the centre of the pentagram. She stood in front of him, her arms by her side.

'It looks like some kind of initiation,' I said.

'Or sacrifice,' Rod responded.

Olwen looked at the other people in the room, and then back to her. 'Why do you come here?' he asked.

'To worship the God and Goddess and do so with the brothers and sisters of my family line,' she replied, her voice timid and nervous.

'Who do you bring with you?'

'Just my true self.'

Olwen nodded solemnly.

'Do you wish to end the life you have known so far?' He said it calmly, and I felt Rod tense behind me.

'You might be right,' I whispered, not wholly serious.

'It might just be symbolic,' came the reply, hissed in my ear, but he sounded nervous.

The drumbeat became slightly faster. Olwen stepped forward and held the knife towards her head. I felt Rod lean forward and his fingers dug into my shoulders.

Olwen cut off a small piece of the woman's hair and tossed it into the flame of a candle just behind him, where it crackled for a few seconds before disappearing as a spark into the night.

Olwen reached out and grabbed her dress, pulled it towards himself. The woman swallowed. The drumbeat quickened even more, matching my heart-rate.

Olwen raised the knife and looked around those present, before slashing downwards quickly, digging the blade into the cloth.

The woman jolted, and then, as she shrugged her shoulders, the dress fell from her. I saw that she was naked underneath. She closed her eyes for a second and I saw her cheeks flush. It was cold and she shivered slightly, her nipples hardening.

She hung her head and the young man who had brought her in stood behind her with a cloth and placed it over her eyes. He pulled it tight, snapping her head back, and then tied it into a knot.

The woman swallowed.

'This isn't looking good,' I said.

Rod just breathed heavily through his nose.

The young man took one of her arms and pulled it

behind her back. When Olwen handed over a length of rope, the man pulled her other arm behind her and bound the woman's wrists together. The length of rope was then looped around the woman's neck and tied, so that any movement on her arms would pull her head backwards.

I saw the woman shiver again, but Olwen did not seem to be in a hurry. He kept his gaze on the woman's face but placed the tip of the knife against the woman's pubic hair, and I saw her mouth open, her cheeks flushed red.

Rod's fingers dug into my shoulders more as he leaned forward. I could feel him edging past me, his movements smothered by the drumbeat, now going at a fast steady rhythm, the others present swaying in time to it.

Olwen traced the blade up the woman's body, making her skin drag, leaving a red line as he went, until he reached her right breast. She flinched but didn't back away, thrust her chest out towards him. He moved the knife across to her left breast, his movements slow, deliberate, making no cuts. I thought I could see moisture on her chest, despite the cold.

The knife lingered on her left breast, and then Olwen moved it down her body, back to where he had started, completing the triangle. She swallowed again, and I saw the sweat spread to her forehead. When the knife reached her pubic hair again, he stopped, and then lifted the knife away. He reached out and put his hand on her shoulder. As he pushed down, she went to her knees in front of him, her arms still bound behind her. My ears were filled with the sounds of Rod breathing heavily, every second making him more nervous, wanting to interrupt, moving forward, the drumbeat speeding up.

I put my hand on his arm and gripped it, just a squeeze to remind him to stay put. I didn't know what was going to happen – maybe the young woman was in danger – but for the story's sake, I wanted to see how it ended.

Olwen put his head back and held his arms in the air, the knife pointed upwards.

'Do you want to feel death in your old life?' he shouted out loud.

The woman paused, and I saw her lick her lips. 'Yes,' she said eventually, her voice quiet.

'Do you want to die now?' the priest shouted.

'Yes,' she said, her voice stronger now. 'I want to die now.'

'What was your name?'

'Julie.'

The woman with the drum banged louder.

'I call upon you, Horned God,' Olwen shouted, his hand tight on the knife. 'Care for this woman in her death. Bring her back to us in life, in our life.'

Rod stepped forward.

'Are you ready to die?' Olwen asked again, his hands trembling.

'I am ready.'

Olwen brought his knife down quickly.

I closed my eyes, and then I heard a scream. I was

pushed to the floor as Rod ran forward, the old door clattering to the floor.

'Stop now,' Rod shouted, his arms outwards. 'Stay right where you are.'

Chapter Fifty-four

Sarah yearned for sleep. The heartbeat sound had come back on and it kept her awake; it was so loud that not even clutching the blanket tight around her head could shut it out. The skin around her eyes felt sore and her stomach ached. There had been no visit since the day before, and so she hadn't eaten all day. She had always been slim, but now Sarah could feel her ribs properly and her face felt drawn.

She stood up, still in the middle of the circle, the blanket around her shoulders, and tried to assess the time, the temperature her guide. She sensed it was night, it was getting colder again, and she knew she had to act. She wouldn't know the answer until either she was free, or else it was too late.

Sarah went to the camp bed and pulled back the mattress. The bed had a tubular frame, with a lattice of metal supporting the mattress, springs holding it in place. It was the springs she was after. They had sharp points at the end, hooks that linked the springs to the frame.

She threw the mattress onto the floor and looked for

a spring that was slack. She rubbed her eyes, tried to blink away the fatigue. They all looked the same.

She gripped the lattice with one hand and pulled at it, so that the springs at one end were less taut. With the other, she gripped a spring and tried to stretch it out so that she could unhook it. Beads of sweat flecked her forehead as she strained, but the sweat on her palms made her grip slippery and she banged her hand on the bed-frame as it slipped off the spring. She tried not to yell out, afraid of attracting his attention, but as she looked down there was blood on her fingers. She sucked at it and then dried the wound on the blanket. Moisture wouldn't make it easier.

Sarah looked upwards, said a few words to herself, just to garner some strength, and then pulled at the spring again.

She could feel it slipping in her hand again, but she gripped it tighter, gritting her teeth with effort. The spring started to cut into her finger, bringing blood to the surface, but still she pulled at it, tried to bring the hook out of the bed-frame. The effort made her face red, but she tried to use the pain as fuel. Her hand hurt, the metal spring cutting into her fingers, but it made her angry. She took a deep breath, let out a screech, and then gave it one last pull.

She heard a ping as the spring jumped out of the bed-frame.

Sarah took some deep breaths and then she worked the spring free of the bed, saw how the hooked end was sharp. She pulled on another spring, the metal lattice hanging a bit looser now, and then worked on another one.

She felt enlivened, three metal springs in her hand. Weapons; tools. They could be useful. Emboldened, Sarah threw the bed-frame the right way up and put the mattress back on top. It was not obvious that the springs were missing. She slipped them under the mattress and sat back down in the middle of the circle. She would need to gather her strength for a few minutes, and then her escape would begin.

Chapter Fifty-five

Everyone looked startled. Olwen turned around and dropped the knife. Some of the worshippers looked towards the door, so I ran out as well and rushed towards it, to make sure it stayed closed. As I got there, I saw some switches by the door and clicked them on. The barn was suddenly flooded with bright light from overhead.

'What is going on?' Olwen asked, his eyes angry, blinking at the lights.

'I'm a police officer,' Rod shouted, pulling out his identification. 'You held a knife to her chest.'

No one said anything. I saw some of the candles flicker as the hands holding them wobbled, and I could feel the anger from around the circle.

'This is our church,' Olwen said, in a voice thick with emotion. 'You have come into our church and broken our circle.'

I looked at the young woman, naked and cold, curled up in a ball, trying to protect her modesty. I took off my coat and walked over to her, hearing the gasps as I walked across the pentagram. I removed the blindfold and untied the knots. When the rope fell down to the floor, I took off my coat and placed it around her. She didn't look at me, but she took the coat anyway, wrapping her arms around her chest.

'What was happening here?' I asked her quietly.

'I was joining the church,' she said, and I sensed sadness in her voice. 'Now I can't. You stopped it.'

'You said you wanted to die.'

She looked up at me, and I saw tears in her eyes.

'I wanted to say goodbye to my past life. Julie was going to die. I was going to be reborn.'

'Don't say any more,' said Olwen. His voice was strong, and I realised that Rod had made a mistake. He had panicked, worried that he was about to witness a sacrifice. Instead, we had stumbled into nothing more than an initiation ceremony.

'No one leaves until I have some answers,' Rod said sternly.

Olwen shook his head. 'You have no power here,' he said. 'You might have broken the circle, but you cannot stop us from leaving. We have done nothing wrong.' He looked towards the other people in the room and held out his arms. 'Go now to your homes. We will speak in the morning. It will be our special day, and we will celebrate.'

Rod looked at me, uncertain, confused, and then at Abigail and Isla. They looked away, avoiding his gaze, and so he nodded at me. I opened the door, and as everyone passed me I tried to catch their eyes, to see who might do an interview, but they all went out with their heads bowed. The naked woman shrugged off my coat and pulled her dress back on over her head before running out, her face down, streaked by tears, her hand holding the torn pieces together. When everyone had gone, Olwen nodded at me to close the door again, and then he removed his copper headband.

Now that he was alone in the bright lights of the barn, I was surprised by his appearance. The ceremony before had seemed sinister, but the man in front of me was ordinary, middle-aged, unthreatening, just the ponytail hinting at a different way of life. His cheeks were filled with broken veins, and the stubble on them was grey. He smelled of cigarettes, and I saw that his fingers were stubby and brown.

'Why are the police here?' Olwen asked Rod. He sounded weary now.

I looked at Rod, and I saw that he was still thinking through his actions. 'I'm not a police officer,' I said. 'I'm a reporter, and I have been asked to find Sarah Goode.'

'By whom?' His voice was rich, cultured.

'By her parents.'

He sighed at that. 'Then we're on the same side. We also want Harmonie back,' he said.

'Harmonie?' I asked.

'Sarah was Harmonie's name in her old life, before she died and was reborn. Her name is now Harmonie.'

'Like Julie was almost reborn?'

Olwen nodded. 'Julie will get another chance. She has waited a long time, and worked hard.'

'Cut the shit, Olwen,' Rod barked. 'You might like your little games, messing around out here in your barn, but people are being hurt, and Sarah is missing. I don't care what happens to the girl from before.'

Olwen looked at Rod for a few seconds, and I saw him take a deep breath to calm himself before he turned back to me. 'So why are you trying to find Harmonie?' he asked. 'Your sense of humanity, of doing the right thing by her?'

His voice was mocking, and I realised that honesty was the only way.

'Because it will be a good story,' I replied. 'Nothing more.'

'And what brought you here, to this barn?'

I looked at Rod, whose face was still blank.

'She is a descendant of Anne Whittle,' I said. I could tell that I didn't have to explain about Anne Whittle. 'Other descendants have met unfortunate ends. It just seemed like a good story, you know, a cursed line.'

Olwen didn't answer, as if he didn't know what to say.

'I could tell that this was some kind of Wicca ceremony,' I said. 'Words like Goddess gave it away. And you don't look surprised by what I'm telling you.'

Olwen was still silent.

'So Sarah – sorry, Harmonie – was a member of your church, I presume?' I pressed. 'Part of the family line?'

He looked down, and I saw him struggle with his doubts about me, wondering whether he should say anything. Then he looked at me, a glistening of tears in his eyes, and said, 'She will die tomorrow,' his voice breaking.

Rod looked at me when he said that, and I saw that he was suspicious.

'What do you mean?' Rod asked.

My mind flashed to the Facebook entry for the next day, 31st October. *I die.*

Olwen didn't answer. He turned to go, but as he went past me I grabbed his arm. 'If you know something about her, you should come forward.' He looked at me but said nothing, and so I thrust a card into his hand. 'Call me if you change your mind.'

He looked down at the card and then at me, before he shrugged off my hand and walked out of the barn.

When we were alone, I breathed out noisily. I turned to Rod and said, 'That was an interesting evening.'

He stood with his hands on his hips, and then he nodded. 'And it's ended. Go home, Mr Garrett.'

Chapter Fifty-six

My house glowed warmly as I approached it, the soft yellow lights of home welcoming me. I heard the sound of the television as I opened the door. Laura was curled up on the sofa in her dressing gown, her hands around a hot drink. She looked up and smiled sleepily.

'How was your evening? All ghouls and ghosties?'

My keys clattered onto the table as I thought about what had happened earlier. 'Do you remember what I said before, that maybe she's not the killer at all?' I said by way of reply. 'Perhaps she is something else.'

Laura nodded slowly. 'This sounds too much like work,' she said. 'I've shaken off my day, so come on, sit down and think of something else.'

'That's not easy when you've seen what I have tonight.'

Laura sat up, more interested now, and so I shrugged off my coat and sat down next to her, then told her about the ceremony in the barn, the chanting, the initiation.

'Your night was more exciting than mine,' she said. 'Was it definitely witchcraft?'

'Yes, and the priest said that Sarah was in the coven,'

I replied. 'We knew there was a connection with witch-craft, because of the family tree and the letters, but to know that she is a practising witch, well, that takes the story to a whole new level. So why would Sarah write those notes, as a practising witch?'

'Guilt? Trying to lay the blame on her hobby, or whatever you would call it.'

'But there is something else as well.'

'Go on.'

'Do you remember the Facebook entry?' I asked.

'Pretty hard to forget: 31st October – *I die*,' answered Laura. 'Why?'

'Because the priest also said that Sarah will die tomorrow.'

Laura looked alert now, her tiredness gone as she became more businesslike, transforming herself back into Laura the detective. 'Why would he say that?'

I shook my head. 'I don't know, and more import-antly, how does he know?'

'The murder squad need to be told,' she said, although when I agreed with her, she added, 'but I'm not looking forward to telling them.'

'You don't think they'll be receptive to witch stories?'

'I don't think they'll be receptive to any idea that isn't their own,' she answered curtly.

Before I had the chance to say anything else, my phone started to ring. When I looked at the screen, I saw a number I didn't recognise. But when I answered, I heard a voice that I'd heard earlier that evening. It was Olwen's baritone, the priest from the coven.

Laura watched me as I gave him directions, and when

I hung up, I said, 'It looks like we might get the answers to our questions sooner than we think.'

'The priest?'

I nodded.

'But he might not talk if a police officer is listening in,' said Laura.

'I didn't tell him you were a police officer,' I said mischievously, 'and you don't look like one right now.' I grabbed Laura around the waist, and as I pulled her towards me she wrapped her arms around my neck. 'This will be strange for you,' I said softly, 'but maybe tonight is the night that you play at being the little woman at home.'

She went to kiss me. 'As long as you don't get too used to the idea,' she murmured.

Chapter Fifty-seven

Olwen looked different when I opened the door. The robes and copper headband were gone. In their place were casual clothes, a rugby jersey and jeans, his stomach straining against his belt.

He gave me a sheepish look as he walked into the house. Laura came down the stairs, still in her dressing gown, deciding to play the part.

'Hello,' she said, trying to sound surprised. Then she looked towards the kitchen. 'Can I get you a drink?'

Olwen nodded that tea would be nice. I showed him to a chair, and as he sat down I saw his thumbs making small circles on his index fingers, showing his nerves.

'What's your name?' I asked. When he paused, I said, 'I mean your original name. I presume it wasn't always Olwen.'

He thought for a moment, and then he said, 'It used to be Michael Smith, but when I was drawn into the circle, I changed my name.'

I must have looked unimpressed, because he added, 'It isn't some hobby, you know, some kind of game we play, where we give each other names and play with candles.'

'So what is it?' I asked.

'It's my spirituality,' he said, his voice weary, as if he was tired of trying to justify himself.

'Witchcraft?'

He nodded. 'It's my faith. The Craft. Witchcraft, Wicca, call it what you want, but that is our church.'

Laura came in with a tray of drinks and a plate of biscuits. She seemed to be overplaying the little-woman act, but when I looked at her I detected a mischievous glint in her eyes.

'And Julie was being initiated into it?'

'Yes. She had waited a long time for tonight, a year and a day, and then you burst in and ruined it for her.'

I held up my hand in apology, but he brushed it away with a shake of his head. 'I didn't come here because of that. I came here because of Harmonie.'

I sighed. 'Can I call her Sarah? That's the name I have for her, and I'm struggling with the change.'

He considered that for a moment, and then said, 'If that's how you prefer it.'

'So why is Sarah going to die tomorrow?' I asked.

'Because it is Samhain, our most sacred day, our main sabbat.'

'Sabbat?'

'Festival,' he replied. 'Those of us who practise the Craft celebrate eight festivals a year. We call them sabbats. Tomorrow is the main one. It is called Samhain.'

'Tomorrow is Halloween,' said Laura.

The priest nodded. 'That is what you call it.' When

298

Laura looked confused, he continued, 'Your Halloween comes from our festival. The Celtic new year was at the end of October. It marked the end of summer, when the harvest had been brought in, and all that lay ahead were the dark months of winter. The church tried to change it, brought in All Saints' Day, but the old traditions held. For us, it's a special time, one for celebration.'

Laura flashed a guilty look to the table, where Bobby's ghost mask sat next to the carved-out pumpkin.

'You said that Sarah will die tomorrow,' I said. 'Would Sarah really kill herself on one of the sabbats, if they are so special?'

Olwen shook his head slowly. 'I didn't say anything about suicide.' When I flashed a look at Laura, he said, 'You told me earlier that members of our coven had died, and that it seemed like we were unlucky.'

'No, I didn't,' I said, correcting him. 'I said that descendants of Anne Whittle had died or disappeared. I don't know who is in your coven.'

He looked at me, and I could tell that he was nervous. I glanced over at Laura. She tried to look relaxed, but I could tell from the sharpness in her eyes that she was listening intently.

'We are the Family Coven,' he said solemnly. When I nodded at him to continue, he added, 'We all practise the Craft, and we all come from a special blood line.'

I thought back to the family tree in Sarah's house, then to the ceremony I had witnessed earlier. 'The Pendle witches?' I asked, faking my surprise.

'We call them the Elders,' he replied, nodding. 'They

died for their beliefs, but,' and he looked confused at this, 'I am curious to know how you worked this out.'

I sensed Laura fidget. I knew that I couldn't mention the letters from Sarah.

'I was looking into Sarah's disappearance,' I said, 'and I was shown her family tree by her mother. She told me how it seemed cursed, that so many of the people at the bottom of the tree, today's generation, had died so young.'

He looked uncomfortable, swallowing and wiping sweat from his forehead.

'Are you all right, Mr Smith?' asked Laura.

He nodded quickly, and then leaned forward as he said, 'What I am about to say is something of the utmost importance to me.'

'Don't ask me to stay silent on it,' I said, warning him. 'I'm a reporter, and if it's a good story, I'll write it.'

'What about identities? Sources?'

I thought about that. 'Names can be worked around,' I said. 'Sources I never reveal.'

I could see his mind working as he wondered how much he should say – but then he sighed, as if he knew he had already made his choice when he came to the house.

'We all took a vow when we joined our church,' he said, his voice steady now, as if he was comfortable with his decision to talk. 'It was one of kinship, of secrecy. The Elders died from saying too much, all those years ago. We will take our secrets with us.'

'But did you promise to protect each other?'

'That is why I am here,' he said, and his eyes flickered

with sadness for a moment. 'We can't allow someone else to die. We've talked about it, tried to work out how to stay safe, but we all knew this time would come, when I would have to break the rule of secrecy.' He took a deep breath. 'But I am the priest, and so I will have to live with the consequences.'

'How many people have died in your coven?'

'Through the years?' he said, shaking his head. 'I don't know. The coven has existed since the time of the Elders, made up of the ones who survived. Secrecy was life or death then. Most of those who went to Lancaster Castle admitted witchcraft, and they died for their confessions, and so those that were left behind stayed silent. Sometimes the coven stayed small, when sensibilities weren't in our favour, but society is different now. We have moved on, and people are prepared to accept our Craft.'

'So that ceremony I saw tonight is four hundred years old?' I asked, fascinated.

'No, it isn't. It is our ceremony, decided by ourselves. Sometimes there were so few people to carry on the coven that the old traditions were lost. And the Craft isn't about re-enacting old traditions. It is a modern faith, so we adopted our own ceremonies. There are no rules in the Craft.'

'How can it be a faith if there are no rules?' I queried.

He smiled, but it was patronising, like a father to a child. 'Your faith rules,' he said. 'Our faith liberates. We have guiding principles, that's all.'

'What like?'

'You tell me something first,' he said. 'What do you think witchcraft involves?'

I thought quickly, but I couldn't get beyond myths and legend, pointed hats and broomsticks. Then I thought of the ceremony I had witnessed earlier.

'It seems like it provides a spiritual outlet for those people who want to have something to believe in, but who want to do something outside of convention,' I said.

'Like a bunch of misguided hippies?'

I smiled. 'I didn't say that, but I think that if witchcraft was the norm, you would all be Christians. The important thing for you is that you live outside of the norm.'

'Do I look like I live outside of convention?'

I looked down at his clothes, at the battered suede shoes and grubby jeans.

'Maybe you're in disguise,' I responded.

Olwen smiled. 'There might be more truth to that than you think. And maybe there *is* something of the hippie in all of us, because peace, love and nature are what we are all about. We have one guiding principle, our "*rede*", and that is "an' it harm none, do what thou wilt".' When I looked confused, he translated it for me. 'Do what you want to do, as long as it doesn't harm anyone else.'

'It seems a strange sort of spirituality, where you can do what you want,' I said. 'How can any of you be sure that you are following the same spiritual path?'

'There are some tenets to our faith,' he replied. 'We all celebrate the same sabbats, and we all apply the threefold rule.' He guessed my question before I asked it, because he added, 'That whatever we do, it will come back to us threefold. So if we use our spells for good, we will be rewarded three times over. If we do them for evil then it will come back at us three times as badly.'

'Sort of insurance against the bad guys,' I said.

'Something like that,' he agreed.

'So you do spells?' asked Laura, sounding sceptical. I knew that Laura's religious views were stronger than mine, that for Laura there was only one God.

'Yes, we do. I know that most people laugh at that, but it is part of our spiritual path, part of my faith, and so I am not ashamed of it. It is no different to saying prayers in church, or taking the wafer and wine.'

'I thought the Pendle witches were just wrongly accused old women,' I said. 'If they are, then your coven has no basis.'

'The bookshelves are full of theories,' Olwen said, shaking his head, 'but what runs through all of them is that the Elders confessed to their witchcraft. If they had been in your church, you would call them saints, dying for their cause. Your church and history prefer to paint them as deluded old women admitting to things they didn't understand. Your church did what it always does to other faiths: it defamed them, and those parts that it couldn't get rid of, it took for itself.'

'But what makes you so right?' I asked. 'You aren't exactly neutral on the issue.'

'Is that different to any other faith?' he replied.

'So how did you get involved with the coven?' asked Laura. 'If it is all about secrecy, I suppose you don't advertise.'

'Someone I had known for a long time sounded me out. It was an uncle. I knew I was a descendant, but

303

I hadn't realised that the uncle had been testing me, trying to gauge my interest. I'm from a different line to Sarah, from Alice Nutter, but we all maintain the family tree.'

'And that's why you use that symbol?' I asked. 'The one on the Nutter grave.'

Olwen paused and looked at me, and I saw him realise that I knew more than I was letting on. 'You've done your research,' he said quietly.

'And how did you recruit Sarah?'

'Sarah came to us,' he said. 'We met her at a pagan festival, and when she realised we were from Lancashire, she stayed with us, said she was looking for answers. I showed her the way, and when I looked into her background I found out that she too was a descendant, and so I taught her the Craft, introduced her to the coven.'

'How old was she then?'

'Eighteen. I think it was her way of becoming her own person. The more she looked into the Craft, the more she realised that our ideals were the same as hers.'

'So you're not a witch because you are a descendant?'

'No,' he said, shaking his head. 'I follow the Craft because those are my beliefs. But our coven is limited to descendants, because we have a bond, a common link. There are thousands of practising witches in this country, we are nothing unique, but we all have different rules of entry for our covens.'

'So why do you think tomorrow will be the day?'

At that, Olwen sat back in his chair and took a deep breath. He looked down when he spoke. He seemed suddenly tired, and he ran his hand over his hair, just a quick stroke of his ponytail. 'Because members of our coven who have been killed over the years have always been killed on one of the sabbats. Tomorrow is our main sabbat, and so that is why I think tomorrow she will be most in danger.'

I went to the table, where I had put the family tree.

'So the ones I have pointed out,' I said, 'the ones on the family tree who have died, were members of your coven?'

He nodded, and then sighed heavily. 'That is why I have come to you. If you have got this far, then you are going to continue, and you would find out all about us. Our vow is secrecy, but if we are going to lose that anyway, then it is time to come out to try to save Sarah. If we can find her, then we might find whoever has been killing our members.'

'Why is secrecy still such a big deal?' I asked.

'In the past, people died because of the Craft,' he said solemnly. 'Now, people won't kill us, but they might ruin us. Some in our coven have good jobs, positions of respectability. We've got a police officer, a Magistrate, an accountant. Sarah is a teacher. People are not always comfortable with the thought of witchcraft. They think it is all about human sacrifice, or stealing babies. We are ridiculed, you know: *hubble, bubble, toil and trouble.*'

I glanced at Laura, remembering her saying the same thing earlier, but she looked away.

'So have you come here to tell me about Sarah because you think she will die tomorrow?' I asked.

He nodded, and then pulled a piece of paper from his pocket.

'This is a list of all the people who have died or gone missing from the coven in the last ten years. The ones who have died often did so on one of our sabbats. Tomorrow is our biggest of the year. If Sarah is in danger, then she will die tomorrow.'

I reached out for the list, and I saw six names. Some of them were familiar from my own research. Some were new.

'What do you want me to do?' I asked.

He looked at me, and he seemed lost, unsure. 'Help us,' he said. 'You are a journalist, so you have a voice.'

'Why don't you go to the police?'

He snorted a laugh. 'Can you imagine how the police would react if I went to them with this? I would be laughed out of the station.'

I noticed Laura look down.

'You can help us,' he continued, pleading. 'Maybe it will be too late for Sarah, we all know that, but you can write about the link and still not reveal the living members. And if you do, the police might take notice and find whoever has been killing us.'

'How do you know that Sarah isn't what the police think she is?' I asked. 'A murderer on the run?'

'Because I know Sarah,' he answered. 'I know how gentle she is, how kind she is, of the promises she has made to us, her brothers and sisters in her coven. The Sarah I know wouldn't do what the police think she might have done.'

He stood up and started to move towards the door.

'What are you going to do for Sarah?' I asked.

'We are going to have our ceremony tomorrow. It is

Samhain and we are going to celebrate. But we will worship for Sarah. If we have faith, it might turn out justly.'

I shook Olwen's hand as he went, and as the door closed I turned to Laura. 'What do you think?'

'I don't know,' Laura replied, 'except for one thing: that if Olwen is right, and Sarah isn't a murderer, then we don't have long to check it out.'

Chapter Fifty-eight

Sarah opened her eyes and took a deep breath. Her body felt weak, worn down by the lack of food, and her fatigue was making her see things, like the walls moving, just pulsing in time with the heartbeats. But she had gained some strength from thinking of those things she was trying to get back to: her parents, the children she taught, her friends. She tried to listen past the noise coming from the speakers, but it was too loud. All she could do was hope that she wasn't interrupted.

She slipped the blanket from her shoulders and stood up, her knees creaking. She stepped over the line of the circle and went to the door. She pressed her ear against it, but the heartbeats were still too loud.

Sarah looked down at the floor. It was dirt, just the same as it was in the rest of the room, but it was compacted hard from footfall. She took one of the springs in her hand and scraped at the floor. It made a groove. She scraped again, this time harder, and the groove turned into a small furrow. She knew her plan: if she could dig a hole deep enough, she might be able to get under the door. She had no idea what was on the other side, but at least it gave her a chance, some hope.

She threw herself to the floor and tried to peer under the door. The gap was tight, but she thought she could get through. Sarah started to dig at the floor harder, and then as the compacted soil began to break up, she used her hands and tried to scoop the dirt from around the door. But it was still tightly packed, and she felt her jagged, broken nails bend back painfully when she scraped.

But still she dug, scraping quickly, loosening the soil until she could pile it up next to her feet. And the hole was getting deeper all the time.

She mopped her brow. It was hard work and she hadn't eaten or drunk much over the previous few days, but she knew she had to keep going. She couldn't think about what would happen to her if she was caught, so she knew that this was her only chance.

An hour passed, maybe more, and Sarah had a hole. It looked deep, and she threw her head and shoulders into it, but it still wasn't wide enough. She had to scrape into the other side so that she had an exit. She could see under though. Steps went upwards. What happened when she got up there was something she wouldn't have long to work out.

She resumed her digging, made the hole creep further into the room as her fingers turned bloody, when the spring caught on something.

Sarah stopped and looked into the hole. There was something white, like a twig, snagged in the hook on the bedspring. She scraped around it so that she could see whether it was an obstacle. The twig got longer, its texture like smooth ivory.

Sarah yelped and scuttled backwards. She sat against the wall, looking into the hole, her hand over her mouth. It was a bone, she could tell that now, clean white in contrast to the dark soil around it.

She returned to the hole, nervous now, and dug around the bone, smoothed the soil away from it, treated it with respect. It wasn't an animal bone, she could tell that, some long-forgotten memory of school biology creeping back. It looked like a forearm. She brushed it clean, and when she saw the elbow joint she knew it was human.

Sarah was crying now, her panic rising. People had been buried here. She wasn't the first.

She began to dig further along the arm, to get the hand free, firstly freeing the soil around the wrist, and then the hand itself. She was careful as the fingers were exposed, long white spindles.

Then she saw something on one of the fingers, like a black metal band. She swallowed, felt her stomach lurch. She guessed what it was, but she had to be sure. Her hands were shaking as she cleaned off the dirt with her spit, but when she had finished she went down on her haunches and began to sob.

She looked at the ceiling, wailing, 'No, no, no, no.' And then, through her tears, she looked at her own hand. There, on the third finger of her right hand, was the same black band, the same emblem. A screaming face, silver on black.

Sarah couldn't dig any more. She couldn't crawl over the grave of the ones who had been before. Instead, she started to scrape at the soil around the body.

Chapter Fifty-nine

My fingers drummed nervously against my knee. I had
spent most of the night thinking about what Olwen
had said, how Sarah was a victim, not a murderer, and
how she wasn't the only victim, and I had ended up
being convinced. The internet had thrown up old newspaper reports and tribute websites set up by friends of
the other victims, keeping my printer busy, and a visit
to the archives in the library had filled in some of the
gaps. Now it was time to see what the police thought.

I didn't expect a good reaction, but I was doing what
I thought was right. What happened after that was in
someone else's hands.

I was in the reception area of Blackley police station,
alone, nothing for company but hard plastic seats and
dog-eared posters on the wall, some of them hanging
loose from a corner or two. I had a bag of news clippings by my feet.

I rubbed my eyes. I wondered whether I was doing
too much, if I had crossed the line from chasing the
story to chasing the girl. But then I thought of the letters,
and Olwen, and the Facebook entry. Sarah could die

today, and that would always be on my mind if I didn't do what I could.

I patted my bag, filled with pieces of forgotten history and the family trees. I chewed on the skin around my nails, so that my fingers were feathered by the time Karl Carson appeared in front of me. There was someone else with him. A quieter man, more measured than the ones who had taken me to the moors.

'Ah, it's the Witchfinder General,' said Carson sarcastically.

'Isn't that your job?' I replied, and I saw a flicker of a smile on the other man's face.

'You know how to make yourself conspicuous, Garrett,' said Carson, walking over to me, trying to intimidate me. His colleague behind him was more watchful, and I could feel him assessing me. They seemed like opposites. Fire and ice. The classic team of good cop, bad cop.

'I can just go,' I said, and then I held up the bag. 'Or you can stop puffing your chest out and I can tell you what I know. The story won't take long to write, so if you want to wait for the front-page edition, you can.'

Carson ground his teeth as I stood there for a few seconds, just waiting out the silence, the bag in my hand. It was obvious he was used to being in charge. He took a few deep breaths through his nose, his cheeks just flashing red, before he said, 'So you've been talking to tree-huggers and inbreds around Pendle Hill. It's tourist stuff, nothing more. Witch shops, walking trails, crap like that. Why should I be interested?'

'Because there's a connection,' I said.

Carson looked at his companion, just a raise of the eyebrows, a doubtful look, before he asked, 'With what?'

'With Sarah Goode.'

Carson stepped closer. 'What proof have you got?'

'Are you prepared to think about Sarah as anything other than a murder suspect?' I asked, still holding up the bag.

'In a murder investigation, you have to play the percentages,' he replied.

'And maybe sometimes you have to get creative,' I said. 'Like, why does a young woman from a normal family murder a casual boyfriend? And what if Sarah is in danger?' Before Carson could respond, I added, 'Sarah Goode is a descendant of a Pendle witch, and she is a member of a witches' coven. Members of that coven have been killed over the last ten years, and I think Sarah might be the latest.'

Carson and his colleague looked at each other, surprised.

'A coven?' asked Carson incredulously. And then he started to laugh. 'I'll tell you something, Mr Garrett: every instance of witchcraft I have come across in my police career is nothing much more than middle-aged men trying to persuade young women to take off their clothes. Sometimes the girls are too young, and so we get involved.'

'I bet you've come across a few vicars who have caused you concern too.'

Carson took some deep breaths, and then said quietly, 'This is all very convenient.'

'What do you mean?'

'Your job is to clear Sarah,' he said angrily. 'You were brought into this by Sam Nixon, her wannabe lawyer. No one knows about her involvement in witchcraft, and then Sam Nixon sets you after her, and suddenly it's all talk of covens and old murders.'

'Why would I want to make something up?'

'Because you hope it will give her a defence,' Carson snapped. 'Maybe Sarah does have a family link, and maybe she does go to some kind of coven. But that means nothing. It's kids' stuff. Hocus pocus, fun in the woods, everyone's at it this time of year. Now that she is in trouble, she is making herself out to be some crazy old witch to get some kind of diminished responsibility defence. Avoids a life sentence,' and then he stared at me, 'and perhaps she even has some lawyer telling her how to sound, because he has sent a reporter to follow the trail she has set.'

'You forget that for me this is just a story,' I responded. 'Think about the other options.'

'What like?'

'We know that the witch thing isn't a coincidence, the letters tell us that. And we know the letters are from Sarah.'

Carson glowered at me. 'Those don't get printed. Understand?' The question was brisk.

'But they make one hell of a story, don't you think?'

Carson pointed angrily towards the door from which he had just come. 'In there, now, Mr Garrett,' he growled at me. 'I think we need to talk.'

Chapter Sixty

Sarah didn't move as the noise of the heartbeat stopped and footsteps sounded on the other side of the door. She sat back against the wall and waited for him to enter.

The door opened slowly, as always, rumbling on its runner. As he stepped in, he stopped, his head tilted downwards, towards the hole Sarah had dug during the night.

He lifted his head and looked over towards Sarah, who stared back at him defiantly. Her fear had gone, because she knew where it was going to end. There was no escape, she knew that now, and with the certainty of her end came strength.

His head tilted back towards the hole. Two skeletons exposed, the bones bright, both with the same ring on one hand. When he seemed to look back at Sarah, just his head moving, she held up the springs in her hand, the hooked ends sharpened by the digging.

'I've been busy,' she said, spitting the words out, her hands digging into the springs.

He didn't answer. He let the silence grow.

Sarah swallowed. She had expected a response.

'No way out?' she asked eventually.

He shook his head slowly, his body still.

'How many more?' she asked.

'Just enough,' was the reply.

'Why are you doing this?' Sarah asked, gesturing around her. 'Why are you holding me like this? I've done nothing to you. Neither had they.'

He moved forward quickly and grabbed a handful of Sarah's hair. He pulled her head to the floor and knelt down beside her. Sarah screamed in pain. His hand strained as he pulled her hair tighter. Sarah's hands flailed at his hood, trying to break free, crying out.

He put his head to her ear and whispered, 'We've spoken about this before. We're not so different.'

Sarah froze. She remembered the last time she had stood up to him.

'But what did they do to you?' she hissed through gritted teeth.

He laughed at that. 'No, it's what I did to them that interests you,' and then he held up his hand. 'Enough. No more kindness,' and then he let go of her hair before walking quickly out of the room.

Sarah put her head to the floor and closed her eyes. She stayed like that for a while, just feeling the coldness of the ground against her head, when she heard something. She looked up and saw the other one, the younger one, the hood looser around his head. He was holding another bag.

'One more letter,' he said.

Sarah shook her head. 'No.'

He stepped forward. 'Now's not the time to be a heroine,' he said.

'But what if I don't?'

He pointed towards the hole in the ground. 'And then there were three,' he said, laughing.

Sarah looked down, thought for a few seconds, and then she held out her hand. He put the pen and paper into her hand, along with some pre-prepared script.

She looked at what he was asking her to write, and then at him. Her mouth was open. 'I can't.'

He nodded. 'You will.'

Sarah looked at the hole again, the view blurring as her eyes filled with tears. She wiped her eyes and started to write, copying what he had brought in. When she had finished, she put her head on her arms and started to sob.

She didn't notice when he left the room. She didn't know how long she had been on her own, but when she looked up again, she knew that she was living out the last day of her life.

Chapter Sixty-one

I was pushed towards a small room with a view onto the street outside, the walls once painted bright white but now yellowed by nicotine. I guessed that it was the room where the police took statements, nothing worse than that. As I put my bag of clippings onto the table, Carson burst in after me, the door smacking against the wall, his colleague just behind him.

'You will print nothing about those letters,' he said.

'I'll write whatever makes the story interesting,' I replied. 'And if you know that the letters are from the witch trials, why are you being so dismissive about the witch connections?'

'Sit down, Mr Garrett,' Carson barked.

'No, I won't sit down,' I snapped back. 'I've come here with information. If you already know it, I'll leave. If you don't, then maybe it will help you to know that Sarah will die today.'

'We know about the Facebook entry,' he said sarcastically.

'There's more than that,' I replied.

Carson opened his mouth to speak, and then he closed it again. His colleague stepped forward.

'I'm Sergeant Joe Kinsella,' he said, and he smiled politely. 'Please tell us what you know.'

His voice was more measured, and I saw curiosity in his eyes.

I looked at Carson and saw that he was still angry, but I noticed how Joe Kinsella had an effect on him, that the quieter man kept him in check.

'Okay,' I said, 'maybe you're right: perhaps Sarah did kill Luke in a lover's rage. His death might have sent her over the edge, made her crazy.' I tapped my head with my finger. 'Maybe she has gone, unravelled.'

Carson didn't respond.

'Or maybe Sarah was already crazy,' I said. 'Perhaps she developed some obsession with witchcraft, and in her madness she killed Luke. Perhaps the letters are a manifestation of that. If you are right, that she killed Luke, then she is a dangerous woman, even to herself, and must be caught.'

Carson nodded with mock-graciousness, but then said, 'And I know reason number three. She killed her boyfriend, decided she needed a defence, so she goes to see her crooked defence lawyer, and he tells her to act crazy. She sends some well-researched letters and waits for a sympathetic jury. She will eventually appear on chat shows as the woman who killed and stayed free.'

'You're too cynical,' I said, trying to retrieve the initiative, 'because that wasn't the final possibility. There is a more obvious one.'

'Which is?'

'What if the witchcraft obsession is someone else's? What if Sarah is the victim of that obsession? Think about it. She comes from a stable background, she's close to her family, and there are no known mental problems.'

'Apart from the fact that she is in a witches' coven,' said Carson, 'which doesn't sound like ordinary-girl stuff.'

'But messing around in the woods with salt and candles does not make her a psychotic knife-woman,' I countered. 'So could killing Luke have sent her over the edge? Well, I'm no criminologist, but I can guess one thing: young women do not kill casual boyfriends without a very good reason, and they were not so close that an argument would send Sarah into a blind rage.'

'So go on,' he said, 'inspire me.'

I ignored his sarcasm. 'If it isn't fraud or madness,' I said, 'there is only one option left.' I raised my eyebrows. 'That someone else is responsible for Luke's death.' I paused. 'It is the witch connection that ties Sarah into all this. And if that is the case, then Sarah is in great danger.'

Carson glared at me for a few seconds, and then he started to laugh, except that it was filled with hostility, meant to belittle me. He walked to the door and held it open.

'Goodbye, Mr Garrett. Perhaps you should call in on your girlfriend. She'll be spending her career filling out lost dog reports pretty soon.'

I swung the bag onto the desk. 'If it's just coincidence, there's been a lot of bad luck in Sarah's coven,' I said sarcastically, and nodded towards the bag, the contents spilling onto the table. 'Missing persons, murders and suicides, scattered around the Pendle area, and sometimes further afield. All different, but linked if you look at them the right way.'

Carson looked at the bag, and then back at me. Kinsella stepped forward and began to pull the papers onto the table.

'Linked how?' asked Kinsella.

'They were all descendants of Pendle witches,' I said, 'and they were all members of the same coven.'

Carson spluttered a laugh, but when he realised that Joe Kinsella wasn't joining in, he stepped forward and pushed hard on my shoulder.

'You'd better sit down,' he said, and he was scowling as his colleague closed the door.

Chapter Sixty-two

I opened the bag and started to pull out the rest of its contents.

'Four deaths, and two missing persons, plus Sarah,' I said. I waved a piece of paper, a print-out of an old newspaper report. 'April Mather. Jumped naked from the top of Blacko Tower ten years ago. Thirty years old.' I glanced at the press picture of a smiling woman with long blonde hair, her head thrown back. It seemed such a waste.

'Naked?' asked Carson.

'So the report says.'

'And what the hell is Blacko Tower?'

'An old stone folly close to Pendle Hill,' I replied. 'Some people think it is connected to the Pendle witches, but it isn't. It is just what it looks like: a small tower on a hill.'

'What did the family say about it?' asked Kinsella.

I scanned the words quickly. 'No direct quotes. She was married, one child, a boy. Her husband just wanted to be left to get over his grief undisturbed.'

'What about suspicious circumstances?'

'It doesn't say. Nothing about how she got onto Blacko Tower, or where she had been before then, or why she was naked. But if I keep on looking, I can find out more.' I reached in for another sheet. 'Rebecca Nurse. A nineteen-year-old girl from Higham, a small village not far from the hill. She set off walking to meet some friends in a pub, but she never arrived. The road is a country road, quiet and dark. She was found near to Sabden Brook two days later.' When I saw Carson look at me, I said, 'Sabden Brook is a small stream that runs to Newchurch.'

'How long after the first one?' asked Kinsella.

'Around eighteen months,' I replied.

'And how did she die?'

'Anally raped and strangled,' I said. 'Her hands were tied behind her back and linked to a thin cord around her neck, so that she was strangled by her own efforts to escape, killed like a dog on a choker. The police thought the brook was just a dumping ground, because there were grazes on her, and it's just soggy grassland down there.'

'Suspects?' asked Carson, although his mind seemed elsewhere, as if he was thinking back.

'I don't know,' I said. 'Her boyfriend was away at university, and the papers don't mention any arrest or descriptions. It even went onto *Crimewatch*.'

Carson spluttered a laugh. 'That's like panning for gold.' When I looked confused, he said, 'You can get rich, but on the whole you get more dirt than nuggets.' He nodded towards the bag. 'Next?'

I pulled out the next bundle of papers.

'Mary Lacey,' I said. 'A nurse from Preston. She had an apartment on the docks, and used to walk home down the hill from the town centre, past all the down-and-out guest houses and hovels. One night, she never made it home.'

'I know that one,' said Carson, folding his arms. 'I'd just joined the murder squad. She was found on the banks of the Ribble.'

'That's right, four days later,' I said. 'And she didn't die in the water, did she?'

Carson shook his head. 'No. Raped and strangled.'

'Just like Rebecca Nurse,' I said.

'No rope used, though,' said Carson, scowling. 'If you're trying to say we missed something, there is nothing to say that they were connected.'

'Both raped and strangled and left by water,' I said.

'But the ties weren't used,' Carson replied. 'That's the signature. Mary had been beaten up, and her walk home didn't take her through the best part of town. The best we could come up with was a random sex attacker – you know, because she was on her own and in the wrong place at the wrong time – and just pray that it didn't happen again.'

'Well, it did,' I said. 'The following spring. Susannah Martin. A shop assistant. She went to work and never came home. She was found in some woods near Skipton a week later.'

'Is that all the deaths?' asked Kinsella.

I nodded. 'The other two are just missing persons.'

Carson's mouth twitched for a moment. 'So why do you think they are connected to Sarah Goode?'

I gave him a look of surprise. 'Four members of the same coven die within a few years of each other, and you wonder about the connection?'

Carson ground his teeth and clenched his jaw, so Kinsella intervened and asked, 'So what about the missing persons?'

'There was a gap after the murders, and the missing persons are more recent,' I said. 'One a year over the last two years. Bridget Bishop. She ran a shop in Accrington, selling Celtic jewellery and crystals, all that New Age stuff. One day she was there, and the next day she wasn't. But the business had been struggling, money was tight, and everyone thought she had run away to somewhere warm where the bank couldn't find her. The same for Lizzie Parris. Bit of a local wild child, just twenty, but she had spent the previous three years hitchhiking to festivals and travellers' camps. She set off on one of her trips and never made it home.'

Carson exhaled loudly and flicked through the paper-work dismissively. Kinsella was stroking his chin, and he looked deep in thought.

'So is this everything?' asked Carson.

I nodded. 'I was given a list of names.'

'By whom?'

'I can't say, but I got all this from the internet and the library archives, so it's no great secret. They were all members of the Family Coven, and they have all died or gone missing in the last decade, starting with April Mather.'

Carson exchanged glances with Kinsella and then went to the door, opening it for me. 'Thank you, Mr Garrett. If you'll leave this with us.'

I smiled. 'No problem.' I stopped myself just before I got to the door. 'Did I mention that the four bodies were found on one of the sabbats?'

Carson's irritation returned. 'What the fuck are you talking about?'

'They are the Wicca celebrations, the special days in witchcraft,' I said, enjoying his reaction.

'What, like we have Easter and things like that?' asked Kinsella.

I nodded. 'A closer match than you might think. In Wicca, Easter is called Oestara, as it was in Celtic times, when it was a festival of balance, the twenty-first of March, when day and night are equal and the long nights of winter are slowly disappearing. It's named after Eostre, an Anglo-Saxon goddess whose symbols are the egg and the hare.'

'Easter eggs and Easter bunnies?' he queried.

'It seems that way,' I replied. 'It looks like our Easter has a background that isn't just about Jesus and the resurrection.'

'So these festivals, these sabbats,' queried Carson, his hand still on the door, 'do they always coincide with the discovery of the bodies?'

'It seems that way.'

'But what do these sabbats represent?' asked Kinsella. 'The Christian festivals mark an event. The birth of Christ, his death and resurrection.'

'You have to put the old Celtic festivals into the context of a world built entirely around crops,' I said. 'If the crops failed, people died. In Wicca, there are four major festivals, all built around the crop cycles and seasons.

Imbolg is the second of February, when the buds first appear. Beltane is the first of May, when the blossom comes out. Lammas is the first of August, when the harvests begin, and Samhain is when the frosts begin.'

'And what date is Samhain?' asked Carson.

I saw Kinsella's eyes grow keen. It looked like he'd guessed the answer.

'It's today,' I said. 'We call it Halloween. In ancient times they called it Samhain, and it was the start of winter. The Celts put a spiritual slant on it. Samhain was the end of the Celtic year, and they said that it was when the veil between the land of the living and of the dead was at its thinnest.'

'So that's why you are saying that Sarah Goode will die today,' said Carson incredulously, 'because it fits in with some ancient Celtic festival?'

I took a deep breath. 'It is quite possible.'

'So tell me how the others fitted into these sabbats.'

'Remember April Mather?' I asked. 'The first one, who jumped naked from Blacko Tower?'

Carson nodded.

'That was Samhain,' I said. 'Ten years ago today. And Rebecca Nurse,' I continued, my hands flicking through the paperwork. 'She was the girl who disappeared on the way to the pub, found down by the brook. That was Imbolg: the second of February. As I go through the list, it is the same thing. Mary Lacey, the nurse from Preston found by the river. Beltane: the first of May. So was Susannah Martin, the young shop assistant found in the woods.' I put down my list. 'Sarah will die today,' I said solemnly, 'and so I'll let you two get on with some police work.'

'And where are you going?' asked Carson.

'Back to the beginning,' I said, and then I left the room. But before I closed the door, I glanced in and saw the two detectives looking at the pile of papers on the desk, and then at each other. Neither of them moved.

Chapter Sixty-three

The wind was blowing crisply through the Pendle valley as I walked towards Blacko Tower. I had my collar hitched up to my ears and my hands thrust deep into my pockets.

I remembered Katie's words: go back to the start. The story has to start somewhere, and Blacko Tower seemed to be the death furthest back. April Mather had jumped from it ten years earlier, and a few photographs might add a good touch. But it was more than that. I felt like I was in a race against time.

The tower was easy to find, about thirty feet high with a castellated top, sitting proudly on a hill that rose out of the Pendle valley like a hump, but I had to clamber over a gate to begin the climb. When I got up to it, the tower wasn't very wide, with just enough room for a winding staircase leading to a view from the top, so that it was like a giant chess piece, the rook, dropped into the countryside. As I looked around, the view was spectacular, looking down onto farm buildings and a few houses from a nearby village. I took some photographs and made some notes, just first impressions, when I heard someone shout. A quad bike headed towards me, the noise of the engine getting louder as it struggled to make it up the hill.

The rider jumped off as he got near, and I saw from the look on his face that he hadn't come over to pass the time of day.

'What the bloody hell do you think you are doing here?'

He looked to be in his fifties, too old to be on a quad bike, but his rosy skin and the redness of his knuckles told me that he'd spent most of his life outdoors.

'Taking pictures,' I said innocently.

'This is private land,' he bellowed at me.

I looked around theatrically. 'I didn't see the sign.'

'Well, look harder.'

'Is it your land?'

The man shook his head. 'No, but I help the owner keep an eye on it. This time of the year, all the Goths and black arts crowd come here to hum at the moon, or whatever they do.'

I smiled. 'I suppose what happened to April Mather must make the landowner nervous.'

He stalled at that, and then looked at me with suspicion. 'Who are you?'

'Jack Garrett, a reporter. I'm writing a story on the tower.' It was a partial lie, but it was too early to tip people off about the story. 'Do you remember the April Mather death?'

He nodded slowly, unsure whether he should respond.

'Did it seem suspicious at the time?'

331

He started to smile. 'Not with all those witnesses.'

'What do you mean?'

'Like I say, Halloween attracts all the local weirdos. Most people go to Pendle Hill, but a few make their way here, and back then, Halloween at the tower was like a bonfire party.'

'And April Mather? Did you know her?'

'Everyone knew April Mather,' he said with a smirk.

'What do you mean?'

'Her father was some local big-shot,' he replied, 'and April seemed to like pissing him off. I used to see her in the pubs round here from when she was fourteen. No one asked her age because she took up with the local biker crowd.' He shook his head dismissively. 'They are worse than the tree-huggers for lighting fires.'

'Wasn't she a bit young for them?'

He chuckled. 'If you were young, attractive and promiscuous, they only cared that you were legally old enough, and she was by the time they got round to her. Just.' He leaned in and whispered, even though there was no one around to overhear, 'The police raided a pub once, because the landlord was serving cheap ale to the local kids. When they got there, they found April Mather lying on a pool table, wearing nothing below the waist but the hairy-arsed biker she was humping, with the rest of the pub either cheering her on or standing there with their dicks in their hands, waiting their turn.' He shook his head. 'She was seventeen years old.'

'I can see why she would be remembered,' I said. 'But

the April Mather I read about was a married woman with a child.'

He curled his lip in distaste. 'She was a mess, in here,' he said, tapping his head with his finger, 'and people started to get sick of her. So she set up with one of the bikers more seriously, kept herself in with the crowd, and they set up a bike workshop together, knocking out custom choppers. They had a little boy, and for a few years she calmed down, but then she started drinking again, and I mean seriously drinking. I saw her a few times staggering along the lanes. Almost hit her once.'

'What, she lived nearby?'

'Aye,' he said, turning round to point at an old stone cottage on a ridge a few hundred yards away. 'That's what drew her here, to the tower. I reckon she saw the bonfire and came over, hoping for a party. She was drunk when she got here, and brought some whisky with her.'

'You sound like you were there,' I said.

He gave me a wry smile. 'I was. That's why I keep people away from here now, because of what I saw.'

'Which was?'

'Some pissed-up biker girl making a nuisance of herself. She was falling around, shouting, flirting, with men and women. She upset a few people, and we would have taken her away, but we didn't want her coming back with a pack of angry bikers, so we just put up with her.'

'So how did she die?' I asked.

He seemed to lose some of his smile at that, the

memory of April's death souring his relish at recounting the tale.

'She started getting all maudlin, like whisky drinkers do, crying and complaining, saying that she was evil. There was some scaffolding around the tower, just for some maintenance work. At midnight, she climbed up the tower on the scaffolding. When she got to the top, she stripped naked and started to shout at us below.'

'What did people do?'

'Laughed, mainly. Some told her to be careful, but we were all drunk by then as well. But what we didn't know was that she had taken a ten-foot length of wire with her and hooked it around a scaffold pole. The other end was in a loop, and it was as sharp as cheese wire. She stood on the edge and made a speech, something about, "Do what you will and it harm none".' He looked down and took a deep breath. 'Then she jumped.' He looked at me, and I saw the pain in his eyes. 'She'd put the loop around her neck, and it took off her head like a pea being popped from its pod.'

I nodded, understanding, attempting to stay calm, but my mind was trying to remember the quotes. It didn't seem like the right time to pull out my notepad, and I cursed myself for not switching on my voice recorder.

'So it was a definite suicide,' I said, almost to myself.

He nodded at me. 'Unless there was an invisible hand that pushed her, she did it all herself.'

I thanked him and set off back down the hill, heading for my next visit. As I got lower, wondering how a suicide fitted in with Sarah Goode and the other murdered girls,

334

I heard an engine start and saw the roof of a white van setting off along the country lane.

I ran to where I had left my car, and just made it over the gate when I saw the van disappear around the corner.

Chapter Sixty-four

I called Olwen before I set off for his house. I owed him an update, although I wasn't sure what I had to report. April Mather had been a definite suicide, and so I was down to three murders. I checked my watch. It was just after one, the day moving on too fast.

I had an address and directions for a house on a country lane, and I almost missed it, just a small sign obscured by long grasses. As my tyres rattled over a cattle grid and then echoed between dry-stone walls, I got the feeling that I had been there before.

Olwen's home had a name, *Tindale Cottage*, not a number, written in bold white on a black sign. It was two-storey, with a centre porch and ivy creeping up the walls, and as I stepped out of the car, my footsteps scraped on stones on the dirt track and I shielded my eyes as sunlight twinkled off the damp grass.

I had been there before, though, I knew it, and I scanned the fields around the cottage, my hand over my eyes so that I could see.

Then I saw it, just a glimmer, a flash of light in the grass.

I ran to the side of the house, away from its shadow, and jumped onto a stone wall to get a better view. 'Shit!' I exclaimed, and jumped down. I was by Sabden Brook, where Rebecca Nurse had been found. I looked further along the lane and I saw where I had been the day before. I had come in the opposite way, that's all.

I glanced at Olwen's house and got a sense that something wasn't right. Why hadn't he mentioned this the night before? Was I being played? And how easy was it to get to the site of the body from his house?

I walked away from his house and towards the brook, and the lane seemed suddenly secretive and hidden, high walls stopping anyone seeing into it.

Sabden Brook was the same as it had been the day before, just a trickle of water, and stones scraped and wobbled as I scrambled over the wall next to it. When I got to the place where Rebecca had been found, I knelt down and touched the ground. I didn't know why. Perhaps it was a desire to make it real, to touch something as solid as a rock, so that it would become more than a collection of old murder stories bundled together by some crackpot theory.

The grass just felt like what it was: coarse strands of moorland grass blowing in the breeze beside a slender ribbon of water. I felt no great connection. Instead, just deflation.

I whirled around quickly when I heard something behind me, a rustle in the grass. Olwen was standing there, his hands behind his back, his ponytail blowing in the wind.

'Did it give you any special inspiration?' he asked.

'What do you mean?' I replied, wondering how long he had been there.

'It's nothing special to you, is it?' he said. 'Just an old story, a forgotten murder in a quiet Lancashire field.'

I looked back at the rock. 'Did you scratch that symbol?'

He nodded. 'People forgot too quickly.'

'But why didn't you tell me that you lived next to where she was found?'

His eyes twinkled. 'The story isn't about me.'

'What else are you keeping back from me?' I asked.

'Nothing else that matters.' Before I could respond, he continued, 'Why did you want to speak to me?'

'Professional courtesy,' I replied. 'I went to the police this morning, told them what you told me.'

'Did you tell them about me?'

I shook my head. 'I don't reveal sources, I told you that.'

He nodded at me. 'Thank you.'

'Do you want to know any more?'

He shook his head. 'You will have done what you thought was right.'

'And what now, Olwen?'

He smiled. 'It is Samhain, and we will pray for Sarah.'

I grabbed his arm. 'Is that it?' I asked, shocked. 'You told me that Sarah will die today, and all you are going to do is pray, leave me to do everything?'

He pulled his arm away. 'Sometimes prayer is all we have,' and then he stepped away, walking back to his cottage.

I didn't move until the door to his cottage closed. I looked around and saw the chimneys of Newchurch in the distance, the church tower in the middle, squat and square. I could see paths worn into the countryside around me, the hikers' trails that headed off in all directions. I realised again why it would have appealed so much to someone involved in murder. So many paths in, so many paths out, but hidden from view.

'There's only one thing for it then,' I muttered to myself as I looked towards the church. 'It's time for some spiritual inspiration.'

Carson glanced over as Joe came into the Incident Room.

'What are you looking at?' Carson asked.

Joe waved some computer print-outs. 'I've pulled some of the information on the names Garrett gave us before.'

'And?' Carson asked.

Joe's mouth twitched, unsure, and then he gave a small smile. 'He might have something.'

Carson put his head back and breathed out noisily. Everyone else looked up, the pressed shirts, the scrubbed faces.

'What do you mean, "he might have something"?'

Joe held up the print-outs. 'I thought it when he said it, that the names were familiar. And he was right, the deaths did happen on the dates he mentioned.'

'That doesn't mean anything.'

'It means it isn't bullshit.'

Carson had his hands on his hips, unsure what to say.

'Do you know something else about East Lancashire?' Joe asked.

'The gene pool gets shallower the nearer you get to the hills?' replied Carson sarcastically. 'I don't know, surprise me.'

'It has the worst record in Lancashire for unsolved murders,' said Joe.

Carson waved it away. 'Populations distort figures,' he countered. 'A couple of rogue cases in a rural area make it look like gangland, but really it means nothing.'

Joe shook his head. 'I'm not talking per head of population,' he said. 'I'm talking absolute figures. The cold-case drawer must be bulging around here.'

Carson paused, thinking about what Joe was saying, and then said, 'It's also the divorce capital of England, so maybe the domestics count for most.'

'They would be easier to solve, by definition,' said Joe. He looked at Carson, tapping his lip with a pen. 'I want to keep digging,' he said. 'And I want McGanity with me.'

'McGanity?' queried Carson, and looked around the room. The faces staring back at him were waiting for his answer, wondering whether Joe would be allowed to make a fool of himself.

'She's the one who can tell us what Garrett is doing,' Joe added.

Carson scowled as he thought about that, and then snapped, 'All right then, but keep me in the loop.'

Joe nodded, smiling, and left the room. As everyone else watched him go, Carson barked, 'If any of you have

340

got any better ideas, then speak to me, but until you do, button it,' and then he slammed the door as he left, heading for the station yard. He needed to be on his own for a while.

Chapter Sixty-five

I walked to the church yard again, looking for the vicar. I remembered our last conversation, and I reckoned he knew things about Pendle's other religion, and Olwen, its apparent leader. The wind was picking up, so the sound of my footsteps on the gravel was drowned out by the crackle of branches as they blew against one another, but the church yard was deserted.

I found the vicarage further up the hill. The vicar was at home, although when he opened the door I saw that he wasn't wearing his dog collar. He must have caught me looking at his throat, because he gave me that icy smile and said, 'It's a collar, not a shackle.' He stepped aside. 'Come in.'

I had to stoop as I walked through his house, the ceilings and oak beams right above my head, the doorways designed for a time when people were much shorter. Local landscapes dotted the walls, and I was shown into a room lined with books. I saw an open one by a high-backed chair in front of an open fire. The heat hit me in a blast, and straight away I felt comfortable. It was a room to fall asleep in, with a view over the fields and the crackle of burning wood by my feet, and I wondered whether the vicar felt closer to God in his room than in his church.

'Do you remember me?' I asked.

'You're the young man from the church yard,' he replied. 'And you've come back.'

'Would you mind answering a few more questions about people from your parish?'

He held out his hand as if to gesture at me to carry on, so I asked, 'Rebecca Nurse. You said you remembered her?'

The vicar exhaled loudly and nodded. 'The girl by the brook. That wasn't very nice at all.' He paused for a few seconds, and then said, 'She was a sweet girl though, but she was going through some wild times back then, just kicking back at her parents. They were good people, but they were occasional worshippers, and so stopped seeing the good in God when Rebecca was killed. Things like that even make me doubt Him, when I see what evil He allows to happen.'

'In what way was Rebecca rebelling?'

'In the way that kids do. They experiment, try to shock.'

'Do you know that she dabbled in witchcraft?'

The vicar's face turned into a frown as he cast his mind back. 'She was one of Olwen's disciples.'

That surprised me, Olwen's name coming up unprompted. The vicar must have spotted my surprise, because he asked, 'Do you know Olwen?'

I nodded. 'We've met.'

The vicar considered me carefully. 'He's a child of the sixties,' he answered.

'What do you mean?'

'Just that. He had a strict upbringing, but he was a young boy when the sixties really got going, and so saw himself differently to how his parents saw him. We knew each other, nodding acquaintances, but as I was drawn to God, he was drawn to the hippie scene, all that dancing in the woods, sitting around campfires and taking drugs – except that around here there weren't many drugs available.'

'But there is something different about Olwen,' I said. 'He's a descendant of a Pendle witch, so maybe that made him feel different.'

The vicar laughed and shook his head.

'What's wrong?' I asked.

'Young man,' he said, still chuckling, 'most of the people around here are related in some way to a Pendle witch, or so they say. Those unlucky men and women were from local families, and so they left other family members. I'm not convinced by most of the claims, and most people rely on a name. Nutter. Whittle. Bulcock. Common names around here.'

'So it's no big deal then?'

He laughed again. 'I could even be a descendant, but the records aren't detailed enough to be sure.'

'I've seen the family tree,' I replied.

The vicar rubbed his eyes. 'Olwen is a fantasist,' he said wearily. 'I've seen that family tree. He has drawn it up himself. I would be surprised if you had to go back too many generations to find the first error. Seeing a piece of paper with names on doesn't make any of it true. All of this lifestyle is made up. He was just plain old Michael Smith back in the sixties, but somewhere along the way he became Olwen.'

'So where did the hippie thing take him?' I asked, curious now.

The vicar considered me carefully. His fingers were steepled under his nose and he looked thoughtful.

'You know where it took him,' he said eventually. 'Witchcraft.'

'Is that widely known?' I asked.

The vicar smiled. 'Everyone knew back then. He conducted ceremonies in the woods, lit candles in the middle of the night. It's a small village – things like that don't go unnoticed.'

'Did he get any trouble from the locals?'

'No, not around here. Pendle Hill attracts people who are drawn to its history. He was no different.'

'So you have heard of the Family Coven?' I ventured.

I expected the vicar to look blankly at me, or to look angry. Instead, he broke into a smile.

'Olwen's disciples, like I told you. Most are getting old now, just more sixties remnants, but he became a bit of a mover in his circle. People who showed an interest in the occult were targeted by him, and it is women he concentrates on – the thought of getting a woman barely into her twenties to stand in front of him as naked as God created her is too strong for him to resist.'

'But isn't he carrying on an old tradition?' I said. 'A line of witchcraft going right back to the Pendle witches?'

The vicar was clearly amused. 'Did he tell you that?' he asked, still chuckling. Then he shook his head and said, 'No, you've no need to tell me, because I can see the answer in your face. He started the tradition sometime during the eighties. He picked up most of it from books and television, carved it out into a sect, really just for his own fun.'

'But he has followers,' I protested.

'He has a few ageing hippies, just like himself,' he countered, 'and through the years a few have passed through his coven, just a phase, a passing interest in the alternative. He shows them some interest and then mocks up some family tree to tie them into a blood line that they didn't know they had.'

'But that would be easy to disprove,' I said.

'Not if you don't want to disprove it,' he replied.

'So you don't believe in witchcraft?' I asked.

'The witch trials of four hundred years ago were just what you think they were, the product of a misguided time. The area moved on, but then people like Olwen turned it into a lifestyle choice. But I don't mind if people like Olwen want to hold ceremonies. Let them, I say. God will be their judge, not me.' Then he sighed. 'This is all linked to Rebecca, I presume.'

I nodded. 'She was in his coven.'

'And April Mather?'

I nodded again.

He looked down, his eyes mourning an old memory. 'A few years on, Rebecca would have grown out of it. Maybe she would have come back to God. My God. Our God.' Then he swallowed, his face filled with sadness. 'April is a more obvious guess though. I knew her parents, good people, but they lost control of her when she got involved with the local bikers. It wasn't their fault, she was always wayward, and I met her husband, Dan, a couple of times. Dan wasn't a bad man. He'd had a rough upbringing himself; his mother ran away when he was a young boy, left him to grow up with his grandmother. But April kept his life steady, and it seemed like he loved her.'

'And she was drawn to Olwen?'

The vicar nodded. 'He preys on people like her. The vulnerable, the confused, the disenchanted. He gives them an outlet.'

'Are you saying it was partly his fault?'

He thought about that, and then he said, 'No. They would have chosen their own path. Olwen isn't a bad man; he is just misguided.'

'Rebecca was found next to Olwen's house,' I said. 'Did you know that?'

The vicar nodded. 'Olwen found her.'

I felt a crackle down my spine, like a shiver, and sweat jumped onto my palms.

'Olwen found her?' I repeated, surprised.

'Yes. He called the police, and they found him hugging her body when they got there.'

I looked into the fire, at the flames as they danced along the black chimney breast, at the smoke being sucked into the chimney.

'I didn't know that,' I said quietly.

'Is there any reason why you should have known?'

I shook my head, and then thanked the vicar for his hospitality, leaving him to his fire and his book.

My phone rang as I got back to my car. 'It's Joe

Kinsella,' said the voice as I answered it. 'Do you want to come back down to the station, to go through what we've found?'

I looked around, at the lines of dry-stone walls, at the dark grass reflecting the mood from the clouds drawn into Pendle Hill. I wanted to get back to civilisation.

'I won't be long,' I replied, and then I climbed into my car. The Stag sounded loud as the engine started, and despite the cold I put the roof down; I wanted to feel the slap of the cold October day across my face. Time was running out, and I was no nearer to finding Sarah.

Chapter Sixty-six

Joe Kinsella was waiting for me as I arrived at the police station. He looked relaxed, composed, much different from the detectives who had taken me to the moors.

There were steps leading to the front door, and as I bounded up them, he said, 'Follow me, Mr Garrett.'

I almost broke into a trot as we walked along deserted corridors, those that the public never walked. It felt strange to be there. When I'd lived in London I had made a few police contacts, so visits to the station were frequent, just for those 'an insider said' talks, designed to get information out there that the police can't say explicitly. Sometimes people need a nudge that the police share their suspicions before they will come forward. In Blackley, the police station was Laura's world, and so I didn't cross the threshold, and tried to keep our working lives apart the best I could.

But this was a development, although I knew the reason was something other than goodwill: it was about control. They wanted what I had, either to use or hold back.

As we walked, it seemed like Sarah Goode was the

only case in town. The corridor was filled with boxes, the rooms empty, most of the regular staff already moved to the concrete and glass building on the edge of town. I could see why they were going. The light was dim, the station networked by long, windowless corridors, and the walls looked tired and dirty. It was packed full of the town's memories, decades of misdemeanours, but it was no place to work.

I heard Joe Kinsella say, 'He's a good copper, you know.'

I stopped. 'Carson?' I asked incredulously.

Joe nodded. 'Yeah, believe it or not. He's a bully – I know that, and he knows it too – but he has a good nose.'

'His nose didn't seem so good on this case.'

'Trust me, if he didn't think there was something in it, you wouldn't be here. He might be old school, but if one of your loved ones was hurt, you would want Karl Carson in charge of the hunt.'

I wondered about that. Maybe I just didn't like mystery tours to the moors and the long walk back.

When I didn't respond, Joe turned and kept on walking. We went past what looked like the main Incident Room, with people looking through paperwork or glued to computer screens.

'Maybe it's time to start again,' said Joe.

I saw that it was meant as an apology, and so I shrugged it off. 'Don't worry about it. Maybe I prefer some old-school policing.'

Joe smiled. 'Good.' Then he saw my laptop case in my hand. 'Writing it up already?' he asked.

'Just getting the basics down,' I said.

'And where is it leading?'

'Do you know Olwen, the coven leader?' I asked.

'I haven't met him yet, but Laura's told me all about him.'

'Is he known to the police? Try the name Michael Smith. That's his real name.'

'Why?'

'He found Rebecca Nurse, the girl by the brook.'

Joe looked surprised at that, and then he began to smile.

'What's funny?' I asked.

'Just a train of thought,' he replied, and then he said, 'You do know what you are suggesting in your article?'

'Pretty much so.'

'That there is a serial killer at work in Lancashire, and that we have missed it.'

'I wouldn't put it so strongly.'

'There isn't another way to put it,' Joe said. 'You are saying that someone has been killing members of a coven for years now, and is still at large.'

'I'm writing a story, that's all.'

'No, you're not,' Joe protested. 'You are treading on people's memories of their loved ones. You have to be careful.'

'Maybe there aren't as many as I thought,' I said.

'Why?'

'April Mather was a definite suicide,' I said. 'I've spoken to an eye-witness.'

Joe nodded thoughtfully. 'There are others though.'

'Yeah, but when you start to lose some out of the list,'

I said, 'the list is less compelling. We have Rebecca, the girl by the brook, and two others, plus a couple of missing persons, who might just be that: missing.'

'So, if there is no one targeting witches,' said Joe, 'we are back to Sarah as a murderer.'

I nodded in agreement.

At that, Joe opened the door to a room that was filled with desks but looked devoid of life. Pieces of paper were scattered on the floor, those scraps that hadn't made the move to the new station, and the yellowing paint was covered in white patches where pictures and memos had once been taped to the wall.

And Laura was sitting in a chair by the window. She smiled at me. 'Hello Jack.'

I smiled back. 'It looks like we've got a good team.'

'Let's go through the case then,' said Joe, 'because we need to know whether you're wrong – because if you're right, Sarah hasn't got long to live.'

Chapter Sixty-seven

Joe put photographs onto a desk, and as I leaned over I saw that they were pictures of Sarah Goode, her auburn hair shining, her smile relaxed. Next to her, Joe placed pictures of Luke's body. My eyes were drawn to the images. The muscular young body, the ribbon of red over the chest, and the dark stain on the sheet. I stepped closer. I saw how he was leaning out of bed, his hand on the floor, knuckles down, his arm flaccid. But it was the middle of the chest that drew my eye; it was the knife, only the handle visible, an ordinary black-handled kitchen knife standing up from the chest like it was jammed in there.

'Does she look like the sort of woman who would do that?' I asked, almost to myself.

'I learned a long time ago not to look at appearances,' Joe said. 'But what about this?' And then he placed some more photographs onto the desk.

I leaned forward and nodded, tried to hide my shock. I knew what Joe was doing; he was showing me that this was more than just a story, that the victims were real people.

The photographs were of a naked young woman, her hands tied behind her back, the cord going up to her neck and round, so that if she pulled with her hands she would make it tighter around her neck. I had seen that knot before, in the ceremony, as part of the initiation. This body was by a stream, and although the colours were faded now, I recognised it as Sabden Brook, next to Olwen's cottage.

'Rebecca Nurse,' I said solemnly, and then looked again.

It was her skin that struck me. Her legs looked too smooth, ill-defined, the muscles no longer working, just pale limbs with no form to them. In the next photograph there was a close-up of her face. Although it was lifeless, it was still possible to see the pretty young woman, all innocence and youth.

Joe dropped another photograph onto the desk. I looked at him, my eyebrows raised.

'Mary Lacey,' said Joe, 'the girl killed in Preston.'

I looked at the picture, Laura looking over my shoulder, and I saw how different the two images looked. Rebecca's body looked ritualistic, symbolic. Mary's body seemed like just another murder victim, her clothing loose, the bruising showing up as dark stains.

I sighed, but couldn't bring myself to say anything.

Joe floated the last one down. 'This is the worst of all.'

I grimaced and turned away, Laura gasped just behind me, but after a few seconds I knew I had to look back.

It was a body, although only just recognisable as that. It was in a small pit, the head unnaturally bent forward, sitting down with the legs pulled up, so that it seemed to be in the foetal position. The whole body was charred, burnt to a crisp, the teeth bared in a grotesque grin, and the bones showed through the skin, making the legs and arms look stick-thin. And there was mud on the body, as if it had just been dug up out of the ground.

I looked at Joe.

'Susannah Martin,' he said. 'Found like this in a small copse just outside Skipton.'

Laura leaned forward and picked up the picture of Susannah. 'It seems different from the other two,' she said. 'They were left on display, but Susannah was burned and buried, wasn't she?'

'All the witch killings are different,' said Joe, 'and so if they are connected, that is why we have missed the link. They are just three unsolved murders, still live, but overtaken by others, waiting for a cold-case review.'

'So Susannah was burnt to destroy the body, to frustrate forensics?' I asked.

'No,' said Joe, shaking his head, and then he tapped the photograph with his finger. 'Susannah Martin was alive when she was set alight.'

I looked away and shuddered, not wanting to see the photograph any more, the image of what she must have gone through.

'How do we know?' asked Laura, her tone cold and professional.

'There was tissue reaction,' Joe replied. When I looked confused, he said, 'If someone is alive in intense heat like that, there is a reaction in the tissue cells, as the tissues are still alive to react.' He exhaled loudly. 'I read the post-mortem report earlier. It makes for grim reading. In high-temperature situations, the tissues can rupture, and splits appear like slash wounds. The pathologist dissected those ruptures to look for the reaction, and he found it.' Joe tapped the photographs. 'All that was going on as she was alive.'

I forced myself to look at the photographs and shook my head. 'He is a cruel bastard,' I said quietly.

'There is something else too,' said Joe, 'but it messes up your theory.'

I looked up. 'What?'

'Rebecca Nurse,' he said. 'The girl by the brook. She was the victim of a serial killer, but her murder had nothing to do with witchcraft.'

When I looked shocked, he added, 'We know who killed her.'

Chapter Sixty-eight

Joe bent down to a box by his feet, crammed nearly to the top with paperwork and files. I could see the sheen of photographs, yellow Post-it notes indexing bundles, maps, drawings, bound reports.

'As you can see,' he grunted, as he heaved the box onto a table, 'I've done some digging around.'

I whistled. 'Are they all the files?'

He shook his head. 'Just the main parts. You know, the summaries, the incident logs, police intelligence prints.'

'How did you know where to look?' I asked.

'Because we know who did this,' Joe said. 'And he harmed more people than Rebecca Nurse.'

I looked at the papers again and licked my lips nervously. 'So what have you got there?'

'Murders, rapes, attacks, attempted rapes,' he answered.

'But he hasn't been caught, has he?' I said.

Joe shook his head. 'No, he hasn't.'

'So how can you be sure?' I asked.

Joe shrugged. 'Just intuition,' he said, and then scattered

more photographs across the desk. As I leaned forward, I saw that they were of different women. Two of them. But the images were similar: young women, slim, light-coloured hair, their hands tied behind their backs, rope around their necks, their clothes dishevelled. Just like Rebecca.

'Who are they?' I asked.

As Laura rummaged through them, Joe picked up two of the photographs. 'These two women were killed within a year of each other, not long before April Mather jumped from Blacko Tower.'

'Any connection with the Family Coven?' I asked, looking at the dead women.

'Only that their killer also murdered Rebecca Nurse,' he said. Joe floated one of the pictures back to the desk. 'The first was from Blackpool, a runner, and her jog took her along the sea-front and all the way to Lytham, when she would turn back at the sand dunes. One day, she never made it back. She was killed and dumped in the dunes, and she died like Rebecca, with a cord around her wrists and up and around her neck. The other girl, Beth Howe, was a student at the university in Preston. One night, she didn't take the student safety bus home, set off walking to her boyfriend's flat, but she never arrived. She was found by the side of the A6, just on the other side of the motorway, killed in the same way, with a cord around her wrists and up and around her neck. Just like Rebecca.'

'You said you know who killed these women,' said Laura.

'Mack Lowther,' Joe replied, and he grimaced. 'A real

nasty bastard. He went for school kids mainly, enticing them in with fags and booze, which then turned into sex. When he was younger, it seemed more like a party and so a lot of girls went along with him, but he took drugs, and so his teeth went, and his complexion went, and by the time he was thirty he looked twice his age. The school kids kept going round for the fags and booze though, but he wasn't getting what he expected. He would get nasty, hurt them, tell them that he would tell their parents if they didn't do what he asked. Until one of them didn't care what her parents thought, and so the police got involved. When Beth Howe was killed, he was living in a bail hostel, waiting for his trial for forcing an underage girl to do things to him that she didn't want to do. The problem is that all the hostel can do is provide a bed and a no-booze rule, and so Mack Lowther spent his time just wandering around. Not long before his trial, Beth Howe was found dead.'

'And so Mack Lowther was the suspect?' I said, guessing the answer.

'Number one,' Joe confirmed. 'The hostel wasn't far from where she had been last seen, and he couldn't account for his movements. And he liked the rough stuff. Ligatures, anal, that kind of stuff. It was all about pain and humiliation, not about the sex.'

'Why wasn't he convicted of Beth's murder?' Laura asked.

'No direct evidence,' Joe said, with a sigh. 'No DNA. No fibre transfer. Beth Howe came up blank, forensically. We knew he had done it, just from the sneer on his face, but we couldn't prove it. He did twelve months for the sexual assault on the young girl, and was then back on the streets. Not long after that, Rebecca Nurse was killed. Once more, he didn't have an alibi.'

'So what was the problem?' I asked. 'Why wasn't Mack Lowther caught for Rebecca Nurse's murder?'

'Once again, a clean forensic sweep, but whatever chance we had was taken away when fate intervened,' said Joe.

'Fate?' I asked.

'In the shape of a hammer, or something similar,' Joe replied. 'He was beaten to death in his crappy little flat; neighbourhood revenge was our guess. And do you know what: no one saw anything.'

I ran my fingers through my hair, feeling deflated now. 'So we've got a suicide, and a murder by some local pervert.'

Joe nodded. 'That leaves two murders connected to the coven – Mary, who was found by the river, and Susannah, found burned – plus two missing persons. And add in this: maybe witchcraft attracts the misfits, the unconventional. Perhaps it takes less to make them run away. Don't forget April Mather's suicide. Maybe some things are just how they seem, some unhappy tales and a coincidence.'

I exhaled loudly, feeling frustrated. Things didn't feel right, and I still had the feeling that Sarah was in danger.

'And what if you are wrong about Mack Lowther?' I said. 'What if he didn't kill Rebecca Nurse?'

'We know that whoever killed Rebecca killed the two women before her; we know that from the way she died, the knots used, the profile of the killer. And the profile is often the best indicator.'

'What do you mean?' I asked.

'It tells us that the person who killed Rebecca and the other two before her was a white man from Preston, just like Mack Lowther,' Joe replied.

I looked back at him, surprised. 'How do you know that?'

'The white-man part is easy,' he replied. 'All serial killers are white, and all violent serial killers are men.' He noticed my expression and added, 'Female serial killers murder in a different way. You know, the nurses who kill while on duty. Female serial killers murder passively. Men kill aggressively.'

'And the white part?' I asked. 'Is that true?'

Joe smiled, the twinkle of his eyes telling me that he was enjoying himself. 'It's a hobby of mine, criminology,' he said. 'Always has been. For as long as I've been on the murder squad, I've kept up to date with all the latest studies and theories. Police work is about playing the percentages, going after the most probable. Understanding how criminals think helps to narrow the odds, and from what I've read, serial killers are invariably white.'

'Why is that?' asked Laura.

'No one knows,' said Joe, 'or else, no one dares say it. But in each case, you have to look at the victim for the biggest clue, and each victim was white.' He pointed at the box of papers. 'They were each found some distance from where they were last seen, so a vehicle was involved, and there seems to be some planning, some watching and waiting.'

'How do you know that?' I asked.

'Because there are no reports in any of these cases of people being abducted in public, no struggles into waiting cars, no muggings in the street. Whoever did these murders would have been driving around, patrolling the streets, maybe watching his victims, waiting for the right time to strike. And how would you describe the ethnic make-up of Lancashire?'

I thought about the faces I saw, the new influx of Poles and Iraqis, the working-class white boys, Pakistani Muslims.

'Diverse,' I said.

'Exactly,' said Joe. 'And what about where they live?'

I smiled, seeing what he meant. The whites and Asians lived separately, in cluster communities, rubbing shoulders but not shaking hands.

'Apart,' I said.

Joe smiled back at me. 'So what chance is there of an Asian or black man being able to patrol white communities, looking for women, without being noticed? No chance, that is the answer. Think of Rebecca Nurse, walking to the pub from her house in Higham. An Asian man patrolling the country lanes around there would be remembered, somebody would have called it in. But for a white man, being white is his disguise – he's inconspicuous, the killer's get-out clause, so he can back out if things don't go as planned.'

'So what makes them, killers like this?' I asked.

'Serial killers are born, not made,' Joe replied, 'but something has to trigger them off. Their upbringings can seem okay on the outside – parents still together, stable families in nice neighbourhoods – but their lives tend to be messed up on the quiet: family histories of psychiatric disturbance, alcohol and drug abuse, with sexual violence in the home, but we don't always know that. They retreat into fantasy, an escapist world they create, and they play out hostilities in that secret world. But then there is a trigger, something that makes them step out of the fantasy world and start killing in the real world.'

'What, so there might be potential killers around that just haven't been triggered?'

'Think of wartime,' Joe said, his eyebrows raised, 'and what ordinary soldiers do. What do you think trauma-tises veterans most?'

'Seeing comrades killed?' I guessed.

Joe shook his head. 'Wrong. It's the people *they* killed, the ones they saw die right in front of them, because that's something they did, on their conscience. In the Second World War, a fifth of soldiers aimed to miss, not kill. But then think of how some behave, in the name of revenge or cleansing, killing and raping civilians. Ordinary people do that, not just generals. You see, some people are born to kill, and others aren't.'

'So how do you spot these people?'

'You can spot them young,' he said, sighing, 'but you can't do anything about it. Animal cruelty, arson, things like that, they're the danger signs, but a lot of kids do that kind of thing.' Then he leaned forward. 'Sometimes, though,' he said, his voice hushed, 'you get a kid, a young teenager, and you can just tell that he's different. When they get in a cell, most kids get angry, or cry, or get scared, maybe even cocky, but sometimes you get one who is cold, who has no emotion, nothing at all, who just sits and stares, and you realise that he did something cruel just to see what it was like.'

'So why don't you keep a database or something like that?' I asked.

Joe shook his head. 'Someone would complain about privacy, that we were pigeon-holing people.' He gave a small laugh. 'But even if we had a database, I'm not sure we would catch anyone. Think of the big ones: Harold Shipman, Dennis Nilsen, Peter Sutcliffe. All caught by chance. Dennis Nilsen wasn't caught by a profile. He was caught because he blocked his drains with human fat. Peter Sutcliffe, the Yorkshire Ripper? He was caught because he went into bushes with a prostitute, and when the police went back there, they found a hammer. And as for Harold Shipman, well, it was his greed that let him down. He forged a will, and that led to his murders being discovered. Wherever you look in recent times, it isn't the criminal profile that catches the man, but witness testimony, or forensic evidence, or just plain chance.'

'And so what chance do we ever have?' I asked.

'None,' Joe said simply. 'If we had a database, the list would be too long. Not all young psychopaths go on to be killers. A lot of people have the capacity, but something has to trigger it.'

'But Mack Lowther is dead,' I said, 'and the murders are still going on. Is it possible that coven members have been killed by the man who killed Rebecca Nurse and the others, and that he is still attacking people today, including Sarah?'

Joe looked at me, and then back at the box. 'I don't think so. The earlier murders were sexual murders. Raped and strangled, the bodies left. Mary and Susannah were kept for a few days, and ropes weren't used. It was more prolonged, more sadistic.'

'Maybe he changed his methods,' said Laura.

I could almost see Joe's mind working as he thought about the contents of the box and then of what he knew about Sarah's case. He shrugged and said, 'It's feasible, I suppose. White victim, with preparation, just like the others. If you are saying that Sarah was abducted, then the snatch took place at just the time that her lodger was away for the weekend. That must be more than mere chance. It suggests that he had been watching her, or perhaps even knew her.'

'It wasn't a very good plan,' said Laura, teasing her hair as she thought about what Joe had said. 'What about Luke? If you plan to take someone against their will, you don't take them when they have a fit and trained gym instructor in attendance.'

'Maybe he doesn't always get it right,' Joe replied. 'Perhaps he didn't see Luke arrive. He wasn't in his car that night. Did Luke arrive at the back door?'

I thought about that, but then I remembered something else Joe had said.

'You said that whoever killed these women was a white man,' I said, 'but you also said he was from Preston. How can you know that?'

'The preparation time makes it likely, as he has to have the time to devote to research, and so he has to be able to get to each location quickly,' Joe replied, 'and

Preston is in the middle of them.' And then he smiled. 'And of course, there is the circle theory.' When I looked quizzically at him, Joe explained, 'Put yourself into the mind of an attacker, or a killer, or a rapist. If you wanted to do the crime and get away without being identified, where would you do it?'

I scratched my chin and thought for a moment. 'As far away from my own home as possible, I suppose.'

'That's right,' Joe agreed, 'but what if you wanted to do it again? Would you return to the same place?'

I shook my head.

'Right again,' he said. 'It would be in people's minds. They would be on their guard. But you still wouldn't do it near your own home, would you?'

I shook my head again. 'No, I'd go as far away again, but in the opposite direction.'

'To throw the police into confusion?'

I nodded.

'Well, there you have it,' Joe said, with a note of triumph. 'You've just created the diameter of the circle. Your instinct was to spread the attacks apart, but as far from your own home as possible. Think how that would look if there were a few attacks, how they would look on a large map. They would form the circumference of the circle, and your home would sit right there, in the middle, as far away as possible from each attack. The first victim was dumped to the west of Preston, the second to the north. Rebecca was found east of Preston. Right in the middle of that was Mack Lowther's home town: Preston.'

I sat back with a smile. I was impressed. A killer

drawing a big arrow to his own home, created by a desire to do exactly the opposite.

But then something occurred to me, and I thought about Lancashire for a moment, a county clustered around the west coast, with the jaded resorts of Blackpool and Morecambe, and further inland the larger cities of Preston and Lancaster. East of all of that, the clutter became countryside, as the concrete turned into the hills of the Ribble Valley and the ruggedness of the moors further south. Running through those scenes was the cotton belt, the ribbon of cotton towns that hugged the Leeds–Liverpool canal until it disappeared into the Pennine Hills and Yorkshire.

'But if you add the coven deaths into the equation,' I said, 'doesn't the centre of the circle change? Susannah Martin was found in a copse just outside of Skipton, much further east.'

'Making it somewhere not far from Pendle Hill?' Joe queried. But before I could say anything, he added, 'You're trying to make the facts fit the conclusion. That's the wrong way round.'

'But the same sort of people are victims,' I countered. 'Pretty young women, and most of the coven members don't fit that description.'

'Most victims are pretty young women,' Joe said, and then he raised his hand. 'Okay, I'll go with this imaginary scenario. He didn't start off targeting coven members. He went after young women, mostly fair-haired and pretty. If he is killing coven members, he is following the same pattern of victim, but just restricting his choice even more. But none of the rest fits, and why would he suddenly move on to members of a witches' coven? None of the other coven members died like Rebecca.'

'Two are missing persons, and so we don't know how they died,' I said.

'Or even if they're dead,' Joe responded.

I breathed out noisily. 'This is heavy stuff.'

'No, it's not,' said Joe. 'It's imaginary. Maybe you're planning one of those press conspiracies, knitting possibles into probables, but I still don't think Sarah has anything to do with Rebecca Nurse, or the women killed before her – and if this is nothing to do with Rebecca, then you haven't got many coincidences.'

'I hope you're right,' I said, 'because it's Halloween, Samhain, whatever you want to call it, and if there is a connection, tonight is the night Sarah will die.'

'I know that,' Joe replied, his face grim, 'but we have no evidence.' He sighed. 'I'll put out a general alert for unusual activity tonight, but the whole county will be filled with masks and lanterns.'

Then I thought of something else.

'I've been followed,' I said.

Laura looked shocked. 'What do you mean?'

'Just that. Someone in a tatty white van, small, an Astra. I started to notice it, and I've been seeing it more and more.'

'Why do you think it has anything to do with this case?' she pressed.

'Because I've been at Sarah's house a few times, and around Pendle, asking questions. That's when I noticed it, when I was in Newchurch.'

Joe nodded and made a note on a scrap of paper,

putting it into his pocket. 'Okay, we'll look into that. If we get some news, you'll be the first to know.' Then he smiled at me and gestured towards Laura. 'The afternoon is nearly over. Take Laura up Pendle Hill. That's what most local people do on Halloween. If you're right, it's about to get really busy around here.'

I remembered the tradition from my own childhood, the torch-lit procession up the hill, excited children in masks and costumes, the hillside filled with lights, like lines of fireflies.

Then I felt my phone buzz in my pocket. I looked at the screen. A text, from Katie. *'Call me please. Urgent.'*

Chapter Sixty-nine

When I pulled up outside Sarah's house, Katie came rushing out to meet me. She wrapped her arms around me, tears running down her face.

'Jack! I'm scared.'

I pulled away from her. 'What's wrong?'

She reached into her pocket and produced an envelope.

'Another letter?' I asked, surprised.

Katie nodded and wiped her eyes.

'Hand-delivered again, when you were out?' I asked.

Katie nodded and sniffled and then thrust it into my hand.

I looked at it and took a deep breath. Everything was coming to a head. The Facebook entry. Olwen's prediction. And I remembered the thread in the other letters, how they started with the accusation, then the evidence, and concluded with the judgement. Only one thing could come next: the sentence.

'Have you read it?'

Katie shook her head but said nothing.

I looked at it, and then at Katie, who was looking

around as if she expected someone to be watching her. I let out a breath, nervous about opening the envelope, but I knew I needed to see what was in there.

'Okay,' I said, 'here goes.'

The envelope was only folded closed, so I flicked it open. I saw a piece of simple lined paper, just like before. I looked at Katie. She had her eyes closed.

I reached in and slid the piece of paper out slowly. As I opened it, Sarah's script appeared again, just a few lines, although it seemed more jagged now, less neat.

I read it to myself first, and I felt my mouth go dry.

'What does it say?' Katie asked.

I looked again at the words and then read out loud, '*I shall go from here to the place from where I came; from there I shall be carried to the place of execution, where my body shall be hanged until I be dead. Sarah.*'

Katie put her face in her hands and began to sob.

'This is it,' she wailed. 'The end.'

As I looked at the words again, I took a deep breath, and realised that there was no other conclusion.

Chapter Seventy

Sarah was back in the circle. She sensed that it was evening, and she was certain about the date. Samhain, her favourite time of year. Dancing with her friends, music, cakes and ale. Her head was down as she tried to think of her friends, to find the strength to meditate, to join with them in spirit, but it was hard. She felt drained, despondent.

She looked up when the door slid open. He wasn't there to bring her food, Sarah guessed that straight away. Although she couldn't see his eyes, concealed as always under the hood, he seemed more animated. He was holding a long piece of cord, and he was swinging it in his hand, the end trailing on the floor behind him. In his other hand he was holding a blue plastic sheet.

Sarah didn't move, except that she looked down at the bones, still visible, like a sign of what was to come. Would her parents ever find out what had happened to her? Or would they always wonder, waiting for her to walk back into the house?

The man grabbed Sarah roughly by the arms and hauled her to her feet, pushing her against the wall, his hands around her throat. Sarah didn't resist. She wanted to fight him, hurt him, but she couldn't make herself, as if she had no fight left. She felt his hands scrabbling at her clothes, pulling them off. Then his hands were behind her, wrapping the rope around her wrists, tying a knot, and she winced when he pulled it tight. He pushed her face into the wall, the bare stone scratching her cheek, and then kicked her legs open, heavy boots against her ankle bone. She felt his rough fingers fumble with her, his hand between her legs, scratching at her thighs, feeling for her. A tear ran down her cheek and she retched, waiting for him. She didn't move or try to get away. Get it over with, she thought, and then she gasped as she felt the jab of something inside her. She closed her eyes.

But then she was confused. He stepped away from her, pulled her away from the wall, and whatever he had put inside her was still there.

Sarah looked at him, scared as to what was coming next. He threw the plastic sheet over her head and pulled her towards him as he tied it around her thighs.

She took some deep breaths, her panic rising, unable to see him or to guess what was coming next. Her breaths came back at her, damp and warm behind the plastic sheet. Then he grabbed her and walked her towards the door.

Her feet hurt as she was propelled up the steps, her toes banging on the stone, and she gasped when she realised that she was outside. The wind was cold against her bare legs, and when she looked down her body she could just see the ground between her feet. It was night-time, her legs in shadow. Sharp gravel dug into her feet as she was pulled along, with no idea of where she was going, but she felt a surge of hope, gained some strength from it. She was outside, no longer in the room. Maybe he was going to let her go, tie her up and dump her somewhere, so that she wouldn't know where she had been. They'd had their games, and now it was the end. She was going home.

Sarah heard a car door open and pulled back, not wanting to go in the boot again, but strong hands pushed her onto the floor of the car, face down, wedged between the front and rear seats. When the door closed, she heard an engine start up, and it moved slowly away.

Chapter Seventy-one

Bobby was pulling on Laura's arm as we got nearer to Pendle Hill. We were walking through Sabden, just along the valley from Newchurch, a collection of stone cottages with peephole windows and small studded doors, and narrow lanes with trailing rose bushes straddling the walls.

There was a crowd ahead, excited children in Halloween costumes and adults holding torches, the night air throbbing with the sounds of footsteps and music coming from car radios, all mixed in with the generators for the burger vans. It seemed like everyone was laughing, the normally quiet village streets brought to life by excited children and Halloween revellers. Older teenagers headed for the hill in outlandish costumes, vampires and horror characters, and parents went along with the game, wearing flashing deely-boppers that they could discard when the children got bored.

I looked towards the hill, at the dark shadow looming ahead. Heading upwards, I could see a long line of torches and lanterns, and the side of the hill flickered in reds, blues and greens from the glow-sticks bought from street peddlers.

Sam Nixon was with us, along with his wife, Helena. He'd called me, asked for a progress report, so we followed Joe's suggestion and headed to Pendle Hill, to get lost in the crowd. But I didn't feel the excitement. All I could think about was Sarah.

Sam and Helena were with their children, two young boys, both young enough to enjoy the adventure of a late-night walk up a spooky old hill. They were pushing each other, spoiling for a wrestle, and so we set off walking, hoping that the trek might quieten them down.

Helena set the pace, talking to Laura, just small-talk about children and school, the pressures of motherhood. Pendle Hill was almost invisible in the darkness, so we just followed the lights and the noise of laughing teenagers, their bags clinking with alcopops, ready for the party at the top. The ground was firm underneath, the night cold and clear, and the stars twinkled brightly over the towns and villages, the streetlights turning the road into orange strips as we got higher.

'How do you think the police are faring?' Sam asked. 'Will they catch Sarah?'

I thought of all that Kinsella had talked about earlier in the day.

'If you're hoping for a murder case, I think you might miss out,' I answered. 'There's a possibility Sarah has been kidnapped.'

Sam looked astonished, and I gave him a summary of what Olwen had told me. He didn't answer straight away, and I didn't push it. We just followed our partners and the children, the night getting colder all the time.

'That will be a relief for her parents, in a strange kind of way,' he said eventually.

'What do you mean?'

'Mr and Mrs Goode are solid people. The thought that their daughter was a murderer was a lot to take in. If Sarah is a victim, then she will remain special, still the gentle girl they know.'

'There's a downside to that,' I said.

'Which is?'

'That if the theory *is* correct, then tonight is the night that Sarah dies.'

Sam looked at me, and I could tell he was shocked, despite the darkness.

'Why tonight?'

'Because of this,' I said, gesturing to the scene around me. 'Halloween. The death may be symbolic, when it comes.'

'And what do the police think about that?' he asked.

I smiled ruefully. 'They're unconvinced, and if they're wrong, then Sarah Goode will be having the worst night of her life right now.' And then I felt a stab of guilt as I thought about how we were enjoying ourselves. 'And her last,' I added quietly.

The journey didn't take long.

Sarah could hear other traffic going by, the noise of everyday lives. She was naked under the plastic sheet, jammed between the seats, sweating and scared.

They hadn't travelled far, just a few turns and a couple of hills, when she heard the road change from the tarmac hum to the scramble of a track, and she was bounced around in the cramped space between the seats, her head banging on the floor of the car.

Was this it? The release point?

She was jolted forward as the brakes sent small stones scattering, and they arrived at their journey's end. She sensed that she was about to get her answer.

Chapter Seventy-two

I was deep in thought, my mind on Sarah, when I saw movement in front of me, sharp and fast, moving from side to side. Then I saw it was Bobby, running towards me, roaring, his face hidden behind a monster mask, a black plastic cape over his coat, a scarred red face and gravestone teeth, the hair coming down in black nylon curls, Laura's torch flashing around in front of him.

'You scared me,' I said playfully, pretending to go to my knees. When he grabbed me, his arms squeezing hard around my neck, I could hear his excitement from the shrieks coming from behind the mask.

'Did the pumpkin get too hot?' I asked him.

'It was too heavy,' he complained. 'I gave it to Mummy.'

I saw Laura lift the lantern ahead of us, and the flicker of the candle inside threw orange shadows over her face.

I heard Bobby yelp as I lifted him onto my shoulders and felt his thighs clamp my cheekbones. People jostled us as they went past us on the path, but Bobby liked it up there, with a good view over the Lancashire countryside, the old cotton towns nestling in the valleys, sometimes spilling onto the hilltops, the farmsteads just dots on the hills, the lights weak and yellow. I guessed that somewhere, in a dark space between those lights, was Sarah Goode, and I felt my mood slide again.

Laura dropped back and slipped her hand into mine. 'This could be quite romantic, if things were different,' she whispered in my ear.

I looked around. I could see the lights and steam from a burger van that was parked further along, just before the track got too slippery.

I squeezed her hand. 'It must be the cold air that makes you so easily pleased.'

Laura glanced over at some teenagers; they were showing off, laughing too loudly at a joke that probably wasn't that funny. 'I wonder what they would say if they knew what could happen tonight,' she said.

I looked at the youths, and then at the other children with their parents, loving the change from the homework routine.

'I reckon they would come out just the same,' I replied.

I could see Sam and Helena further up the hill as they let their children run around, yelping and squealing, and Laura followed my gaze.

'I love you, Jack Garrett,' whispered Laura. 'You know that, don't you?'

I squeezed her hand. 'I like it when you remind me.'

'Do you think we'll ever be like that?' she said, looking towards Sam and Helena. 'Our own children, I mean.'

I felt a jolt, unsure what the right answer might be, but then I realised how Laura's hand felt in mine, comforting, warm. 'One day, I reckon,' I said softly, 'but we'd have to get married first.'

Laura looked up at me, her eyes gleaming, and then she kissed me. For a moment, it felt like it had the first time, the flutter of nerves, that tingle down my spine, and then I felt Bobby kick his legs against my chest.

'What are you talking about?' he demanded.

I squeezed his ankles. 'Just telling your mummy that she is special.'

Bobby giggled at that.

'You'll keep me safe, won't you?' Laura murmured in my ear.

'That's your job,' I said. 'You're the one with the truncheon.'

Laura laughed at that and linked her arm in mine. In that second, some of the stresses of the past few weeks lifted, and it felt like we were a brand-new couple again.

Sarah felt another blast of cold air as the car doors opened. Rough, callused hands grabbed at her legs and started to pull her out of the car. She shouted out as she landed on the ground, her shoulder taking a jolt, and then she felt cold gravel beneath her as she was pulled to her feet. She was gripped tightly by the arms, making her cry out in pain, and then she was pulled down the track, stones and grit scraping the soles of her feet as she did her best to keep her balance. Her captor was silent. The noise of the traffic was louder now, like it was overhead.

Was she about to be left? There had been too many opportunities back in the room to kill her. Any time, she could have been tortured, killed, dismembered, disposed of, never seen again. Like the bones in the dirt. She was different now, away from the room.

Sarah wasn't taken too far. Her feet hurt, cut by stones, and when they stopped, her chest ached and her legs felt weak. Sarah listened, and she thought she could hear water, just a light trickle.

The plastic sheet was torn off her head. Sarah blinked. She couldn't wipe her eyes as her hands were still bound.

She saw flickering lights. The stars were bright, her first view since she'd had a different life, but then she saw more lights, headlights as they swept the sky above her. She could see the concrete supports, the motorway, a bridge over a river. Sarah tried to look around, to take in her surroundings, and she saw houses not far away. There was a glow of a conservatory, the clean lines of a modern cul-de-sac, and streetlights that led away, up a hill.

She was about to shout out when a cord was wrapped around her neck. It was pulled tight so that a small knot dug into the back of her neck, and then she was turned around as it was connected to her wrists. She tried to pull away, acting on instinct, but it made her gasp as the cord around her neck went tighter.

'Even the start of a scream, and I'll kill you right now,' he whispered into her ear.

He turned her round again so that she was facing him. The wind was cold, and she was naked. He pulled her closer, one hand behind her, clutching her bound wrists. She could smell cigarettes, and could feel his erection pressing hard against her stomach.

'What do you see?' he hissed at her.

Sarah shook her head. She couldn't speak.

He yanked the cord down, pulling her head back. 'Tell

me,' he said, and brought her right up against him, so that his hood was brushing her face. Her chest hurt; she wanted to take a breath, but couldn't, the rope squeezing her throat. Sarah looked up to the stars. She thought they were moving, streaks not dots.

'Tell me what you see,' he said, angrier now.

Sarah shook her head again. He sounded more distant now, his voice an echo.

'Tell me, tell me,' he said, and he tugged at the cord.

She let out a strangled gasp and her vision became speckled, her chest aching for air. She thought she saw herself on the grass, underneath him, and then she saw her mother crying. Her knees started to give way and his voice faded, her terror replaced by calm.

As she fell, she thought she heard him groaning. It sounded like moans of ecstasy.

Sarah wasn't sure how long she had passed out for. The sounds came back slowly and she lay on her side on the cold, hard ground for a while, stones cutting into her arm, coughing so that her chest hurt as she gulped in the cold air. The cord seemed looser around her throat.

'What did you see?' he asked, just behind her, his voice quieter now.

Sarah took some deep breaths, tried to think about where she was. 'Are you going to let me go?' she asked.

He chuckled.

Sarah didn't say anything, so he jumped to his feet and yanked on the rope binding her wrists.

Sarah yelped and stood up slowly. Tears started to stream down her face. She no longer felt the cold. Her life was going to end soon, she knew that; she was about to die at the hand of someone she didn't know. She strained on the rope to get away, but he yanked her back, pulling her to the floor, hurting her neck.

'Let me go, please,' she pleaded desperately.

'What, you won't tell?' he said mockingly. He kicked her. 'Forget it, because my little helper has prepared me a treat.'

Sarah tried to pull away, her feet scattering stones, blood on her toes. 'No, no, no!' she wailed.

'Do you want to know what you've got between your legs?' he continued, enjoying himself now.

Sarah remembered him putting it there, his rough hands, his force. She could still feel whatever it was inside her. She shook her head slowly and said nothing.

'Gunpowder,' he said simply. 'We're experimenting, branching out. He's got a thing for explosives. This is a new idea of his. Gunpowder and ball-bearings, jammed into a condom.' He chuckled. 'Like a small bomb.'

Sarah's mouth dropped open. She went pale, cold. She began to sob, and then she began to thrash on the rope, trying to get away, knowing what was coming, but it went tight around her neck again. She thought of her parents, thought of home. She tried to scream, but he shot forward and put a rag in her mouth. It was soaked in petrol. Sarah coughed and gagged.

'You've got a little string in there,' he said, the excitement making his voice higher.

Sarah's head hung down, tears falling onto the ground.

'Works like a fuse,' he said, and then he began to laugh as he walked towards the car. Sarah looked around, tried to figure out what to do, to quell the panic so she could work out how to get away. She looked back to the houses, the security of the lights, the lantern glow of trick-or-treat children on the cul-de-sac. She could get there, make a run for it. She was young, fit.

She set off, her bare feet pounding on the cold, hard ground, her hands still behind her back. Her chest hurt and she was weak from hunger, but terror drove her onwards, her head thrown back, just the noise of footsteps in her head.

But the ground was uneven, it was difficult to keep her legs upright. She hit a dip and went down hard, with nothing to break her fall. As she turned around, panting, crying, looking up, she saw him over her, laughing at her, something in his hand. A canister, large, like a fuel can.

She struggled to her feet, ready to run again, but he was moving too fast. She heard movement, a shout, and then felt a splash. It was petrol, the stench sweet in the clean air, filling her nostrils.

And then she saw him flick the lighter into life.

She screeched through the rag in her mouth, knowing what was coming.

He laughed and then tossed the lighter towards her. The flame came arcing at her, spinning slowly, yellow and blue stars dancing in the air, and then it hit her in the chest, cold metal. The pause was only for a fraction, but in that moment she saw everything. Her house, her friends. Her parents smiling. Last day at school. Her first time. The last time. Kisses. Fights. Laughter. Tears. Then she looked down and saw the flames spread in a flash, and then that was all Sarah could see.

A deep breath sucked in flames and the heat poured into her, igniting the cloth, drowning out her screams. She stumbled around, her thoughts slashed away by pain, tearing at her as the fire raged. Then the world went black as the gunpowder caught hold.

The last sound Sarah heard was the noise of her body falling to the floor as her hips exploded and her legs left her body.

Chapter Seventy-three

I saw the lights first.

We were sitting on a blanket, watching the small dots move and shimmer: the orange of the towns, and then the white of car headlights. But then there was another colour: flashing blue. I pulled away from Laura and looked over to Sam Nixon. I knew what it was straight away. Laura looked confused at first, but then followed my gaze to the lights of the police cars racing along the country lanes.

Laura got to her feet and went further away from the crowds, to stand on a dark patch of grass. I held on to Bobby's hand and called over to Sam, pointing into the distance when he looked over. I saw his shoulders slump and knew he had seen them too.

'I think we need to check that out,' I said to Laura.

Sam must have heard me, because he said, 'We'll look after Bobby. Just keep me informed.'

Laura and I nodded our thanks, and then we made our way back down the hill, running into the beams of the oncoming torches. But my mind was filled with the lights we had seen from the top of Pendle Hill. Blue flashing lights, at least four vehicles, converging on a spot not too far away. Something had happened, and we all knew that our questions about Sarah Goode were about to be answered.

Halloween traffic delayed us from reaching the scene, the narrow roads jammed tight by people who had come to enjoy some spooky fun, but it got easier as we got away from Pendle Hill. As we drove down a long, dark lane, the blue lights lighting up the scene ahead, we saw a police car in the road, blocking our way. A motorway bridge went overhead, and there was a patrol car on the hard shoulder, to stop people having a look from there.

I pulled over and turned off the engine. As I reached for the door handle, Laura put her hand on mine.

'I need to go there on my own,' she said.

'But this is my story,' I protested.

Laura looked at me and shook her head. 'Let me do my police work. There'll be a crowd here soon. You work that, see if you can get any information they won't tell the police. Maybe I'll even wait for you if you want to speak to people at the scene later, but right now, they won't let me near if I have a civilian with me.'

I nodded my agreement, feeling suddenly like an outsider. Laura kissed me on the cheek before she left the car. 'Thank you, Jack,' she whispered.

Chapter Seventy-four

Laura saw the darkness lift as she got nearer, the crime scene illuminated by a large lamp. Blue and white tape had already been stretched across the road, and further in she could see a white gazebo, standing head-height like an emergency latrine. There were two people inside the flap, hunched over something black. The sudden flash told Laura that someone was taking photographs, and the brightness illuminated the white forensic boiler suits and the masks over the faces of those inside.

Laura saw a small group of people standing to one side, turned in to each other and deep in conversation. A uniformed officer came over towards her, concerned that Laura was just a curious onlooker, but her ID allowed her through.

'Is it what I think it is?' she asked the uniform.

He grimaced, just visible in the police lights. 'Not very nice, so I hear.'

Laura pointed over to the group of people. 'Who's over there?'

'The Home Office pathologist, and a couple of big-shots from the murder squad.'

Laura looked over as there was another flash from the camera and she saw Carson's outline, tall and broad, the light reflecting off his bald head. She took a deep breath and wondered how Carson would react to being wrong. She set off towards him.

As she got closer, Carson turned around, and when he saw her, he folded his arms, his body language defensive. Joe Kinsella was behind him, his toe making circles in the autumn leaves.

'Your boyfriend not here to gloat?' Carson asked, his voice bitter.

'He's not far away. I can call him if you want.' When Carson just scowled in response, Laura pointed towards the forensic tent. 'Not much to gloat about anyway,' she said.

Carson looked away, his hands jammed into his pockets.

'I'm sorry that you don't think much of Jack Garrett,' said Laura, trying to sound conciliatory, 'and if I was in your shoes, I would maybe think the same, but he is a good journalist. If you get him on your side, he'll write it up how it is.'

'What, that I got it wrong?' he snapped. 'I can't wait for that edition to come out.'

'It's not about you, sir,' said Laura, her dislike for Carson showing through. 'There is a dead woman just over there. The blame game isn't that important right now.'

Laura braced herself for the response, but she was shocked when Carson's shoulders slumped and he said quietly, 'I know that.'

Before Laura had the chance to respond, a voice boomed out, 'Detective McGanity, how glorious to meet you again.'

Laura looked up and saw a lanky figure advancing towards her in a paper boiler suit, the face mask around his chin. Her lips twitched with the beginnings of a smile.

It was Doctor Pratt, a Home Office pathologist. She'd met him before, and, like most pathologists, he seemed to enjoy his work more than appeared normal. She'd attended one of his post-mortems, when he wouldn't start until the stereo play-list was sorted out. She knew that most pathologists liked to slice up to music, but it had to be appropriate. He wanted Pink Floyd, it was turgid enough, but the assistants complained about it being old-fashioned, although there was a consensus that dance music was too frivolous.

'Good to see you, doctor,' she said, and pointed towards the forensic tent. 'What have you got over there?'

His eyes widened and he shook his head. 'Damn nasty,' he said.

'Sarah Goode?' she asked.

The doctor pointed towards Carson. 'He is convinced,' he said, and then he leaned in conspiratorially. 'It hasn't improved his mood though.'

'We received a call from the fire service,' Carson said, trying to take the spotlight from himself. 'They thought it was kids, you know, Halloween pranks, setting rubbish alight. The residents from over there reported it, said they could see a glow near the river. When they got here, they found Sarah, naked and burning. It looks like somebody stripped her, poured something on her, and set her alight. She was dead when they arrived; there was never any doubt.'

'Ah, but you've missed out the strangest thing,' said Doctor Pratt, his eyes wide.

'What's that?' asked Laura, turning to Carson.

'She was burnt out,' said Carson, scowling at the doctor, 'but half of her abdomen had exploded. It looked like someone stuck a giant firework into her and lit it.'

Laura felt her stomach roll over and she closed her eyes, trying not to think of how it must have been, but she found herself clamping her thighs together. She took a few deep breaths and asked, 'Do we have any witnesses?'

'No one yet,' Carson replied. 'We've got the people who saw the fire once it was going, but no one has come forward to say they saw it start. There are officers doing the door-to-door, but it's not looking good.'

Laura looked around the scene, at the houses nearest to it, all the windows now filled with faces.

'He parked over there, we think,' said Joe, his voice weary, pointing towards a scrap of land just underneath the motorway bridge. 'There are some tyre marks in the gravel, but they might belong to the fire crew or the first patrol car on the scene.'

'Any speed cameras around here?' Laura asked. 'Sometimes people can't stop the panic when something like this happens.'

'On the main road, I think,' Joe answered, 'and we'll check them out tomorrow, but nothing on the back roads.'

Doctor Pratt grinned. 'You haven't spotted the joke, have you?'

'I don't see anything funny,' Carson replied.

'You said that this is all to do with witchcraft,' the doctor said. 'Look at the location.'

'What do you mean?' asked Carson, looking around.

'Cuckstool Lane,' boomed Doctor Pratt. 'This is where they used to duck witches back in the Middle Ages. You know, all that sink or swim stuff, on ducking stools. This is where they did it: in the river at Cuckstool Lane.'

Carson looked at Joe, who looked back at Laura but said nothing, although Laura thought she could see apology in his eyes. Carson looked tired. 'Great,' said Carson wearily. 'A killer with a sense of humour.'

Laura looked back to where Sarah's body had been found, charred and twisted in death a few yards away, and thought of the bad news waiting for her parents.

'Go home,' said Carson softly. 'Tell that reporter boyfriend of yours that he did well, that he was right and we were wrong. If we'd done more digging, maybe we would have found her.'

'What about you?'

'Oh, I'll be here for a while yet.'

'Who's going to tell Sarah's parents?'

Carson took a deep breath. 'I'll do that. I want them to know that I'm not going to dodge whatever comes my way.' He looked at Joe. 'Neither of us will.'

'And what about me, sir?' asked Laura.

Carson thought about that, and looked at Joe, who nodded to him. 'Can you make it to the station for midnight?' asked Carson.

'I'll be there, sir.'

He nodded. 'Good. Now go back to your family. Spend some time with them.'

Laura walked away, but she stopped for one last look back and wondered how the final moments must have been, so close to town, to safety, but filled with terror, pain, fear. And loneliness, kept away from her loved ones.

Laura turned away again, realising that she didn't want to think about it too closely.

Chapter Seventy-five

I woke when I felt Laura's hand on my hair.

I was asleep at the table, my laptop dark, the battery long dead, papers strewn in front of me.

'What time is it?' I murmured.

She kissed me on the top of my head. I could smell the remnants of a long night on her, bad coffee and too much sugary food to stave off tiredness. When I looked round I saw dark rings under her eyes. I checked my watch. It was six o'clock.

'Are you okay?' I asked.

'Yeah,' Laura replied, her voice a drawl. 'It was a long night, and I get this way sometimes when people die, you know – I'm watching a new day that someone else didn't see.'

I took her hand and kissed it. I knew the feeling. I had lost both my parents, and I remembered that feeling of guilt when the new sun rises, that life is just starting over again.

'How's your story?' she asked.

'It's a struggle,' I said, stretching. 'I might try later, if I can keep my eyes open.'

'Too close to the action?'

I gave a little laugh. 'Something like that.'

'Bobby okay?'

I nodded. 'He's fine.'

Laura went into the kitchen and I heard the kettle click on. I turned on the television, flicked through to the news channels and waited for the local angle. I needed to know if my story was about to become public property.

As Laura passed me a cup of coffee and settled down beside me, a young reporter set the scene, learning his trade when no one was watching. Carson was brief, just something about keeping an open mind, spoken in that brusque police-speak.

The scene flashed back to the studio, the presenter looking appropriately sombre before turning to a story about a dance contest in Blackpool. I flicked off the television.

'Is that it?' asked Laura.

'He's being cagey,' I said, pulling at my lip. 'Was he like that at your midnight meeting?'

'You know I can't talk about that, Jack. Let Carson tell you the secrets.'

'What about the custody case?' I asked. 'Are you okay to be on the team?'

'Jenny will have done the report by now. We have done all we can.'

I slumped back in the chair and rubbed my face with my hands. I knew I had a good story, filled with local intrigue and murder, but I felt frustrated that I hadn't found Sarah in time, that the story was not complete.

The telephone rang. We exchanged glances before Laura answered it, and as she spoke, I went to the window and watched the rising sun paint the fields with colour, greens coming out of the black. Laura wasn't saying much, but I could guess what it was: the murder team was getting together again, and so she had to be at work early.

When she put the phone down, she looked at me, surprised. 'They want you there,' she said, her eyes wide.

'Who are "they"?' I asked.

'Carson, the squad.'

I turned back to the window. As I looked into the valley below me, I saw that the houses had come into view. But they were still dark, just indistinct blocks, and around them I saw shadows.

Karl Carson waited for me on the canal towpath, the police station close by. He looked preoccupied, watching the sunlight reflect off the water. He didn't look round as I got near, staring into the canal instead and saying to me, 'It looks nice, doesn't it?'

I looked along the canal, saw how it disappeared around a corner, past bramble bushes and the high walls built over a hundred years ago. Lavender bushes overhung the canal on the other side and brushed the surface, although the flowers were long gone, the branches just long spindles. I could see birds sitting on fences further along. I knew that barges cruised along here sometimes, with bright primary colours and tiny windows.

'Yes, it is,' I agreed. 'Very pretty.'

'It's filled with crap,' he said calmly. 'It looks good

from here, but get under the water and it's filled with old bikes and tyres, made dark by algae.' Then he looked at me and said, 'Thanks for coming down.'

That took me by surprise. 'I know why I'm here,' I said.

He looked at me warily.

'It's so I don't say anything,' I said.

'You're a reporter, and you've made it clear that I can't control you.'

'You're trying, though.'

'How do you mean?'

'If you keep me close,' I answered, 'you're hoping that I won't write the story yet. I'm the only media in the know, and so if you let me think that there is much more to come, by giving me access, you hope that I won't write what I have already, perhaps worried about how you'll come out of it.'

'And people call me cynical,' he said, shaking his head. 'You can say many things about me, but I don't cover up.'

'So what is going on?'

'It depends on what you want,' he said. 'So how do you want to play it?'

'What do you mean?'

'Free access to the rest of the investigation, when you want it, or are you going to go with what you've got?'

'You know how I'll answer,' I said, 'otherwise you wouldn't have invited me down.' When he shrugged his agreement, I asked, 'So let's start with an interview. How do you feel, knowing that you missed what was going on?'

He flinched, but didn't dodge the question. 'Someone has died. I didn't kill her, but I didn't stop it either. That will never leave me.'

'What about Sarah's parents? What will you tell them?'

'The truth. It is always the best place to start. They are in the station right now, being updated.'

I blew out a whistle. 'That won't be easy.'

Carson sighed. 'When someone dies, it never is,' and he looked distant for a moment before adding, 'particularly when they might be able to blame me. What are they like?'

'A decent couple,' I said, suddenly feeling sorry for him. 'She's in charge, but they are good people.'

Carson stayed silent for a moment, looking back into the water.

'Are you going to go public with the witch connection?' I asked.

Carson shook his head. 'Not yet.'

'Why not?' I asked.

'It's an operational decision.'

'Or a trap?'

Carson smiled for the first time that day. 'It's an operational trap.'

'Who made the decision?' I asked.

'I did, on advice.'

'Joe?'

'I had to give him something to do.'

'He was wrong yesterday,' I said. When Carson shot me a wounded look, I asked, 'What's the new plan then?'

'Joe thinks we have to mislead him,' said Carson, 'to make him think we haven't spotted the link. It might bring him out of hiding, and forensics might not be enough.'

'How?'

'Simple. Appeal to his vanity. Who are we to him? Small-town plods. Let him think he's too clever for us, too subtle, then maybe he'll show himself, send a more obvious sign.'

'Do you think it will work?' I asked him.

Carson thought about his answer, and then said, 'Joe Kinsella thinks it will.'

'It doesn't seem the most complex trap.'

'No, it isn't, but I've known Joe a few years now, and he's right most times. He thinks the killer is unravelling, losing his control. The letters sent to Katie are a first. None of the other murders had coded clues. So why were they sent?'

'To taunt you?'

Carson shook his head. 'That's what Joe thought at first, but now he's not so sure. You see, the letters were sent before Sarah Goode died. I would go with the taunting thing if they arrived now, the day after her death, but not then, when Sarah was still alive. So they can only mean one thing.'

I raised my eyebrows in query.

'We were supposed to stop him,' Carson said ruefully. 'Things have changed. He warned us what he was going to do, and why he was doing it. As we didn't stop him, he may get back in touch, to blame us.'

I pondered on that. I looked away from the canal, and I could see into the streets further away from the police station, on the hills that rose above the town centre. People were going about their daily business, and I could rejoin them. My job was done. I had no reason to feel guilty about not finding Sarah, because she'd been beyond discovery. I felt sure Carson would tell Sarah's parents how much I'd helped, and eventually they might appreciate that, and I knew, deep down, that I had done all I could. I had no reason to feel guilty. I should file it all away in that drawer marked 'bad day' and forget about it. I could write up the feature and sell it before the killer was caught, or maybe write it up for a book.

But I sensed that the story could only get better.

Chapter Seventy-six

We walked back to the station in silence. The scene was busier than the day before, more local officers drafted in. Detectives criss-crossed the corridors with pieces of paper in their hands, looking earnest, and I recognised one from my trip to the moors. He looked away as I got near.

Carson marched into the packed Incident Room ahead of me. I was about to follow when I saw some more people I recognised through an open door further along the corridor. Sarah's parents. I knew by now that Carson was focused on the case, not me. I was a distraction, and so he wouldn't notice if I was no longer there.

I walked towards Sarah's parents, expecting to be challenged, but I made it all the way to the doorway. Next to Sarah's parents, taking notes, was Sam Nixon.

They looked round, and gave weak smiles when they recognised me.

'I'm sorry I didn't find her in time,' I said, my voice soft, leaning against the doorjamb.

Mrs Goode shook her head. 'It's not your fault, Mr Garrett,' she replied.

I didn't recognise the police officer in front of them, but he was high-ranking, judging from the embroidery on his shoulders. He shifted in his seat and looked uncomfortable.

I smiled my thanks, and then tilted my head to Sam Nixon, to get him to come out of the room. He excused himself and came into the corridor.

'How are they?' I asked, as he closed the door.

Sam glanced back to the room, and then replied, 'Not good. It's strange, though – they feel almost vindicated, that Sarah wasn't the murderer the police thought she was.'

'And that's your murder case gone.'

'Sometimes it isn't about the money.'

'I thought with lawyers it was always about the money.'

Sam put his hands in his pockets and sighed. 'When most lawyers start off, it's about justice, or something close to that. The money becomes important later on. But occasionally the old Sam Nixon comes back, and I try to do what's right. What's your next step?'

I thought about that. I knew the story wasn't finished yet, so I didn't want to write it up, and I knew I had the run of the Incident Room, the chance for an insider's view before the nationals came sniffing round.

'Write the story, I suppose.'

He smiled at that, and patted me on the arm. Then he opened the door to go back into the room, leaving me on my own in the corridor.

I looked around, at the flaking paint, the worn paths in the carpets, old dents and chips in the paintwork. I could see the history of the town in the walls, in the floor, in the smell of the place. Sarah's parents were in the room behind me, their lives ruined, trying to come to terms with the death of their only child. How many times had that scene played out within these walls?

I walked back to the Incident Room and looked in. Carson was pointing at people, talking fast, his eyes animated. Then I heard the rumble of chairs and saw that people were getting quickly to their feet. The squad would be heading out soon to begin their enquiries. I stepped to one side as people filed out, in groups of two, imbued with a sense of urgency. As Laura followed, in step with Joe Kinsella, I put my hand on her arm.

'Where are you heading?' I asked.

'Katie Gray,' she said. 'She might remember some more about Sarah's whereabouts, who she spoke to, where she went.' When she saw my raised eyebrows, she said, 'Don't worry, I won't play the angry girlfriend.'

'And what about the rest of the squad?' I asked.

Laura looked at Joe, who nodded, and so she said, 'They're going to make an arrest.'

'Shit!' I exclaimed. 'That was quick. Who?'

Laura looked uncomfortable. 'Olwen.'

I thought I felt the blood drain from my face. 'Olwen? He was at our house the night before.' And then I looked at Joe. 'Do you think he was playing us?'

'We just want to see what he knows,' he said.

'What do you mean?'

'He went to you, not us,' Joe said. 'Maybe that was about control. That's how killers like this operate. Remember Rebecca Nurse, the girl by the stream. Olwen called it in. He found her, so he said, and I bet he even

404

handled the body, just to frustrate the forensic search. But no one notices, so he carries on, picking off his recruits, persuading young women to join his club.' When he spotted my sceptical look, he said, 'We were wrong about Mack Lowther, and I'll always remember that.'

'And so you stopped looking,' I replied curtly.

Joe's mouth just twitched. 'Maybe we've got it right this time.'

'No,' I protested, shaking my head. 'It can't be Olwen.'

'Why not?'

'Because it's too neat,' I said. 'Why would he kill his own members? The letters were sent as a message. The dumping of the first body will have been a message too. And I've met Olwen. He seems gentle, kind.'

Joe laughed, but there was little humour in it. 'I've met some very pleasant murderers. Don't take that as a sign. That's part of the control, he exerts it even over himself. You ask anyone who ever met a serial killer, and they will all say the same thing, that he was such a quiet, gentle man. It's a trick. They are all about control. It was Olwen who sought you out, wasn't it?'

'Only after we gate-crashed his ceremony.'

'But still he came,' said Joe. 'He brought the names. He led us to all of this. Maybe he has been controlling this all along, right from when he dumped Rebecca Nurse by that stream and we didn't spot it. Did you say that he was initiating someone else?'

I nodded. 'A young woman. Blonde hair, pretty,' and I went quiet as I said the words. Just like all the others, I thought. 'Sarah's replacement?' I queried.

'Maybe,' said Joe.

'And if you're wrong?' I asked.

'Then we'll say sorry,' he said and then he rushed away, the corridor echoing with the clatter of the door as he barged through it.

Chapter Seventy-seven

The tension was high in the police station. Calls were still being taken, leads being pursued, but everyone was twitchy, looking up at every engine noise, waiting for Olwen to arrive.

I was standing by a window in the Incident Room, my camera ready, my visitor's pass stuck to my shirt. He would have to come into the station yard and then be walked across the cobbles to get in. I would get a picture as he went. I could syndicate that, because it would be the image that would be splashed across the papers, the rights to it owned by me. They're the money-spinners, the pictures that become part of the mythology.

I felt uneasy. This had become more than a story, and it didn't seem right that I should profit from it, but my conscience didn't have to wrestle with itself for long. I heard the sirens, and then the blue lights bounced off the walls of the station yard as three cars raced down the ramp. Chairs scraped on the floor as people rushed to the window, wanting to see Olwen as he was brought in.

Olwen was in the middle car, and when he was brought out, his eyes scanned the yard quickly, his shoulders hunched, looking scared, confused. His pony-tail was untidy, and his jogging bottoms looked creased, as if he had just been dragged out of bed. He was hand-cuffed at the front, and two officers grabbed an arm each and started to walk him to the station door.

As he walked, I clicked away. He looked around, as if he was trying to make sense of what was going on, and then he looked up and saw me. He stopped. I saw something in his eyes that I couldn't read. Was it anger? Or maybe betrayal?

I put my camera down and looked away. I checked my watch instead and thought about what to do next. Lunchtime. I knew the police would be tied up with Olwen for the rest of the day, and nothing much would happen until they had finished. Maybe it was time to get some more quotes.

I picked up my bag and headed for the door.

I stood at the gate of Sarah's parents' house, nervous about going in. I had looked for them at the police station, wanting to finish my piece with a quote, but they had gone home. I had a sense of what they must be going through, as my own father had died suddenly and violently, and so I felt guilty for badgering them. But I had a story to write.

I tried Laura's number, to see how she was getting on with Katie, but there was no response. I would call her when I got out.

The gate creaked as I opened it. I had expected a few more reporters to be there, but the story was still too new, and there was an arrest to distract them.

The door opened before I got there. It was Mrs Goode. She looked pale and drawn, apart from the flush to her cheeks that had resulted from crying. She was wearing the same clothes as before, when I had seen her at the police station.

'Come in, Mr Garrett,' she said, her manners on automatic.

As I went into the house, I was struck by the silence. In the living room, Mr Goode was just staring ahead, his face etched with disbelief, holding a picture of Sarah, one of her as a child, a grinning young girl with her arms around her father's neck.

I tried not to be put off by it. I was doing something I found hard to justify, bothering the bereaved, but the readers wanted the human reaction, the parents' grief. Shame is not part of the reporter's make-up.

'I won't stay long,' I said softly. 'I just wondered whether you could sum up how you feel right now. I know it feels like an intrusion, but if it engages with the reader, it could encourage more information.'

Mrs Goode gathered her thoughts for a while, before she said, 'I feel like I've nothing left. My whole reason for being here has gone.' She looked at the floor. 'No, it's more than gone,' she said, her voice more strident, tears rippling into her eyes. 'I feel angry. I feel empty. I feel cheated.' When she looked up again, I saw a loss in her eyes as deep as anything I had ever seen. 'But, most of all, I just don't know how I'll get through the rest of my life.'

I breathed out noisily, feeling some of her emotions, a lump in my throat. I scribbled some notes, and then asked, 'Did you know that they'd made an arrest?'

She looked up at me, and I could tell that it offered little comfort. 'Who is it?' she asked.

'Someone called Olwen. He styles himself as a modern-day witch. He runs a coven near Pendle Hill.'

She thought about that, and then asked, 'Was Sarah involved in it?' When I nodded, she said, 'I thought she had some secrets. It didn't make her a bad person, though, did it?'

'No, it didn't. It seems a pretty gentle thing,' I said softly. Her head drooped to the floor and I could tell that the conversation had ended. I had all I needed, though – the quote from the family.

'Take care,' I said, and as I stood up to leave, I reached out to take her hand. It trembled in mine.

'I don't think I can,' she said meekly, her voice breaking, letting go of me.

I took a deep breath. These people didn't deserve this.

I was just about to head towards the front door when I thought about where I could go next for a quote. Katie was the obvious one, and it would give me the chance to catch up with Laura.

I turned and asked, 'Has there been any contact from Katie, Sarah's lodger?'

Mrs Goode looked up at that, and I saw some colour flash into her face.

'Sarah didn't have a lodger,' she said, almost a snap.

I paused, unsure that I'd heard it right. I felt a moment of confusion, an image of Katie in my head, in her room, at Sarah's house.

'What do you mean?' I asked.

'Just that, Mr Garrett,' she said firmly. 'Sarah did not have a lodger.'

'But I met her,' I said. 'Katie Gray. I interviewed her at the house. She had been lodging with Sarah.'

Mrs Goode shook her head, and she seemed angry, tears flashing across her eyes. 'The police told me that, and I told them the same as I am telling you. But they didn't believe me, told me that daughters do not tell their parents everything, patronised me. I was going to go down there and have it out with her, but I was told that I would be arrested, that Katie was a witness. I didn't matter, you see, because they thought my daughter was a murderer.' Then she leaned forward, and looked right into my eyes. 'Sarah did not have a lodger. We were close. I had been in her house a few days before she died. Only one person lived there: Sarah.'

'But Sarah had secrets. You said that.'

'A lodger isn't a secret,' snapped Mrs Goode. 'It's a living arrangement.'

I thought about Katie. The jumble of clothes, no real organisation. No photographs. How Katie had found Luke. The different accounts of Luke and Sarah's relationship given by Katie and Callum, Luke's friend.

And then I thought of Laura. She was with Katie. I felt my brow go cold, and the hairs stood up on the back of my hand.

'So who is Katie Gray?' I asked, confused, alarmed.

'I don't know,' came her reply. 'But if you find her, ask her what she was doing in Sarah's house.'

Chapter Seventy-eight

I looked back at Mrs Goode's house as I got to my car and saw her in the window, watching me. I rubbed my hands together, suddenly edgy. I thought back to my meetings with Katie. I had seen her in Sarah's house. She had a key. She had reported Sarah's death to the police.

Was that the control Joe had talked about, keeping herself involved in the investigation?

No, of course it wasn't. Serial killers are men, that's what Joe had said, and if she had killed those other women, then she was a serial killer. So she couldn't be responsible for Sarah's death.

And would a woman have killed Sarah in that way? It was too graphic. Too intimate.

Forget about it, I told myself. Mrs Goode didn't know that Sarah had dabbled in witchcraft. Why should she know everything about Sarah?

But as I thought back to Sarah's house, I realised that there hadn't been much of Katie in there. I didn't remember seeing any photographs of her on the wall or sills, and it had struck me how her things seemed sort of thrown down.

But it wasn't just the story, I knew that. It was almost as if a doubt that had always been there had just surfaced for the first time: that Katie's behaviour wasn't right; she was too provocative, like she enjoyed the tease.

I tried calling Laura. No answer.

I put my car into gear and set off quickly.

I went to the college first, entering the foyer at a run, moving too quickly to be stopped by security. I had tried to call Joe, but he was still tied up with Olwen and would be unavailable for a few hours.

I must have looked wild-eyed and out of breath, because the woman behind the administration desk stepped back when I got there.

'Katie Gray,' I barked at them, out of breath. 'The police will need to know about her. Just get out her file and have it ready.'

'Why would the police want it?' she asked, and she glanced towards the security guard, who started to walk over. She began to say something about data protection, but there must have been something in my eyes that told her that this was no time to hide behind regulations.

The security guard appeared next to me as she tapped on the keyboard.

'Is everything okay?' he asked her, looking at me all the time, his chest puffed out.

The administrator paused for a moment, but then she asked, 'How do you spell Gray? With an "e" or an "a"?'

'Try both ways,' I said.

The security guard placed his hand on my forearm,

wondering whether he should try and eject me. I shrugged him off, and just before he could make a better grab, the woman shook her head.

'There's no file to get out,' she said. 'We don't have any female students called Katie Gray, or Kate Gray or Catherine Gray. Are you sure she's a student here?'

I told her that I wasn't sure of anything any more, and then ran out of the building.

Once outside, I thought about where to try next. I called Laura again, but once more the phone went to voicemail. Perhaps she had gone back to the station and was in the interview with Joe?

But I knew that wasn't right, I sensed it.

Go back to the start. Those had been Katie's words. Had it been a clue, a hint? Had she been playing a game all the time? I had doubted Mrs Goode's story that there had been no lodger, but now it seemed that Katie was no student either.

Go back to the start . . . But what was the start? Olwen was locked up because he had found the girl by the stream. Was that the start? Were they both playing games?

I thought about Olwen's list. Rebecca Nurse. She was the first murder he had mentioned. I should start there, and then work backwards.

Chapter Seventy-nine

Rebecca Nurse's parents' home was a modern detached house in Higham, a small village a few miles from Pendle Hill. Once a farming village of stone and slate, Higham was now a commuter magnet, its size doubled by the curves and cul-de-sacs of modern housing, close to the motorway, but near enough to the hills for the faux country set.

As I approached the door, I saw the curtains were drawn. The doorbell rang out in an electronic tune, slow and loud. It was a while before anyone came to the door, but just as I was about to turn away, I saw a shadow behind the frosted glass.

A woman opened the door, in her fifties, thin and pale, her hair grey and unkempt.

'Mrs Nurse?' I queried.

'Yes?' she replied, her voice nervous.

'My name is Jack Garrett and I'm a reporter,' I said. 'I'm writing a story on the murder of Sarah Goode, and I think it might be connected to Rebecca's death.' Her face twitched when I said Rebecca's name. 'I'm sorry to intrude, but I wonder whether you would be willing to talk to me.'

She looked back into the house, and I got the sense that she wasn't alone. After a few seconds, she turned to go inside but left the door open. I guessed I was meant to follow.

I was led into the living room, all flowered carpets and patterned wallpaper. There was a picture above the gas fire, large and framed, a teenage girl in a school photo. I recognised the face. Rebecca. I looked around the room and I saw other photographs. Baby photographs. Rebecca as a toddler, a young girl, a gawky teenager.

As I turned around, I saw that Mrs Nurse was watching me.

'It's not what you think,' she said quietly.

'How do you know what I'm thinking?' I said.

'You'll write it up that the house is a memorial to Rebecca.' Before I could answer, she continued, 'But it's not like that. We loved her, you see. She was our daughter, someone special, a beautiful young woman. If she was alive today, those photographs would still be there.'

I nodded and smiled my apology. I understood.

'Why are you here about Sarah Goode?' she asked. 'The man who killed our daughter is dead.'

There was no way to dress it up.

'Maybe not,' I said bluntly.

I saw her fingers clench and her eyes fill with tears. 'Mack Lowther murdered my daughter,' she said quietly. 'I know that.'

'How?'

'The police told us. They couldn't prove it, but they were certain.'

'And if they were wrong?'

416

Mrs Nurse sat down heavily and I thought I could hear movement from the back room. Was someone listening in?

'There have been more deaths,' I said. 'The police think he killed someone last night. Sarah Goode.'

Mrs Nurse looked confused for a second, and glanced towards the back room. 'I don't understand,' she said, her voice quiet.

'More women have been killed, Mrs Nurse,' I repeated, 'and it looks like the person who killed Rebecca also murdered them.'

Mrs Nurse went pale, and she looked distant, as if she were going to faint.

'Mrs Nurse? Are you okay?'

She looked at me, and then towards the other room. She shook her head. 'Can you leave please,' she said to me.

'Mrs Nurse?'

'Now,' she insisted.

I did as I was asked, but as I looked back towards the house, I knew that something wasn't right. Something I'd said had troubled her, more than I expected. And who had been in the back room?

I checked in my pocket for my camera. I wanted to know who had been listening in. I looked at the house, just to check that no one was watching me, and then I walked quickly up the driveway to the garden, my camera in hand, past the garage, the door of which was slightly ajar. I peered round the back of the house, checking that there was no one there. I saw just a small patch of lawn and a conservatory made out of white PVC. I couldn't see anyone, but when I turned to go I saw a glimpse of something that made my palms break out in a sweat.

I walked towards the garage, just to check, and peered in through the gap in the door. It was the same, I knew it straight away. It was the white van, an Astra, shabby and old, the registration number ending in DDA, the one that had been following me for the past few days.

Before I could do anything else, I heard a voice behind me.

'What are you doing round here, Mr Garrett?'

Chapter Eighty

Carson was angry as he walked quickly down the corridor. Olwen was in his cell, waiting for the first interview, the forensic swabs done, his hands, his fingernails, the humiliation of the penis swab, but now there was someone to see him who could give him an alibi.

As Carson strode into the Incident Room, someone pointed to a uniformed officer sitting by a window. Carson marched towards him, and was about to bark something at him when he spotted the pips on his shoulder.

He stopped himself just in time. 'Inspector. What can I do for you?'

'Hello, Mr Carson.'

'Have we met?'

'We have, but you probably don't remember me,' the inspector said. 'I was just the local hierarchy when you breezed into town. My name is Rod Lucas, and I believe you have arrested Olwen for the murder of Sarah Goode.'

Carson nodded and waited for Rod to continue.

'I know where Olwen was last night,' Rod said.

Carson didn't respond at first, knowing that the conversation was going to take a turn he didn't like. Then he asked, 'Where was he?'

'The same place he had been the night before, in a coven ceremony,' Rod said.

Carson sighed wearily. 'Between what times?'

'All evening,' said Rod. When Carson didn't look convinced, Rod added, 'I was watching him. I'd been there both nights,' and then he told Carson all about the attacks on the old women in the area. 'I knew there was some link with Olwen, or else he could end up as a victim, and so I watched him. The only place he went was to a barn, and some of his coven members were there. They were having a bit of a party, food and drink, and they conducted a ceremony. I was still there when I heard about Sarah's body being discovered.'

Carson looked down and took some deep breaths, and then asked Rod whether he could put that in a statement. Then he headed towards the door, barking as he went, 'Will someone fill in the inspector on what we know.'

The room stayed silent at first, just the echo of the slammed door. Rod coughed and said, 'So who's going to start?'

There was a man in front of me. Rebecca's father, I guessed. He looked nervous and upset.

'Why have you been following me?' I demanded angrily.

He stepped closer to me. 'Mr Garrett, it's not what you think.'

'You don't know what I think,' I responded.

His hands were stretched out in front of him, tears in his eyes. 'Please don't be angry,' he said, pleading softly.

'You've been following me,' I stressed. 'I want to know why.'

'I wanted to know what you were doing,' he said, fidgeting as he spoke.

'Why didn't you just ask?' I replied. 'I haven't made it a secret.'

He took some deep breaths and bent over.

'Mr Nurse?' I asked, my tone softer now, worried. 'Do you want to sit down?'

He straightened himself. 'You said this person is still killing people, that Mack Lowther didn't kill my daughter.'

I nodded. 'The killer is more specific than that. He's attacking members of a local coven.'

He looked surprised, and then he leaned against the wall, his face pale. 'Rebecca got involved in that,' he said quietly. 'Just a bit of fun, she said.' He looked at me. 'And you think that's why she died?'

'That's the working theory.'

'That girl last night,' he asked, 'are you sure that it was done by the same person who killed Rebecca?'

'Pretty much so.'

He took some more deep breaths.

'So Mack Lowther was innocent,' he said, almost to himself. 'God help me.' Then he turned back and looked at me. 'Please leave,' he said, echoing his wife's plea.

I watched him for a moment, and then I saw his wife appear behind him. She took hold of him and put her arms around him, and he began to sob into her shoulder. I turned to walk back to my car, looking backwards as I got there, and I saw Mrs Nurse watching me. I smiled at her sympathetically, but she put her eyes down and avoided my gaze.

I tried Laura again. Still no answer. I tried the police again, and this time I was put through to Joe.

'Jack? Have you heard about Olwen already?'

'It isn't that,' I replied. 'It's Laura.'

'What about her?' he asked, but I could tell that he sensed some panic in my voice.

'Katie Gray wasn't Sarah's lodger,' I said, 'and she isn't a student. Laura is with her, and I can't get through to her.'

There was silence on the other end for a few seconds, but then he said, 'We'll put out a call. Where are you going?'

I thought about Katie's words, to go back to the start. Was it a clue, a tease? And the witch link started with the death before Rebecca, with the woman who had jumped from Blacko Tower.

'I'm going to see April Mather's family,' I said, and then I threw the phone onto the passenger seat before screeching away.

422

Chapter Eighty-one

I drove quickly towards Blacko Tower. I knew I could see the Mather house from there, a small white house on a rise, and so I weaved between fields bounded by stone walls that were brushed by large branches hanging over the road. There was no path, just steep grass verges, so that I had to drive the Stag onto the grass whenever a car swept around one of the bends. I could see the house in the distance, silhouetted on a hill, but then it would disappear from view until a break in the wall allowed me to see it again. I was getting nearer all the time, though, and then as I passed through a cluster of trees, the house suddenly appeared in front of me.

From Blacko Tower it had been a pretty white house on a rise. Now that I was closer, it looked more isolated, almost on a ridge, set against the grey sky. The white walls looked dirtier as I got closer, with a tumbledown extension and old grey tiles. There were no trees on the field in front of it, and a track snaked towards to the house, winding its way through the dark grasses and the brown soil of mole-hills.

As I jumped out of the car, I looked over my shoulder

and saw Blacko Tower, the tall folly high on a hill. I saw how close it was to the house. April Mather had killed herself from the top of the tower, and her husband had seen a reminder of that every time he came out of his house. What was his name? I cast my mind back to the meeting with the vicar. Dan, that was it. Why had Dan Mather stayed there, so close? Then I remembered that he'd had a son. It was mentioned on the plaque in the church yard. How had it been for him? How old would he be now?

I took some pictures of the house, tried to get the outline against the sky, the rural isolation making it a good angle for the urbanites, and then I took a deep breath. What made April jump from the tower?

I left the Stag abandoned on a scrap of grass. The gate to the property was locked shut by a large chain and padlock, and it jangled as I scrambled over it. The path was long and seemed to wind its way to the house, and would make me pass in front of the windows. There would be no element of surprise. I looked for signs of Laura as I walked, but I couldn't see any. The curtains looked drawn, and there was nothing that indicated whether or not anyone was at home. No smoke from the chimney or lights from inside the house.

As I got closer, though, I started to get a view around the back. There were some cars there, a battered old Fiesta and the ubiquitous Land Rover, along with an old grey van with the side windows blacked out. The Fiesta looked familiar, but I couldn't remember where I had seen it.

I looked quickly back to the house. I thought I had

seen movement ahead, a flash of someone ducking behind a wall. I swallowed, my mouth felt dry. A rook cawed from one of the trees at the back of the house, like a warning, but other than that it was silent.

I paused for a moment and wondered whether I ought to carry on, but then I realised that I had probably gone too far anyway. And it was something more than just the story. I wanted the answers, and to get them I had to keep going.

I came to some steps, the final part of the approach, as the track for the cars swept away from the house and went around to the back. They climbed steeply, and ended on a gravel path, so that my footsteps crunched loudly as I got near the door. I turned around and saw where I had just come from, and looked back towards Newchurch. I could see the huddle of cottages and the square block of the church. In the other direction, Blacko Tower stood out on its hill, like a fantasy tower, with a small window and its castellated top.

I pulled out my camera and took shots of the approach. I turned back around and walked towards the door, getting ready to knock, my stomach churning, when I heard a voice from the side of the house.

'Jack?'

I whirled around and opened my mouth to say something, but then I stopped, surprised. It was Katie. What was she doing there? My mind tried to quickly work things out, the possibilities, but they came at me too fast.

'It's all right, Jack,' she was saying, and she walked towards me, her hands stretched out. 'I can explain everything.'

What was she doing there? I set off towards her, not saying anything, but too late I heard the sound of footsteps on the gravel behind me. I tried to turn as I saw a blur of movement and raised my arms, but then the sound of the rook went faint as something heavy thudded into the back of my head. I looked back towards Katie, but she was blurred, out of focus. I reached out with my hand, and I thought that she was covering her eyes, but the horizon tilted and my feet didn't go where I wanted them to go. I heard footsteps behind me again, scrambling towards me, and then came another bang to the head, and the ground rushed up to meet me.

The gravel dug into my cheeks. I tried to look towards Katie, but it was all blurred again, like a bad television reception. I tried to say something, tried to work out why the view was tilted, why I was down on the ground, but then my thoughts dimmed and the pain faded.

The last thing I saw was Katie smiling.

Chapter Eighty-two

Joe Kinsella and Karl Carson were in the Incident Room when they heard footsteps. They looked up. It was one of Carson's henchmen, tall and muscled, normally confident, but he was coughing nervously.

'Any sign of McGanity?' Carson asked, his tone brusque.

'We've heard nothing so far, sir, but it isn't that.'

When he said nothing further, Carson barked, 'What is it then?'

'I know that we are just looking at coven members here,' he said, looking down at some papers in his hand. 'Well, I looked at the other murders too, the ones we had down for Mack Lowther. There were two before Rebecca Nurse, you know, who weren't witches.'

'Go on,' barked Carson, 'or do I have to prise it out of you?'

The detective lifted up the pieces of paper. 'I found these summaries in the file. They're just an update on suspects, that kind of thing. It's just that I remember that April Mather was on the list, the woman who jumped from the tower.' He waved the pieces of paper. 'Her husband was a suspect in both murders.'

'What?!' shouted Carson, who snatched the papers from him and began to read quickly.

'His car matched a car seen nearby,' the detective continued, 'but his wife, you know, the woman who jumped from the tower, she gave him an alibi both times, so he was eliminated from the case. He drove a similar car, that's all.'

Joe and Carson exchanged glances, and then Joe asked, 'How much time elapsed between the murders and April Mather's suicide?'

Carson skim-read the pages. 'The second murder, Beth Howe, was about a month before,' he said.

Joe looked up, surprised. 'That close?'

Carson nodded.

'And there's something else,' said the detective. 'Katie Gray, our witness. Do you remember that she had been in trouble a couple of years ago?'

'Shoplifting,' said Joe, nodding. 'She received a caution for it.'

The detective nodded, his mouth set, his face a little pale. 'So did Tom Mather, April Mather's son. They were together.'

Joe and Carson exchanged shocked looks, and then they ran for the door.

Sounds came back to me like soft murmurs. I tried to move, but was stopped by a sharp pain in my head. I groaned and clenched my fist, and I felt dirt between my fingers.

I took some deep breaths until the pain faded slightly, and then I heard Laura's voice, but it sounded like a dream, a distant echo. I lifted my head towards it and the pain came back, but not as sharp this time. I put my hand to my head, felt the blood there.

I heard Laura's voice again, but nearer now. 'Are you okay?' she was saying softly. 'Jack, it's me, I'm here.' But her voice wasn't right. It was muffled, slurred.

I opened my eyes and I saw nothing. It was pitch black, with no source of light anywhere. I reached out and my hands felt something soft and warm. Clothes. A body. Then I felt someone clasp my fingers, and I realised why I had heard Laura's voice. She was there with me.

'What are you doing here?' I asked, my voice slow and sluggish.

'I don't know,' she replied. 'I went to speak to Katie, but when I went into the house, something hit me.' Her voice sounded strained, as if it was an effort to talk. 'I don't know where I am, Jack.'

Someone had hit Laura. 'Are you okay?' I asked, alert now, angry, and I rushed to my feet, but too quickly, so I wobbled, my head spinning.

'My cheekbone hurts,' she said, and she winced as she spoke. 'I can't touch it. It feels like it moves when I open my mouth.' I could hear the pain in her voice, like she was speaking through gritted teeth.

I went towards her, but she heard me move.

'No,' she wailed, surprising me, and I heard her shuffle backwards. 'It hurts too much,' she said.

I thought about Katie. I remembered her outside. Then I remembered the battered old Fiesta. I hadn't seen her drive it, but I remembered where I had seen it: outside Sarah's house.

'Katie has got something to do with this,' I said. 'She wasn't really Sarah's lodger, and she wasn't a student either.'

'So who is she?' asked Laura.

I didn't have an answer for that.

My head still hurt, but things were getting clearer. I put my hand to the back of my head and it came away sticky. We both stayed silent for a while, as I considered what we should do next.

I thought about the people who had died through the years, the ones we had talked about just the day before. Then I thought about why I had come here. I had followed the trail set by Katie, and now Laura was trapped in here too, hurt.

Then I thought of how Sarah had been kept hidden before she died. And what about the two witches who were still missing? Was this the room? I remembered how remote the house was, set far back from the road, the nearest neighbour a few hundred yards away. I reached out with my hands, away from Laura, and I hit the wall, testing it with my fists. It felt solid and cold. The floor beneath me was just dirt, and I realised that I must be in some kind of outbuilding. Or cellar. It seemed far-fetched, but my thoughts went to Josef Fritzl. He had abused and held his daughter captive for twenty-four years, and she bore him seven children, all from a cellar in the middle of an Austrian city. Keeping people captive here would be easy. Who would ever visit?

'How did I get in here?' I asked.

'There's a door, and then some stairs.'

'Are there any other ways out?'

Laura didn't answer at first, and then I realised that she was crying.

'Hey, hey, don't cry,' I said. 'If you get weak, you don't think. Don't get beaten by this.'

'That's why I'm like this,' she said, her voice breaking. 'I'm the policewoman. I'm supposed to be strong, able to defend myself.' She stopped for a few seconds as she groaned with pain, before she continued, 'Look at me. Captured by some kid. And what about Bobby? He'll wonder where I am.'

'We'll get back for Bobby, don't worry,' I reassured her, although I wasn't convincing myself. I thought back to Katie. 'She isn't acting alone,' I said, reaching out to Laura slowly. When my hand brushed her shoulder, she came towards me carefully and put my head gently into her chest. 'I ended up here the same way,' I said. 'One minute I'm looking at Katie, the next minute I'm eating gravel. She's not acting alone. All she did was sucker us in.'

Before we could say anything else, the door opened and a burst of light made me blink. I couldn't make out who was there, as the glare put his face in shadow, but a deep voice growled at us, 'One of you, come out, and slowly.'

I looked at Laura. Her right cheek was swollen, and I could see in the light that it was bruising badly.

'I don't know what they are going to do,' I whispered to her, 'but I think I might be in better shape than you to stand it first.'

I thought she was going to object, a copper's pride, but then she looked away and I saw a tear roll down her cheek.

I kissed her on her head as I stood up, and then I moved towards the door. As I got close, I felt a sharp blade stick into my back.

'She won't be watching, so forget about the macho stuff,' he said.

As we got outside the room, I glanced around. He smelled of tobacco and bad breath, and had a ratty face and sallow skin, his hair long and pulled back into a greasy ponytail. He was taller than me, easily over six feet, and his hands were large and calloused, ingrained with oil and dirt. I could smell body odour, and there were sweat stains under his arms.

I felt another jab in my back, so I looked to the front and climbed the stairs slowly. I felt like the condemned climbing the gallows' steps, and as I got to the top, I wondered whether the room would be the last I would ever see.

Chapter Eighty-three

Carson drove quickly along the country lanes, Rod Lucas in the back, giving directions, Joe talking into his phone.

'Should we get more people here?' asked Rod.

'We will, but if we get there first, we are going in,' replied Carson.

As Joe hung up, Carson asked, 'Developments?'

'Sort of,' he said, looking stern. 'Rebecca Nurse's father has just walked into a police station and confessed that he murdered Mack Lowther.'

Carson looked grim-faced at that, his jaw clenched.

'Why would he do that?' asked Rod.

'What, kill Mack Lowther, or confess?' Joe replied.

'Both, I suppose,' Rod replied.

'Because someone told him that Mack Lowther had killed his daughter,' Joe said, his voice filled with regret. 'More importantly, if he did kill Mack Lowther, maybe he has just realised that he killed an innocent man.'

'Any intelligence on Katie Gray?' Carson asked.

Joe shook his head. 'Blank, so far. And Laura McGanity hasn't called in yet.'

As they rounded a corner, Rod told Carson to stop,

and then they saw the red Stag. A car flashed its head-lights further along. A patrol car had got there first.

'What's Garrett doing here?' asked Carson.

'Hopefully it's just an interview,' said Joe.

Carson looked up at the house, and then at the gate, saw the chain and the padlock. He parked on the grass verge, just behind Jack's car, and stepped out. He shivered slightly and wished he'd brought his coat. The air was much fresher than it had been in Blackley.

'So what are our choices?' asked Rod.

'Limited,' Carson replied. 'McGanity is missing, and the person she was last with is linked to that house.'

'Remember that the old women were attacked with booby traps, small home-made bombs,' said Rod. 'Shouldn't we wait?'

'If McGanity is in there, do you think she'll be in any less danger if we do?' asked Carson.

Rod shook his head.

'That's right,' said Carson. 'He's already gone past the point of no return.' He took another look at the chain on the gate. It was thick metal, and would take more than hardware-store bolt-cutters to get through it. He took a deep breath. 'Let's hope he's in the mood for visitors,' he said, and started to climb over the gate.

I glanced around, tried to get a better look at my captor. He was wearing steel-toe-capped boots, the glint of metal showing through the scuffs at the front, and a worn black leather waistcoat. Although he was lean, his arms looked strong, used to hard work. He looked to be in his late forties, and there were streaks of grey in his ponytail.

He smiled at me, which surprised me, although his eyes gave him away, cold and cruel. His teeth were dirty and brown.

'Don't look so shocked, Mr Garrett. This is your story. The hook, the climax. Reporter in peril.' Then he laughed. 'You'll make the front page at last.'

I heard someone else in the room, and when I whirled round I saw Katie against a wall at the back of the room. There was a young man with her, and he looked familiar. He was young, early twenties, grinning excitedly.

Then I remembered. He had been at the initiation ceremony. The young man who had brought in the girl.

'You're in the coven,' I said.

He stepped forward, and as he got closer, he said, 'I'm Tom Mather, April's son, so I'm a descendant, just like the others.'

'You make a sweet couple,' I said sarcastically, looking towards him and Katie. Then I nodded towards my captor. 'And this must be Daddy.'

I felt a slash on my arm, sharp, like a burn, and I stared at the cut, blood spreading onto my skin, running towards my wrist.

I looked at Dan Mather, at the knife in his hand.

'It's all I've got, Garrett,' said Dan. 'Rush me. The door's only there,' and he pointed with the knife. I could see my blood on the blade.

I glanced towards it, and then at the window.

'You can go,' said Dan, taunting. He stepped to one side. 'I won't stop you,' and as I looked at the door again, he added, 'but then I'll have Laura to myself.' He looked at his son, and then at Katie. 'We all will.'

I put my head down. I knew I had no choice.

'Consequences,' said Dan, stepping closer, shaking his head. 'You're so weak. You want to go, to save yourself, but you're scared of the consequences, worried how they'll write it up. You'll be the coward, the man who left his girlfriend to die. You know how it works. You'll sell papers, the latest villain.' He was right next to me, and I could smell his breath on me, fetid, unclean. 'No, you want the big romantic tale, the white knight saving his belle. Or maybe you just fear the middle of the sleepless night, that pricking of your conscience at the knowledge you left her with me, that her little boy will grow up without her. Two lives ruined.'

'So what would you do, if it were you in my place?' I asked.

'I would go,' he replied in a whisper, his dirty teeth bared. 'I would embrace life, enjoy whatever happens next.'

I turned away, not wanting to look at him any more. I could feel my face flush from the adrenalin, my nerves keen. I looked around the room instead, trying to get a sense of my surroundings.

It was a cottage, just as I had seen on the way up, but it was dark, not cosy. The walls were papered, but it was starting to peel at the top, and the decorative border which ran around the centre of the walls was hanging off in places. It looked shabby, with the curtains threadbare in places, dirty and faded, and mud trailed across the floor. Motorcycle parts were propped up in one corner, and the furniture was dated and worn out. There was an old oak table but no chairs, and the settee had foam showing through some of the cushions.

I turned back to Katie. She looked amused, excited, all part of the game.

'Why are you doing this?' I asked her.

Before Katie could answer, Tom Mather interrupted me. 'Because it fucking excites her,' he said, stroking her hair.

'No time for questions, Garrett,' Dan Mather said, his smile staying on his lips, but I thought it faltered. I sensed that his son was someone he couldn't control.

I leaned back against the wall and asked, 'Why, what's the rush?' trying to get myself some thinking time, working hard at controlling my fear. There was a jab of pain when my head touched the wall, and when I put my hand there, my fingers came back sticky with blood again. As I looked back around the room, I saw a hammer on a shelf, blood smears around it. At least I knew why I had a headache. 'I came here to ask questions. I'm a reporter, it's what I do.'

'Let's talk about you first,' Dan replied. 'Can I call you Jack?'

'You've got the girl,' I said, nodding towards the stairs, to where Laura was still held, 'so I suppose that gives you the choice.'

'Do the police know you're here?' he asked.

'It won't take them long to guess.'

Mather turned to his son, and then to Katie. 'So this is it,' he said. 'It's the end.'

As I watched Katie, I thought I saw her smile slip.

Chapter Eighty-four

Carson stood on the other side of the gate, looking up at the house as Rod and Joe scrambled over and landed next to him, Rod puffing slightly, too old for that kind of thing.

'Is that it?' said Carson, almost to himself. It looked like any old farm cottage, dirty and ramshackle. The field in front was virtually barren, apart from one dead tree, its trunk split open, just a gnarled old branch pointing upwards.

'What did you expect?' asked Rod. 'Barbed wire?'

'Hang on,' said Joe, and then he reached into his pocket for his phone. Rod and Carson looked at each other as Joe listened.

'This doesn't have a good feel,' said Carson.

When Joe ended the call, he looked at them both, and then up at the house. 'McGanity hasn't picked up her child from school,' he said.

Carson took a deep breath and ran his hand over his head. 'Garrett is in there, so maybe McGanity is in there too?' He looked up at the house again. 'I missed Sarah Goode. I'm not missing another. Come on, get walking.'

* * *

'Why did you do it?' I asked.

Dan Mather rolled his eyes in mock-boredom. 'Here we go,' he said. 'The confessional.'

'But you hurt people. I want to know why.'

Dan smirked. 'Why do you want to know?'

'I'm a reporter. If I ever get the chance to write this up, my readers will want to know the answer.'

I was trying to distract him. I had seen what he could do to people.

Dan Mather thought about that for a few seconds, and then he said, 'What words would you use to describe me? Not the psycho-babble stuff you'll put in the book you want to write. Give me the tabloid version, the screaming headlines.'

'Evil,' I replied. 'Inhuman. Monster, maybe.'

'So why do you want to live off me?' he asked. Before I could respond, he said, 'You call me inhuman, but you want to feed off me, make money from the things I have had the courage to do.'

I glanced over at Katie. She was biting her lip nervously as Tom Mather paced around, his cheeks flushed, looking agitated.

Dan waved his hand at me. 'Don't feel bad, Mr Garrett. Do you think the police will be any different?' He smiled and shook his head. 'Of course not. They'll be just the same, churning out some ghost-written memoir to be read on the beach, like this is all throwaway stuff. And the judge?' Dan laughed. 'He'll be kept awake by what to call me, how to define me, the cutting words that will be remembered through history. His wife will get sick of his dinner-party talk, how I looked at him coldly before they took me down, blah fucking blah. Fucking parasites, all of you. So cut the shit and just ask me the question that you really want to ask: how does it feel to kill someone?'

I tried not to react to that – didn't want to play his game – but it was hard. I felt sweat prickle across my forehead.

'But it wasn't about death,' I said. 'It was about sex. You fucked them first. Did you tell them that?' I looked over towards Katie, and then at Tom, hoping for a re-action, but there wasn't one. 'Why did you do that?'

'That's not what you're interested in,' Dan Mather said. 'You've fucked people, you know how it feels. You can just ask the little slut we've got downstairs. No, it's the killings you want to know about, how it feels to watch someone take their last breath. What do they feel? Fear? Acceptance? Relief?'

'So that's what it's all about,' I said. 'You get off on their fear.'

Dan Mather laughed out loud at that, turning to look at Katie, and then at Tom. Katie was emotionless, but Tom grinned. Then I noticed that he was gripping Katie's arm, as if worried that she might run out.

'It's my story,' I said, turning back to Dan. 'I want the full truth. I could tell it for you, get it out there. What you think, why you did it, how it felt.'

Dan whirled back to me.

'I'll give you the choice,' he said. 'If you want to write your story, tell the world about me, you can. I'll let you walk out of that door when I've told you everything.'

I was suspicious – but then I realised the catch.

'What about Laura?' I asked.

Mather stepped right up to me again, making me push my head back into the wall.

'That's your choice, Mr Garrett, because today is the final day. If you want to write your story, you can, because it's a simple question for you: one of you is going to die very soon. You, or Laura. But I am going to give you the choice. That'll be some story.' His eyes looked into mine, his eyebrows raised, the stare hard. 'Who do you think it will be?'

'That's no choice,' I said quietly.

He kicked out at me, his mouth in a snarl, the steel toe-caps catching me on my shin. I shouted out and bent double in pain.

'It's your only choice,' he snapped back at me. 'One of you will taste the fire. The other will tell the tale.' His grin came back. 'So who will live and who will die? You or her?'

'But why now?'

'Because the time is right,' he said. I felt the blade under my chin, its tip sharp, cold, pushing against the skin. 'If the choice is you, then I could do it now. A quick slice and it's done. Laura walks.'

I moved my head away.

'Is that your choice, Mr Garrett? Laura's the one?'

I shook my head. 'I haven't decided. I need more time.'

Mather nodded. 'Okay, you've got more time, but if you leave it too long, it's game over. You both die.'

I closed my eyes.

'Let me see if it's a good story first,' I said, trying to

441

draw him out. 'There might be nothing to tell. So go on, what is it like to kill someone?'

Dan Mather spluttered a laugh. 'Do you really want to know?'

'I asked the question.'

He was quiet for a moment before he answered. 'It's never quite what you think it will be.' When I looked surprised, he continued, 'Have you ever thought of something so much that when it happens, it's an anticlimax?'

I nodded.

'It's just like that,' he continued. 'The fantasies, the dreams, those times I've thought of my hands around someone's neck, squeezing tightly, seeing the pleasure in their eyes at first, just a game, but then the fear kicks in. And then they see it, that knowledge, the end, their lives about to be snuffed out. What do they think of, what do they see?'

I saw that his cheeks had flushed and his breaths were heavy. He licked his lips.

'Better in your head?' I asked. 'In real life, there was no pleasure for them.'

'You're catching on,' he said, grinning again. 'They don't piss and shit in my dreams, or cry for their mummies.'

'So why do it again?'

'Have you ever chased your fantasies?' he asked me.

'Not if it meant hurting someone,' I answered, and then I looked him in the eye, tried to show a lack of fear. 'So in your dreams,' I said, 'were they pretty young women, or were they coven members? It seems like you crossed between the two?'

Dan rushed towards me. I put my head back as the knife dug into my neck. I could see sweat on Mather's face, his fingers straining around the handle.

'It's not as simple as that,' he said.

'So now you're complicated? Bit of a cliché, isn't it?' I mocked, trying to ignore the blade against my neck, hoping I could unsettle him, but it was a perilous game. I felt the tip of the blade break the skin. I swallowed, tried not to move.

Then Katie shouted, 'There's someone here.'

Mather looked at her, the blade drooping as he was distracted. 'Who is it?' he shouted.

Katie went to the window. 'It's the police,' she shrieked. 'Carson. What do we do?'

He looked towards the window, and then he grinned. 'Tom, you deal with them.' When Katie looked shocked, he said, 'It's time.'

Tom ran to a locked cupboard and opened it. He pulled out a shotgun and a box of shells.

'What are you doing?' asked Katie, her eyes wide.

'Target practice,' said Tom gleefully.

Katie looked at me, and I sensed that her excitement had now mutated into alarm. 'You can't kill the police,' she said. 'They won't stop hunting you.'

Tom Mather looked at his father, and then at me. Both of them started to laugh. 'There will be nothing to hunt,' Dan said. 'This is the end. This isn't just fantasies to fuck by, you silly little girl. Did you really think it would be any different?'

Tom went to go to the stairs, but Katie shouted, 'You said it wouldn't come to this,' her voice filled with panic.

When Tom ignored her, she looked towards the door, to the way out.

Dan Mather shook his head. 'Don't be stupid, Katie.'

I saw sweat appear on her lip.

'She's right,' I said. 'If he shoots at the police, you will have no chance of getting out.'

Dan went to the window and looked out. 'There's the door, Garrett,' he said, 'if you're worried about getting caught up in it. Just remember that Laura will definitely die if you go – and I won't make it nice.'

I knew that wasn't an option. I looked at Katie. 'You don't look like the suicide type,' I said. 'We've seen it before. Brady and Hindley. Fred and Rose West. Impressionable young woman meets exciting psychopath. She goes along with it, enjoys the ride. It's nothing new.'

'It wasn't like that,' she said, squirming.

'So what was it like?' I asked. 'Myra Hindley got the children into the van. They trusted her, she was a woman. What about you? Did you do the same?'

Katie shook her head.

'You played me all the way through,' I said. 'Why?'

'Maybe I enjoyed it,' she said, mocking, but I sensed a quiver in her voice, saw that her eyes were on Dan, not me.

'But you took a risk,' I continued. 'You brought yourself out in the open by writing those letters.'

'What letters?' asked Dan, as he whirled around, looking angry now.

'Didn't you know?' I asked, surprised.

Katie looked away, suddenly scared, her mouth hanging open.

'Sarah wrote letters,' I said. 'Katie handed them in, pretended that they were delivered to her.'

Dan looked at her, and he took a long, slow deep breath.

'Just part of the game?' I queried. 'Not fun any more, is it, Katie?'

'What did the letters say?' growled Dan.

'Tell him, Katie,' I said.

She backed away from Dan, shaking her head.

'They were all about the witches,' I said, answering for her. 'And when the police didn't realise the connection, you used me to translate them, didn't you, Katie. That's what led me here. That day in the library, when you found all the passages. Just another set-up. You played me well. The flirt, the tears.'

'Why?' asked Dan, and he sounded confused. 'You betrayed us.'

'We talked things through,' she wailed, crying now. 'It was Tom's idea.'

Then we heard a noise upstairs.

Chapter Eighty-five

'Who designed this driveway?' complained Carson as they got nearer to the house. 'It takes forever to get there.'

Joe looked around carefully for anything suspicious on the hill or in the house. 'Maybe that's the point,' he said, and then he put his hand out. 'Stop!' he ordered. 'There's someone there.'

'Where?' asked Carson, looking towards the house.

'Upstairs, at one of the windows.'

Rod's eye shot to the house, and then he shouted, 'Get down!' just before there was a loud bang, the sound of a shotgun. They all ducked. Rod cried out.

'Fuck, fuck,' shouted Carson.

'Keep down,' Rod shouted back, his voice hoarse with pain, his face contorted.

There was nowhere to shelter. The path was open, with no bushes or trees, just a stone wall along one side, dividing Mather's land from the one next door.

They all ducked again at the sound of another blast, but it missed, sending up a shower of dust from the path. Then there was silence.

Carson looked at the other men, saw the sweat on

446

their brows, all of them breathing hard, Rod pale, grimacing.

'Are you hit?' Carson asked, concerned.

Rod nodded and pointed to his trouser leg, shredded and bloodied. He pointed towards the wall. 'We're going to have to get out,' he said through gritted teeth.

'Can you remember the training?' Carson asked.

'Move quick and stay low,' replied Joe. He looked at Rod. 'Can you do it?'

Rod nodded, sweat on his lip, his face pale. 'I'm not waiting for him to reload,' and he set off at a fast hobble towards the wall.

Carson almost smiled, before he set off on a run across the grass.

Tom Mather ran down the stairs, excited now, waving the shotgun.

'Got them,' he shouted manically, his hands tight around the shotgun stock, his face flushed. 'They know we're in here now.'

'Tell me about the letters,' Dan growled at Tom.

Tom stopped, his face turned pale. 'It was just a game,' he said. 'To tease them.'

Dan took a deep breath. 'We're all going to burn,' he said, his voice filled with menace. Then he turned to me. 'Have you made your choice?'

'I haven't decided yet.'

'You'd better be quick, because today we die. You can join us, if you wish.'

I nodded towards Katie. 'Does it include her too?'

Dan smiled at me. 'Especially her,' he said.

Katie was shaking.

'She doesn't want to die,' I said. 'This has been an adventure, that's all, a bit of excitement, riding with the wild bunch.'

'I can speak for myself,' Katie shouted at me.

'Go on then,' I replied. 'Say what you really think.'

Tom strode forward and put the shotgun under my chin. 'This isn't your show,' he said through gritted teeth.

I swallowed, tried to ignore the feel of the steel against my chin. 'The problem with hostages,' I said, 'is that once you lose them, you don't have a bargaining chip. So you need to be careful with that gun.'

I could feel the tremors in the metal as his finger squeezed on the trigger, his eyes tight with anger. Then Dan reached across and put his hand on the barrel.

'Not yet,' he said calmly. He nodded towards the stairs. 'Get the slut.'

Tom looked at his father and then glared at me, before lowering the shotgun and running off to the stairs.

I closed my eyes and swallowed when I heard heavy footsteps, not wanting Laura in the room. Then I heard Laura cry out as she was brought up the stairs.

I opened my eyes and saw that Tom was gripping Laura by the hair. Her face was swollen, there were violent bruises on her cheeks, and one of her eyes was just an angry red slit.

I jumped, wanted to go to her, but I told myself to stay calm, not to provoke them. Dan must have seen my reaction, because he started to grin, spittle appearing in the corners of his mouth.

'You bastard!' I seethed at him.

Laura looked at me and gave a small shake of the head. *Don't antagonise them*, she was saying, *concentrate*.

Tom jumped forward and rammed the butt of the gun into my knee. I dropped to the floor, my teeth gritted, pain shooting through my leg. I squirmed around so that I could see him properly, to make sure that he couldn't come at me from behind, taking deep breaths to drive away the pain.

He stepped over to me again. I shuffled away, my leg dragging and throbbing in protest as I moved in an arc to put my back against the wall. He stared at me intently, wanting to see my fear, the pain in my eyes. He wasn't going to get either. I stared back at him, angry, challenging.

He snarled at me and stamped on my hand, his boots heavy. I shouted in pain and felt my fingers swell. My head hung to the floor, black spots flashing in front of my eyes. Was this it? Was this how it was going to end, slowly and in pain?

I stopped crawling and lay down, out of breath. I looked over at Laura, who had her eyes clamped shut and was slumped against a wall. I thought I could see tears through the swelling of her eyes. I looked at Dan. He was leaning against the wall, just watching.

Tom Mather pulled a wooden chair towards me and sat down, so that he was looking down at me as I lay on the floor, panting. He pointed his gun at me and slowly brought it towards my head. It crept closer, the chasm of the barrel getting darker and more hypnotic as it came closer, drawing me in.

The gun only stopped when it reached the tender spot between my eyebrows. He pushed against it slightly, so I could feel it there, could sense the menace. It was cold.

He looked down the barrel at me and smiled.

'Katie?' he shouted, never taking his eyes off me.

'Yeah?'

He tilted his head towards Laura. 'Get me some rope to tie that bitch up.' When Laura glanced towards the door, he added, 'If you run, you'll hear your boyfriend's brains hit the wall before you reach the grass outside.'

Tom got to his feet and turned his chair so that the back of it was facing the door to the room. He grabbed Laura by the hair again and pushed her down into the chair, back-to-front, so that she was facing the door, her legs splayed around the back of the chair.

Katie passed Tom some cord. 'What are you going to do?' she asked.

'Improvise,' he said, his eyes never leaving me.

He put his gun on the floor and took hold of Laura's arms.

'If you rush me,' he said to me, 'I'll pick up that shotgun in a second, and the first person to die is her.'

I didn't move. I glanced over at Dan, who was watching his son in action, a proud smile on his lips. I turned back to Laura, and watched as Tom bound her arms to the back of the chair so that they were sticking out in front of her. He rummaged in a drawer and pulled out some parcel tape. He strapped Laura's wrists together with it. Before I could work out what he was doing, he rushed to a drawer and pulled out a handgun.

Tom looked at me and said, 'It's not real, but it should do the trick,' and then he laughed to himself before strapping it into Laura's hand. He glanced round to his father. 'What do you reckon?'

Dan nodded in approval. 'I like it.'

I looked at Tom again, searched for a sign that Laura was about to die, but there was nothing. Tom picked up his gun and joined his father by the window.

Then I realised something that made me feel sick. He wasn't going to shoot Laura, I knew that now. He was going to make someone else do it. Tom had put the handgun between Laura's bound wrists, so that from a quick glance it would look like someone holding and aiming a pistol. And it would be the first thing the police would see when they burst in, rushing, adrenalin pumping, looking for a target to shoot at. They wouldn't see it was Laura. They would just see a gun pointed at them, arms outstretched and forward, and they would shoot. Quick reaction, self-preservation. They would mistake Laura for the enemy and shoot her, riddle her so full of bullets it would take a public inquiry to work out who fired the fatal shot. The Mather family's last joke.

Laura tried to lift her head, but Tom went to her and slapped her on her swollen cheek. Laura's head fell forward onto her arms and I could hear her groaning, blood gushing from her swollen lips. My good fist clenched, and I started to kneel, getting ready to launch myself. Tom must have sensed my thoughts, because he pressed the shotgun against Laura's head. 'Don't,' he warned.

I looked at Dan and said, 'I've made my choice.'

'What choice?' asked Dan, stepping away from the wall.

'The one you gave me. Who dies, me or Laura. I choose me. Just let her go.'

Laura lifted her head and looked towards me. She shook her head. I could see blood running from a cut above her eye.

Dan Mather started to grin. 'The game has changed. You need to keep up. We're all going to die. This is the day.'

'You bastard,' I whispered.

He waved me away. 'This is no time for compliments. Just be glad that you'll die together.'

Chapter Eighty-six

Carson peered over the wall as he tried to work out the layout of the house. They had made it back down to the road. Rod was on his radio, calling for the firearms unit. Joe was pacing around, trying to decide on the next step.

The house looked dark and dirty, just a two-storey stone cottage, the white paint old, with small dusty windows and a tumbledown extension at one side. The field leading up to it was steep, but the house wasn't quite at the top of the ridge, so that the bottom part of the house was built into the hill. If there was a cellar, then it would be a good place to keep someone captive, the landscape providing the soundproofing.

Carson worked out the windows. One at the front downstairs, and a door next to it, with another window at the side. One room, two windows, was his guess. Upstairs, there were two larger windows, one with frosted glass. The bathroom, he presumed. Five places from which they could be shot at.

Rod shuffled along to join him, grimacing in pain, a tourniquet fashioned out of his shirt sleeve wrapped around his thigh. 'Firearms are on their way,' he said. 'Will be twenty minutes, maybe more.'

'And an ambulance?' asked Carson.

'I bloody well hope so,' said Rod. 'Your bedside manner isn't doing me much good.'

Carson smiled, but it faded when he looked back towards the house. 'How did this turn into a hostage situation?' he asked, almost to himself.

Joe arrived next to him. 'By us not realising the danger,' he replied.

'So what now?' asked Carson.

'We wait.'

'Did Dan Mather never come up on your radar?' asked Carson, looking at Rod.

'I don't know any more than you,' Rod replied, gasping.

'This doesn't feel good,' Carson said.

'It's worse than that,' said Joe. 'If McGanity is in there, this is a desperate last stand.'

'But why?'

'Because he knows we are on to him,' replied Joe. 'He has already killed, if we are right, and so he has nothing to lose.'

Carson didn't respond to that, all his attention focused on the house; he looked round only when he heard Joe speak into his radio.

'Are you sure about that?' Joe asked, his eyes wide.

Carson waited impatiently as Joe listened. They had found something.

When he signed off, Carson asked, 'What have you got?'

Joe turned to look at Carson, and then said, 'It's his son, Tom Mather.'

'The shoplifter?'

Joe nodded. 'There was more on him than on his father. His school called the cops a couple of times, thought he had killed some of the school pets. But they had no proof, just schoolboy rumours. And anyway, his mother had killed herself not long before. He was bound to be a bit screwed up.'

'There's a young man in the coven,' said Rod, suddenly remembering. 'He would be about the right age.'

Joe whirled around. 'Tom would be a descendant, just like his mother.'

Carson looked at Joe. 'What the hell are you thinking?' he asked.

Joe bit his lip, his thoughts flowing fast, and looked towards the house. 'He's the scout,' he said. 'He tells his father who's in the coven, the pretty ones.'

'But why did he turn on the coven?' asked Carson, confused.

'Resentment about April's suicide would be my guess,' said Joe in reply. 'Remember that April Mather gave her husband an alibi the first time the police asked questions about a murder. Perhaps she believed his story, that it was nothing to do with him? When it happened a second time, Beth Howe's murder, did she realise that she'd got it wrong, that she had allowed him to kill again? Remember that April was a witch, all about harmony and nature, doing things for good. She died on Halloween, her special night, the first time it came around after the second murder. After some booze, maybe the guilt came out.'

'It would fit,' said Rod.

'What would fit?' asked Carson.

'With what she shouted when she jumped,' Rod replied. '"An' it harm none."'

'How do you think Dan Mather felt about that?' Joe asked, and then he answered his own question. 'Betrayed would be my guess, and all because she was in a coven.'

Carson sighed and looked at the house again, at the clouds gathering just behind it. 'How the hell are we going to unravel this mess?'

Chapter Eighty-seven

Tom Mather was carrying empty paint tins from the back of the house and placing them around the room, ten in total. Then he brought in a large oil can. I guessed they had a diesel store at the back somewhere. He had put the shotgun down on the floor while he moved the tins, but I knew I would never get to it before Dan.

I slumped back against the wall. 'So why did you do it?' I asked Dan. 'If it was never the high you expected, why carry on?'

He watched his son for a while as Tom half-filled each tin with oil, before turning to me.

'You wouldn't understand,' came the reply.

'Try me,' I said.

Dan shook his head. 'This isn't your show.'

'But what did you enjoy most?' I pressed. 'I want to know why, and what you got out of it.'

Dan watched Tom again, who was carrying a bucket and dragging some wires along the floor.

'You want to get the thrill without the risk,' said Dan. 'Like all the rest, cowards until the end.'

'No, it's not like that,' I protested, trying to keep up

the diversion, to postpone the final moment. 'I just want to expand my knowledge, so that I can understand people like you,' I added, pandering to his ego.

'But you'll never understand people like me,' Dan Mather said, arrogance creeping into his voice. 'People like you can't, because you can't see beyond your own little world, where everything is safe, no fears, no dangers.'

'Or maybe there is nothing to understand,' I snapped back at him. 'Perhaps you just never stopped being the little boy who liked torturing animals; not for any reason, but just because you've got a cruel streak you can't control.'

Dan Mather stepped closer to me. His teeth were bared, spittle peppering his lips.

'Have you ever imagined jumping from a building?' he said slowly, quietly. 'Alive all the way down, but with no way out, the ground getting closer all the time, rushing towards you. Tell me, what would go through your head?'

I thought about that, tried to engage him. 'Could be many things,' I said. 'My family?'

'But why not think of them before? Suicide is such a selfish thing.'

'Okay, so what about acceptance, or regret,' I said. 'Some sorrow for how my life ended up? Maybe fear of what is about to come, that split-second of pain?'

Dan tugged on his lip, began to smile. 'You're getting the game now. How does it feel?'

'Interesting, I suppose – but I can live without knowing.'

'But I want to know,' he said gleefully. 'That moment, life or death, realisation in their eyes, fear. I want to know that moment, want to see inside them, to taste that final thought, the glimpse into the abyss.'

'So is that your high?'

He chuckled. 'If you chase the high, you are never happy.'

'So why was it only young women who interested you?' I asked.

He flinched. I saw Laura shake her head. She knew what I was doing, but *Take it slow* was the message.

'That's what troubles me,' I continued, knowing I had to take a risk, try to provoke him, knock him off balance. 'If you wanted that knowledge, why not vary it a little? What's so special about the last moments of pretty young women?'

His eyes narrowed. 'It wasn't about that.'

'So what was it about then, the girls you strangled and raped? It was more than just witches, wasn't it? Who were you really striking back at?'

Tom put the bucket onto the floor. It was filled with black powder, which he began to scoop into the cans of oil, watching us all the time.

'It's just that moment that counts,' said Dan, his voice quieter now, 'that final few seconds of panic when they know they are dying, like a flash of their life in front of my eyes.'

'But what do you want them to say?' I pressed. 'Do you want them to say sorry?' Dan looked uncomfortable, and so I carried on. 'Whose face do you see when they are dying? Your mother?' When Dan shot me an angry look, I added, 'She left you when you were a boy. I know that, brought up by your grandmother. Is it her you are killing, just wanting her to say sorry for walking out on you?'

Dan looked away, his jaw clenched tightly.

'You're saying too much – you don't have to tell him anything,' interrupted Tom angrily, as he attached the wires to some small discs. He placed each disc in a paint tin, the wires trailing out, which he then bound together, all intertwined, ten wires joined into one. 'Do you know what this is?'

'You're changing the subject,' I said. 'I was talking to your father.'

'Look around,' Tom said. 'This is our show, and so we change the rules.' He lifted the wires. 'So come on, what is it?'

I played along. 'At a guess, some kind of primitive bomb.'

He laughed. 'Nothing primitive about this. Once I've attached the wires to a detonator, one press of the button and we're fucking bird food.'

I looked at Katie. Her excitement was long gone now. She looked back at Tom, and then at the tins spaced out around the room. It looked like there was to be no escape.

'So when do we go bang?' I asked, keeping my gaze on Katie.

'Pretty soon,' said Tom. 'We just need a few more of those people outside in here.'

'Why don't you just give yourself up?' I asked. 'Go out there now. At least you'll live.'

Katie began to edge towards the door.

460

Tom shook his head. 'No. We all die.'

'So you can feel the moment, that final thought? Pity you won't be able to tell your father about it.'

Dan laughed and then gestured towards Laura. 'I'll be looking into her eyes when we go, wondering about her thoughts.'

I didn't look over, tried to keep focus. And anyway, I knew what Laura's thoughts would be. They would all be about Bobby, how he would grow up without her.

Then we all saw something against the wall. A flicker. Blue lights. And then I heard the sirens.

'A few more for the party,' said Dan, his voice calm, looking out of the window.

Tom lifted up the wires and pointed around the room. 'We can start the fireworks early.'

Katie looked at me, and I saw fresh panic in her eyes. She looked around at the paint tins. I saw her get closer to the door.

I glanced towards the window. I could hear the vans outside, could see the blue lights flickering off the walls. If Katie could get out, she might tell them what was going on. I didn't trust her to be truthful, but it was our only chance. So I had to keep Tom and Dan distracted.

'So how did it happen?' I asked Dan. 'Did you get them randomly, or was it watch and wait?'

'Who do you want to know about?'

I remembered Rebecca's father from earlier. 'I don't know. What about the local girl, the one you left by the brook? Just an innocent young girl walking to the pub.'

Dan laughed, mocking. 'Innocent? She wasn't fucking innocent.'

'What do you mean?'

'Why wasn't someone with her?' he said. 'When I saw her, it had just started to rain, and so I stopped to give her a lift. Why not? Would you let her walk in the rain?'

'So what happened to turn it from a favour to a murder?'

Dan waved his hand dismissively. 'I had no choice. She was going to tell lies.'

'What lies?'

'That I raped her,' he said, his eyes wide. 'I helped her out, showed her some kindness, but at the end of it, she just wanted my money, tried to blackmail me.'

'How so?'

'I saw her, and I stopped, gave her a lift. Then, when we got further down the road, she started to come on to me, wanting to fuck me.' His lip curled slightly.

'And did you?' I asked.

'Of course I fucked her,' Dan continued, sneering. 'And Christ, she enjoyed it, shouting and crying out.' But his face was screwed up with distaste, like it was a bad memory. 'But you know what it's like afterwards with these sluts. Things got nasty. She said that she would tell my wife if I didn't give her money. She said that she would tell the police that I had raped her. Who would want that?' he said, his voice getting quieter, meaner. 'I had no choice. I strangled her, watched her life end right in front of me, tasted that final moment.' He looked at me, as if he was appealing for under-standing. 'I put her body down by the brook so someone would find her.'

'That's bullshit,' I said. 'Is that what you told Tom

462

here, to justify it? April was dead by then. How could Rebecca say anything to her?'

Dan faltered at the words.

'And what about the others?' I asked. In my peripheral vision, I saw Katie's hand slip onto the door handle. She was watching me, her face paler than before. 'What about the ones before,' I pressed, 'and the ones after? What about Sarah? Did she want to fuck you?'

Dan didn't respond.

'Because don't take this the wrong way,' I pressed, 'but I don't think women act like that, begging for sex from strangers.'

Then there was a noise, the door opening. I looked up. It was Katie. 'I'm sorry,' she said, tears in her eyes. 'I love you, Tom,' and then she was gone.

I sat back and said a silent prayer.

Chapter Eighty-eight

Carson walked quickly among the police vans, dark blue, three of them, with grilles on the windows, lights flashing. A driver's window went down on one and a large man with a crew cut smiled and asked, 'Having trouble?'

'You missed off the "sir"', snapped Carson.

The smile broadened. 'Seems like I did.' He pointed round to the other side of the van. 'Go round the other side, so that there is no line of sight from the house.' When Carson got there, Rod and Joe just behind, the driver jumped out and joined them.

Carson was a tall man, used to being intimidating due to his size, but even he was forced to look up. The man in front of him was over six foot six, his chest and shoulders broad, with biceps like bowling balls, his hair light and thinning. His ears gave away the rugby history, swollen and misshapen, and his nose seemed to be pushed flat to his face. 'Ged Flynn,' he said, introducing himself. 'So what have we got?'

'Someone shooting at us from the bedroom window,' said Joe, stepping in. 'A shotgun, I think, and there may be hostages inside.'

Flynn looked towards the house. 'Who lives there?'

'Father and son,' Carson replied. 'Dan and Tom Mather. They have killed people already, and so they'll do it again. And they know that when we get them, they're under arrest for murder.'

'So this is a last stand?'

Joe nodded. Then Rod stepped forward. 'He's used explosives before too.'

'What sort?'

'Ammonium nitrate. Just enough to injure so far, but they seemed like stunts.'

Ged Flynn whistled. 'Crazy then,' he said. Then he looked around. A car was trying to crawl past the scene, a young family, the children with their faces against the windscreen. 'Get this road blocked off,' he said to Carson. 'Half a mile either side.'

'What about residents?'

'Get them out.'

Joe started to direct some of the uniforms to close off the road, but then he heard someone shout. He turned around, saw something moving quickly. It was someone running away from the house, a young woman. Carson saw her at the same time, and he watched as she ran at the gate, her hair wild, her eyes frightened.

He reached out and pulled her over the gate, and then dragged her behind the wall. She put her head back against the stone, panting hard.

'Katie Gray,' said Carson. 'You've got a few questions to answer.'

*   *   *

'She's gone,' I said to Dan Mather. 'What now?'

Tom looked at the door for a few seconds, unsure what to do, and then he turned to his father.

'She was always going to go, forget about her,' said Dan, and then he turned to me. 'It looks like the story will get told now, so you're sort of redundant.'

'But Katie will be the one telling it,' I said. 'We're your only hope of making the story even.'

'What do you mean?' asked Dan, curious.

'She'll tell it her way, to make her seem the innocent, make you two out to be the terrible ones.'

Dan laughed. 'Oh, we're terrible all right, and you can think what you like of me, but she fucking revelled in it. You know, sometimes the newly converted are the most enthusiastic.'

'So that's why she was the one in control,' I said. When Dan looked confused for a second, I added, 'The letters. You didn't know anything about those. She has brought you out into the open, willing you to be caught. You see, Katie didn't enjoy it, not really, not deep down. It was a thrill, the talking about it, but she didn't really want to do it. The letters were a way of the police finding you, because when I started asking questions, she was the one who decided that Sarah ought to write another one. That's right, isn't it, Tom?'

He shuffled nervously, glancing towards the door, hoping that she would come back was my guess.

'She was the one who led me round the library,' I said, 'looking at transcripts, because she knew I would work it out.'

Dan held up his hand. 'Stop,' he said quietly.

'Am I getting near the mark?'

'I said Stop!' Dan was shouting now. He walked to the window and looked out. When he turned back, he looked at Laura, and then at Tom. 'What the fuck were you doing?' he demanded.

Tom shrugged, tried to feign calm, but I could see his fingers drumming nervously on his leg, fast and nervous. 'We thought it would liven things up,' he said.

'Katie's the one outside now, talking to Karl Carson,' I continued. 'You're still in here, getting ready to blow us all to bits. Now tell me, who was in charge?'

Dan picked up the shotgun and pointed it at me. 'You're good,' he said, mocking. 'Very Clarice Starling. But do you want to know who is in charge?' and he waved the barrels at me. 'Run at me and find out, you might just get to me in time.'

Laura tilted her head to the side and I saw movement, just a shake of the head. *Don't*, she was telling me. *Don't do anything he wants.*

'No,' I said, 'I won't run at you.'

Dan stared at me for a few seconds, and then shook his head. 'A coward to the end.' He lowered the barrels and passed the gun back to Tom, who was getting edgy, pacing up and down, his footsteps getting faster, like he was winding himself up.

I looked at Laura. She opened her eyes and tried to smile at me, tears running down her face.

Dan Mather pulled a phone from his pocket. He stared at the keypad. I looked at the cans dotted around the room. Bombs, I knew that, home-made and crude. How were they detonated? As he moved his finger to the keypad, I remembered the description of Sarah's blown-out body and I squeezed my eyes closed, waiting for the bang.

Chapter Eighty-nine

Carson shoved Katie into the tactical response van. When she winced as her arm hit the side, he said, 'Don't think about a complaint. I'm not interested.'

Katie moved onto a seat at the back, rubbing her arm. Carson climbed in next to her, with Joe and Ged Flynn just behind him.

'Talk,' barked Carson.

Katie started to cry. 'Don't I have any rights?' she asked.

'Not right now,' Carson replied. 'Just tell me what's going on.'

'He made me do it,' Katie said, her voice strained through the tears.

'Who?'

'Tom,' she replied. 'He made me go along with it. Sarah Goode, the lies I told you, everything.' Katie put her face in her hands. 'He said his father would kill me if I gave him away. I had no choice.'

Carson peered through the van windows. 'How many people are in there?'

'There's Tom and his father, plus the reporter. And his girlfriend, the detective.'

'Are they still alive?'

Katie nodded as she wiped her nose.

Carson grabbed her by her collar and lifted her up in her seat.

'There's no time for that,' he snarled.

'I didn't want this to happen,' she cried, tears streaming down her cheeks.

'It's not about you,' he said, still gripping her collar. 'It's about what's happening in there. So you are going to talk. Firstly, why did you lie?'

Katie took some deep breaths, tried to compose herself. 'I told you, he made me do it.'

'Made you do what?'

'Live in Sarah's house,' she said. 'I didn't know he was going to kill her. I didn't know about the others.'

'So what did you think it was about?' asked Carson.

'I don't know,' she wailed. 'I came back to Tom's house and she was there, and Dan said that if I didn't do what he asked, he would kill her, and if I gave him away, he would kill me.' Katie sniffled and wiped her nose. 'And I didn't want to lose Tom.'

'So you did it for love?' Carson said sarcastically.

Katie nodded.

Carson knelt down in front of her. He spoke quietly, made sure he had her attention. 'You'd better do something now for the people in there,' and he pointed towards the house. When Katie didn't answer, he grabbed her chin and lifted her head up. 'You'd better co-operate, or else I'll turn you into Britain's most hated. It only takes a few damaging leaks before you'll need to claim a new life abroad to survive. Remember Maxine Carr?' When Katie looked at him, her eyes filled with tears, he asked, 'What's the scene in there?'

Katie took some deep breaths, tried to compose herself.

'Laura is strapped to a chair,' she said quietly. 'She's tied up so that it looks like she's going to shoot.'

Carson thought about that. He realised that it was a trap, that it would make Laura a target for the firearms squad. But he realised something else: that Dan Mather would know that the trick was blown, with Katie in the van. What would they do next?

'Is she hurt?' he asked.

Katie nodded. 'She's been beaten up. And Jack too.'

'How is he?'

'He's alive,' she said, and then added, 'You don't know what you're dealing with.'

'You're going to tell me. But how do I know you're not just another trick?'

'What do you mean?'

Carson gave a sharp laugh. 'You moved in after Sarah was kidnapped, and you pretended to be her lodger and friend, and then it turns out that she never had a lodger. You played us all, lied in your statement – just part of the game, was it? How do I know that he didn't let you out to mislead us?'

Katie swallowed and wiped her cheeks. 'You don't,' she said, 'so it's your gamble.'

'You're a sweet little bitch, aren't you,' Carson sneered at her, but he knew that she was right.

Dan Mather had taught her well. 'Where was Sarah kept?' he asked.

'There's a cellar, split into two halves,' Katie replied.

'How many ways in?'

'Just one. It's the part of the cellar nearest to the hill-side.'

Carson thought back to what Rod had told him, about the coven members being targeted, and then he thought about how Sarah had died. 'What's his thing with explosives?' he asked.

'That's just Tom,' she replied. 'He likes blowing things up. I caught him once emptying the gunpowder out of fireworks. He keeps experimenting.'

'Is that all he has up there?'

Katie looked down.

'Miss Gray, you'd better say something.'

'He's been buying fertiliser, just in small amounts, but now he's got quite a pile. And blasting caps. He's got some of those. I think he's building up to something big.'

'Has he tried it out yet?'

Katie nodded. 'He blows up bottles, just behind the house. He mixes the fertiliser with oil and then sets off a blasting cap. It makes him really excited.'

Ged Flynn spoke up. 'Ammonium nitrate?' he asked, and his face had turned serious.

'That's it,' said Katie, nodding. 'It was in the shed at the back, but he's filling tins with it.'

'What do you mean, "filling tins"?' asked Ged.

'Just that,' Katie replied. 'He's put paint tins all over the house, and he's filling them with oil and that fertiliser. They're under the windows, everywhere.'

'Shit!' exclaimed Flynn.

'Ammonium nitrate is serious stuff,' said Carson.

Ged Flynn nodded. 'If you mix it right,' he said, 'and easy to get hold of.'

Carson paused for a moment. 'Is he going to kill himself?' he asked Katie.

Katie nodded. 'And everyone else in there.'

Carson stepped out of the van and looked back towards the house. It was booby-trapped, and he knew that Dan Mather was prepared to kill. Then he turned around when he heard a phone ring. Katie looked at him for a moment, and then reached into her pocket. As she pulled out her phone and looked at the screen, her eyes opened wide. She tried to turn it off, but Carson beat her to it. He pushed her against the side of the van and looked at the screen. The caller ID simply said 'Dan'.

Carson pressed the answer button.

Chapter Ninety

'Dan Mather? This is Karl Carson from the Lancashire Police.'

Carson didn't know what to expect as he introduced himself. He thought that there might be some desperation from Mather's end, and he knew that he had to stay calm, not startle him.

'Hello Karl. This is Dan.' His voice was calm, almost serene. Carson was surprised. But then Dan said, 'She found you then.'

Carson set his jaw and looked at Joe. Dan Mather was too calm, as if the call was about a parking ticket. Joe held out his hands as if to say, 'Calm down. Take it slow.'

'Yes, I'm with her now,' Carson said coolly. 'I know that you have got one of my detectives in there. How is she?'

There was silence for a while, Carson straining to hear anything going on in the background. Dan's voice returned eventually. 'She's still alive.'

Carson almost grimaced. 'She's still alive' covered too many possibilities.

'Is she unharmed?' he ventured.

'She's still alive,' Dan repeated, and Carson sensed that he was enjoying himself.

Again, there was silence as Carson tried to evaluate the position. Joe was scribbling furiously on some paper, and then he passed the paper to Carson. It said, 'All about control. His pace, not yours.'

Carson nodded. He understood. 'What do you want us to do?' he asked.

There was further silence.

Carson moved the phone away from his ear and shrugged his shoulders at Joe. Joe made a hush sign to his lips. Carson stayed quiet. Instead, he looked at Katie's phone, searching for the hands-free button. He found it, and the next time Dan spoke, his voice was like a tinny echo around the van. 'I just want some of you in here,' it said.

'That's not going to happen, not unless you let the other two people leave first,' Carson answered, his mouth close to the handset so Dan wouldn't know he was on speaker-phone.

'You've made your choice, Inspector.'

Carson glanced over at Joe, who held his palm outwards and then lowered it, telling him to take it slow. There was silence again. Carson thought about Laura, and he wondered if she could hear the call. There were experts at this kind of thing, but he wasn't one of them.

His relief wasn't to last long.

'My son is pointing a shotgun at your detective's head, and he's a little bit trigger-happy,' said Dan, sneering. 'So I want some of you in here. You come, and she can go.'

'And what about the explosives?'

Dan laughed at that. 'The little bitch didn't take long, did she? So you might as well know that if you mess me about, I will set those fuckers off, and you'll have to explain to your police officer's family why she has been pureed. I'm not doing deals. I want you in here, or wish your colleague goodbye.'

Carson looked over at Joe and said, 'Can I call you back?'

Dan was silent for a few moments, and then Carson heard him agree. 'Five minutes,' he said, and then the line went dead.

Carson gave a heavy sigh and thought about Joe's one word of advice: control. Let Dan believe that he is in control. Don't bullshit him or underestimate him. He looked down at the phone. His hand was sweating. This was it. The next thirty minutes could save or cost lives.

When Dan put down his phone, I asked him, 'You're determined to die?'

He looked at me, and I saw that some of the arrogance had gone, that in its place was an acceptance of his fate.

'The letters were Katie's idea, not yours, we know that,' I said. 'But why did Tom go along with it?' I glanced over at Tom, who was still pointing the gun at Laura, but it didn't seem like he was listening, the barrels drooping slightly. Was he thinking about Katie, how she had betrayed him?

'He wanted to be stopped too,' I continued, 'and that's why the letters were sent. He isn't like you.'

A smile flickered at the corner of Dan's mouth. 'Maybe not,' and then he looked back out of the window, to where Katie had run. 'Sometimes a woman wants a taste of the wild life, but it's just a game, because when things get too wild, they want out.'

'Is that how it was with April?' I asked.

Dan shook his head. 'April was different. She didn't know.' He looked over at Tom. 'Katie changed him. A man's first really good fuck does that. A man should move on, find someone else, because women like that are trouble – when the man can't deliver, the woman moves on.'

'How much did Katie know?'

'She knew everything,' Dan said angrily. 'I saw the excitement in her eyes, the flush it brought to her cheeks.'

'And now she is telling her story,' I said. 'What now?'

He looked down and scratched his cheek as he thought, and then he looked around at the tins, filled with fuel and powder. 'We go next, I suppose.'

'But you could tell them all about her, otherwise she'll get away with it, blame it all on you.'

Dan shook his head. 'Do you think it would make a difference? I kill people, as does Tom.'

'But why? You sound like you know it's wrong.'

He sighed and clenched his fists, screwed his eyes up tight, like he was fighting against his own personal demons. I looked over at Laura. She nodded at me almost imperceptibly, and I could tell she thought I was getting somewhere.

Dan took a deep breath. 'Do you know what it's like to live with someone who won't leave you alone?' he said, his eyes squeezed shut. 'It's like that in my head, a voice, always pestering me, driving me to carry on, like a constant tap-tap-tap in my fucking head, non-stop. I kick against it, tell it to leave me alone, but it won't stop, constant, in my ear all the time, telling me to feel it, to know it, someone's last second, facing death in an instant, just a glance at the end. And I don't want to listen but it doesn't stop, and so I give in, and I see what the voice means, the pleasure, the rush.' He opened his eyes, gave a little laugh. 'But do you know what? When it happens, I don't remember much, like it's old movie footage, black and white, flickering, going too fast.' He laughed again. 'What kind of fucking irony is that?'

'But if you know it's wrong,' I said, 'why do you carry on?'

He shook his head. 'If you were pestered constantly to kill, you would give in, I can promise you. Just after, it's like a release, silence.'

I pointed towards the window. 'Let them understand you. It might stop it happening to someone else.'

Dan followed my gaze, and for a moment I thought he was tempted, but then his phone rang, and the spell was broken.

He looked at it, then back at me, but when I saw his sneer return I realised that the moment had gone.

'Carson. I'm glad you called back.'

Chapter Ninety-one

Carson heard Joe whisper 'Good luck' as Dan answered the phone. He tried not to think about whether he needed the luck. He felt isolated, but he wanted it that way. Just himself and Dan Mather, a meeting of minds. If he messed up, he would be the one answering the awkward questions at the inquiry.

'Mr Mather?'

There was just silence.

'Is that what you want me to call you?' asked Carson, waiting for the answer.

Joe gave him the thumbs up. *Good*, it said. *Let him take the helm.*

'You can call me Dan,' came the response, the voice echoing around the van again.

'Good, Dan,' Carson said. 'You called Katie's phone for a reason, so what do you want to talk about?'

'Well, it isn't about the fucking weather forecast, is it,' came the sarcastic response, followed by a low chuckle. 'I wish you could see her now.'

Carson's stomach turned over. 'How is she?' he asked. It was a lame question. Then he heard a grunt, some kind of exertion, and then a yelp, a female cry, echoing around the van. He guessed it had been a kick at Laura, maybe a punch.

'I keep telling you, she's alive,' answered Dan, amused.

It didn't seem like much, but at least there was still some hope. Joe whispered at him to stay calm, but the thought entered his head that if Laura was alive at the start of the call, and then dead before its end, it could be his fault. Carson took a deep breath to push it to one side.

'It looks busy out there,' said Dan. 'How about losing a few?'

'What do you mean?'

'Get them to retreat. I want every police car out of sight.'

'I don't know if I should do that.'

'What you ought to do is whatever I ask you to do, Carson. You're no longer in charge.'

'Don't worry,' whispered Joe. 'Tell him it's okay, you'll give it a try, and then shout at everyone to move their cars.'

Carson nodded in agreement. He dropped the phone to his chest and shouted for everyone to move back, waving his arms at them theatrically. He heard the crackle of static as the message went through the radios, and then the movement started. The cars and vans edged slowly backwards, until the only vehicle still there was the van with Joe and Carson inside. But Carson knew that there would be men still stationed behind the wall, waiting for a good line of sight.

Before he had the chance to speak, Joe gave him the thumbs-up signal.

'See, Carson, do you see the power I have?' said Dan, laughing. 'I know they will be crawling along the walls, but I got them to move.'

Carson stayed silent. Perhaps Joe had underestimated Dan Mather.

'Do you want your detective back?' asked Dan, taunting.

Before he had a chance to answer, Joe made cutting motions with his hands. 'Don't say yes,' he hissed. 'Preserve the status quo.'

'I just want her to be safe, that's all,' said Carson.

'Well, she can be. It's in your hands, Karl Carson. Fuck up, and you have blood on them.'

Carson felt a flash of anger, but Joe shook his head. *Don't say anything. Let him lead.*

There was silence for a while, although Carson thought he could hear harsh words spoken over the whisper of stifled sobs. He felt a bead of sweat trickle onto his lip.

'Send the little bitch back,' said Dan, 'and then we'll talk some more.'

'If you mean Katie, we can't send her back,' Carson answered. 'And you know that.'

'But don't you care about your detective?'

'Yes, I do, but why do you want Katie back?' asked Carson.

'C'mon, you've seen her. Pretty young thing, isn't she? And it gets lonely in the countryside. Send Katie back, and make it all right for Laura. She wants to go home. You can help her.'

'Why don't you help her? Just let her go, Garrett too, and take your chances in court. It might work out for you.'

There was silence again, and Carson wondered if something he'd said had angered him. And then the phone went dead. Dan had hung up.

Carson glanced along the road, to where the other police vehicles were, just out of sight of the house.

'You're doing okay,' said Joe. 'Give it two minutes and ring back. Just don't agree to anything we can't deliver. Let him agree his own surrender. Start to explain the positives in letting Laura go.'

Carson looked back towards the house, and he felt angry. He was being held to ransom by a bike mechanic from the hills. This wasn't what he had expected when he'd started the day.

But he knew the drill in negotiations. Concede some to win some.

He looked at the phone in his hand, said a silent prayer, and pressed call.

The phone rang out seven times before it was answered.

'Is that you again, Carson?'

'Yeah, it's me.'

There was a moment's silence, so he decided to press on.

'Look, Dan, this is difficult for me, and I suppose it will be for you too, but I think we can work this out.'

A bitter laugh came down the line. 'There is no "we"

involved. I tell you what we want, and you do it. If you don't, I kill Laura, and then I kill Jack Garrett.'

'What do you want out of this?' Carson pleaded, but the phone went dead.

Chapter Ninety-two

Tom Mather was bouncing on his heels, the gun barrels swivelling around like a tank turret.

'This place is going to blow like fucking Etna,' he said, his eyes wild.

I looked towards the window and wondered what was happening outside. And I began to wonder whether I should run for the door, try and get outside to warn everyone to stay away. I would die in the process, I was certain of that, but if I did nothing, I would die anyway.

Then I thought of Laura. If I ran, she would certainly die. It could be what made him set off the explosives. Laura was still alive, and for as long as things stayed like that, I would co-operate.

I looked at Dan. He was smiling.

Rod thought about what he could do. The ambulance wouldn't come any nearer, not with an armed stand-off, and he wouldn't leave. Carson had taken over the negotiations, but this was his area, he felt some responsibility. He had been told what Katie had said about ammonium nitrate in the house, confirming what he knew. He had been around enough farmers to know about fertiliser.

He looked over to the firefighters, who were standing by their engines, looking restless. They were further back than the police vans, clustered at the entrance to a field. Rod hobbled over to them, wincing all the way, looking for the person in charge. Rod found him pacing at the back of a fire appliance.

'We can't just sit here all day,' he complained to Rod, glancing at his watch. Then he looked down and saw Rod's trouser leg, now soaked through with blood.

'I know that,' Rod replied, his voice calm. 'Tell me this, though: would you go near that house if there was a fire in there and you knew that there was some ammonium-based fertiliser inside?'

The fire chief opened his eyes wide. 'Not a chance,' he replied. 'And I know there's fuel in there. I heard the girl before. Do you remember the Oklahoma bomb?'

Rod nodded.

'That was ammonium fertiliser. Blew the front of the building off, and that wasn't some old cottage in the hills. That place will be blown into nothing if it goes up.'

'So how do you deal with it?' Rod asked.

The fire chief scratched his head and thought for a moment. Then he said, 'Get it wet. Really wet.'

Rod smiled. He'd thought as much.

'Tell me one more thing,' Rod asked.

The fire chief gave a wary smile. Police officers in this mood usually meant trouble.

'Could your hoses break glass?' Rod asked.

The fire chief looked surprised. 'What do you mean?'

'Can the pressure from the hose break a small pane of glass?'

The chief looked at Rod quizzically, weighing up whether it was wise to answer truthfully or not, before cracking a smile. 'If it isn't too big, I reckon they could make a mess. Depends on how strong the glass is, I suppose.'

'What about if we break it first? Could you get a good stream going, enough to knock a man over inside?'

The fire chief's smile widened. 'Those hoses can blow. If you got in their way, you'd know about it.'

Rod smiled. He had what he wanted.

Chapter Ninety-three

Carson was tense. The officers nearby waited for his signal, but he was putting other professionals at risk. The firefighters took risks every day, but then the enemy was fire, something they had been trained to contain. This was something different. Their safety depended on decisions he reached, and on the reactions of the madman in that house.

Everyone knew Rod's plan. The first step was the distraction.

Carson pressed dial and heard the ring of Dan Mather's phone in his ear. There were seven rings before it was answered.

'Yes?'

'Just seeing how you were doing?' Carson said, and then he nodded at the officers standing nearby.

The plan was to get the explosive wet, very wet, so that it wouldn't matter if sparks started flying. There were three units of police officers, and in each of them were two men holding riot shields to the floor, and another two holding theirs so that they overlapped the others, but higher, so that each unit consisted of a two-by-two bulletproof shield, protecting the men behind them. Each four-man riot shield allowed a small gap in the middle. Behind that gap stood a line of three firemen, one behind the other, the front one holding the high-pressure water hose, the two behind helping, with the nozzle of the hose protruding through the gap, the shields clamped like vices around it to limit any way through for bullets. Just behind the firemen were two tactical response officers. They were carrying their guns across their chests, the settings on rapid fire.

'I'm just fine,' replied Dan. 'McGanity doesn't look too good though.'

Carson gave the nod to Joe, who radio'd the command, and then watched nervously as the air was filled with the sound of shields banging together and heavy feet shuffling through long grass.

The lines advanced slowly, the officers with the shields moving carefully, making sure they stayed together as a solid wall. Two units shuffled towards the windows of the main room in the house, vulnerable in the open space at the front. Another unit headed towards the house from the side, sneaking along the wall that formed the boundary.

Carson lifted binoculars to his eyes and looked at the house. There were no signs of movement. A curtain flapped around the upstairs window, but everywhere else was as peaceful as a Sunday morning. Sweat prickled his forehead, despite the November cold, and his shirt stuck to his back. He put the binoculars down and looked at the control van. All eyes were trained on the house.

'Let me know that they are both still alive,' said Carson, trying to keep Dan's concentration on what was happening inside the house, not outside.

The units crept forward at a pace almost too slow to see. Each unit was waiting for the signal to pull back if there was any sign of adverse movement from inside. Carson had given his men clear instructions not to put the fire officers' lives at risk under any circumstances.

Each line came to within ten yards of its intended target. There was nothing from the house. The countryside around was quiet, except for the buzzing of radios clipped to jumpsuits, everyone waiting for the signal from Karl Carson.

Tom Mather stood up quickly when he heard something outside.

'They're coming!' he shouted.

Dan Mather looked at his son, and then glanced outside, saw the riot shields. I made a dash for him but my knee gave way, and so I fell to the floor, grimacing with pain. I heard my cheekbone crunch as Tom jammed the butt of the shotgun hard into my face. I yelled out in agony. My face felt like it was on fire, my cheekbone cracked in half.

I almost passed out, but as everything went distant I heard Laura straining on her bindings. I fought the image to vomit, but before my vision cleared Tom had me pinned to the floor, the gun pressed against my shattered cheekbone, making my vision speckle as the pain took me over.

I took deep breaths, tried to clear my head, to see

489

through the panic and the nausea. I could feel my cheek-bone moving around under my skin, every breath making it click and grate, and I felt a jab of pain run through me, as sharp as a sword.

Tom got his face near to mine. 'Getting brave, Garrett?' he snarled. 'We die together.'

At that moment, I knew that he was probably right. I summoned up all my anger, all my venom, tried to get past the pain, and spat at him. It landed on his face, bloody and angry, and he swiped me across the face with his free fist. I groaned with the pain, and for a moment I sensed myself drift off, but I tried to shut it out, determined to stay conscious.

I started to stand but fell down again, my head spinning out of control.

'You are one sick bastard,' I said to him, blood spewing from my broken mouth, every word agony. 'At least I know that no one else will die after today.'

I collapsed back onto the floor, panting, my outburst draining me. Tom's gun followed me, the dark barrels tracking my forehead. I saw Dan appear behind him.

'So that's it,' said Dan, strangely emotionless. 'Your final words. Not good.' He bent down towards me, tried to meet my gaze. 'How does it feel?' he said. 'Not long. Your life gone. What are you thinking?'

I spat blood onto the floor, panting, struggling for breath. I closed my eyes. 'Mostly, I'm thinking "fuck you".'

Dan smiled at me.

'And there's something else too,' I said.

Dan nodded at me to continue.

'I just want to know why your wife killed herself,' I said. 'Tom's mother. What was behind that?'

'She was weak,' came the reply. 'Like the little slut who just ran out, when it came to it, all her wild talk meant nothing in the end.'

I thought I saw Tom wince as his father said it. Something occurred to me, a chance. Divide and conquer.

'But didn't she think about young Tom here?' I asked. 'He was left behind.'

Dan shook his head. 'She didn't care about him. She was selfish to the end.' And then he laughed. 'She was hard to shift though.'

'What do you mean?'

'The whining little bitch used to moan that it had all been just a game, sex talk, that she didn't really want anyone to die,' replied Dan. 'But that was bullshit. She used to like the dirty talk, my hands around her neck, describing what it would be like to kill someone, the big squeeze, her face full red, eyelids fluttering.' He grinned at me. 'If you've never tried it, you're too late now.'

Tom looked uncomfortable. He was looking at the floor, shifting his weight from one foot to the other.

'So to her it was a game, but for you it was just practice,' I said.

'Something like that.' He sighed. 'She couldn't handle it, but she knew it was partly her fault, that she had stoked the fire, and then when I couldn't stop, well, she was desperate. It didn't take long to persuade her to jump.'

I noticed Tom's head snap up at that.

491

'You made her jump?' I queried loudly, making sure that Tom could hear me.

'She was going to tell,' said Dan, 'but I had other plans,' and he tapped his head. 'I've told you, if the voice keeps on fucking tap-tap-tapping, non-stop, then you give in; you obey.'

'But it was your voice in her head?'

Dan laughed. 'Genius, don't you think?'

I heard a noise behind him, and I saw that Tom had raised his gun and he was pointing it right at me. I saw his bared teeth as he began to squeeze on the trigger.

Carson looked over at Joe, who seemed pensive for a moment. Then he glanced at the fire chief, who appeared worried but proud. Carson spent a second or two surveying the scene, and then unclipped his radio and shouted, 'GO! GO! GO!'

The firefighters by the appliances turned the water on quickly. It coursed down the three hoses, making them stretch and writhe and buck like live snakes on a grill. As the firefighters braced themselves behind the shields, the tactical response officers burst out from behind the shields and sprinted towards their targets, one set for the door, the other two taking a window each. The door went in with a kick, the windows needed just a jab with a gun. The officers dived to one side just as the water rocketed out of the hoses and into the house.

Chapter Ninety-four

The window smashed behind me.

I whirled around in panic. I saw a flash of light reflecting off police shields, and then I saw movement in the grass behind them. I threw myself against the wall, driven by instinct.

Tom tracked me, surprised by my movement. Then he looked at the window, and then back at me, his face filled with surprise. He raised the shotgun once more.

And then the water came through.

A torrent shot across the room, catching Tom in the chest like a liquid battering ram. The gun flew out of his hand and skittered away from him. He went down hard, and then tried to scramble for the gun, but he slipped in the water gathering on the wooden floor.

Tom got to his feet quickly and looked around. I saw fear in his eyes. Laura started to pull at her ropes, screaming for help.

A second burst of water came through the side window, glass scattering across the floor. Tom turned to face it and screamed.

Water was crashing off two walls, moving across,

taking down pictures, clocks, books. Wallpaper began to look sodden, started to wrinkle and peel. The tins of fuel tumbled over, the contents lying in a sheen on top of the water before soaking through the gaps in the floorboards and away.

Tom scrambled to his gun once more and moved back towards me, and I braced myself for the shot. I heard Dan shout at him, 'Kill him, you useless little bastard!' It was barely audible above the noise of water crashing around the house.

I shut my eyes and waited for the end.

But then the water must have moved across. Tom had been near its path as the jet roared across the room, soaking everything in its way. The roar had a steady rhythm, a deafening drumming on the opposite wall, but for a moment I heard the sound change. It went for a second to a high-pitched smack, and as I flung my eyes open I saw Tom hit in the face by a spear of water coming in so fast that it snapped his head back hard. He thrust out his arm and pulled on the trigger. The blast from the shotgun made my ears ring and knocked me off balance, and then he slipped to the floor.

I glanced around quickly, tried to see what he had hit. I looked at Laura. She was panicking, strapped to the chair, being thrashed against it, trying to keep her head out of the water, but the power of the spray was too much for her. I tried to get up and go to her. I was knocked over by the water, taking a hit in the back like a punch from a heavyweight. Dan was moving towards me, keeping low, the water still coming into the room hard. I tried to shout for him to stay still, but the sound was lost.

He fell towards me, and then I heard a moan. It was the sound of breath being expelled, and I could feel it hot on my cheek. I pushed him off, and he tumbled to the floor. As I looked down at him, his gaze seemed hollow. He gasped, his hand clasped to his chest. I glanced down and I saw his shirt billowing red. He'd taken the shot in his stomach. Blood was soaking into his trousers, running down his arms, pushed around by the water on his body, diluted, keeping the blood flowing.

He looked at me, his eyes becoming distant. He'd been hit. Tom had shot him. Was it an accident?

I tried to get a good look at his chest, but didn't lose sight of his eyes for fear it was a trick. I reached down onto his chest with my good hand. His shirt felt like tarpaulin, thick and oily with blood. I pressed hard onto his abdomen and I felt him buck beneath my hand, his teeth gritting and rolling, his voice an almost silent roar.

I could see holes in his shirt where the blood was thickest. I looked back into his eyes, my hand still over the wound. I ignored the sound of glass smashing as the water jets knocked things over, taking out more window panes. My mind was only on Dan Mather.

I glanced at Laura, still strapped to the chair, and let my anger run wild. I thought of Sarah, the girl I'd never met. I thought of her parents, mourning their daughter, nothing left but old photographs and heads full of memories. I looked down at Dan Mather, and I wanted him to suffer.

I gritted my teeth and went looking for the wounds. I stared into his eyes as I felt along, my hands wet and sticky, his breaths coming quicker, his eyes widening as I pressed and prodded.

I found holes in his stomach, just a short reach apart, his flesh torn ragged.

I looked at him hard in the eyes. I thought I saw a plea for mercy.

'Why didn't you blow us all up?' I shouted over the water, my voice angry.

He shook his head weakly.

'Because you are a coward,' I said, 'just like all of us.'

And then I plunged my thumb hard and deep into one of the wounds, jerking my hand upwards as I did it, my teeth bared in anger. I moved my thumb around, backward and forward, Dan's eyes wide with pain, his mouth open and screaming. I could feel him tight around me, could feel every second of pain with every push of my thumb. He put his hands around my neck, tearing at my hair.

I was snarling by now. I kept my thumb inside him but went searching for the other wounds with my index finger. I found one and plunged my finger in deep. He dug his nails hard into my back, drawing blood, increasing my anger. I forced my middle finger in there, and I felt him push himself hard against me, his eyes rolling in their sockets.

I was gripping him like a bowling ball. I could feel him around me, the wetness, the movement of pain as he screamed and bucked against my hand, my fingers and thumb hard and straight inside him. I could feel tissues, veins, muscles between my fingers. I looked into his eyes and I could see fires burning. I hoped they were the fires of hell, ready for him. I felt his body between my fingers, his agony in my grasp.

Then I clenched my fist hard.

He opened his mouth to scream some more but only blood came out, a stream covering his chin, and he started to shake.

I helped him. I shook him by the tissues and muscles I gripped in my fist and I screamed for him. But my scream wasn't a cry for help or a scream of pain. It was a shout of victory, for Sarah, and Rebecca, and April, and all the rest.

I yanked out my hand, making the two wounds one, still holding parts of him in my fingers.

Dan slumped back and stared at me in disbelief. He fell back into the water, the splash lost in the roar as he landed in the growing pool of red. He tried to lift his head and I saw the end in his eyes. I knew at that moment he was dying. And I saw that he knew it. I could see it in his pleading, his silent cry for help.

His eyes looked away from me, and as I followed his eyes I saw his gun.

I knew what he wanted. He wanted out.

The water was still crashing into the room. It was six inches deep now; the flow in was too fast for the flow out. The old wooden floor had become treacherous.

I scuttled over to the gun, splashing through the water, my clothes now heavy and wet, blood from Dan Mather mixing with my own. I grasped it and wondered what to do. I looked back at Dan Mather, who was breathing death breaths, his chest racking itself for air, his mouth open, his pallor white and laboured.

The water kept me awake. I couldn't close my jaw and every breath in and out was like the draw of a sword. The pain twisted my thoughts, made me angry. I saw Laura being knocked by the water, and I saw her knees sagging, as if she was beginning to lose consciousness.

I threw the gun down and rushed to her, put my arms around her, and pulled the chair to the floor, out of the line of the water. I was kneeling on the floor, cradling Laura, the water coming in above my head. Pictures were gone from the walls and I could hear glass smashing in the kitchen.

Then the water stopped.

The house became deathly still, silent apart from the dripping from the ceiling and shelves.

I realised I was cold.

Dan Mather looked at me, pleading.

I shook my head and smiled. 'What do you see?' I said quietly, mocking. 'Now you know the final moment, enjoy it.'

I plunged my hands deep into the water to soak away his blood, and then I heard the door crash in.

I lay in the water as it slowly seeped through the floor-boards, my arms around Laura, still strapped to the chair. The water cleaned the blood off my hands and cooled the pain in my cheek. I could hear the shouts of the police officers as they ran through the house.

Dan Mather was still alive, just. I lifted my head up. The pain almost sent me back down, but I had to see. He was breathing short breaths, his chest going hard like a piston, trying to draw air in. His cheeks had sunk hollow and his eyes rolled in their sockets. I could see his blood painting the floor red.

There were two police officers standing over him, each with their gun trained on him. But Dan was looking at me. Someone was talking to him, asking him how he was. He smiled, thin and weak. He knew he wouldn't need them.

I heard the tear of Laura's bindings as someone cut her free, and she fell into my arms. I could hear running footsteps, shouts and yells, and someone appeared with a blanket. I thought I saw a paramedic.

I looked back at Dan Mather. He groaned and his chest rose one last time, his back arched, his eyes wide and scared, one last effort for air.

I closed my eyes as the pain shot through me. 'Rot in hell,' I hissed, before collapsing back down.

I heard footsteps around me and I looked up. It was Karl Carson.

'You stupid bastard,' he said.

I managed a smile. 'Thank you.'

And then it all went dark.

Chapter Ninety-five

I heard the letterbox clang as a letter dropped onto the mat.

I checked my watch. It was still early, dark outside, but I hadn't been sleeping well. Every time I fell asleep, I saw Dan Mather's face. But it wasn't the look that he'd had when he was hurting me that kept me awake. It was the look as he'd died that was in my mind, that final knowing glance. I could still feel his flesh on my fingers, cold and wet, and I could have tried to save him.

I groaned as I slid out of bed. I'd tormented myself for too long. It had been a month since Dan Mather died, but my body still ached, bruises and swellings all over my legs, and a plate had been inserted into my cheek to hold my cheekbone together, the same for Laura. There was little feeling there now, just numbness. I knew it was worse for Laura, because it had hurt her professionally as well. She had been signed off for a couple of months, and would be on light duties after that, but she was restless, wanted to go back.

I hobbled down the stairs, saw the Christmas tree in the corner of the living room. We were trying to make it normal for Bobby. He had been quiet at first, and I knew it was worry over Laura.

We had some financial security now. The story had been sold, and an exclusive with a tabloid had paid off the mortgage. It had come at a price, though, and I tried not to think of Rebecca Nurse's father as he struggled with prison, waiting for his trial for killing Mack Lowther. He was going to argue diminished responsibility, try to win the hearts of the jury, that he wasn't in control of himself, but I knew that his heart wasn't in it. He was tormented by the thought that he had killed an innocent man. The other prisoners were fine with him, told him that Mack Lowther had deserved what he'd got for the other lives he'd ruined, but that didn't help him. He had killed Mack Lowther to avenge his daughter, twisted by revenge, but he'd got it wrong.

As I walked to the front door, I saw a familiar envelope. It was from Laura's solicitor. I was nervous as I picked it up, knowing that its contents might decide whether Laura and Bobby stayed in the north or not. I thought about saving it for Laura, but as I held it in my hand, I knew that I wanted to be prepared for whatever was contained in it.

I slipped my finger into the fold and opened the envelope. As I spread out the letter, I saw the neat typeface, covering a whole page, and took a deep breath. I started to read it.

When I had finished it, I felt my eyes go wet, and a tear ran down my cheek. I read it again, just to make sure, and then I looked towards the stairs, to where Laura was still sleeping.

I put my head back against the wall and closed my eyes.

It was going to be all right. The Court Welfare Report had recommended that Bobby should stay with us. Geoff had decided that he couldn't afford the final hearing, that it would be a waste of money, and was going to withdraw his application for custody.

I heard movement behind me, and then I felt Laura's arms go around me, felt her pull my head into her shoulders.

We were going to be all right.

Enjoyed *Last Rites*? Read on for an exclusive peek at Neil White's new novel, coming soon . . .

May 1988

The two police officers had the car windows open as they came to a halt outside Claude Gilbert's house. They were down to their shirt sleeves, the interior stifling from the first real promise of summer. When they turned off the engine it seemed quiet, the bustle of the town centre out of sight, just the long curve of the street in front of them, the houses bordered by high walls, ivy-covered, with the black iron railings of a Victorian park on the other side.

Mick Roach looked at the house next to their car, a large Edwardian house with sandstone walls and white corners, roses creeping around the edges. 'One day,' he said. 'I can see me in one of those.'

Bill Hunter shook his head. 'Not in this job.'

'You've no ambition,' Roach replied, and he stepped out of the car. 'Who wouldn't want to live up here? All I can see of Blackley is the moorland.'

'That's why the best houses are up here,' said Hunter quietly. 'It kept the professionals out of the smog when the mills were running. It was peasants like us who had to live in the valley, where the smoke from the chimneys choked us every day.'

'Oh, give it a rest, old man,' Roach said wearily. 'Do you remember the miners' strike? Well, that was the end of the class war. The revolution ended with a brass band soundtrack, so let's rest the working class hero shit. Thatcher won.'

Hunter joined him on the pavement. 'So you covet all of this, do you?' he asked.

Roach looked at the house and then nodded approvingly. 'Yeah, maybe I do,' he said, almost to himself, and then turned to Hunter. 'And what's wrong with that?'

'Because when I joined the force all those years ago, I had different ideals,' Hunter replied. 'Just the old-fashioned stuff, like making a difference, something to make me proud that I joined up.'

'And look at you now. You're not exactly a career advert,' Roach said, shaking his head. 'The only person who will help me is myself, and so if I can get myself a big house I'll will, and fuck everyone else.' And then he set off walking to the gates, pausing only to let Bill Hunter catch up with him before giving them a push.

They swung open slowly, creaking on old hinges, until they banged against the brick pillars that supported them. They stepped onto the gravel drive that led towards the house. The only noise as they walked was their footsteps and the swish of branches in a light spring breeze, blowing the confetti of cherry blossom against their shoes.

'Turn the radios off,' Roach said, smiling. 'I wouldn't mind hanging around for a while. They might serve us strawberries on the lawn.'

Hunter laughed. 'You don't know Claude Gilbert.'

'Some barrister, so I heard.'

'How long have you been in the job now?' Hunter asked, stopping.

Roach ran his fingers through his hair; it was getting long, ready for the months ahead working undercover on the rave scene, his youth his asset. Saturday nights spent chasing around the Lancashire countryside, trying to work out the venue, ecstasy the new pill on the block.

'Three years in August,' he said. 'Why?'

'Because when you've been in it a bit longer, and you've been spat on and punched and uncovered sudden deaths, then maybe you'll look at lawyers' houses and wonder why they get so much for doing all the dirty work.'

Roach shook his head. 'No, I won't. It's just all part of the game. You're just bitter that it slipped you by.'

'Yeah, I'm bitter all right,' Hunter replied. 'My mother worked on this street as a cleaner at one of the houses further down. I've given twenty-five years of my life to this force, and do you know what I've got to show for it? Grey hair, a semi-detached house, and a crappy old Sierra. And I'm fighting for the good guys. Gilbert sets free some real wicked bastards, and he doesn't lose a minute of sleep.'

'It's a great view though,' Roach replied, looking along the lawns, and when he heard Hunter grunt his disapproval he added, 'You're a dinosaur, Bill,' before walking towards the double wooden doors at the front of the house. 'When were they last seen?'

'Five days ago,' Hunter replied, breathing heavyily as he rushed to keep up.

'So it could be a holiday,' said Roach.

'His chambers don't think so. He missed the start of

a big fraud case, and they pay well.' Hunter smiled. 'Like you, he's a greedy bastard.'

'What, you think they've run away?'

'It depends on why he's gone,' Hunter replied. 'Bit of a gambler so I hear. Maybe he's had a big loss. If Mrs Gilbert is used to this lifestyle, she's not going to settle for nothing. They could have emptied their accounts and gone somewhere.'

Roach wasn't convinced. 'House prices are rising. There'll be plenty of money tied up in this place.'

Hunter took a step back and looked up at the house. All the curtains were shut. 'Maybe he got too involved in a case? Lawyers think they're immune but they're not, they are dealing with some real nasty people. I know judges who have been threatened, just quiet words when they are out with their wives, thinking that no-one knows who they are.' He stepped forward and pressed his face against the stained glass panel in the front door. 'There's a few letters on the floor, so they're not in.'

'What do we do?' Roach asked, looking around. He could see an old man watching him from the other side of the road.

Hunter followed Roach's gaze. 'Go ask him if he's seen them,' he said.

Roach paused for a moment, and then he shrugged and walked away. He hadn't gone too far when he heard a smash of glass. He whirled around. Hunter was brushing his arm.

'Slipped,' he said, before reaching in and turning the Yale lock.

Roach walked quickly back up the path. He got there just as Hunter was pushing the door open.

'Get the post,' said Hunter. 'See how far back the post-marks go.'

It was dark inside. The hallway stretched ahead of them with stairs leading upwards, the stained glass around the doors casting red and blue shadows along the wall. They both crinkled their noses. The house smelled stale.

Hunter looked into the living room to his left. Nothing unusual in there. Two sofas and a television hidden away in a wooden cabinet, crystal bowls on a dresser, nothing broken. There was a room on the other side of the hallway dominated by a long mahogany table. There were place settings, plates on mats, a jug of water on the table.

'No sign of a disturbance,' he said. 'What about the letters?'

'These go back a couple of days,' replied Roach, flicking through them. 'Bills, credit card statements.'

Hunter went along the hall to the kitchen at the back of the property. It was long with high sash windows looking along the garden. There was a yellow Aga and a battered oak table with china mugs hanging from hooks underneath dusty cupboards.

'They hadn't planned to leave,' Roach said. When Hunter turned round, Roach was holding a half-empty milk bottle. 'This is like yoghurt. They would have thrown it away.'

Hunter scratched his head. He ambled over to the window and looked at the two lawns, green and lush, separated by a gravel path. There was an elaborate fountain in one corner of the garden with a wide stone basin and a Grecian woman holding an urn, and a steel and glass summer house in the other. Hunter could see the bright fronds of plants.

He heard Roach join him but he was looking down at the floor and the walls. Hunter was about to say something when something drew his eye, some detail in the garden that didn't seem quite right. He looked closer, wondered what he'd seen, when he realised that it was the lawn. It was flat all the way along, green and even, but he noticed that there was an area near the back wall where it seemed dirty, as if soil had been piled on it.

'What do you think to that?' Hunter asked, before turning round to see Roach kneeling down, examining the skirting and the wall. 'What is it?'

Roach looked up, his brow furrowed, his cockiness gone. 'It looks like dried blood,' he said. 'And there's some on the wall.'

As Hunter followed his gaze, he saw it. Just specks, and some faint brown smears on the white tiles, as if someone had tried to clean it away.

'What do we do?' asked Roach.

Hunter looked at him, and then he pulled his radio towards his mouth. 'You can forget about your strawberries,' he said.

Hunter and Roach were outside, Hunter sneaking a cigarette as the scenes of crime officers scraped at the blood on the skirting. There was an unsmiling detective watching him, watching them both, blaming them for wasting his afternoon.

'We can't just rip up a barrister's house because we've found some old blood,' Roach said to Hunter.

510

'Because he's a barrister?'

'Yes,' Roach answered, 'he can make trouble for us if we get it wrong.'

Hunter ground out his cigarette and marched over the patio, heading towards the garden.

'Where are you going?' Roach shouted.

'Gardening,' came the reply.

Hunter walked quickly down the path, looking at the grass at the end of the garden, just before the path wound towards the summer house, the last thing before the high garden walls. As Roach joined him, Hunter pointed. 'Can you see that?' he asked.

Roach looked and shrugged. 'Can I see what?'

'Soil,' Hunter replied. 'On the grass and there on the path,' and he pointed at some more dark patches. 'Someone's been doing some digging round here,' he said.

'It's a garden,' Roach said sarcastically. 'It's what people do.'

Hunter ignored him and strode onto the soil beds, dragging his foot along the ground, his face stern with concentration. Then he stopped. He looked at Roach, and pointed downwards.

'It's looser here,' he said. 'Crumblier, less dense. And there is soil on the lawn and the path. Perhaps they thought it would be washed away with the rain, but it's been dry all week.' Hunter saw the detective watching him from the patio doors. 'Get some spades from that shed over there.'

Roach looked uncertain. 'Just the flower bed,' he said warily, 'nothing more.'

When Hunter nodded his approval, Roach went to the shed and after a few seconds he came out holding two spades. When he rejoined Hunter by the soil bed, he asked, 'Do you think we should? I mean, what if there's nothing there?'

'Do you think Gilbert would rather we did it and then filled it back in again,' Hunter countered, 'or should we get the diggers in, just to make a real mess of the garden?'

Roach pondered that for a moment, and then sighed before thrusting the spade into the dirt.

It was hot work, but it took them just thirty minutes to empty out the soil; it wasn't very compacted, and it only went to a depth of a few feet before Roach's spade hit something hard. They looked at each other and began scraping the soil away silently.

When they had finished, Roach climbed out of the hole and looked down. He glanced over at Hunter. 'What the fuck is it?'

'That's not the real question, is it,' he replied.

Roach exhaled loudly. 'Who's going to look first?'

Hunter nodded to him. 'You dug the hole.'

Roach shook his head and held his hand out to Hunter. 'Seniority.'

Hunter grimaced and then dropped into the hole. In there was an old chest, painted red, with the initials *CG* on the lid. It was about four feet long, and just a couple of feet wide, but it was deep. It was fastened with a metal clasp, clogged up with soil. Hunter spat on it to remove the dirt. He clicked open the clasp and looked back at Roach.

'What do you reckon?' he asked. 'The family silver?' and then he opened the lid slowly. It only came half way open before he recoiled and quickly put his forearm over his mouth.

'What is it?' asked Roach, getting to his knees.

Hunter took some deep breaths and then reached out to open the lid again. This time he threw it open and scrambled out of the hole.

Roach gasped. The patio door opened at the other end of the garden and they heard the footsteps of the detective making his way down the path.

'Fuck me,' said Roach, almost in a whisper.

In the chest was a woman, squashed in, curled up on her side, her face blue and her dark hair over her face.

'There's blood on the lining,' said Roach, pointing to some staining just above her head.

As Hunter looked he noticed something else. He went to the floor again just to have a closer look and then struggled back to his feet. He looked at Roach. 'It's worse than that,' he said, his face pale.

'How can it be worse?' Roach asked.

'Look at the lining, near her hands,' Hunter said, his face ashen. 'Can you see it, torn and shredded, the fibres all pulled out?'

Roach didn't answer.

'She's got the same fibres around her fingers,' Hunter continued. 'I can see them under her fingernails.' He turned to Roach. 'Do you know what that means?'

Roach nodded slowly, his face now pale too. 'She was buried alive.'

Present Day

It was the start of another ordinary day. Clear skies and rolling Lancashire fields, the sunlight turning the grey of Turners Fold below me into quaint Victoriana, the canal twinkling soft blue, bringing the summer barges from nearby Blackley as it wound its way towards Yorkshire.

Turners Fold was my home, had always been that way, or so it seemed. I'd spent a few years in London, a small-town boy lost in the bright lights, but home kept calling me, and so when the rush of the city wore me down, I headed back north. I had lived in Soho, and as I now looked over strips of stone housing, at the cars heading towards the motorways and industrial parks, it made me realise how different my life had been then. I used to enjoy walking the London streets, feeling the jostle of the crowd, just another anonymous face, but the excitement faded in the end. It didn't take me long to pick up the northern rhythms again, the slower pace, the bluntness of the people and the lack of any real noise. And I liked it that way. It seemed simpler somehow, less complicated, not as much of a race.

The summers made the move worthwhile. The heat

didn't hang between the buildings like it did in London, trapped by exhaust fumes, the only respite a trip to a park packed out by tourists, never really enough space to unwind. The tourists don't visit Turners Fold, so it felt like I had the hills to myself, a private view of gentle slopes and snaking ribbons of drystone walls, the towns in the valleys just blips. But they had character, tough little towns of millstone grit. I smiled as the breeze ruffled my hair and I felt the first warmth of the day, in anticipation of a perfect June afternoon. I heard a noise behind me, the shuffle of slippers on the stone step. I didn't need to look round.

'I thought you were staying in bed,' I said.

Laura put her arms around my waist, and I felt her lips brush my neck.

'I want to take Bobby to school,' she replied, her voice hoarse. 'Early shift next week, so I won't get chance then. What are you doing?'

'Just enjoying the view,' I said.

Laura rested her head on my shoulder and let her hair fall onto my chest. She had grown it over the winter; dark and sleek, it was past her shoulders now. I looked down. Cotton pyjamas and fluffy slippers, she looked a long way from the sharp-suited detective she transformed into when she went to work.

'When are you going to work?' she asked.

'Soon,' I replied, 'but I'm not rushing.'

'Court?'

I nodded. 'I've made the call, and there's not much from the cells, but I'll have a snoop around and see what I can find.'

'You could always spend the day here.'

I smiled. 'I might just do that, but I'll make sure we can pay the bills first.'

She gave me another squeeze and then went back inside. I listened as she grabbed Bobby when he skipped past, now seven and getting taller; his face getting slimmer, losing the nursery cheeks. It felt good, my favourite type of morning, carefree and unarranged, Laura happy, Bobby laughing. He wasn't my son, but he was starting to feel like it and I realised how much he brightened the house. I wondered for a moment about children of our own, the complete family, but I shook it off. I wasn't ready for that, wasn't sure when I would be.

I thought back to work instead, about what I might find at court that day. I'm a reporter, freelance, writing the court stories, always enough crime to keep the local newspaper happy. People always like to know what other people are doing.

But if I was going to get the stories, I knew I had to go to court. It was the enthusiasm I was lacking, not the work.

I turned to go inside, was about to shut the door, when I heard a noise. I paused and listened. It was the steady click-click of heels, a woman's walk.

I stopped, curious. There were no other houses near mine, and the shoes didn't sound like they were made for walking. Working the crime stories can upset people, names spread through the local rag, reputations ruined. The truth doesn't matter when court hearings are written up. The only thing that mattered is whether someone in court said it. Unexpected visitors made me wary.

The clicks got closer and then she appeared in the gateway in front of me.

She was middle-aged, bingo blonde, in a long, black leather coat, too hot for the weather, and high-heeled ankle boots.

'You look like you're a long way from wherever you need to be,' I said.

She took some deep breaths, the hill climb taking it out of her, her hands on her knees. She stubbed out a cigarette on the floor.

'There are no buses up here,' she said, and then she straightened up. Her breasts tried to burst out of her jumper, her cleavage ravaged by too much sun, her thighs squeezed into a strip of cloth that was three decades too young for her.

Before I could say anything, she looked at me and asked, 'Are you Jack Garrett?' Her accent was local, but it sounded like she was trying to soften it, exaggerated femininity, but the bluntness of the vowels slipped through.

'You've come to my door,' I replied warily, 'so you go first.'

She paused at first, unsure what to say, before she blurted out, 'My name is Julie Bingham, and I'm looking for Jack Garrett.'

'Why?'

'I've got a story for him.'

I sighed. That was the line I heard most, but usually it turned out to be some neighbourly dispute, or a problem with a boss, wanting to use the press to win a private fight. Sex, violence and fame sell national papers, they want the headline – the grabline, not the story – but local papers are different. Delayed roadworks and court stories fill the pages.

But I knew one other thing, it pays to listen first before you turn people away, because just as many people don't realise how good a story can be – they see a rough-cut diamond as cheap quartz.

I opened the door and stepped aside.

Bobby went quiet as Julie came in, suddenly shy.

'Can you tell Mummy I've got a visitor?' I said, and as Bobby ran towards the stairs, I gestured for Julie to sit down.

She looked around. 'I like your house,' she said. 'Sort of cosy and dark.'

I knew what she meant. The windows to the cottage were small, the sunlight not making it far into the room, just enough to catch the dust swirls and light up the table in the corner of the table where I write up my stories.

'We like it,' I said.

Julie went to get another cigarette out of her packet but I gave a small shake of my head. 'I'm sorry,' she said. 'I didn't mean to be rude, but I'm just a bit nervous.'

'That's okay,' I said.

Julie smiled. The powder on her face creased, and as she showed her teeth, I saw a smudge of pink lipstick on the yellowed enamel. I'd guessed Julie's age at over fifty when she'd first arrived, but she seemed younger now she was out of the sunlight.

'So what's your story?' I asked her.

She sat forward and put her bag on her knee. She looked like she was unsure how to start. I raised my eyebrows. *Just say it.*

'I've seen Claude Gilbert,' she blurted out.

I opened my mouth to say something, and then I stopped. I looked at her. She didn't laugh or give any hint that it was a joke.

'*The* Claude Gilbert?' I asked.

Julie nodded, and her hands tightened around the handles on her handbag. 'You don't look like you believe me,' she said.

'There are Claude Gilbert sightings all the time,' I responded. 'Do you know what the tabloids do with them? They store them, wait for the quiet news days when a false sighting will fill a page, the same old speculation trotted out. Newspaper offices are full of stories like that, guaranteed headlines, most of it padding. The Moors Murderers, the inside story on Rose West, all just waiting for the newspaper rainy day.'

'But I saw him.' She sounded hurt, frustration creeping into her voice.

I looked at her, saw the blush to her cheeks. I wasn't sure if it was shame or the walk up the hill, but as I looked at her, I knew that I would be a fool to turn her away. What if she was genuine? If Gilbert was alive, he had to be spotted eventually. And anyway, I thought to myself, perhaps the truth doesn't matter as much with the Claude Gilbert story.

'Wait there,' I said, and I shot off to get my voice recorder.

What's next?

Tell us the name of an author you love

| Neil White | Go ▶ |

and we'll find your next great book.

www.bookarmy.com